The Last Convict

Anthony Hill is a multi-award-winning, bestselling author. His most recent book for adults, *Captain Cook's Apprentice*, was published in 2018.

His novel *Soldier Boy*, about Australia's youngest-known Anzac, won the 2002 NSW Premier's Literary Award for Books for Young Adults. The children's version of *Captain Cook's Apprentice* won the 2009 NSW Premier's Young People's History Prize. It follows *Soldier Boy*, *Young Digger* and *Animal Heroes* as further testimony to his remarkable ability to extensively research historical material and, from wide-ranging sources, piece together a moving and exciting story.

He is also the author of two novellas, the beautiful *Shadow Dog*, and the award-winning *The Burnt Stick*, illustrated by Mark Sofilas, as well as the picture book, *Lucy's Cat and the Rainbow Birds*, illustrated by Jane Tanner.

After 40 years living in Canberra, Anthony and his wife, Gillian, have moved to the Mornington Peninsula. Their daughter, son-in-law and granddaughter, Emily, live in Melbourne.

anthonyhillbooks.com

Also by Anthony Hill

Young Digger
The Story of Billy Young
Soldier Boy
The Burnt Stick
For Love of Country
Animal Heroes
Captain Cook's Apprentice

The Last Convict

ANTHONY HILL

MICHAEL JOSEPH
an imprint of
PENGUIN BOOKS

MICHAEL JOSEPH

UK | USA | Canada | Ireland | Australia
India | New Zealand | South Africa | China

Michael Joseph is part of the Penguin Random House group of companies,
whose addresses can be found at global.penguinrandomhouse.com.

Penguin
Random House
Australia

First published by Michael Joseph, 2021

Text copyright © Anthony Hill, 2021

Cover design by James Rendall © Penguin Random House Australia Pty Ltd
Cover images courtesy Trevillion (figure) and Shutterstock (beach, boats, ship and oar)
Typeset in Sabon by Midland Typesetters, Australia
Printed and bound in Australia by Griffin Press, part of Ovato, an accredited
ISO AS/NZS 14001 Environmental Management Systems printer

A catalogue record for this
book is available from the
National Library of Australia

ISBN 978 1 76089 446 7

penguin.com.au

MIX
Paper from
responsible sources
FSC® C009448

For Richard Morris,
in friendship.

And to the memory of my great uncle, Edward Waring,
who left me his books.

Do not go gentle into that good night.
Dylan Thomas

CONTENTS

FOREWORD

The Last Convict is a work of historical fiction based on the life of Samuel Speed, who believed himself to be – and is widely accepted as – the last of the transported convicts to survive in Australia. He lived into the modern era – dying in November 1938, on the eve of the Second World War.

Very little is known about him: even his true identity is uncertain from the many Samuel Speeds born in England during the 1840s. I have reconstructed his story on the basis of the fairly meagre established facts on the public record, and an interview he did with a Perth newspaper only a few months before his death. The whole book, indeed, is built around that August morning when he gave this interview to the *Mirror* reporter.

While it remains an historical novel, for interested readers I have included in the Appendices the full interview as published (complete with errors as noted), the report of Speed's trial at Oxford in 1863, and a timeline of the known details of his life. I have also included a set of chapter notes to help separate historical fact from the historical fiction.

Anthony Hill
Canberra, 2020

I

OLD MEN

Perth, Western Australia, August 1938

It wasn't me!

The old lag stirred uneasily on his dormitory bed: at liberty in sleep, yet imprisoned still within a frail body and held by the shackles of memory.

He'd been dreaming, as he often did, of smoke. And fire. The gum-scented pleasures of a billy boiling in a bush camp, and a yarn over the coals after a day's labour. Sweet dreams . . .

. . . shifting, in the way they do, to an image of hot cast iron and an ember glow that sweated but never warmed you, as too many broken old men huddled around the stove on a winter's night . . .

The aroma of salt beef boiling in the mess deck copper on the transport *Belgravia*, drifting with the sea breeze to the convict decks below. Food that filled yet failed to nourish . . .

And before that . . . a smell of dry grass and sulphur, for the ghosts had become more disturbing. A wicked yellow flame. And a pale spectre of smoke that rose in the darkness to billow and surround him – acrid and flecked with black burning cinders – until he could see nothing else and cried out in his fear:

It wasn't me!

Samuel Speed woke up. Frightened, as always, by the old vision. The blanket was in a tangle and the sheets damp, as if he'd wet himself in the night. Not uncommon now, at his age, though he hoped it was only perspiration and not the result of a too-vivid nightmare. Incontinence was frowned upon.

I'm sorry, he'd have to tell Matron, *but what do you expect in my nineties?*

Samuel felt his breath laced with the panic of wrongdoing, for he was still caught in the shrouds of the past. He lay in the narrow bed, eyes closed a little longer to let himself return more gently to the present and the waking day. Lying on one side, he carefully brought his knees together in a foetal position, and with elbows and feet slowly levered himself onto his back. It was one way to avoid the agonies of leg cramp from any sudden movement, and eased the strain on both groins from his double hernia and the pressure of what remained in his bladder. He could sometimes manage it without assistance or pain; and succeeding this morning, Speed allowed the sense of accomplishment gradually to displace those lingering feelings of dread ignited by the phantom bonfire.

No phantom though!

He opened his eyes. And, for a moment, Sam Speed imagined himself still enveloped by the smoke cloud. The morning light coming from the window was white and opaque, through which only shadows moved. Like fog on the Swan River outside, or the Thames at Chatham. Until he realised he was also incarcerated in his blindness – or very nearly so. The bad eye had been scarred as a boy, and from then on was permanently misted, like pale opal. The authorities put it down to a cataract, not knowing that cataracts are usually another affliction of age. The other eye had been all right until his middle years, when it also began to fail.

But, praise God, I can still see a little, Sam thought, in silent morning prayer. Enough to read the newspaper, anyway, with the help of a large magnifying glass, once the eye settled: hunched over a table in the day room, the page six inches from his face, like some decrepit Sherlock Holmes. He laughed. Not that it was worth the bother, filled with talk of Depression and now war, though he could still get a chuckle from the comic cartoon.

Books were out, however. Had been for a long time. It was too hard to maintain the sense of them, squinting at the tiny words through that thing. So, thank heaven for Braille – as Sam returned to the Almighty – and the man who invented it, for allowing him still to have stories at his fingertips. And also, as a postscript, for the person who thought of putting the new 'talking books' on gramophone records.

Samuel was never one to let himself dwell too much on the hardships of life. Such things were better left to his dreams. To the outside world – even to his Maker – Speed tried to adopt the cheerful countenance of his literary namesake, Mr Samuel Smiles. And thus, he lay there thinking and letting his good eye adjust to the patterns of the day.

'Good' was a relative term, of course, for Sam's sight was such that anything much beyond the end of his arm was a blur. The best he could manage this morning was to concentrate on the contours of his right hand, stretched limply across his chest. A thin, brittle hand, wrinkled like tissue paper, through which the bones stuck out as ridges and the blue river veins ran as if through a painted landscape, mottled brown with freckles like the summer country around the Vasse. An old man's hand that had seen much – done much – these ninety years or so. The strength that once allowed him to lift a chaff bag or dig a garden bed had departed long ago, however, as had the interest in his own anatomy.

Besides, as vision failed, his other senses had become more acute. And as the emotions roused by smoke and fire receded into the darkness, they were replaced in Samuel Speed's consciousness by the early morning dormitory sounds of those about him. The old feller in the next bed grunting as he strove to stay asleep. Coughs and mutters. Somebody urinating into the metal chamber-pot. A magpie started to sing outside the window. 'Break o' day birds', they used to call them – and one chap, in need of conversation during those lonely weeks out as a shepherd, even taught one to speak. He was happy, so they said. Unlike those two at the other end of the ward, quarrelling as one tried to cadge a smoke.

'Get way with yer. It's me last . . .'

'Bastard.'

'Bludger.'

Ever the same.

Somebody farting.

'Jesus!' from the next bed. Taking the Lord's name. 'Open the flamin' winder . . .'

The odour of his own body. A kind of stale, fetid sickliness that never scrubbed out. An old man's stink – but more than that, Samuel . . .

It's the whiff of too many bodies crammed together in one place for far too long, experience told him. *And that is something you have known all of your life.*

Indeed. He'd become used to it. Had to. In the workhouse. In prisons from Oxford to Fremantle. The *Belgravia.* Convict Depot. Boarding houses he had known. Braille Society Rest Home at

Victoria Park. Perth Hospital. And now back in the crowded ward of the Old Men's Home at Dalkeith, Silly Sam Speed had been in an institution of one kind or another for the better part of his ninety-odd years. And the smell of it never went away, not even using laundry soap in the bath last night, and they'd given him clean clothes again.

What was that for?

There was something . . . something about today . . . Samuel's mind tried to search the possibilities. This forgetting was the worst of growing old. Something he had to do . . . The trouble was not just the disintegrating body; the cobwebs of age were spinning a cocoon over the brain as well, so that the past generally seemed more alive to him than the present.

Church? No, that was only a few days ago, a service in the dining hall, and he'd had a bath on Saturday night. Only one a week allowed, so why two . . .? Were they going to tell Sammy he'd won the lottery? There was a piece in the paper not long ago about an old-timer who'd scooped up a fortune. But no . . . he didn't gamble. Yet the paper . . . that was it! Some feller from the newspaper was coming to see him today. Wanted to do an in-ter-view with him, so of course he had to be clean-smelling and all smartened up.

Mr Rust had told him about it only yesterday, when he was called into the Superintendent's office.

'It's a reporter from the weekend *Mirror*, Sam. He wants to talk to you.'

'What about?'

'Oh . . . about yourself, and the old days, and what it was like. Take a photograph, too, and publish it in the newspaper.'

'I'll break the camera!' Sammy was always ready with a laugh. 'And why me, Mr Rust?'

'Well . . . because of who you are. He's heard that you're the last of the old ex-convicts still among us. The last of the expirees – so far as we're aware, anyway.'

Expirees. That was a word rarely heard nowadays – an ugly word, as if he had already expired and gone to his grave. Certainly, it was something Samuel Speed rarely talked about to anybody else, except when he had to. Tried to keep hidden, in fact. The others had gone – and even after all these years the shame was still palpable: in the looks and small, distasteful shifts of the body if anything were said to the respectable. 'Swan River lags', they used to be called in contempt, back east. They even tried to stop them from entering the uncontaminated air of South Australia after they'd served their time; and Samuel Speed, convict indent number 8996, wasn't at all sure he'd want his past exposed on the front page of a newspaper. The secrecy of his iron bed was enough to bear.

'It's a good story, Samuel.' Albert Rust could see the doubt on his inmate's countenance. 'You're a piece of living history. Here we are in 1938, seventy years after transportation to Western Australia ceased, and you're still alive. Hale and hearty . . .'

'Don't know about the "hale", Boss.' It was the name they all called him. 'I'm falling apart, held together with me truss straps.'

'Hearty, anyway. Never without a cheery word, Sam. And you don't have to tell them everything. Nothing too grim. Just the amusing things, little anecdotes that people like to read. You'll be famous. And besides,' as the Superintendent turned from flattery to self-interest, 'it would be a big help to the Home.'

'How?'

'Well, it's always a struggle to raise donations from people to buy those extra comforts we like to give our inmates.' Rust was a large, expansive man and spread his hands wide. 'Books, and another wireless, and little treats . . . Especially in these times. A nice article about you, Sam, will bring us to the attention of readers and perhaps even encourage them to be generous. As we have – er – been very generous to you over the years . . . As you well know.'

He smiled broadly, as officials ever do when tightening the moral screws.

'So I told him to come tomorrow. In the morning, when you're not too tired. If that's all right?'

It would have to be.

'I suppose so, Mr Rust. If you wish it.'

With a little bow and knuckle to the forehead, as always, to those in authority. And to be fair, the Boss was a decent-hearted man – far better than many workmasters and superintendents Sam Speed had known in his life. If he thought it a good thing and Sammy could help.

Still, he sought to put the interview out of his mind for the rest of the day, and even tried not to think about it last night. Which perhaps was why his dreams had been so intense. But lying here this morning before the quarter-to-seven getting-up bell, the sounds of other men about him, Sam couldn't help but rehearse the sorts of things he might say. Nothing unpleasant, Bert Rust had advised: and if nothing else, during his nine decades on this Earth, Speed had become adept at burying his secrets deep and telling people only those things he wanted them to hear. Not lying, exactly, for that would be sinful. But a small exaggeration here, a gloss about his age there, tossed off with a joke.

And some things he could truthfully tell the reporter from the *Mirror*.

'I've never been in a chain gang,' he murmured to himself. 'My back bears the scars of no whip.'

No, by God, for the penal system had put the fear of Christ into Samuel Speed – quite literally – though that was something he would also keep to himself.

'I learnt me lesson,' was the most he would say, 'and came out of it a well-travelled man. It brought me halfway round the world, eh?'

Sam was still chuckling at his prepared jest, when the bell began to ring. Fifteen minutes to breakfast and the orderlies would be on their rounds. His whole life had been governed by bells, the man's free will replaced long ago by their insistence. When to eat, work, sleep and rise determined by official regulation. There was a certain comfort in that – knowing these essential routines of life were taken care of by somebody else, and you didn't have to worry about them like you did outside. Nevertheless, the old man still occasionally felt the need to rebel: and so he lay there, refusing to get up and face the day, even though all around him thirty men were creaking out of bed, piddling in the pot, grumbling, dressing, lighting the first fag of the day and squabbling over the wash basin. You didn't want to be late for a meal!

'Sammy . . .'

He heard the voice of an orderly. Felt him touching his shoulder, and a little shake.

'Wakey-wakey, Sammy. Time to rise and shine, mate. It's your big day.'

'Yes . . .' A long pause as the old chap dragged his thoughts back from the past imperfect to present indicative. 'Howzit, Bob?'

'Bit cloudy. Still cool and a chance of rain, they reckon. Easy there, Sammy . . .' as the old man felt Bob's arm slide between his shoulderblades and the kapok pillow, and begin to lift him. 'Hold on to me other arm, here.'

With bony elbows, knuckles and feet acting as secondary props, Speed hoisted himself up. That was always the hardest part of the day, and he sat there catching his breath and looking at Bob's shadowy presence.

'Thanks, cobber. Could you pass over me falsies?'

Bob picked the dentures from the bedside glass and put them in Sam's hand. A nice enough feller, he couldn't be much more than half Sam's age. One of the 'Tuppenny Orderlies': an inmate like himself, but still with his strength and reliable, who did all sorts of jobs around the Home. In the hospital block, kitchen, yards, helping old codgers in the wards who were past it. There were quite a few of them here. In return for which they got paid twopence a day. Tuppence, see? And a plug of tobacco. Well, they all got that. Clay pipe, too, in the old days.

'Oh, Sammy. Have you pissed yourself in the night?' The orderly uncovered the old bloke's limbs and prepared to set him upright.

'Sweat, I reckon, Bob. I felt hot . . .' Samuel fumbled putting the teeth into his mouth. They were a nice set, too; a pal got 'em second-hand from a jumble sale.

''Course it was. Excitement, more like. All right, I'll take the sheets to the laundry for yer. They won't know.'

He helped Sam swing his legs over the edge of the bed. And holding him under the arms, rather like mother lifting a child out of the bath, gradually coaxed and manoeuvred him into the vertical position. He stood there giddily a moment – skinny shanks, poking beneath the old cotton nightshirt he always wore, trembling with the exertion of it all. Shrunken chest heaving, as mind and body laboured to restore equilibrium.

'Have you got me stick handy, Bob?'

'Right here.'

Grabbing it and balancing on his three legs, like an unsteady tripod: Samuel Speed the very picture, in his dotage, of Shakespeare's seventh age of man, remembered from those days when that clever old sot, Clarrie Short, would recite to him, *sans teeth, sans eyes, sans everything*.

Or almost everything.

'Have you got the chamber-pot there, Bob?' For he still had to pee.

'Coming right up.'

An awfully tedious business however, as it dribbled out in tea-spoonfuls. Another measurement of age. Sometimes he'd have to ask for the receptacle three or four times in the course of putting on his clothes. His midriff bursting to go, and then nothing happened. Though this morning, Sam was glad to sense, the stream seemed reasonably plentiful. Perhaps he'd need it only twice.

He sat back on the bed as Bob helped him dress.

Relieving himself had eased some of the pressures on Samuel's abdomen – but the mere fact of standing created others, especially for his old trouble, the hernia.

'The belt, Bobbie – quick!'

The nightshirt had rolled up about his waist, and he looked down at his willy, a poor, flabby bit of gristle these days, just visible through the mist. Useless for anything, except passing water, and had been for years. Difficult to remember when he'd last known a woman, other than Matron and the nurses – but you never looked at them like *that!* And Sam had never known a wife. Always down by the river, or a back alley somewhere he was ashamed to remember God . . . His shrivelled balls and tuft of body hair were hemmed in now by swellings, as parts of his intestine bulged through the abdominal wall into each groin. Hence the truss to push them back, for the hernias could be very painful, especially if they descended into his scrotum. They had put Sammy away several times: indeed, he'd come back to the Home from the Braille house at Victoria Park only last month, after another spell in hospital. And he was far too old to operate.

But really, it was like getting into harness, as Bob guided his feet through the leg straps and raised the contrivance up to his waist. Clinging on to the man again to stand as the orderly tightened the belt, the pads on either side of his privates helping to push the intestine back inside. What a thing! What a way to end up – his scrawny frame kept intact, as he'd told the Boss only yesterday, by the girth of a hernia truss.

'You deserve every one of those tuppences, Bob,' as he eased himself back onto the bed.

'Worth *four* pence a day having to put up with you, y'old bugger.' They sniggered.

Hands up, as Bob pulled the nightshirt over his head. Sam glanced down at what he could see of his aged torso, more bone than flesh now, the few wisps of hair on his sunken chest, sallow belly sagging in his nakedness. He'd never been a tall fellow: not much more than five foot three in his prime, but sturdy and toughened by hard labour. Now, in this seventh age, he'd be lucky to make five foot – like his mother, he seemed to recall – and his head a hollow skull with a layer of sunburnt skin stretched over it.

Hands up, still, as Bob pulled the flannel undershirt over his head and eased arms into the sleeves. Sammy always wore his flannel, regular as a prison uniform.

'Well, I'm used to it and feel the cold. And don't forget me long johns. I got no reserves of fat left on me, Bob,' as the underwear was pulled up and buttoned. His brown trousers and loose jacket, courtesy of the government, freshly washed and pressed from the laundry to make him nice for the interview. Linen overshirt courtesy of the charity shop.

'The shirts used to be stamped W.A.G., Bob. Did you know that? Western Australian Government. And us old lags called ourselves the old "wags". Pretty funny, eh?'

'Hilarious, Sammy. And keep still while I put on yer shoes and socks.'

'I wish it were boots. I always like boots.'

'They said shoes for the gentleman.'

'I can still tie me *own* laces if I get the foot close enough up to me eye.'

'It will take you all day, mate. That reporter will have come and gone. Talking of which, the breakfast bell's already gone. We'd better move if you're to get some tucker.'

'They're greedy about their food, them blokes. Always have been.'

'Do you want me to scrounge something from the infirmary, or shall we try the hall?'

'Oh, the dining hall, Bob. They're all sick and ailing at that other place.'

Unlike himself.

'Then best foot forward.' Bob took hold of Samuel's arm.

'I can find my own way,' as the old man tried to shake him off, independent as always.

'It will take forever, chum, limping along with yer stick.'

'But me beanie, Bob. You said it was cool, and I need me beanie.'

Bob sighed. He picked up the striped knitted object from the end of the bed and gave it to Sam, who adjusted it like a tea-cosy over his bald pate and the tips of his ears.

'Look all right?'

'You'll do. You can splash yer face as we pass the basin. And hurry up.'

Arm in arm, once more, they set off to find what was left of breakfast and to discover what the rest of the day would bring.

2

BREAKFAST

The food had pretty much gone by the time the late-comers made it to the dining hall. They had a good hundred yards or so to go, Sam's stick tapping down the dormitory's limestone wall, across a covered walkway and along the hall verandah to the middle door. Despite the security of Tuppenny Bob's arm and his urgings to 'step on it', for the morning was bleak, the old chap liked to take his time and be *sure* of where he was going. He never trusted anybody else completely: it was the great lesson of life – and a mark that his individual human spirit was still kicking.

Thus the porridge bowls had been scraped clean when they arrived, but there was still a last slice of bread and butter, and a little stewed tea to be squeezed out of the large enamel teapot on the far table.

'Shove along, you lot,' Bob instructed the unwilling occupants from the centre aisle. 'Make a space for the old feller.' He helped Sam take his seat on the long refectory bench, painted white with a high rail back to prevent any unstable residents from falling off.

'And stow it!' sharply to one man who reached out to grab the remaining bit of bread. 'That's reserved.'

'Why?'

'Because I said so.'

'I got as much right to it as 'im.'

'You've already eat some breakfast. Sammy ain't.'

The orderly placed the slice firmly in his hand.

'Sorry about that,' as he poured half a mug of lukewarm tea. Black, two sugars, a legacy from the bush.

'It's all right, Bob. I know what things can be like.'

Certainly, he did. Samuel Speed knew all about overcrowded mess rooms and hungry men fighting over crumbs. In the struggle for survival, only the self mattered. And this place was full.

The Home had been built to sleep 400–500 destitute old men in three rectangular accommodation blocks. Originally, they were all relics of pioneering days, when men had far outnumbered women in the colony. But once the Depression started there'd been half as many again. The wards had been crammed, blokes sleeping on verandahs and even in humpies in the nearby bush, only coming inside to eat. Numbers had been dropping lately, but even so . . .

And it wasn't just the aged and infirm, either, but younger men like Bob, who'd lost his job and his home and everything, admitted by Albert Rust because he had nothing. One of many, their small sustenance benefits were paid into the Home to help support them, with a little left over for the canteen and pub. Plus their Tuppences.

It was decent of people like Albert Rust to do as much as they could to help those in distress. But that was the sort of man he was. Rust had started the 'Sunshine League' to raise money for the needy and was 'Uncle Tom' in the *Daily News* for the orphan children. But it was still charity – still a handout. And Samuel Speed knew that expectations of gratitude filled no stomachs. Indeed, for many men it only fed resentment, because hunger can make you do almost anything . . .

Can't it just! You wouldn't be here, otherwise.

He pushed the unwanted thought away and turned his almost sightless eyes down the white painted table, where neighbours were still whingeing about Sammy's purloined bit of bread. Sharp ears picked up muttered phrases: 'It's not fair', 'shoulda come earlier', like so many upset birds on a roost settling their feathers.

So, to provide a diversion, the old chap spoke up in his high, quavering voice, 'Do you fellers know what's happening in the cricket?'

It was a smart move. If there is any one thing that can unite Australians in riches or poverty, it is talk of sport: and especially, during a Test series, of cricket. Attention turned immediately to the Fifth at Kennington in faraway London.

'Hutton's still smashin' us,' one feller said, two across from Sam and yesterday's booze still reeking on his breath. Sam had been teetotal from . . . well, for as long as he cared to remember, and could smell it anywhere. 'I found a newspaper in the rubbish bin.'

'Triple century and close to beatin' Don Bradman's record,' from further down.

'Yeah, but that were Tuesd'y,' in Samuel's ear. 'It's worse'n that.'

'Why . . .?' a small chorus interrogated him. 'What's happened?'

'Bradman's hurt his foot. Slipped while bowlin', and out of it now. Tommy Senior heard it overnight on his crystal set.'

Tommy had once run his own electrics shop before he fell on hard times.

'That's right,' confirmed Tuppenny Bob. 'It was on the wireless news this morning.'

And the conversation moved from crusts to a diagnosis of the mighty Don's injury, its cause, consequences and prognosis for the outcome of the 1938 Test series, Bradman himself, and the very future of Australian cricket. This group of down-and-outers, reduced from whatever degree of former self-worth to penury and disgrace, animated for a little by the great leveller of cricket. No amount of money could buy the prowess of a Len Hutton or Jack Fingleton – let alone the Don – and anyone could express an opinion as good as the next man.

Which they did, up and down the breakfast table and elsewhere in the hall. Samuel listened for a bit, munching his bread, for he liked the game, though he'd never actually played it. Eyes. And impoverished working-class boys like him didn't play cricket in those distant days. But whenever the Tests were held in Australia Sammy liked to listen in.

The Boss had bought the Home's first wireless in the late twenties after a charity drive: a great contraption of a thing with a battery cabinet set up on the stage in the hall, and a huge horn like a gramophone coming out of the top. Only Mr Rust, of course, was allowed to fiddle the dials, but the inmates would sit on the benches listening to the broadcast of every over – the sound of bat on ball conveyed by the tap of a studio pencil – the fall of every wicket. And then a few years ago he'd raised the money to buy their first electric wireless. There was one in the recreation room you could listen to of an afternoon. But things were harder, except for the most dedicated with crystal sets, when the Tests were in England: for the night bell would ring and lights out at nine o'clock, when the day's play in 'Pommie Land' had barely begun . . .

Which was how Sam thought of it now. England. Somewhere foreign. Some other place with which Mr Speed barely felt any connection.

Except that you have to!

Shut up.

And it wasn't just the wireless. Not long after he bought that first one, the Boss built a projection room over the servery from the kitchen, so they could show pictures. The silent ones at first, though they weren't of much use to Sam because they were just moving shadows accompanied by Mrs Sheridan on the pianola. And then the new talkies when they came in. Mr Rust persuaded some rich people to donate a yacht and a motor car for him to raffle and raise funds for the projector and all the sound equipment. The Boss was a corker at that. And the Home was the third place in Perth to show talking pictures. Twice a week at six o'clock after tea, and so much better because you could hear what was going on, even if the dialogue didn't mean a lot without vision and fellers got cranky if you asked what was happening. But there was always the music – what did they call it? – the soundtrack. Better than the pianola.

And Sam Speed loved music! It was one consolation for not being able to see much. He couldn't say he liked those jazzy, jitter-bug tunes they usually played on the radio nowadays. Too noisy. Too energetic. They made you want to dance, and that was impossible on a walking stick, even if you could find a girl to dance *with*. No, but sometimes they would play nice things – an old-time waltz, say, or a song that meant something. 'Home Sweet Home' – if there'd ever been such a place – or 'Danny Boy'.

Remember . . .? The concert parties that used to come out regular in the years before the War? Troupes of young ladies and gentle-men – and a few older ones, too – would hire a ferry from town, berth at the jetty down the embankment outside, and entertain them up there on the stage with songs and piano solos and comedy duets and recitations.

Some of them were pretty good, too. Even Dame Nellie Melba came to the Home once and sang to them, because she supported the Boss in his work – not just with the old blokes, but the orphan kiddies as well. Though some of their entertainers could be hopeless. Remember that lot who came down with a beer keg on board? They were pickled when they arrived, and got worse as the performance went on. Forgot their words . . . slurred their songs . . . tottered about the stage . . . It got so bad the audience started to leave, muttering insults and tripping people up with their crutches and wheelchairs. The Boss had to bring the curtain down in the end. Called the whole thing off. And the concert party was so offended, they refused to stay for the special supper that he and Mrs Rust had prepared for them at the Superintendent's house.

Samuel laughed to himself. Such times! You didn't need to see very well to enjoy them, and most of the entertainment was up to a standard. Such a pity they hardly ever had a concert now, not since the pictures and the wireless. But when the concert parties did come, Bert Rust would often wade into the river with a tin tub tied to his waist, catching prawns and crabs and fish – enough to feed all his guests afterwards, when the inmates had gone to bed.

Such a considerate feller, the Boss. 'Make life easy for the old men, and they'll make life easy for me' was the rule he ran the Home by. Contentment all round. So very different to that arrogant booby, Mr Wade, who'd been the first Master here (as they called him then) and at the old Mount Eliza Depot before that. The Perth Convict Depot it used to be, when Sammy first arrived on the *Belgravia*.

Oh, how it will keep intruding . . .

That feller Wade, though . . . as one thought slid by association to another in the old man's mind . . . he carried on like the workhouse beadle, Mr Bumble, in *Oliver Twist*. Truly. Sam knew the type from his youth. Even the newspaper called Wade a character out of Charles Dickens. He'd strut around in a swallow-tail coat, high boots and cocked hat, an exacting disciplinarian to both deserving and undeserving poor alike. Cruel, too. He kept all the gates locked, to stop inmates wandering through the bush and up to the pubs. It was like being back in prison again.

Well, Albert Rust opened the gates, and they've never been shut since. That's what he meant yesterday about being generous to the old blokes. Besides everything else. And it was true.

I owe him a lot. We all do.

Samuel let the observation percolate in his head. He didn't shove it away this time, but left it sitting, only half-aware of the cricket chatter around him . . .

'Even if Hutton keeps on beltin' us, the series will still end in a draw.'

. . . and considering that, if they *were* all in Mr Rust's debt one way or another, then what followed?

Only this:

If he wants me to talk to this feller from the paper, well, it's the least I can do to help him. I've nothing else to give: no yacht or motor car. No money any more. And keep it sweet 'n' simple. Just like he advised.

There.

Sam had said it to himself. Meant it. And come what may.

The dining hall was emptying of men, voicing last-minute certainties on Bradman's ankle as they departed. Sam, too, got up slowly from the bench, feeling for his stick.

'Here y'are,' as Bob handed him the cane and prepared to take charge once more.

He was under orders from the Boss himself to look after the old fellow for the day. Spruce him up; attend to his needs; settle him ready for the interview. For the Superintendent was well aware of Sam Speed's reluctance to provoke the ghosts of his convicted past, which some people would still find shocking. Understandably reticent. But Speed was the last one left who could remember from the *inside*: and if that might lead to a little public sympathy as well, and prise open a few more purses by way of donation, surely it would benefit everybody associated with the Old Men's Home?

In the twenty-eight years Albert Rust had been running the place, he'd raised over £10000 to improve the amenities. The cinema . . . four-rink bowling green . . . the recreation room . . . He'd been a journalist himself in a former life, as well as a man who devoted himself to helping those in need, and Rust knew all about the mechanics of extracting money from the public in a good cause.

Thus he'd given Bob the orderly instructions to take particular care of Samuel. And first thing, after he'd eaten, was to attend to his toilet.

'I don't think I need to go yet, Bob.'

'Well, we've got to go back to the dormitory to tidy up . . . fix yer bed and whatnot. Why don't you make your way up there now? I'll nip over to the laundry store to get your clean sheets and meet you up there. We can decide then.'

'Righty-oh.'

It took Samuel a lot longer to retrace his halting steps to the ward without Bob's guiding arm. A cool breeze was springing up from the river, and he could smell rain. But he relished the freedom of independent action – craved it, indeed, and he had all the time in the world. Sort of. They'd put Sam in the hospital here at the

Home for a few days when he returned from Perth last month, just to keep his hernia under observation. But he hated the restrictions. And then to the infirmary where the really frail aged lived, reliant on help for everything. But Speed had insisted he return to a general dormitory – near the hospital, just in case – where other old 'uns like himself lived with some autonomy. In their 'twilight years', to be sure, but not yet utterly useless. And it was one step further away from the inevitable.

Still, they weren't completely free of the need for some assistance – especially with all those little housekeeping chores that occupied this part of the morning, before the nine o'clock bell sounded for the able-bodied, who'd been assigned work, to get started, and for the rest of them to find something to occupy the long hours of the day ahead. Some to go into the remnant scrub to relive, for a little, the old days. Some to find their way to the nearest pub and offend the neighbours. Some to play bowls or throw a fishing line from the jetty. Some just to sit and think. And for one of them to confront the meaning of his long life.

There were quite a few orderlies about the ward when Sam arrived. Bob was already among them, helping with the sheets and the white cotton bedspreads with a red stripe down the centre branded W.A.G. to stop pilfering; tidying the bedside cupboards and removing bits of food that might be hoarded inside. That's why the bread was always buttered before it was put on the table: some of the old 'uns would pinch the butter and any other eatables, leave it in their lockers, and forget about it until the stuff went rotten and stank. And then make a fuss when their 'possies' were taken away. It was the result of many years living on hard rations.

'Do you want me to give you a hand, Bob?' Samuel proffered his assistance, anxious to be useful still.

'Thanks, Sammy, but quicker by meself. Why don't you go outside and sit down for a bit?'

'If you say so.'

He shuffled out the side door and found an empty chair among a few other ancients sitting on the verandah in the lee of the wind, but still catching a few patches of winter sun that slipped through the scudding clouds. They exchanged greetings and murmurs, but soon settled back into that silent inner world of old age: one that might *seem* solitary, but was in fact populated with far more incident and memory than the present could ever be.

The sound of the orderlies going about their work indoors stole through the open windows. And to be honest, Samuel thought, the place would be nothing without them. Before the Depression there'd been a paid staff of more than forty people, including orderlies: but when things went bad, they were reduced to a handful, even as the numbers of inmates rose.

Whatever would we have done without Tuppennies like Bob? Samuel wondered. And as he sat in the shelter, contemplating a question to which he could provide no answer, he nodded and drifted into a snooze, made all the more pleasant after last night's broken sleep.

'Sammy . . .'

Bob was nudging his shoulder again.

'Having a little nap, eh? I'm ready for you now . . . the bathroom.'

'I still don't think I need to go, Bob.'

'I think you should try, Sam, in case. Don't want to have an accident afterwards, do we?'

We? Samuel felt himself start to bristle, as Bob eased him up from the chair and led him towards the toilets and washrooms halfway along each side of the accommodation block. Why, he wondered, do people like nurses and orderlies always talk to children and the infirm in the plural? Was it power – or just condescension? Either way the old man disliked it, though he was as equally helpless to do anything about it. *We?*

To be sure, it was a joint operation in the cubicle as they man-oeuvred to get his trousers down and sit him on the porcelain. But still Sam sat there, straining away with not much to show for it, and resenting this dependence. Talk about the Bard's *second childishness and mere oblivion . . .*

'You finished yet?'

'Nearly.'

Then the struggle recommenced to get him up, wiped and trous-ered again – and next propped by the basin to wash his face and hands with a flannel and soap. A mere splash from the dormitory basin would not suffice today. The water was warm, at least. Always was, from the artesian bore.

'Do we need a shave, Bob?' With just a hint of sarcasm.

'Had one yesterday. Yer face is still smooth as a baby's bum.'

True. Even his stubble had stopped growing much nowadays.

And staring at the pallid, distant reflection of himself in the mirror, as if through a haze, Samuel felt his irritation subsumed by some more immediate sensation in his guts. Nerves, probably, and the forthcoming interview. He'd tried to ignore the reporter's visit until breakfast time. But now that he'd made up his mind to go ahead with it, Sam began to worry if he'd not unwittingly agreed to appear before the Inquisition? Like poor old Galileo. And wondered if he'd also condemn himself in the eyes of the world from his own mouth.

Don't be silly. Just stick to the funny stories. Tell 'em about Moondyne Joe . . . you've been doing that for years . . .

'What time did you say this chap is coming, Bob?'

And the Fenians' escape on the Catalpa. *That always goes down well.*

'Mid-morning, I were told.'

'Ah.'

But what if he tries to make me confess things?

What things?

The truth of it . . .

'Yes.'

Bob removed Samuel's beanie, passed a comb over his skull, and covered it again.

'We can go into the recreation room if you like, Sam.'

'I'd rather go to the library. They've got books there. And it's nice and quiet.'

Six thousand books, all collected from donations by the Boss. Some had even been given by Sam himself, when his eyes gave out. They had a few Braille ones, too, that the nice Society ladies brought round on loan, with a couple of those new 'talking books', besides.

'The library isn't open yet. P'raps later. You could look at the paper in the rec room?'

'I can't read the morning one any more, Bob. The *West Australian* print is too small, even with the glass.'

'There'll be yesterday's *Daily News*.'

'That's right. They have a good comic strip, eh?'

And at that moment it occurred to Sam there was also a right way to consider the reporter.

He's only a journalist – not the flaming Pope.

Samuel brightened a little at that. Things would be fine – until the next thought reminded him that journalists are also trained to ask questions. Not very penetrating ones usually, but often quite personal and dogged if they sensed something was being hidden.

What if he takes me places I don't want to revisit?

And they also carried a lot of weight. Look at the Boss. He was still 'Uncle Tom' in the paper, and not long ago persuaded the Governor to give two full-sized billiard tables from the vice-regal summer residence at Albany to the recreation room here at the Home. Walter Lindrum had even given exhibition matches. That showed the extent of Bert Rust's influence.

Samuel moistened his lips and his hand trembled a little.

He'd been placed in this predicament by other people. And while he was still willing to help the Boss, he began to wonder if there was anything he could do to restore the balance a little? Rather than passively allow himself to be chief witness at his own indictment, perhaps he might be able to tilt the situation slightly more in his favour?

Vulnerable old men can sometimes be quite good at playing vulnerable old men . . .

'All ready, Sammy?'

'Good as I'll ever be, Bob.'

'Feeling all right?'

'A bit chilly, Bob. That breeze is right off the water – and there's not a lot of me, you know.'

He sniffled and allowed a drop of moisture to dangle from the tip of his nose.

'The walk will warm you up.'

'Yairs. I hope so.'

They set off once more in the direction of the hall and recreation room. Walking in silence apart from the stick, and the wind, and the patter of a passing shower on the iron roofs. Until Sammy asked, 'What do you reckon that chap from the *Mirror* is doing now, Bob?'

But he didn't really care or expect any answer. Samuel Speed had conceived an idea.

3

THE JOURNALIST

As it happened, the journalist was himself out of sorts that morning. In part, it was a case of a new set of twins who had Joshua Cribben and his wife up half the night. One baby was screaming, and the other wasn't; and the dilemma that faced the inexperienced parents was, Which infant is sick?

They'd therefore picked them both up and walked around the tiny flat for hours, trying to pacify the one, reassure themselves that the other was yet alive, and mollify the neighbours. No sooner had they got back to bed than the other started crying, and the performance was repeated. Having waited through the worst of the Depression years until their early thirties to get married, Mr and Mrs Cribben were of sufficient age to be a little set in their ways, and found the trials of parenthood exhausting.

Josh Cribben had consequently slept in, missed several buses and arrived at the newspaper office to find that the photographer, with whom he was to get a lift to the Old Men's Home at suburban Dalkeith, had already gone.

'He's got several jobs on,' said the chief-of-staff. 'You'll have to take the bus.'

'Is there another office car?'

'We've only got one, and that's spoken for.'

'It will take hours in the bloody bus.'

'Thirty minutes,' replied the chief decisively, 'and a nice ride. It's only Wednesday. We don't need your copy until Friday. I'd get cracking, if I were you.'

Another irritation to add to Mr Cribben's tiredness, and not much soothed by the chief-of-staff's parting words. 'We plan to give it a decent run, you know, and expect a good job.'

'I always do a good job,' the reporter muttered to himself, gathering his hat and coat again from the peg. 'That's why you bloody hired me.'

Joshua Cribben had grown up in the country around Toodyay, north-east of Perth, left school at fourteen, and got a job with the local rag. Starting as a copy boy and general dogsbody, as good newspapermen always did, he learned his trade from the ground up.

Small paragraphs on the district sports results and weather led to more substantial stories from the weekly stockyard sales, social events, the magistrate's court and shire council. Journalists on rural papers have to be adept at pretty much everything: by turn their own editors, secretaries, photographers and salesmen – and friends with everyone from the local mayor and policemen to the town drunk.

Joshua thrived on it, and discovered that printer's ink flowed thickly in his veins.

He learned the need for accuracy from his mistakes – as when he muddled the brides' names at two Saturday weddings and was threatened with legal action; or inadvertently killed someone in a motor accident who'd only been injured. 'Dad's not dead, he's sitting up in bed with a bowl of soup.' He developed a nose for news. A woman's routine application to the JP for a maintenance order against her estranged husband turned into a juicy scandal when the local priest offered Cribben a bribe not to report it.

The story, in fact, led to his being recruited to the city and into another league altogether. But the young man had held his own, worked his way up through the grades on several newspapers until he'd ended up at the weekend *Mirror*, where Joshua specialised in writing 'colour' pieces and human-interest stories. The rag was devoted to them, and the more colourful, human and interesting the better. Which was why he'd been selected to interview Sam Speed at the Dalkeith Old Men's Home, said to be the last of the convict expirees still alive in the state.

Cribben wasn't so sure how much colour or interest his readers would find in such a tale. Nude bathers arrested at midnight in the Dalkeith hot pool was more the *Mirror* style. Only a few months ago the paper had led with EXCITING 'BOIL-OVER' at the hot pool, when two couples, each cheating on the other, had inadvertently gone swimming at the same time – recognised their partners – and began brawling in the water 'with fists and legs flying in the vimful battle', as the breathless scribe put it. And emerged wearing nothing but black eyes.

Walking to St George's Terrace to catch the bus, Joshua laughed out loud at the memory and wished he'd written it himself. The pool was on the riverbank, near a camping ground just down from the Home. It had been formed some years ago when a pipe, carrying hot artesian water up the embankment to the old men, had broken. Hundreds of thousands of gallons had spilled out, creating a pleasure pond for bathers, especially for 'birthday-suiters' after dark, and a never-failing source of steamy hot copy for the *Mirror*.

The Home had since had a pump installed. But perhaps, Cribben wondered, he could entice Sam Speed to tell tales of old men frolicking in the pool in a state of nature. Just to spice the story up a bit. Then again, as he conjured up the vision, perhaps not.

He bought the morning paper at the bus stop and stood bemused, as he always was, at the vast spread of classified advertisements that occupied the front and second pages of the *West Australian*. It was so old-fashioned: a sea of black ink with nothing to catch the reader's attention. No entertaining high jinks like the *Mirror*. Even something responsible to provoke alarm would help rouse interest – a strike, say, or the latest news from Europe, where Adolf Hitler was making trouble again. But nope – just ads.

As Cribben turned the page and prepared to enter the bus (tucking the ticket safely in his wallet to claim against expenses), he noticed that Wirth's Circus was in town. The twins would like that when they were bit older. They'd just bawl through it at the moment. *Cassidy of Bar 20* with William Boyd was opening at the Grand, and Josh liked a good western. Perhaps Mollie would be tempted for the weekend, though she'd probably want to see *Maytime* again with Jeanette McDonald and Nelson Eddy, and who would look after the baby daughters? He would.

On and on through the dense pages: Woman's Realm, On the Land, local sports news, State Parliament, two differing views from people affected by Hitler's takeover of Austria last March. One, a Jewish opera singer who'd escaped, had just arrived in Perth saying that Austria was 'like a cauldron stirred by witches'. The other, a letter from an ecstatic German woman in the Sudetenland of Czechoslovakia, telling the world that Hitler 'knows but love and wants to make everybody happy'.

Tell that to the monkeys, Cribben thought. Anyone with half a brain could see that war clouds were gathering over Europe again. And here was the paper's editorial calling on the democracies – and especially the trade unions – to stand up to the dictators and get behind the rearmament program if another war was to be averted. They were right about that – even if Joshua Cribben, feature writer, knew in his bones that within a year or two he'd be filing altogether more serious articles as a war correspondent.

The bus jolted through the city streets towards Mounts Bay Road.

Oh. Here on page twenty was something. A daring double-column intro and a bold four-stave headline: RECORD SCORE. HUTTON MAKES 364. BRADMAN INJURED. A HOPELESS POSITION.

Page twenty! Cribben gave a small, contemptuous, journal-istic guffaw. He knew what the *Daily News* would splash this afternoon . . .

He looked out the window. It was a pleasant enough drive cer-tainly, even on a damp, overcast day. The road skirted the river: the rippling waters of the Swan on one side, the winter green of King's Park on the other, then past the Swan Brewery site. If Joshua remem-bered from his reading-in for the story, the Convict Depot had once been near here, later used for destitute old men. Well situated for the drunks among them – and a reason, apart from the prime value of the land, it had been moved thirty-odd years ago. Past the university, the bus emptying of students, and into the suburbs. Rather posh, expen-sive suburbs they were, too. Crawley, then Nedlands, with Claremont a little further to the coast. Dalkeith and the Old Men's Home on an exclusive 22 acres high above the riverfront near the point.

The place had been quite isolated when first built in 1906: surrounded by bushland on three sides, with the nearest houses (and pubs) a good mile away. But since the Great War the streets and modern brick residences of suburbia had encroached up to it. Increasingly pricey residences, too, built for people attracted by the water views, easy distance to town, and proximity to the coastal beaches and Fremantle. Prospering people, to whom the presence of the Home and so many destitute old men among them, was an unceasing embarrassment.

Josh Cribben laughed to himself again. This suburban angst was another source of good copy for the *Mirror*. Residents were always writing to the authorities complaining about intoxicated old men on the streets – who used the Claremont tram shed as a lavatory, swearing and shouting in public – and demanding proper supervision of the inmates. Worrying that their land values would be diminished if the place gained an 'unsavoury reputation'. Fat chance of that, Cribben thought, with houses here selling for £1300 and more – well above anything he and Mollie could afford. One upset householder had even written to the Minister a few years ago, saying it was 'most objectionable' for anyone to have to look at an old man in the street with some kind of paralysis, and even worse if he was 'in liquor'.

Of course, Albert Rust defended his charge by observing that some of the drunks were not his inmates – that the Home was not a prison, and once the old men were outside the gate they were as free as any other citizen and could be arrested if they committed an offence. Which they quite often were, and Rust had to spend a day in court to have them returned to his care. From a newspaper-man's point of view, this battle between virtue and vice was always an entertaining exercise in 'conflict journalism'; and from the *Mirror's* particular angle it offered, like the hot pool down the road, an opportunity to at once report scandalous goings-on in shocked tones and mock the pious self-interest of the respectable classes.

Hypocrisy has ever driven a printing press.

'Next stop, sir,' as the bus slowed on Birdwood Parade.

'Thanks!'

And just as he was getting off, Cribben remembered there was a wooden hut at the Home said to have come from the original Convict Depot, near the brewery, where the worst of the derelict old men were supposed to be housed.

Perhaps, if nude bathing was out, he could persuade Samuel Speed to tell him a few yarns about drunken brawls among the derros instead . . .

Sam had spent a good half-hour in the recreation room – coughing and blowing his nose in mounting crescendo – as he stooped over yesterday afternoon's newspaper with the magnifying glass and his almost-useless spectacles.

Much of it was sport, largely the disasters of the Fifth Test compounded, in his mind, by the news at breakfast time. But the headlines were large and easy on his semi-good eye. Something about Franco. The new bridge being built at Fremantle. There was a big photo on the back page of a little boy marching beside the King's guards in London. That was nice! And a cartoon about finding a missing necklace under a fat woman's double chin: not a problem skinny Sam Speed had ever faced. But otherwise, the writing on the Popeye comic strip was getting just too small, and the same for Brick Bradford . . .

Samuel looked around to where Bob was practising a shot at the Governor's billiard table, saw his opportunity, and all of a moment he sneezed loudly – once – twice. Sniffled extravagantly. And fell back into his chair.

'Are you all right, Sammy?' Bob put up his billiard cue and came over to the table by the window.

'Think so, Bob. I just had a little turn, there.' He sneezed again. 'And feeling the cold.'

'Let me have a look at yer. You got a hanky?'

'In me pocket,' for his nose was running again.

Bob felt for a handkerchief – found it rather mucky – and used a fairly clean one of his own.

'How yer feeling now?'

'A bit better, thanks, Bob. Sorry to interrupt your billiards, I know how you like them.'

'That's orright.'

'Remember when the Boss played a game here with Walter Lindrum? And won. Though of course Lindrum gave him a 400 start in a 401 game.'

Another cough and a heavy sniff.

'I don't know what come over me, Bob . . .'

Though of course he did.

'Are you all right for this interview? Still feel up for it?'

'Oh . . . I *think* so, Bob. Think so. Just a little giddy, there. Except . . .'

'What is it, old-timer?'

'Well, I'm feeling rather chilly. The breeze and that last shower, you know. And the heating's none too flash in here during the daytime.'

'No better in the library, neither.'

'I know. The only really warm place for these old bones is back in bed.'

'Bed? You want to go back to bed?'

'Yairs . . .'

'How will this bloke talk to you in bed? Take yer photo?'

'He can sit beside me in a chair, Bob. I'll be warm. He'll be comfy. And we'll both be pretty private. Not many people about in the ward at this time o' day.'

'What will the Boss say?'

'You'd better ask him, Bob. But you know . . .' after another dramatic sneeze and wheeze '. . . if I have to stay out here in the cold, I don't reckon I'm up for talking to anybody at all. Not today and worried about another turn. It's me ticker. I think you'd better tell that to Mr Rust as well.'

So it was, when Joshua Cribben arrived at the Old Men's Home, he was taken first to the Superintendent's office, then to the ward in Block C, where he found Samuel Speed in his nightshirt, flannel and knitted beanie, a shawl around his shoulders (courtesy of the infirmary) and cradling a mug of tea, sitting tucked up in bed and waiting.

'Sorry about this,' Albert Rust explained as he walked his visitor up to the ward, 'but the old chap felt the weather this morning – the cold snap.'

'That's all right,' Cribben replied, 'it will help give the story a bit more colour to see him in his – er – habitat.'

'Overexcitement, I suspect.' The Super smiled. 'I had the nurse look at him, take his temperature, fuss about him a bit. She says he's fine. You have to expect these things at his age.'

'What *is* Sam's age?' the journalist asked, hoping to establish the basic bread-and-butter facts at the outset.

'Well, that's rather an elastic commodity.' Rust's genial good humour broadened into a laugh. 'I've seen it put variously at ninety-two, ninety-eight – and even one hundred and five. We generally reckon around ninety-five.'

'I'll ask him.'

'By all means. But he's often a bit vague about his early days. Understandable, of course, looking back over nine decades – and perhaps there are some things he'd rather not remember. Forgetfulness can be a great blessing . . . Hello, Sam!' Albert Rust called as they entered the long ward. It smelt strongly of calcimine paint on the plaster walls and carbolic soap on the floor. And as they walked down the double row of beds, 'This is Mr Cribben from the paper come to see you.'

'Howzit, Mr Cribben?' a thin but supple voice greeted him from the skull under the knitted nightcap. 'You come with your list of questions like a policeman? Ha ha!'

'Just a little chat, Sam, about the old days. Something to interest our readers.' Joshua took the bird-like claw proffered from beneath the shawl.

'A few reminiscences, like we talked about,' the Boss reminded.

'Then why don't you sit yourself down on the chair here beside me, so I can see you with me good eye.'

The journalist removed his hat and coat, pulled a reporter's notebook from his jacket and a pencil from his shirt pocket.

'Would you like me to stay?' Rust asked, a little uncertain what Samuel might say.

'No, no,' both subject and interlocutor hastened together.

'I've got Bob here if there's anything I need,' the old man added.

Rust turned to the reporter. 'Then call in to see me when you go. There might be a few outstanding things I can help you with – one journalist to another – and give you a cup of tea.'

'Bob's already brought me a mug from the infirmary,' Samuel piped up. 'And a biscuit.'

'Thanks,' Cribben replied to Rust. 'I'll do that. And could you show the photographer up here when he arrives? I hope to get a lift back to town with him.'

'Certainly,' as the Boss departed down the ward.

The hat and coat deposited on one adjacent bed, and Bob the Tuppenny Orderly watching proceedings from the other, Josh Cribben opened his notebook to a clean page and sat down on the bedside chair – from where, Samuel Speed was gratified to observe, he was a good head higher than his interrogator. And hoped he cut a pathetic figure, for he'd removed the dentures to give his face a gaunt, collapsed appearance, and to blur the words a little.

'When were you born, Sam?' First things first.

'I were born in Birmingham in 1840,' Speed replied, sounding very confident. He'd thought about what he should say.

'So that would make you – ah – ninety-eight?' Josh Cribben used his fingers. Numbers were not his strong suit.

'Something like that . . . if you say so.'

There was a pause as Cribben wrote it down.

'Birmingham is a place in England,' Sam added helpfully. 'Pommie Land.'

'I know.'

'A big town, even in those days. Lots of factories, chimneys belching smoke and steam. Well, it's on the edge of the Black Country . . . coal pits and ironstone mines . . .'

'You have any family, Sam?'

'I had a brother . . . and a sister. She got married and lived in Birmingham, too.'

'Parents?'

'Yes, I had parents.' Pause. 'A mother and a father.'

He tried to picture them, but the faces were faded and blurred almost beyond recognition, like an image dissolving back into the metallic surface of a tintype photograph.

'They were working people . . . oh, it were hard work in the pits and mills. But they always took us children to Sunday School. Chapel in those days. That's where I learned my letters.'

And came, too, the fragment of a workhouse – a hard bench in a schoolroom – and a severe woman with a stick as he read out loud from his primer:

A is for Apple. B is for Book. C is for . . . for . . .

The stick striking the back of his hand to hurry him up with *Cat*. But Samuel was very small, and he wouldn't mention that. So he said instead, 'I like a good book. Do you read, Mr Cribben?'

'Have to in my trade, Sam. More than is good for me, sometimes.'

'You can never have too many stories. Dickens has always been a favourite.'

Great Expectations – and Magwitch, the terrifying convict, lying hidden in the marshes. Though he was to come much later. As a child Samuel learned enough of his letters to read the simpler texts hanging in the grimy workhouse. Repeating over and over the shorter syllables – *er-er*, *the-the*, *en-en* – SUFFER THE CHILDREN and GOD IS LOVE above his cot. Sufficient to recite the Lord's Prayer by rote and even to follow some of the easier words painted large on the chapel wall. *Our Father which art in Heaven . . .*

'Did you keep in touch with your family, Sam?'

'Well, my parents died.' Much safer to return from his father and mother in heaven to this world. 'A hard life, like I said. And we all had to go out to work at an early age. Some of the pit boys, you know, were only nine or ten. Younger. But I didn't like it underground, I got cloister . . . cluster . . . what is it? Afraid . . .'

'Claustrophobia.'

'That's it. Little boys and girls in the darkness for twelve hours a day. Pushing heavy coal trucks down narrow passages where the ponies couldn't go. It were terrible. They wouldn't know what it was like, these days.'

'No, indeed. They passed a law against it.'

'Yes, but that didn't stop them. Not where we were. Not when I was young.'

'So, what did *you* do?'

'Oh . . .' Samuel sought to look down the vista of the sepia-coloured years. 'I couldn't stand the mines, Mr Cribben. Or the factories. I needed space. Open air. And then I hurt me eye.'

He turned the blind optic towards his visitor.

'How did that happen?'

'Don't know, properly. A stone chip flying up . . .'

I can still see that carriage going hell-for-leather down the road and the gravel flying.

'Something like that. An accident, anyway, and it left me with a scar under me ear and unable to see a lot out of the left peeper. Oh, I could still read a bit and there was the good eye. Any interesting little pieces from the penny magazines, you know, if I found one lying about in the street and the words weren't too hard. Especially if it had pictures. But it was no good in the pits. Or the mills. As soon as I could I left Birmingham and found work on the farms. I liked that. Out in the fields with the plough and horses or bringing in the crops. That was lovely in a good year . . . a big "harvest home" in the barns, with a fiddler and dancing and everything . . .'

He could see the revels still in pale shades of brown and black and white. Funny that these memories had no other colour in them.

'I was never a very big lad, but it put meat on me bones and roses in me cheeks.'

'Did you still see your brother and sister at all?'

'Oh, sometimes if it weren't too far I'd get a ride with a wagon into Birmingham to see my married sister. But then not so often as I began to grow up and had to find work further afield. There were some bad years, and I was on the road a lot. Out past Warwick . . . down towards Banbury and Oxfordshire . . . So no, I didn't see her much then. And after that – well, after that came my trouble, and I've never seen my brother nor my sister since.'

'What happened, Sam?'

So, now we come to it. Magwitch, in his prison rags and irons, seizing Pip in an overgrown graveyard and snarling, 'Keep still, you little devil, or I'll cut your throat.' *Scaring the boy half to death.*

'Can you tell me about it?'

And through the smoke-grey clouds of memory came the sudden strike and flare of a scarlet flame.

4

FIRE

'Sam, can you tell me about it . . .?' Cribben asked once more into the long silence.

Ah.

'There's nothing much to tell. A pal and I set fire to a stack of barley in a field. At Woodstock, near Oxford. Got caught.'

Rick-burning was taken pretty seriously in country parts, Cribben knew: certainly was around Toodyay. The journalist's nose sensed the making of a storyline.

'Was it a political act, Sam? Were you and your mate protesting against the government? Against the corn laws . . . the new machines?'

'No, young feller. Nothing like that. It was because we were starving.'

Sam allowed another small silence to fall between them. Before going on:

'We *wanted* to go to prison . . . to get something to eat. Regular meals, like.'

Oh. Was that all? Joshua felt the story slipping away from him.

No grand, defiant gesture here. No heartless landlords or cruel tyranny. Samuel Speed was no Luddite: just another criminal.

'And I suppose you could say,' the old chap waved any further discussion away with a laugh, 'that we got what we asked for. Years of meals provided courtesy of the government!' And he sipped the lukewarm dregs of hospital tea in his mug.

So few words. So much left unspoken behind them. Nothing much to tell – or *would* tell. Yet in his mind Sam travelled that whole livelong day again. He could guess the disappointment in Cribben's eyes that he had not something more newsworthy to tell his readers. But in that one day – on that one act turned the whole pivot of his life. Striking a match and setting it to the barley stack had led Samuel Speed to seventy-two years' exile from his native land.

And he was back there now, tramping the slippery road from Bladon village that Saturday afternoon in early August 1863. Sam and his mate, Tommy Jones, a baker with the army who'd lost his place some weeks ago: the two of them so hungry from lack of work and money, that every step felt a burden. And there was Tommy cooking up such vivid pictures of currant buns with icing, and bread smoking hot from the oven, you could almost eat his words! Until they dissolved the moment Samuel reached out to take them.

Would they never get a job? Anything would do – just a few shillings in the pocket, or even a good meal from a farmer's wife to fill the stomach in return for helping with the pigs or the hay stooks. But the answer was always the same. Nothing.

Only half an hour ago the two had gone into a yard back down the road, the dogs barking and the farmer eyeing them suspiciously as they came through the gate. Sammy couldn't blame him – not in retrospect – for the two young men were both pretty ragged and not very clean. Shifty, too: for when you are desperate, the desperation always shows.

'We were wondering, sir, if you was looking for a couple of hands about the place?' Tommy began. The two had not been together long, but being the elder and a former military man, he usually took the lead. 'Both good workers . . .'

'Sorry – but I have all the help I need.'

'Strong, willing, useful in the fields . . .'

'Barley's already in,' the farmer countered, 'and wheat's not ready to cut. Been a poor start to summer.'

'Milk the cow for you . . . bit of thatching . . . drainage?'

'I told you,' the man became threatening, for he knew a couple of vagabonds when he saw them. 'I've got all the help I need.'

'We've got *nothing*,' young Samuel pleaded.

'Then the Union workhouse is just up the road at Woodstock. Built for people like you.'

'We've been there before. And they sent us on our way.'

'Well, go somewhere else. Now, be off with you – and close the gate.'

The same everywhere. And to be sure, Samuel knew the summer had not started very well. The farmer spoke truly, there.

Spring had been fine: good rain and a little warmth for ploughing and sowing, and work had been reasonably plentiful for an itinerant labourer in Oxfordshire. The farmers had even been talking of a bumper year. But then had come a long, dry spell – and word along the wayside and even in the weekly paper, when Sam found a torn page, turned to fears of drought. Not as he was to know months – years – of drought in Western Australia, but bad enough, in English terms, to raise concerns for the harvest. The wheat so far had been soft and unripe – the meadow grass, without rain, slow to grow for

haymaking. And so, in the nature of things, the casual rural work
Speed depended upon had also dried up.

The thirty shillings he'd been able to save began to evaporate
as well.

Sam set his face down the road from Banbury, his few possessions tied in a bundle, like the swags of later years. He was lucky to
get a short day's work from time to time; but mostly it was sleeping
rough in the hedgerows or under stacks, and eating quite literally
into his little store of reserves, until his money had almost gone. And
being young – still in his teens, whatever Samuel told the journalist
Cribben – his youthful self-confidence had started to fail with it.

It was about this time, in late July, that Samuel fell in with the
unemployed baker, Tommy Jones – *Tom Jones!* – another scallywag
from his stories. At twenty-four and formerly with the Royal
Engineers, Tommy had much more experience of life. They got on
together; pooled what little they had; shared the crusts of daily bread
and half-pints of small beer they were able to buy; went halves with
the few coins they managed to beg and the odd jobs they scrounged.
But it was never enough for one man, let alone two. And by the time
they reached the market town of Woodstock, Speed and Jones were
both utterly destitute.

Their only recourse was to the Woodstock Union workhouse,
which they found a short way up a lane leading off the High Street.
It was a large, two-storey building in the local stone, glowing a
soft dun colour in the sunlight, constructed on a kind of elongated
H plan: one end wing for women, the other for men; the reception
area, Master's rooms and offices in the middle; the dining hall, facili-
ties and another accommodation block behind. It was not much
more than twenty years old, with recent additions, having been
built at the time when responsibility for the Poor Laws shifted from

individual parishes to collective groups of them, known as unions: the new and larger workhouses sheltering the poor from a much wider district under an elected board of governors.

They also had some room for itinerant travellers in want, such as Speed and Jones – 'vagrants', as they were generally known – and the Master allowed them to stay for a few days.

'Thank you, sir. We're very grateful to you.'

'Mind you,' the Master went on, 'you will have to look for work while you're here. We're pretty full as it is with our own people. If you've found nothing after three or four days, you'll have to move on.'

Whatever the broader intent behind the reformed Poor Laws, in practice they were still guided by a parochial spirit. Each union took care of its local indigents supported by the poor rate, and strangers – outsiders – who did not contribute, were not wanted.

But for Sam and Tom Jones, they had at least several days' respite. They'd missed midday dinner – but they slept that first night in a dormitory with a number of other homeless men, having a little bread and cheese in their stomachs, rich as any Christmas feast after the hunger they'd known. Yet work in town was nowhere to be found for them: not for a baker with such undoubted gifts as Tommy possessed, nor for a willing young jobbing labourer like Sam. They went down byways into the countryside around, knocking on farm doors and even cottages. But the answer was unvarying: nothing available.

At length the workhouse Master told them their time was up and they'd have to leave in the morning.

'I should try the Oxford Road if I were you. Most of the other fellows head there. Bigger place.'

But the pair had already been down the main thoroughfare a little way without any success, and it seemed foolish to follow everybody else along a bleak path to disappointment. Thus, a mile out of town the next morning, they decided to turn down the road that led to Bladon and the villages beyond.

The problem was, however, that the road skirted the Blenheim estates of the mighty Duke of Marlborough, and most of the farmers were his tenants. Indeed, Sam and Tommy passed the imposing entrance gates as they left Woodstock, just near the police station, and could see down the long drive to the vast baroque stone pile of Blenheim Palace, said to be the greatest house in England. Inspired by Versailles, Blenheim was so grand, that envy was beside the point. They had, in fact, already been to the estate office asking for work; but the Duke – or his agent – gave preference to local employment, especially in lean times. There was nothing for a couple of vagrants, when so many of their own were in need, and this rule followed them all the way down the Bladon road.

For nearly two days Speed and Jones had barely eaten, except for the few scraps they'd been able to save from their workhouse rations. To add to their misery, it started to rain at last. Good for the crops and the prospects for future work, but at present all it did was wet them through, until eventually they had no choice but to turn around and head back towards Woodstock. Through Bladon and past St Martin's church, where members of the ducal Churchill family were buried. Closing one more farmer's gate as the dogs were almost set upon them.

'I told you – I've got all the help I need.'

'We've got *nothing*.'

And thus, with hunger-driven steps, the pair reached the Oxford road again.

By rights they should have turned towards the university town, but that was ten miles away, and Woodstock was only one.

'We've got to go back to the work'us,' Tommy said.

'But they told us to go.'

'It's late and we're starving. They'll *have* to take us in, at least for the night.'

'I don't know about that . . .'

'Come on!'

And with Jones in command they headed back towards Woodstock.

The two hadn't gone very far when they met a townsman – a youngish man like themselves, but in altogether happier circumstances – walking the other way. He worked as an assistant in a drapery store, and was coming home that Saturday afternoon to a wife and child with the week's wages in his pocket. Church, tomorrow, at St Andrew's.

'Excuse me, sir,' Jones began, 'but would you be able to spare us a little change? We've not eaten for two days . . .'

'I haven't very much.' The man hesitated, for drapers' assistants were not paid a fortune.

'Anything . . . please,' Samuel begged.

'Wait a moment.'

Remembering his duty of Christian charity, the young man fumbled in his pocket and produced a halfpenny.

'I'm sorry, it's all I can spare. I have a family depending on me.'

'Thank you, sir, we're grateful to you.'

'Very.'

At least they could buy one of those currant buns with icing to eat. But Jones cautioned against spending it too quickly. They'd go back to the workhouse first, get a bed for the night and supper, and keep the halfpenny against future requirements.

Yet the workhouse was not as accommodating as Tom Jones had supposed.

Night was closing in by the time they arrived, and the Master was away for the evening, attending a private dinner in town. But one of the porters, Charles Ferrabee, was on duty in the vestibule when Speed and Jones rang the bell at the front door. He opened it, and by the light that shone on their faces from the hall lamp recognised them at once.

'Oh, it's you two, is it,' he growled.

A workhouse inmate himself once, who owed his present employment entirely to the Master's goodwill, Charlie Ferrabee was wise to every trick in the repertoire of indigence. He'd done them all.

'You both back agin? What yer want?'

'We need a bed for the night . . . something to eat.'

'We've given yer a bed and fed yer for several nights already. Master's told yer to go. Said to make for Oxford.'

'We went down the wrong way.'

'Then more fool you. But you won't fool me. Go on – you've been told to leave.'

'Just one night – please. Where's the Master?'

'Master's out.'

'Then who's in charge?'

'I am. I do what the Master says. And I'm telling yer – git orf!'

And he slammed the solid wooden door in their faces.

Sam Speed and Tom Jones stood on the workhouse step for a few moments, not knowing quite what to do. Rejection and despair had so reduced their natural spirits, that the mind seemed unable to grasp the enormity of their situation or suggest any possible way out.

'Tommy,' Samuel whispered low, almost with a whimper. 'What now?'

He felt as if he wanted to curl himself up small and cry, as he had as a child into his mother's lap. Or worse – as many a sheep, about to go under the butcher's knife, ceased all struggle and resigned itself limply to fate.

'What are we going to do?'

'I don't know. Yet.' Tommy tried to kick his more adult mind into some kind of motion. What would the Royal Engineers do in this emergency?

'We could use the halfpenny to buy a couple of plain buns,' Samuel said at length. 'There's a shop open in the High Street. Find shelter in a barn somewhere.' For the rain was threatening once more.

'No.' Tommy Jones was anticipating things more quickly. 'No, Sammy. I got a better idea.'

'What?'

'Move aways up the lane 'ere,' for he'd spied Charlie Ferrabee looking at them through the lighted window. 'The thing is, Sammy, if we buy a currant bun with that halfpenny now, it might last us the night. But what about tomorrer? And the day after tomorrer? We'll be no better off. Back where we are now.'

'So . . .?'

'If the work'us won't have us . . .' (how like *Oliver Twist* he sounded as Samuel, in his old man's bed, heard Tom Jones speak down the kaleidoscope of years), '. . . if they won't give us something to eat, there's only one place that will.'

'Where's that, Tommy?'

'Prison. They got to feed you there. Gov'mint regulation. Meat. And potaters. And cocoa. And half a pound loaf o' bread a day. I know, becoz I'm a baker.'

'Hot soup?' Such a feast of piping food Tommy's words had

conjured up. 'The police station's just down the lane. Will we ask them there?'

'It don't work like that, silly. You got to do somethin' wrong first. Get yourself arrested.'

'What sort o' wrong?' Vague memories of the Ten Commandments came back to Samuel from his childhood days in Sunday school. 'Break a winder? Pinch something?'

Thou Shalt Not Steal painted on the wall next to The Lord's Prayer.

'Not sure we're up to that, Sammy. I hardly got enough strength left to chuck a brick. But there is something . . .'

'What's that?'

'The other day I noticed a stack o' barley in a field just along of here. If we was to spend that halfpenny on a box o' matches and set fire to the rick, they'd *have* to arrest us then.'

'And give us a meal in jail?'

'Yeah. Quite a few meals, actually.'

'They serve you with a long sentence, eh?' But his humour fell flat, especially with the arrival of second thoughts. 'I don't know, Tommy . . . it seems to be taking things a bit far. We could be in real trouble.'

Samuel tried to remember if *Thou Shalt Not Set Fire to A Barley Rick* also appeared in the Ten Commandments, but he could not visualise it on the painted list.

'Have you got a better idea then?' Jones suddenly turned on the lad with a savagery, bred of hunger, that Sam had not heard before. 'If so, spit it out.'

'No . . . I don't know.' His resistance had been brought so low by the shock of Ferrabee and distress, that in the moment Samuel couldn't formulate anything much by way of an idea at all.

'Then are you in wiv me or not? If you *are*, say so. If not, shove off and go your own ways by yerself.'

His defences quite demolished by Tommy's violent words, Speed could only surrender and give his assent. Now, with a plan of action in mind, they traced their steps back down the lane – moving very quietly in the shadows past the workhouse and the porter's lamplit window, creeping by the narrow stone houses at the end, until they turned into the high street. The shop was still open. They went in; resisting the display of currant buns, Jones asked for a small packet of lucifer matches; handed over the halfpenny; and the pair returned as quietly as they'd come along Hensington Lane.

Soft their footsteps might have been, but Samuel's heart was beating in his breast like a hammer. This was the first truly bad thing – the first crime – he'd have committed in his life; and here, on the brink of it, the incendiary voices of guilt and fear from chapel, desperation and survival in the present were clashing inside his head. What would happen? Would he be hanged, perhaps? Transported? Whipped? Who could tell? But at least, sweet reason soothed, it would be with a full belly.

Turn back. Turn back, discordant conscience warned. But it was too late, for already they were past the workhouse and standing at the barred, wooden gate that led into a field where stood the barley stack, silhouetted dark against the sky.

'Will I stay here and keep watch?' Sammy asked – a last, feeble struggle against sin as Jones undid the peg and the gate swung wide.

'No. You come wiv me, boy. We're in this together. Remember?'

Footsteps crossed the damp grass to the rick. Hands rummaged past the outer stook to a dry place further in, where the rain had not penetrated. And with an evil yellow flare, the first match was struck and set among the tinder. A smouldering moment of hesitation.

Another flash. Then it caught and licked a crimson tongue of flame into the darkness. Flickering as a serpent, and hissing with joy as it fed, the sparks slid from one stalk to another, spitting and spreading dragonfire until the barley began to burn with its own delight. A plume of thin, white smoke spiralled upwards, quickly filling as the stack ignited, and became a vast cloud – a thing of nightmares, threatening and storming in memory, lit by lightning and cinders and roaring flames.

'Oh Christ! What have we done?'

But Tom Jones merely turned to the lad and laughed.

'Now, Sammy, we can go to the police station.'

A few minutes later, Charles Ferrabee happened to look out of his window again to see if those two vagrants had gone – noticed a curious orange glow in the night – and going outside, saw the blaze.

He at once raised the alarm, shouting 'Fire! Fire!' into the street, and running back inside began to ring the workhouse bell. By the time Tom Jones and Sam Speed reached the end of the lane, the cry had already been taken up, and people were running towards them.

'Bring buckets! Call out the fire cart! Jo Heynes' rick is on fire! We'll catch who did this! Hurry! Hurry now! We'll get 'em!'

'But Tommy, it wasn't *me*,' Samuel whispered when they were around the corner and out of earshot. The magnitude of what had just happened – and its consequences – began to bear upon him, far more terrifying than even the prospect of starvation had been. 'I never done it. I never lit no match.'

'Oh yes, you *did*! You were wiv me, young Sammy.'

Jones turned and, seizing the lad by the throat, pushed him roughly against the wall.

'You had your chance to git. You stayed. You were as much part of it as me. And if you try to 'peach on me, Samuel Speed, I will tell the police it was *you* who begged the halfpenny. It was *you* what suggested the matches. It was *you* that threw 'em away back up the lane. And I'll show 'em where. You understand that? Boy?'

'Yes . . . yes, Tommy.'

But I never did!

'Well then, I hope you do.'

He released the lad, still shaking, and together they crossed the Oxford road and walked towards the police station. Where they waited outside, summoning the last bit of courage required to go inside.

It was then that Inspector Lewis Coates came out of the building, buttoning up his jacket. He'd heard the alarm and, quickly finishing his tea, was on his way to investigate when he saw the pair standing by the stoop.

'What do you two want? Is it about the fire . . .?'

'Yes, sir.' Jones spoke first.

'What can you tell me about it?'

'Well . . . just to say we done it.'

'You lit the fire? Where?'

'Stack o' barley, up past the work'us there.'

'And what did you do with the matches?'

'Threw 'em away. On the road, just outside of the gate.'

'And you?' The inspector turned to Samuel Speed. 'Were you involved with this too?'

'Yes, sir.'

'And you're turning yourselves in? Why?'

'Because we're starving. The workhouse turned us away, and we've nothing to eat.'

'I see.' Inspector Coates drew his breath. He'd rarely solved a case quite so quickly. 'Well then, you'd better come with me.'

And he escorted them inside the police station. He took their statements and particulars which they signed, for both Samuel and Tommy could write their names, albeit rather slowly and awkwardly. Samuel even made a careful show of reading his statement first. Words like *rick*, *matches* and *fire* were easy enough. *Workhouse* he could mouth to himself phonetically, even if things like *Ferrabee* and *feloniously* tossed him. Still, Samuel understood the gist of it and attached his name to the paper in ink.

'Can we get some food now?'

There were still the last procedures to complete. Inspector Coates formally laid charges of suspected arson against each man. And deciding to go up the lane with a lantern to look for the box of matches, told his Sergeant to lock them in the cells.

Though, supper having already been served, Tom Jones and Sam Speed had to remain hungry until morning. With only the crumbs of self-doubt and recrimination to feed them for the first night of their long incarceration.

5

TRIAL

'We shoulda bought that bun . . .' aged Samuel Speed murmured softly – almost inaudibly – to himself.

It takes pages to write it down, but mere seconds for memory to relive the whole experience and return Sam to his bed and the ward in the Old Men's Home, with some other young feller – a reporter – asking the questions.

'What was that, Sam? You want a bun?'

'Eh? No, no, nothing like that. Bob brought me a sweet biscuit already!' With a laugh.

Joshua Cribben looked down at his notebook, just like that Inspector Coates.

'So, you handed yourself in and went to court. Where was that, Sam? And the sentence . . .?'

'We were taken to Oxford Castle. The judge give us seven years. And we knew at once that meant transportation.'

'How?'

'Anything under that, you served your time in England. Otherwise it was bye-bye . . .'

So lightly the words floated between them, borne on the wings of Sammy's little chuckle and caught on the tip of Mr Cribben's pencil. So quick and easily spoken. But how to convey, even if he wished to, the sense of dread that hung over both Speed and Tom Jones as they realised the full weight of the law descending upon them once they turned themselves in to the Woodstock police?

To be sure, after that first ravenous night in the lock-up, breakfast had been brought to them: thin porridge, a slice of bread and a mug of lukewarm tea, no worse than any workhouse meal they'd eaten – and considerably more satisfying, after almost three days without anything apart from rainwater. The hard bench and dingy surroundings were familiar enough from other dosshouses – and a lot more comfortable than sleeping under brambles in the wet. It was only when they saw the morning light through the high barred window and watched the iron shadows cast by the rising sun creep across the stone wall, that they grasped – really understood for the first time – they were not free to go outside into the day. A solid door strapped and studded, a metal lock without a key, and an observation slot stood between them and the freedom of the open road – and this was the price of the porridge they'd just eaten to stave the pains of starvation.

'Tommy, what do you think will happen to us?' Sammy asked, as his mind sought to adjust to these new circumstances in his life. 'What will they do?'

'I'm not sure, boy,' Jones replied, speaking softly. 'I've never been in this situation afore. But I tell you one thing,' and a sense of urgency crept low into his voice, 'you *remember* what I told you outside.'

'Promise, Tommy, I won't 'peach on you.'

'I know you won't,' with a small gloat. And then more seriously, 'I meant the other.'

For standing at the threshold of the police station last night, just before Inspector Coates appeared, Jones had taken sudden pity on the lad. He'd frightened Samuel enough to acknowledge his part in the crime; and by way of reparation he offered the lad a little advice.

'Listen, Sammy. I don't know how old you really are . . .'

'I'm only . . .'

'I don't care, but whatever it is, you tell 'em you're eighteen. Got it? Eighteen. The law can be very cruel to youngsters.'

'How cruel?'

'Never mind. Just remember what I said.'

And so, in the cell that first morning, Jones reiterated his words. 'Eighteen. Remember it.'

'I won't forget.'

Thereafter, whatever his true age, Samuel Speed was forever branded on the official records as being eighteen years old at the time of his arrest and trial.

That first day, being Sunday, they were kept in the cell, from where they could hear church bells ringing, fragments of hymn singing and prayers – no doubt being said for the comfort of Joseph Heynes, the victim of last night's arson attack and a popular local man, who ran a good inn. Not much, Samuel assumed, by way of solace for *his* soul, however penitent he now felt with something solid in his guts.

Not until the following morning were they handcuffed – 'My first pair!' Sammy joked to Tom Jones to keep up spirits – and they were taken to Inspector Coates again.

'I went up Hensington Lane and found the packet of matches where you said you threw them,' he said, stern of voice. 'I consider that proof enough of your statements that you lit the fire. And we have evidence from Ferrabee, the porter, that he saw you both standing outside the workhouse and going towards Heynes's gate shortly before the blaze broke out. The charges therefore will be upgraded from suspicion to the fact of arson.'

'Yes, sir.'

'I can tell you,' the detective went on, leaning back in the chair and putting his fingers together in an attitude of official sanctity, 'there is quite a strong feeling here over Saturday night's fire. Mr Heynes is well liked. If this were America, from all I've read of that country, we might well have a lynch mob after you by now.'

He paused to allow the effect of those words to do their work. And when Coates could see they had done so, he added: 'However, fortunately this is not America, fighting a murderous civil war, but a peaceable, law-abiding nation. Nevertheless, I think it would be better for everybody – including yourselves – if you were removed to Oxford as soon as possible.'

Oxford? We're going to university?

But Inspector Coates's next words were no laughing matter.

'I've therefore arranged for the magistrate to convene a sittings today, where you'll be arraigned. You won't be required to plead, but we'll request you be remanded in custody to a later session of the Assizes at Oxford. You should be in the castle prison by late this afternoon.'

So it transpired. Rain had come on again as the horses pulling the covered police transport – the 'Black Maria' – splashed their way down the last of the Woodstock road, and began to rumble with the ominous sound of drums over the cobbled streets of the ancient university town. Speed and Jones, sitting cuffed and hobbled in the back, could see nothing very much, except the receding view of buildings through the small, grated rear window. Down St Giles and Magdalene Street – glimpses of town and gown as the wagon threaded its way through the grey, damp light – until at length they stopped and heard voices close by. The sound of gates being unbarred and swung open. Movement. And then, through the rear window, their vision was filled with an arch in a wall of grey stone, like a maw being filled as the gates were closed again, shutting off the last green glimpse of a grassy hill.

Oxford Castle. And the first thing Sam and Tommy saw, as they were unloaded from the police wagon, were the high, square battlements of St George's Tower brooding over them.

Like a doom! And it was, too.

Being, as they were, on remand and legally regarded as still innocent, for the next three months Speed and Jones were in a kind of penitentiary limbo. They were subject to the regimen of the jail like every other prisoner: sleeping in cells, sometimes with several other remand men; their lives ordered by the ringing of bells for eating and sleeping; and their every action under the strict supervision of warders.

But they did not have to wear the grey prison uniform, marked with the government broad arrow (which, given the pitiful state of their own clothes, they began to regret as autumn drew on). Nor did they have to work at the mind-numbing hard labour the authorities deemed so essential to reforming the criminal mind – picking oakum or winding the capstan. Instead, they had time in the exercise yard, and access to legal advice to prepare their defences for the pending trial, should funds permit it. Which, for Sam and Tommy, they clearly did not.

Nevertheless, the closed, confined world of Oxford Castle still bore down upon them like a press. For Samuel it was especially hard, and his adolescent spirit began to falter. It wasn't the rigorous discipline of daily life so much – not the discomfort of cold brick and stone, a hard bed, and plain food. As a rural labourer, such things were a normal part of existence: indeed, watery potatoes for midday dinner with the occasional scrap of meat, however poorly cooked, were a luxury only dreamed of but recently when he'd been starving on the road. In that respect, as Sammy jested to the journalist, their plan had been a success. Tommy Jones was right: three meals a day, provided courtesy of Her Majesty Queen Victoria!

No, it wasn't the physical privations that so reduced him, but the psychological ones. The high walls and medieval ramparts. The towers and barred windows. Stone and steel and iron gates, beyond which he could see the sky and scudding clouds, but which prevented him from going out to meet them. The world had been open to him before. Now it was denied – and for Sam Speed, it was the mere fact he was no longer free that so began to crush him. Without work for his hands and, being on remand, denied access to the prison library or schoolroom to occupy his mind, the hours between meals stretched into a boredom that only fed his anxiety.

Their trial had been set down for the sittings at the end of November, and as the date approached, Samuel quite visibly began to lose heart. There hadn't been much of him when he was arrested, God knows, reduced after days of hunger and privation. But now, having put on weight after a regular prison diet for several months, he began to lose it again. His face acquired that sunken pallor, so familiar in the visage of every prisoner, and his manner became more withdrawn, more nervous. He debated with himself, over and over, whether the certainty of three meals a day was worth the deprivation of his liberty – and deciding (again, with a full belly) that it was not, Sam became increasingly depressed by the thought that, so far as the law was concerned, he would lose that argument and be sentenced to spend eternity in this place.

A week or so before the trial, Jones found him one afternoon standing very disconsolate by himself in a corner of the exercise yard.

'Cheer up, Sammy,' he remarked, 'it ain't as bad as all that.'

'But it *is*, Tommy. Trial's on Monday, and I didn't do it. I didn't . . .'

'Come on, Sam-u-el, you know what happened.'

'Yes, but I can't abide the thought of being here forever. I can't . . .'

'The food's all right. It's what we wanted.'

'But it ain't worth it, and I never . . .'

'And it won't be for always. Chap told me that, seven years or more, and they send yer to Australia.'

'Botany Bay?'

The horrors of that hellhole were imprinted on everybody's imagination.

'Not anymore, no . . . the other place . . . Swan River . . . Western Australia.'

It was scarcely an improvement. The idea made Speed so distressed he was almost weeping – and Tom Jones, to his great surprise, found himself touched by it, as an older person may for a younger in travail. Whatever the truth of the rick-burning, therefore, and whatever he may have said or done at the time, Jones put a comforting hand on his mate's shoulder.

'That's all right, Sammy,' he said. 'I can see you're in a bad way. If you want to change your story . . . to plead Not Guilty when you go before the judge, I'll back you up in it. I'll say I threatened you.'

'And so you did.'

'Yes . . . well, that may help things a bit for yer, though I can't guarantee nothing, you understand.'

'No, but I'll tell 'em. I'll let them know I'm not guilty . . .'

'You do that, Sammy. You pass the word through the warders to the Guv'nor.'

And satisfied that he'd given his young companion a week of hope at least, Jones let it go at that – though he remained quite perplexed as to why he'd done so.

Mr Justice Crompton was in a genial mood that Monday morning.

He had travelled up with his associate, tipstaff and servants from the circuit court at Reading on Saturday – in the same train, as it happened, as the Crown Prince and Princess of Prussia (otherwise known as Victoria, the Princess Royal, eldest daughter of the dear Queen), who were paying a private visit to the university. They'd been welcomed at the station with all due expressions of loyalty and ceremony by Canon Stanley of Christ Church Cathedral, who was to show them around the principal attractions of Oxford.

The majesty of the law also received every proper observance, with his Lordship met on the platform by the High Sheriff, the Under Sheriff and a retinue of gentlemen from the faculties and profession, who escorted Sir Charles Crompton with much respect to the County Hall and Court, in New Road.

The building had been erected only twenty years or so earlier: a curious confection in the local stone of Norman turrets and battlements, combined with late-Georgian high-arched windows and spacious rooms. Some people described it as 'quite the most abominable pseudo-Gothic Assizes Court in all England', but in this they were perhaps being a little unfair. It was located right next door to the prison – the view from the Jury Room looked out to its walls – and the architect no doubt was trying to emulate the authentic early Gothic of the original Norman castle. In any event, convenience, not style, was the predominating factor. So handy was the court-room, an underground tunnel with barred gates at either end had been constructed from the jail to the holding cells below the dock, thus saving the trouble of having to convey prisoners anywhere else and minimising their chances of escape.

Here, on a large, velvet-upholstered chair, his Lordship took his seat on the Bench. A carved canopy was suspended above his head, the Royal Coat of Arms on the wall behind him. The legal frater-nity packed the well of the court and the public galleries above, like a dress-circle audience at the theatre. The Commission, opening these sittings of the Oxford Winter Assizes, was read; speeches of welcome were made; and after the civilities and a light luncheon, the learned judge was escorted to his lodgings in St Giles. Where, later that afternoon, he was waited upon by the Mayor and city authorities, together with representatives of the university, who pre-sented him with the customary gift of a pair of white kid gloves, fringed with gold, as a symbol of fidelity and loyalty. The following morning, Mr Justice Crompton attended Sunday service at Christ Church, where the Reverend Doctor Stanley preached an eloquent valedictory Assize sermon to a full congregation on the subject of divine peace, truth, charity and the ideal principles of a university.

It had all been very satisfactory and, at the age of a trim and healthy sixty-six, Sir Charles felt in particularly fine form in his judicial wig and robes when the court assembled at ten o'clock on Monday for the sessions.

The Grand Jury was called and empanelled: a distinguished selection of twenty-one upright County gentlemen – landowners,

commercial and professional people including three Members of
Parliament, one of whom was the foreman. Before bringing up
the accused, however, Mr Justice Crompton turned to the jury
and delivered his opening charge on the matters that would be put
before them.

He'd been through the papers and thought they'd find them
all pretty clear cases, except one or two which he brought to their
attention. There was the matter of a respectable workhouse official
charged with forging receipts (a hanging offence not so long ago,
though being a man of liberal principles, Sir Charles was glad it was
so no longer); a rather painful case of manslaughter; and several
cases of rick-burning, where the jury would have to judge from the
demeanour of the witnesses whether to believe them or not.

It might sound strange to modern ears for a judge to run over
the list to the jury *before* a trial. But that was the way of it. And
indeed, to the intense misery of Sam Speed and the other prisoners
waiting below, who could hear the words wafting down the staircase, through the open door, kept by a warder, and the barred cell
gate, his Lordship reserved his strictest remarks for the rick-burners.

'I must say to you, gentlemen, that a vast proportion of the crime
here in Oxford and Berkshire, is rick-burning, as I find it's become so
prevalent all over the country. There were six cases in Reading last
week, and *eleven* are to be brought before you today. Almost universally they appear to be strangers to the County who, in a state of
destitution, resort to the crime apparently for the purpose of being
put in prison and sentenced to penal servitude. Indeed, a long time
in prison seems to be just what they want!'

A little pause for this moment of judicial levity – before the words
became more severe. 'And in my opinion, a *short* term of imprisonment would do nothing to mark the enormity of their crime.'

Enormity? The word struck Samuel, listening in the cell below, with all the force of a gallows drop. *It was bad to burn Heynes's stack, I know, but enormous? We didn't hurt anybody. Nobody lost a life, unlike the sad case of manslaughter the judge just mentioned.* But then, of course, the law always regarded crimes against property as far more serious than crimes against the person.

'Well, I hope these people will not find penal servitude as pleasant as they seem to expect.' His Lordship, in scarlet and ermine, continued his remarks to the Grand Jury above. 'It did occur to me in Reading, gentlemen, that if we, as a community, are to resort to corporal punishment at all, it might be for such cases as rick-burning, where it could have some effect in preventing men from committing the crime . . .'

And preventing them from starving? But his Lordship didn't pause to consider that question.

'However, the law does not permit the administration of corporal punishment except to persons under the age of sixteen . . .'

How wise of Tommy Jones to warn me!

'At Reading I was able to order a boy to be flogged . . . and in a case to come before you today, there is a child of nine here charged with arson.'

Samuel looked down at the ragged imp, John Smith, beside him in the cell, his hands in irons, as were they all, and crying to himself. He'd had not one visitor in the prison since July, except the magistrate who'd committed him there. And Sam felt the same compassion for little Johnny – as an elder to a younger – that Jones had shown Sam when he offered to testify for him. And Speed would have put his arms around the boy for comfort, too, had he been able.

'Evidently it would be of no use to keep such a child of nine in prison,' the judge's words came floating down.

The birch awaits you, laddie.

'And I believe it is a subject for consideration whether corporal punishment might not be extended to others, older than sixteen, who commit this particular crime.' Certainly something for the Members of Parliament sitting among them in the jury box to think about.

Sentence first – verdict afterwards!

Old Sam Speed, in his bed, could hear these words from Lewis Carroll's *Alice in Wonderland* echoing three-quarters of a century later. *Sentence first – verdict afterwards!* in the court of the Queen of Hearts. And it occurred to Samuel, with a laugh, that they had been written by an Oxford don at much the same time of his own trial, where their author would have had every opportunity to see Mr Justice Crompton in action.

The Grand Jury having been nicely primed, the hearings began. They did not take long. As each prisoner's name was called by the clerk, repeated by the usher and called by a guard down the stairs to those below, a warder unlocked the cell gate, the accused stepped forward and had the handcuffs removed. It was a concession to the presumption of innocence that every person had before they ascended the narrow wooden stairs, a guard fore and aft, to the waist-high barrier of the dock – but only a concession. Everything else that architecture, interior design, costume and ritual could do to overawe the prisoner, had been done. The presiding judge on his high dais in front; the suited jurymen in their box to his right; the clerks and lawyers wigged and gowned at the bar table (whom very few could afford in their defence), all united to focus attention and prejudice on the sad and solitary figures of those who'd been charged.

Intimidating it might have been, but the leniency shown by the Court in the first few cases gave heart to Sam Speed and his fellows listening below. The man charged with manslaughter pleaded guilty, but as he was defending his mother and had not meant to kill her attacker, Mr Justice Crompton sentenced him to three days' imprisonment from the start of the Assizes and had him released immediately.

Three cheers downstairs!

Three men who robbed a jewellery shop were given only twelve months, because there'd not been much damage to property or terror caused to the inhabitants. Even nine-year-old John Smith, whose head could barely be seen above the rail, had his whipping deferred and was sent back to prison to wait for another few months until a missing witness turned up.

But then came the arson cases. The first three were each sentenced to six years, accompanied by a lecture from the judge in similar terms to the one he'd given to the jury.

'You say you did it to get victuals, but it's a shocking thing to destroy property in this way. You might suppose you'll have a pleasant time as prisoners getting into public works, but you'll find a good deal you don't like before you get there, and I hope that in a little while it will be made much more disagreeable than people in your position have any idea of.' A further hint to the Members of Parliament on the jury concerning the benefits of the lash as a remedy against those who took hunger to extremes.

Still, it was only six years, which meant their sentences would be served at home. Yet the next was for seven – undoubtedly transportation – for Mr Justice Crompton was getting into his stride. 'Crimes of this kind must be severely punished.' And it was with sinking spirits and sombre steps that Sam and Tom Jones took their turn to ascend the steps, as if to a scaffold, where fate was waiting.

How bright the light seemed after the gaslit gloom below.

Late autumn sun streaming through the windows – faces turned expectantly towards them – the hum of voices that rose as each new performer took their place, as it were, in the theatre of the court. The two men seemed momentarily disoriented, as perhaps they were meant to be, standing with hands on the wooden bar of the dock, a warder on either side. A little confused, as the voice of the clerk came to them through the shining light, and silence fell.

'Thomas Jones and Samuel Speed, you are each of you charged with arson, in that you set fire to a barley rick, the property of Joseph Heynes, at Bladon, Woodstock, on the eighth of August last. How do you plead?'

A pause to digest what was being required of them. A nudge from the warder.

Then, 'Guilty' from Thomas Jones.

'Not Guilty, your worships,' from Samuel Speed.

Followed by a voice from the judge.

'Very well. The pleas having been recorded, I will reserve sentence against Jones until the case against Speed has been heard with his defence. Mr Sawyer, I believe you are prosecuting?'

'I am, my lord.' A wig and black gown rose at the bar table, and briefly outlined the facts of the case to the jury. Charles Ferrabee was called to the witness stand and, without going into the detail of what had happened beforehand, told the court he'd seen the two accused outside the Union workhouse, and going up to Mr Heynes's field a few minutes before he saw the fire out of the window.

'Does the defence have any questions?'

But Samuel had no counsel, except his own, and he couldn't think at that moment of anything to ask.

I should have said about Ferrabee turning us away that night . . . but I didn't. Should have said he was cruel . . . but I forgot.

Inspector Coates then took the stand and described how he'd seen the prisoners by the police station on the night of the fire, the admissions they'd made, and of finding the box of matches where Jones said he'd thrown it in the lane.

'Any questions?' But again, there were none.

It were too dangerous to go there . . .

'That is the case for the prosecution, my lord.'

'Thank you, Mr Sawyer. Speed, what do you wish to say in your defence?'

It was my moment on the stage in the spotlight, but I managed to fluff my lines.

Samuel's hand trembled on the bar, and his voice rose in pitch as nerves took hold.

'I only want to say, sir, that I didn't light the fire,' he began. 'I went up to the field with Tommy Jones, as I told the Inspector, but I stayed by the gate when he went in by himself . . .'

There was a long pause as a question – yet unasked or answered – hung in the judicial atmosphere.

What did you think he was going to do?

'I thought he was going for a pee.'

Shock. Gasps. Titters.

I just blurted it out. And it were *funny. But a blunder, all the same.*

'The prisoner will mind his language.' Sir Charles spoke sternly from the Bench. 'There are ladies present in court. You say you thought he was going into the field for a different purpose?'

'Yes, sir. "A different purpose".'

Another silence, in which Samuel knew he was supposed to say something further in his defence. But nothing came to him, in this *extremis*, except the truth.

'I went up to the field with Tommy, and he threatened me to say that I lit the fire with him.'

And I promised I wouldn't 'peach on him . . .

'Is there anything else you wish to add?' Mr Justice Crompton asked.

'No, your lordship.'

'I'm advised that the co-accused, Jones, wishes to speak on Speed's behalf. Do you wish to make a statement from the dock, or go into the witness box where you may be cross-examined?'

Tommy Jones hunched his shoulders.

'I'll stay here, thank you. I just want to say, sirs, that it was my doing. All mine. I lit the fire by meself. And I threatened Sammy to say that he had done it as well, just as he told you.'

The court waited to see if Jones had anything more to add, which seemed to be expected.

'We were given a halfpenny on the road, see, like the Inspector said, and instead of buying something to eat with it, I thought we should buy matches . . .'

Another blunder.

'. . . but it was my idea, and Sammy didn't have nothing to do with it. And that's all I want to say.'

'Very well. Mr Sawyer, do you wish to add anything for the prosecution?'

'Very little, my lord. The case seems clear enough.' Mr Sawyer at the bar table turned to face the jury and spoke to them in conversational, almost familiar, terms.

'Gentlemen, we've heard the essential facts from the porter at the workhouse and Inspector Coates, and their evidence has not been contested. The prisoner has admitted to being at the field gate but says he had nothing to do with lighting the barley stack, and only confessed to the police because Jones threatened him. In his evidence, Jones acknowledged that he'd purchased the matches with a halfpenny the pair had been given on the road.

'Because the prisoners gave their statements from the dock, the court has had no opportunity to question them. But I think in your deliberations you are entitled to ask yourselves this: did Speed and Jones not discuss among themselves what they should do with the halfpenny? Should they buy bread, or should they get matches? Did the subject never come up between them? And if you believe that it probably did . . . and as we know, from Inspector Coates, Speed was present in the shop when the matches were purchased . . . I suggest the only sensible conclusion is that Speed knew perfectly well for what purpose they were intended. He was just as culpable as Jones in lighting the fire. He admitted as much to the police at the time and only now, late in the day, is he changing his story.'

But I never did. It was true all along.

Mr Sawyer sat down, and the judge briefly gave his summing up. The basic facts were not in dispute, as the prosecution had stated, and the only matter for them to consider was whether the prisoner Speed had lit the fire with Jones, or knew he was going to do so?

'It is for you, gentlemen, to either accept or reject his denials. You may retire to consider your verdict.'

The jury did so, for appearances' sake, but not for very long. Ten minutes and they were back.

'Have you agreed upon a verdict?' asked the clerk.

'We have,' from the Parliamentarian foreman.

'Do you find the prisoner Speed guilty or not guilty of arson?'

Samuel shaking like a moth before the candle.

'Guilty.'

'Thank you, gentlemen.' Followed by another short lecture from Sir Charles on the heinous crime of rick-burning, the prevalence of hunger as a motive, the merits of the whip to suppress it, and the fond hope expressed that Speed and Jones would find incarceration a lot less pleasant than they seemed to think it would be.

Seven years' penal servitude. Each. The first two in England. After that ...

Transportation.

And as the light began to dim around them the ushers rose, the curtain fell and the audience disappeared from view.

'Take the prisoners down!'

6

OXFORD CASTLE

'The judge was right about that . . .'

Samuel stretched his limbs under the bedclothes, and turned towards the journalist, Cribben.

'The prisons in England were not very pleasant places at all.'

'In what way, Sam? What were they like?'

'Oh . . . they were hard, you know. Tough.'

'I suppose they have to be.'

'Yairs . . . You'd expect that.'

'Not holiday camps.'

'No, definitely not that,' as the old man felt himself starting to fall again, like Alice, through a tunnel dark and strewn with griefs into his past. 'No holiday . . . Though whatever stories you hear,' as he made one last effort to stop the descent, 'the screws . . . the officers . . . were pretty good to me. There are no scars on my back, and there was plenty of food . . .'

Liar.

Once you went to prison, there was enough to keep you alive and able to work – such draining, pointless work, for the most part!

But the food was coarse, tasteless and hard to swallow, as it was meant to be. Suet pudding with greasy lumps. Meat full of fat, and stale bread. The whole system was based on punishment and degradation. On breaking the spirit – the old pattern of moral turpitude that had led you there in the first place – while attempting transformation to a law-abiding life through prayer, hard labour and a basic education.

For some convicts it had this desired effect. Sammy Speed liked to think he was one of those who profited. Not in any material sense – *For look at me*, he thought, *propped up here in the Old Men's Home with nothing, though some others did nicely for themselves* – but within himself. Spiritually, if you want to put it that way.

God found me in the end, and I've never reoffended, not even for being drunk and disorderly. Never been drunk, except once, from the day I entered Oxford Castle.

But for so many others, Samuel knew, the penal system merely broke them, and their lives were never put together again.

Cribben looked at the old chap leaning back against the pillows, his eyes closed and lips moving as if he were talking to himself, though no words could be heard.

'Is he all right?' The reporter spoke to Bob the Tuppenny Orderly, sitting on the other bed. 'Has he gone to sleep?'

'I don't think so . . .'

Bob stood up and lightly touched the old bloke on the shoulder, just as he had done at getting-up time this morning.

'Sammy . . .'

Samuel opened his one good eye, looked at Bob a moment, then shut it again.

'No, he's orright. Just collecting himself. He's old, you know, and gets a bit forgetful.'

Forgetful? What nonsense you talk, Bob.

Who could forget? Even if that were possible.

I'm there again, Bob, and you know as well as anyone that we can live a whole lifespan in a few remembered seconds.

And Samuel *was* there in memory, returning down the long, dim tunnel – no Wonderland metaphor, this – from the cells below the Assizes Court and into his new existence as a convict condemned to seven years' penal servitude. Sir Charles Crompton had conducted his business briskly, and the sittings were all over by three o'clock. The gentlemen of the Grand Jury had been thanked for their labours and dismissed. The judge retired to a hearty luncheon. And the prisoners below were put back in irons and returned to Oxford Castle, whence they came.

'Tommy, what do you think will happen now?' Samuel spoke softly to his mate in front of him, as they clinked in single file through the enclosed brick twilight, warders front and back and on both sides.

The words of his Lordship, addressed to three other arsonists among their number, were still resonating in his ears. 'You might suppose you'll have a pleasant time as prisoners getting into public works, but you'll find a good deal you don't like before you get there.' Retribution was in the air, and Sammy didn't know what it meant.

'What will they do to us?'

Yet his words were overheard by a guard, who spoke to him swiftly. 'Silence! There will be no talking. You've said all you had to say to the judge, and there'll be no more words from you for a long time.'

In such manner was Samuel Speed introduced to the silent system of the English penal regime – and within the hour to the separate system, too.

Arrived back in the prison yard, the convicted prisoners no longer enjoyed the relative freedoms within the jail they had on remand. They were instead taken to the penitentiary reception area, their crimes, sentences and personal details recorded in the ledger.

Samuel Speed, No. 139, 5 feet 2 inches, brown hair, fair complexion, grey eyes, 18, can read and write (R&W), round shouldered, scar under left ear, cataract on left eye, labourer, 7 years Penal Servitude (PS). All entered in the appropriate ruled columns.

From then on within the prison he would always be known as 139 – the identity of a name removed from him – until such time as he was taken elsewhere and assigned another number. Within a few years the Oxford prisoners' photographs would also be taken, but not yet in 1863.

After the clerks, they were stripped of their clothes, hair cropped close to the skull, and made to wash in a deep bath, smelling strongly of carbolic acid, or phenol, as it's usually known, used as a disinfectant and a means to disguise foul odours.

The object was twofold: in a practical sense, to remove the dirt and vermin accumulated on the bodies of poor men (and women, in their section) to whom soap and water were comparative strangers; and in a more abstract sense, to cleanse them of the impurities of their former ways, and prepare these prisoners for the more virtuous life into which it was intended the system would eventually guide them. For this, not only were clean bodies necessary, but clean clothes as well. And from the bath house, Samuel and his fellows were issued with their prison uniforms. A coarse white jacket branded with the convict's broad arrow. Grey trousers tied at the back, for no belts were allowed in case prisoners hanged themselves with them in despair. Socks. Boots. And a square, pillbox hat. All the same. No names. Just numbers. All traces of individuality removed, and their humanity pared back to the bare essentials on which, it was hoped, the reformers could get to work.

In all this introductory business, it was unavoidable that some speech had to be permitted, if only to give orders and answer questions. Allowance, too, for the prison Governor who addressed his new charges briefly in severe terms, advising them to follow every order promptly and cheerfully, lest their lot become even more burdensome. He was followed by the chaplain who told them that, through daily prayer and diligent reading of their Bibles, it was expected they would be led to repent the errors of their ways and avoid sin in future. His tone was softer, though a thread of steel ran through it; and there was no doubt among his listeners that this also was intended as an instruction.

No conversation or questions were permitted among the men themselves. And once they were led to their separate cells in the new and modern wing, constructed on principles of the model prison – three tiers of brick and stone and iron-studded doors rising either side of the central walkway under a high, vaulted roof – absolute silence was enforced. As it was in almost every aspect of their future lives.

For the reformers knew perfectly well that a bath and fresh clothes were only symbolic first steps in the cleansing process. If these unfortunates were to really change their lives, they needed time to reflect in silence on the nature of their crimes. To become truly penitent, before they could hope to find salvation. And to do so not only silently but also separately, removed from the company and influence of their erstwhile associates.

Not for nothing were these new prisons called Penitentiaries.

Hence, for the first nine months of their sentences, convicts were required to be kept in separate confinement. Alone in their cells for

some twenty-two out of every twenty-four hours, with only Holy
Scripture to ease their minds, hard labour for occupation, and just
their conscience, the warder on his rounds to bring work and meals,
or the occasional visit of the prison chaplain and schoolmaster for
companionship. In some prisons, inmates even had to wear veiled
caps over their faces in the exercise yard so they should not recognise each other, sit in separate stalls in chapel, and universally to
refrain from speech or any attempt at communication by sign or
gesture, even in the common workroom after their nine months in
the separate cells. It wasn't solitary confinement in the strict sense.
That was reserved for the 'refractory' prisoners – the bad ones – who
sometimes spent days or even weeks in the 'dark cells'. But separation was near enough, and still drove some of them mad. Indeed,
by depriving men and women of their vital humanity and social
instincts, the system more often than not destroyed the very spirit it
hoped to redeem. Leaden obedience rooted in fear, not divine love,
was the most it usually achieved. Which perhaps is what officialdom
wanted all along.

Such, at least, was Sam Speed's experience – number 139 above
his cell door – as he endured his separate confinement in Oxford
Castle. Fear, certainly – and also hatred diluted with a certain
capacity to manipulate the system for his own purposes.

For the first few days Samuel was merely in a state of shock –
disbelief that this had happened to him. He'd found it hard enough
to bear before, in the remand section, where prison walls and gates
stood between him and all he'd known of fields and woodland and
the streets of a town. But at least he'd had the liberty of the exercise
yard. Now, he was enclosed by the whitewashed walls of a brick
chamber ten feet by six, a high barred window through which only
fragments of sky and a few night stars could be glimpsed, and a

door bolted and locked, with an eye slot through which a warder could see his every movement. An iron bed, a table on which sat a Bible (as yet unopened), a stool, washbasin and toilet bucket. And this, for 139, was to be his shelter for the next how many months.

Shelter? It was a cage, which Samuel paced up and down like a wild animal in captivity – hour after hour on that first day, until he knew every crack and stain on the walls and floorboards – by turns bemoaning his fate and cursing those who'd put him here.

'Tommy! Tommy, you bastard, you never told me it would be like this! Why didn't you say? Damn you and bugger you, everyone. Mr high-and-bloody-mighty judge. God rot you all!'

His Lordship merely laughed.

I said that you'll find a good deal you don't like . . .

But all this, of course, in the silent echoes of thought.

Once or twice Samuel did cry out in his anguish.

'Tommy! Where are you?'

The first time was followed by a banging at the door and orders to be quiet. The second, by a warder unlocking the door and entering the cell.

'You know the rules, number one-three-nine. No speaking. If you breach them again you will be taken outside and whipped. Understand?'

For along with cleanliness and time for private meditation, the reformers also knew that mortification of the flesh was another sure path to virtue. Birch sticks, soaked in water for maximum flexibility, and beaten on the bare buttocks for maximum effect. Flogging with the cat-o'-nine-tails, for the truly recalcitrant.

The warder didn't wait for an answer. To reply would have been against the rules, anyway. So Samuel was left to rage and burn like the dumb. Grief and anger and helplessness simmered inside him, like a pot on the stove – until they'd boil over and the tears spill down, Sammy striking his body with his own fists for lack of anyone else to hurt.

'I hate the lot of you! Everything!' But only to his inner demons.

His misery was compounded the next morning when he was introduced to the servitude of picking oakum.

It was still early dawn as Sam's restlessness was disturbed by the sound of a bell ringing and doors opening further down the catwalk. This was the time fixed by the regulations hanging on every cell wall for prisoners to rise, wash, dress themselves, fold the blankets neatly and prepare for the labours of the day. Hastily he got up and was still putting on his boots when the cell door opened, and a warder entered carrying a lantern and a wooden tray. Samuel supposed it was his breakfast, but instead it contained only several short lengths of ships' rope, tarred and weather-stained.

'This is for you, one-three-nine,' the warder said, placing the tray on the small cell table. 'Oakum. You are to tease out each separate strand from the rope and place it in a neat pile back on the tray. I will expect it completed by this evening.'

'What's it for?' Sam couldn't help asking.

'To keep you busy. And to caulk the decking planks of ships and such like. Now be silent and get to work. Your meals will be brought later.'

Samuel pulled the small stool to the table and, sitting down, began the first of many endless days' labour picking apart hempen rope. It was stiff and tough, and difficult to even find a loose strand with which to start. His fingers hurt, and his nails cracked and split as little by little he prised out the first threads and placed them beside him on the table. Hard to see, too, in the dingy light. The sky through the window square was pale and overcast, and the gas lamp gave little illumination, for it was placed high on the wall, above a man's reach even standing on the bed, to prevent any attempt at suicide by gas poisoning.

Oakum picking therefore required all Samuel's attention, bent over the table pulling the wretched stuff apart, strand by strand, until his fingers were blistered and his back ached as if he'd been flogged already. Nor did he dare stop for any length of time to ease his body, for the warders were constantly on their rounds, looking through the peephole to make sure he was not slacking – and Sam knew what awaited if he was caught. The most he was allowed was an occasional stretch, and a walk to the toilet bucket to relieve himself.

'You've not done very much today, one-three-nine,' said the warder when he brought the evening meal. 'I expected this to be finished.'

'Sorry . . .' Downcast and soft of voice.

'Still, this is your first day at it. You'll get better. Practice makes perfect, eh?'

And with a sneer he left and locked the cell.

However tiring the work, Sam could find little release in sleep. For the first month of their confinement, prisoners were not issued with mattresses. Only three wooden boards were provided to lay on the frame of the iron bed, and these permitted no repose. They were intended, perhaps, as another summary aid on the path to contrition; but for Samuel, all they added was one more torture to his life. Lying on the hard slats at night, with only a rough blanket between him and the cold of Christmas, unable to ease his aching bones or soothe his mind, he'd think on the soft, lice-ridden straw palliasse of a workhouse, the welcoming hay of a barn, or the downy perfumes of a bed under the hedgerows, with the field creatures for company and a lark to wake him. At length, he'd fall into a fitful kind of unconsciousness for an hour or two, until the pain in his joints and muscles and mind would rouse him again.

'Tommy! Why did you get me into this?'

And the cycle of blame and woe and fury would begin all over again.

'Oh God . . . please help me . . .'

Samuel did see Tommy Jones from a distance each morning, when they were taken out of their cells to attend prayers in the chapel, and sometimes again during the hour in the exercise yard. As far as possible the warders tried to keep known associates in separate groups, but it was inevitable the pair would occasionally find themselves in the same line of prisoners walking mechanically around the yard under the watchful eyes of the warders. Sometimes even making eye contact, Sammy sending out sparks of hostility.

'This is *your* fault!'

But nothing more. All was silence, except for the tramp of sullen feet on the cobbles: grateful to be out of their cells and in the company of fellow beings, if only for an hour, but not one of them who wasn't praying fervently to the god of prisoners – whoever that might be – that these same boots might be taking them anywhere out of this place.

'Blast you all to hell!'

Yet anger cannot be maintained forever. Even the most active volcano will eventually subside into smaller, less frequent eruptions, with only the occasional release of steam to let you know the molten core is still there and liable to spew forth at any time. So with Samuel Speed and every human spirit. As the new year turned and he was given a coarse stuffed mattress to sleep upon, Sam's more violent emotions began to moderate a little. Not into acceptance or resignation, certainly; but to a broad realisation that the God he kept calling upon was not going to help him. Nor was anybody else. That he was here, in this prison, for the duration – or at least until such time as the authorities decided to take him to another one. Silent resentment, rather than fury, now took charge of his mind – though the Vesuvius of his anger was not extinct, but merely lying dormant.

The warders on their rounds, and especially the prison chaplain, the Reverend Mr Gregory Hartnett, began to notice the change in him.

For the first few weeks, Sam wanted nothing to do with the chaplain. He'd look up from his oakum picking at the table as the man in black entered his cell, and stare as Hartnett proclaimed, 'I have come to pray with you, one-three-nine, for God's forgiveness.'

'I done nothing . . .' out loud, until the prisoner remembered and spat out the rest as a whisper, '. . . to forgive.'

'Oh, but you have.'

'I told the judge.'

'Who decided otherwise. Turn now to Him who can forgive everything.'

'Go away.'

And as prisoner 139 turned back to his work, the chaplain fell to his knees and began to pray to God who can see into the hearts of all men.

'Come, one-three-nine.'

'No.'

'It is an order.'

And knowing that prison orders had the authority of the birch and cat to support them, Samuel knelt beside the padre with reluctance, but throughout continued to look around the cell and twist his hands together in agitation.

'I see that the Bible on your table has not moved from where it was first put,' Mr Hartnett remarked as he left the cell after his second or third visit. 'I advise you to open it. *Isaiah*. Chapter Sixty-One. Verse One.'

The Bible stayed where it was.

It wasn't until a subsequent call, when Hartnett indicated that reading the Bible might also be considered a requirement, with all its ramifications, that Sammy took up the Book. And opening the page at the desired passage, stumbled over the words: *He has sent me to bind up the broken-hearted, to proclaim liberty to the captives, and the opening of the prison to those who are bound.*

'Rubbish.' Nobody was going to open the prison to him, bound or unbound.

And he closed it up again.

Still, the chaplain was gratified to see on his next visit that prisoner 139 had heeded his advice, and urged him to profit by continuing to study the Holy Scriptures during that hour of solitary recreation before the gas lamp was turned off at night.

'You will find much in it to comfort you. Consider the psalm: *The Lord gives freedom to the prisoners.*'

Samuel didn't believe a word of it but knew enough not to say so. It was instead with a note of humility in his voice that he replied, 'Trouble is, sir, that I find some of the words too difficult.' He spoke softly, so as not to disturb the warders outside, even though the chaplain's visit always carried a small dispensation from silence.

'Eh?' Mr Harnett seemed surprised. 'I thought you could read and write. It says so . . .'

'Yairs . . . but not very well. Don't you have any books with stories and pictures in them?'

'The Bible is filled with hundreds of stories. The parables of Our Lord . . .'

'But no pictures. No interesting things about the real world.'

'Well now!' The clergyman brought himself up short. 'Of course, we do have a library in the prison with all kinds of useful and uplifting books. Some of them even have illustrations.'

'Can't I read those?'

'I am afraid, one-three-nine, they are only available – one at a time – to those prisoners who can demonstrate to me that they are able to read the New Testament.'

'Ohhh . . .' A small nucleus of thought stirred at the back of Sam's mind. ''Course, I *can* read a fair bit of it.'

'Let me hear you.' Hartnett picked up the Bible from Sam's table and leaved through the pages to a favourite test passage. *St Mark*, Chapter 15, verses 5–6, where Jesus is brought before Pilate: *Now at that feast he released unto them one prisoner, whomsoever they desired. And there was one named Barabbas, which lay bound with them that made insurrection with him, who had committed murder in the insurrection.*

'Read it for me. Out loud.'

Samuel began to do so – slowly – though cantering confidently enough along the course to begin with, for the first words were easy. But he tripped at *re-lea-sed*, which came out as three distinct syllables, as did *pr-is-on-er* with four. *Whomsoever* and *Barabbas* were hurdles almost too high to jump. And at *insurrection* (twice) and *murder* in the final straight he made several attempts – baulked – and at last fell down completely.

'Well, at least you didn't overstate your ability, one-three-nine.'

'So what can I do, sir?' Samuel smiled, just a little too slyly. 'I'm ever so anxious to read the Good Book.'

Gregory Hartnett was not a fool, and he recognised an opportunity for a little evangelising when he saw it.

'Clearly you must improve your reading of the Scriptures before you attempt any other – er – good books from the prison library. It's too soon into your sentence to attend classes with other prisoners in the schoolroom, but I could send Mr Martin to visit you.'

'Mr who?'

'The schoolmaster. Surely he's been to see you already?'

'Yairs. But I sent him away. Shouldn't have done that.' Remorsefully.

'No, indeed. But he is permitted to instruct some men confined to their separate cells on my recommendation. Shall I ask him to call on you again?'

'Oh, please sir, yes.' Brightening, at the prospect of some relief from the drudgery of the oakum tray and his inner turmoil.

'Very well. Mind you, I will keep a close eye on your progress, and hope not to be disappointed in you, one-three-nine.'

'No, sir. Never that. I promise . . .' And Samuel Speed bared an artful smile.

Thus, a day or so later, Mr Martin came to the cell with a couple of reading books to gauge the extent of Sam's capacity, help him improve his skills and thereby, in time, to navigate successfully the tricky shoals of the New Testament before entering the happier waters of the prison library. Amos Martin was an older man, grey of countenance and manner, whose intellect had not enabled him to rise higher, in the competitive environment of a university town, than the Oxford Castle schoolroom. But within these confines, he was a diligent, methodical teacher, who took Samuel through his lessons for an hour or so several days each week.

Carefully going over the syllables of each new word: *dis-o-be-di-ence* . . . *straw-ber-ry* . . . *at-ten-tive* . . . *o-bli-ging* . . .

Explaining the meaning of words Sam had never heard before, such as *in-sur-rec-tion* which, when he grasped it, pretty much reflected the suppressed desires of his own heart.

Reading beside his pupil as Sam began each new lesson from the primer: *When Martha Dunne lost her parents, she was put under the care of an old woman, named Molly Flint* . . . Morally uplifting little stories on the whole but they frequently had pictures, and sometimes touched on things with which Speed was familiar. The difference between a horse's hoof and a cow's cloven foot . . . sheep with wool and goats with hair . . . the first visit to the country by a boy, also called Sam, who sat on a rock and praised God for making so many *bea-u-ti-ful* things. A rather extreme reaction, Samuel thought – but on reflection, alone in his ten-by-six brick cell, he understood it perfectly.

Samuel repeated passages with Mr Martin until he could read them fluently, recognising the difficult words and parsing them more confidently – even the ones in the chaplain's verse from St Mark that threw him: *Barabbas* and *murder*. It was not permitted for the teacher to leave his lesson book in the cell, but he did suggest passages from the Testament for Samuel to study in that free hour before lights out, and prepare himself a little better for the chaplain's next test of his progress.

It was the first time since he was a workhouse child that Sam had received any regular schooling. He had a quick head, and with a definite goal in mind he looked forward to Mr Martin's hour of instruction. Day after day, as one week followed another, and winter outside in the exercise yard began to thaw into spring, Samuel felt himself beginning to improve. Tracing the letters with his finger on the damp wall beside his bed at nights: *con-fid-ent . . . wish-ful-ly . . .* And muttering under his breath as he tore at the rope end during the day: *Verily, verily I say unto you your sorrow shall be turned to joy.*

If only I can string along Mr Hartnett a bit more.

The chaplain and warders observed the change in his manner and were pleased. It was quite normal for the behaviour of a convict to progress in this way, under the influence of prison rules and scripture. For the clergyman it was an indication that 139 had meditated upon his sin – was beginning to purge it and would soon seek God's forgiveness. For the prison officers, it was merely a sign that his spirit was beginning to break at last, and yield to the strictures of discipline.

In some sense they were both correct. Samuel was certainly full of repentance – or at any rate, regret that he'd been involved with the rick-burning or had ever met Tommy Jones. Sorrow that they'd led to this miserable confinement and the likelihood of transportation. Resignation, too, that he'd never escape from the Castle. He'd looked often enough at the high walls and locked gates, during his brief glimpses of the outside world from the exercise yard – as had they all – and knew there was no way out except in a prison van. Or a coffin.

The alternative was to try and use the system to his own advantage, and Sammy Speed was uncomplicated enough to know how it might be done. Finding the route to escape – at least in imagination – through the books in the prison library was an end, and the regular visits of the schoolmaster to his cell provided not only the key to that room but a short release from the toils of the oakum table. So much so, indeed, that even as his reading improved, Samuel always took care to falter over his New Testament when he came to read for the clergyman, lest he be thought ready for a library book too quickly and the lessons finish.

So, when the officials looked at Prisoner 139 bent over his table, they saw contrition and acceptance. What they did not understand was that, while Speed's loathing continued to stew beneath the surface, it was kept in check by his need to play them at their own game. He became the penitent from necessity, not desire. Sam smiled thinly and they saw remorse – when he really meant contempt.

Many years afterwards, in Western Australia, Sam Speed was to read a book about the penal system called *Moondyne*, written by John Boyle O'Reilly. He'd been a convict, like Sam, who was working in the Vasse at the same time as him in the later sixties. One of the rebel Fenians – and one who *did* escape. To America. And in his book O'Reilly remarked that, for a prisoner, the year is not made up of three hundred and sixty-five individual days. It is the same day endured three hundred and sixty-five times.

'He spoke from the heart, there.'

But for Samuel Speed it was not entirely so.

Toiling at the oakum table in his Oxford cell, he certainly sometimes wished the hemp rope he was teasing apart might be used instead to hang him. But just as the dead weight of depression was about to settle on his soul, Sam would think that his teacher might visit him today with a story in his reader about one of those strange pouched creatures in that distant country to which Sam was to be deported. *Mar-su-pi-al*. Perhaps it would have a picture. Or maybe Mr Hartnett would come to pray over him and recite a verse from the Testaments.

He brought them out of darkness and the shadow of death, and broke their chains in two.

Rot, of course. What about *my* chains? But at least he knew how to spell it.

Old Samuel chuckled softly to himself in his bed and murmured, 'No holiday camp . . . No, not that.'

And he looked at the journalist, Cribben, with reproachful eyes. As if he could possibly understand what it was like.

THE CRANK

Sorrow turned to a thin smile on the old man's lips. Something funny had occurred to him.

'The Boss knows about prisons,' Samuel said.

'Albert Rust?' Josh Cribben, the reporter, sounded incredulous. Was this a news story?

'I don't mean from the inside. No, no. But he understands. It's why he's never run this place like one. No prisons here . . .'

Which wasn't quite true, either. For Sammy well knew that the Old Men's Home always had a padded cell – and the Depot before it – where they put the fractious and quarrelsome drunks to sleep off the booze and come to their senses. It was on the other side of this block. The lock-up may not have been intended as a punishment – rather it was for the men's 'own protection', the Boss said – but that's what it amounted to. And Bert Rust knew this from experience.

Sam's grin broadened as he remembered it.

There was one old sot, Freddy Gammon, who was a regular guest in the padded cell. Always coming back with a skin full, and argumentative. He'd spent one memorable night in the cell – and the

Boss, coming on his rounds early next morning to let him out, was horrified to see Freddy lying stiff and motionless on the stretcher. Fearing that he might be dead, Rust went into the cell, hurried across to the corpse and touched it. Instantly, Freddy sprang back to life; grabbed the Boss, threw him to the ground, and ran out of the cell, locking it behind him.

He was stronger than he looked, that Freddy. Anger can do that for you.

When the Boss had not returned for breakfast, or even to start the day's work, search parties were organised. But there was no sign of him for over three hours until the Deputy Superintendent, Charlie Brick, passing the padded cell, thought he'd look through the eye slot. And there was the Boss, sitting on the edge of the stretcher with steam coming out of his ears.

Released from incarceration, Bert Rust went outside to find Freddy Gammon sitting on a bench and enjoying the morning sun.

'What the devil did you do that for?' the Boss demanded to know, the words tumbling out in a passion. 'Why did you lock me in that cell? Eh?'

Freddy was unmoved.

'Did you like it in there, Boss?'

'No, I did not. I didn't think much of it at all.'

'Well, neither did I,' Freddy responded laconically. And the retort so threw Bert Rust off balance, that he began to laugh. Though in future he always made sure he had somebody else with him, when he released an inmate from the padded cell.

Samuel laughed with him, and wondered if he should tell that to the newspaper reporter.

'Nothing too grim,' Mr Rust had briefed him for the interview yesterday. 'Just some amusing little anecdotes that people like to read . . .' Here was one. But shrewdly glancing at the reporter with pencil poised over his notebook, Sammy wondered if the Boss would like to be the butt of a joke told against himself? Decided that he wouldn't. And let it pass.

But still . . . if three hours in solitary could do that to Mr Rust, imagine what months of separate confinement did to me.

'How long were you in prison, Sam, before you left for Fremantle?'

'Two years and a half nearly, Mr Cribben. And you know, I never got to enjoy any of it!'

Anything grim was smothered under a laugh. Though it didn't disappear.

Enjoyment, of course, had nothing to do with it. Survival, in the confined world of a prison, is everything – and not least the small stratagems every inmate learns to help them bear it. Samuel had his reading lessons to break the painful monotony of oakum picking, and even there, he found a ruse to help prevent the worst of the damage to his calloused fingers.

One morning, walking briskly in a double circle around the exercise yard, he noticed Tommy Jones coming towards him with his fingers moving in a strange way, as if he were doing some sort of aerial knitting. Their eyes met; and while Sam's blazed with his usual anger, he sensed the hint of a smile in Tommy's countenance, and a quick, downward glance, as if directing attention to his fingers. Initially, Samuel supposed it was just nervous agitation – perhaps even the first signs of prison madness. But the next time they passed there seemed something more intentional – deliberate – about it. And the third time, he noticed a small twig, sharpened at one end, held almost imperceptibly between Tommy's thumb and forefinger.

What was he doing? Until, in a moment, it occurred that he was pretending to pick oakum, using the twig as a kind of spindle to loosen the strands instead of his broken fingernails. Clever! Something Tommy must have learnt in the army. As they passed on the next circuit, Samuel touched the side of his nose briefly, to let Jones know that his message had been understood, with thanks. His eyes softened a little in return, and so did some of Sam's hatred. Another beginning. While it took a few more days for Samuel to find and surreptitiously pick up a twig of his own in the exercise yard, hone it to a point on the rough brick of his cell wall and hide it, when not in use, behind the toilet bucket, thereafter his hands didn't hurt half so much. His output increased. And the warder collected his nightly offerings of hemp a happy man.

So, too, was Prisoner 139. Another small victory.

As for the reading, it was improving all the time – and also becoming increasingly hard to disguise that fact from Mr Hartnett. In part it was Sam's daily practice and mental repetition of words and spellings as he picked at the rope with his little twig. He even began leafing through the New Testament, during the hour before bed, to find words that were quite unfamiliar to him: *Gen-tiles* . . . *Ti-ber-i-as*. He'd learn them and ask Amos Martin what they meant at his next lesson, picking up a little history at the same time. This in turn stimulated his interest, especially when they began reading about exotic animals – lions and elephants from Africa, tigers from India – which Sam may have heard of but never seen, though he gleaned something from the pictures in his book. Journeys through story to places in Europe, much closer to home. *Co-pen-ha-gen* . . . *Swi-tz-er-land* . . . *Ver-sai-lles* ('Ver-sails' which, to his amazement, was actually pronounced *Verse-eye*). Speed had barely any sense of geography, so Mr Martin brought a small pocket map to these lessons. It not only opened an idea of the world to Sam – including distant Australia and the Swan River Colony – but served further to prompt his curiosity and desire to read even more.

Hence the difficulty in hiding his abilities from the chaplain during his formal, stumbled readings of the New Testament. Gregory Hartnett was in any case well aware of what was going on. He was briefed by the schoolmaster on 139's progress, confirmed by quietly listening to the lessons sometimes from outside the cell door. And while the prisoner was not yet fully competent in the more difficult reaches of the New Testament – the *Book of Revelations*, say – the clergyman was content to let Sam think he was being deceived. The system was not so inflexible that it couldn't encourage some genuine attempt at self-improvement.

It was as well that Mr Harnett felt that way. For six months after Samuel entered Oxford Castle as a convict, he was moved to Aylesbury Prison in neighbouring Buckinghamshire.

He was given no warning about it. Sam was merely told by the guard, when he brought in his breakfast gruel on the morning of 3 May 1864, that there would be no more oakum picking that day. Instead he was to be taken to another penitentiary with a batch of prisoners, to serve his remaining two-and-a-half months of separate confinement. As he was cuffed and shackled and taken down to the black prison van, Sam wondered if Tommy Jones would be among his fellow passengers. He wasn't. And this was probably for the best, for Prisoner 139 was now thoroughly ambivalent about his erstwhile mate. On the one hand, he still resented the man who'd placed him in this predicament, and couldn't trust himself not to attempt violence were they to be put in company; on the other, he was grateful for Tommy's attempts to make amends at his trial and in the matter of the twig, and was half inclined to let the friendship stand.

As it happened, Jones was himself moved from Oxford a week later to Millbank Prison in London: a large and fearsome place by reputation – the Fenian, O'Reilly, who wrote *Moondyne*, knew it well. Convicts bound for Western Australia's penal stations were often sent there before transportation. Not that Sam Speed could know this at the time; and jolting in the Black Maria along country roads, such as he'd often tramped in his days of liberty, the young fellow was thankful only that he was no longer with Tommy, and didn't care if he never saw him again.

Aylesbury Prison was new in every sense. New to Samuel – and new in that it had been built only sixteen years ago: not in the brooding, castellated style of Oxford, but in the more elegant, red-brick manner of Queen Anne with smart, white-painted quoins and sash windows. That was only the facade, however. As the prison van drove through the arched gateway in the late afternoon – halted, the prisoners unloaded and led into the reception area – the interior revealed itself as having the same, familiar severity.

Samuel was certainly given a new number and became Prisoner 50. But at eighteen, his age remained the same. And so was the vaulted 'model' cell block, three storeys high, with catwalks either side. The whitewashed cell was the same. The rule of silence. The iron cot with three wooden boards. The stool, basin and toilet bucket were all familiar.

Like coming home.

Yet there was something else that was new to Sam.

Against the wall, on a small platform, stood a machine of some kind. On top of an iron pedestal sat a large, rectangular box from which a crank handle protruded. Samuel couldn't see that it was attached to anything, and having an eye for the new agricultural machines that were then coming into use, asked the warder what it was for.

'It's for you, laddie. To turn. Twelve thousand turns a day. Sometimes more. Four sessions. Morning, afternoon and night.'

'But what does it do?'

'It is to punish you. Exhaust you. Teach you the error of your ways.'

'But . . .'

'It's enough that it keeps you occupied. The crank has no other purpose. Now, silence. Get to it now and show me how the work is done.'

Samuel stepped onto the platform, took the handle with both hands, and began to turn it. He could feel the resistance as the paddles on the other end pushed their way through sand inside the box. It was monotonous but not difficult, and in any case during his labouring life the lad was quite used to repetitive work on the farms. The difference was that it always had some worthwhile point to it. This had no use at all, though it wasn't hard. Not like oakum picking.

'Wait!'

The warder moved across to the machine and turned a screw to adjust the system of weights and brakes inside the box. The effect was to slow the rate at which the paddles moved through the sand, and consequently made the effort of turning the crank handle that much harder.

'Now see how you like it.'

Samuel didn't.

'Good. I'm glad to hear it. There is another hour until I bring your supper. You will continue to work on the crank until then, prisoner fifty. Half an hour for your meal. Then work on the crank from six until eight o'clock. An hour to read, and gas lamps out at nine o'clock.'

'Yes, but . . .'

'Silence! And there will be constant inspections to make sure you are doing it. And if not, I can assure you there are further punishments available.'

The warder left the cell and locked it. He didn't exactly depart, however, for Samuel at the crank handle could sense a pair of eyes staring at him from the observation slot.

As the minutes passed, he could also feel himself beginning to tire, for a whole new set of muscles and sinews were now brought into play than had been required for oakum picking. Legs and arms, unused for so long to such gruelling exercise, were stretched, started to tighten, ache and before long were stabbing pains to both mind and body. His back felt it was about to break with the strain of it. Yet Prisoner 50 dare not stop this senseless grinding, for fear of what might happen if he did. The warders all wore felt on their shoes, so you couldn't hear them coming. Like cats, along the walk. And behind them lay the authority of the whip: the cat, indeed. They'd enter the cell suddenly, from time to time when Samuel was on the crank, to either tighten or loosen the screws: tighten, generally, as the day wore on. Hence the name 'screws', by which they've been widely known ever since. Nor did Sam have the comfort of knowing for how long he had to keep turning the crank until he could stop. One hour, the warder said. But he had no way to measure that time without a clock to tell the passing minutes, except to count the seconds with each revolution of the handle.

One-f—-you-bastards . . . two-up-your-fannies . . . three-go-to-buggery . . .

A small satisfaction there, in the filthiest language Sam knew under his breath. But how to maintain it and keep tally of the minutes, when his body was crying out for relief and the brain was going numb? Valiantly he sought to keep alert by repeating words and phrases from his last reading lesson, but it was exhausting nonetheless.

Twenty-f—-you-bastards . . . twenty-one-con-ster-na-tion . . . twenty-three-no-is-it-twenty-four?-Con-stan-ti-no-ple-I'm-forgetting-God-thirty-two-no-start-again-f—-the-lot-of-you . . .

Here was punishment indeed, as the screw had promised. There was nothing about the crank – or its communal sisters, the tread-wheel and capstan – intended to redeem or improve the prisoners. The contraptions were meant to so humiliate and terrify them, they'd never wish to reoffend and suffer the experience of jail again. For a new spirit of vengeance was abroad, subsuming in many ways the older policy of individual reform and rehabilitation. Alarmed by an apparent rise in the crime rate, people were starting to say the prison system had become too soft – too 'pleasant', as Mr Justice Crompton told the rick-burners in his court – when what was required was a heavy hand. Discipline. Harshness. 'A good deal you don't like,' in the words of his Lordship. And the government agreed.

The face of this new approach was a military engineer, Captain Edmund DuCane, who was appointed director of convict prisons in 1863, the same year that Sam Speed and Tommy Jones were tried and sentenced. He'd had considerable experience of convicts, having spent five years as a young man in the Swan River Colony with the

Royal Engineers at the time they were building Fremantle Prison. This was a place Samuel would come to know well – although DuCane spent most of his time up country supervising convict stations in the Toodyay and Guildford districts, with which Tommy Jones would become acquainted. DuCane had therefore developed firm views about the way convicts should be treated when he became director at the age of only thirty-three, and they were fully in accord with public sentiments.

'Hard labour, hard fare and hard board,' he promised would be the rule in his establishments.

So it transpired – and Samuel Speed was among the first cohort of prisoners to feel the effect of it, even if the earlier efforts at some amelioration were still evident in his time.

The system got worse as the century wore on, until the poet and playwright Oscar Wilde, who was imprisoned at Reading Gaol for gross indecency in the 1890s, cried out in anguish:

> *With midnight always in one's heart,*
> *And twilight in one's cell,*
> *We turn the crank, or tear the rope,*
> *Each in his separate Hell . . .*

As ever, Sam thought when he came to read the *Ballad* and weep with his own infernal memories many years later, it was left to writers and artists to express the truth of the social conditions from which crime and punishment sprang and had their being: something that rarely seemed to occur to the Cromptons and DuCanes of this world. Fear of consequences was all.

In such ways did Prisoner 50 endure his own consequence of having been starving, for another two long months at Aylesbury, where every hour seemed a day, and *each day like a year* as Wilde knew so well. Every day Sam followed the same routine, laid down by regulation. Rise, work at the crank, breakfast, prayers, exercise, work, dinner, work – with sometimes the oakum tray for variation – supper, work, an hour to read his Testament and find new words to dream of in a fitful sleep and ask the prison schoolmaster about . . .

For his reading lessons did continue, and so did the brief respite from Sam's labours granted by a visit from the teacher to his cell for an hour or so three or four days a week. Gregory Hartnett had written to Aylesbury, advising of Speed's progress and trusting he'd be allowed to attempt the Biblical test and gain entry to the paradise of the prison library. To the resident master, one Oliver Tweedie, the idea of books and instruction were more in the nature of a purgatory to be endured. A young man of small learning and less means, he'd been a pupil-teacher in his youth, and as education was the only trade Mr Tweedie knew to support himself and a new wife, he approached his job at the prison without much by way of enthusiasm or erudition.

Still, he had more knowledge than Sam, who, in these sessions of relief from the crank, absorbed the much more difficult passages from the *Fourth Book of Lessons* as avidly as the parched earth soaks up the spring rains. Descriptive Geography and short pieces on the British Isles, North America and the colonies of Australasia. Extracts from Natural History and things Sam didn't realise he already understood – like the Animal, Vegetable and Mineral Kingdoms. *Quad-ru-ped* . . . *au-ber-gine* . . . *iron-stone*. And subjects from the section on Political Economy with which he was all too familiar. Wages. Rich and Poor. Letting and Hiring. On such topics, Samuel Speed knew from experience that he stood at the end of every queue.

Fifty-eight-f—you-all . . . fifty-nine-Or-in-o-co . . . sixty-Cinn-
a-mon-and-Zan-zi-bar, one-stick-it-up-you . . . two-med-i-cine-and-
cook-er-y . . . three-bark-of-the-Cin-ch-o-na tree . . .

Mr Tweedie had never heard of quinine or the Cinchona tree –
or how it was pronounced (with a hard middle *K: sin-co-na*) – or a
disease called malaria. And neither did he care very much. Samuel
did care – as the farmhand was naturally interested in every useful
plant – and this was the difference between the prison teacher and
his pupil.

There were very few pictures in these more advanced readers,
and Mr Tweedie was unable to explain with any satisfaction those
matters which were beyond his ken – the *lyrebird*, for instance,
to be found in the land where Sam was to be transported, or even
what a *lyre* was. *(I asked him if it told fibs!)* The best Oliver could
manage was to say that he'd heard Australia was a dry, hot place,
with poisonous snakes and dangerous blacks, and 'I'm glad it's you
what's going there and not me'.

Sam persevered in the face of such discouragement for as long
as he could. His interest was engaged in reading about the world
around him; and besides, the worth of Mr Tweedie's visits in
breaking the monotony of the crank and oakum tray (assisted by yet
another small twig) was as valuable as ever. Still, as the weeks went
by and became high summer, Sam realised that his time in separate
confinement must surely be coming to an end. Soon he could attend
the prison schoolroom with other inmates for a few hours each
week, and should he also gain access to the library he'd be able to
instruct *himself* a little from the books he might borrow.

Thus, he decided to drop all pretence and pass his reading test
of the Bible. The rapidity with which Sam's skill consequently
improved at their weekly session quite astonished the resident

chaplain. 'Prisoner fifty seems to have transformed himself almost overnight,' he confided to the Governor, 'a sure sign, I think, that the Spirit at last is with him.' And certainly, within a fortnight, the clergyman was able to praise God and report that Speed had passed his trial with ease, and especially that troublesome passage from *St Luke* Chapter 4: *He hath appointed me to preach the gospel to the poor; he hath sent me to heal the broken-hearted, to preach deliverance to the captives, and recovering of sight to the blind, to set at liberty them that are bruised.*

Samuel didn't have to believe it: merely recite it. But if he thought that success would hand him, if not the keys to heaven then at least those to the Aylesbury prison library, the young man was mistaken. It was the chaplain who decided which book would be delivered to each approved prisoner once a week; and in 50's clear case of devout inspiration, he thought a volume of sermons would be most acceptable. It wasn't. When Samuel asked instead for something with stories and pictures, the clergyman gave him a bound copy of *The Saturday Magazine* with a sigh. Most prisoners asked for books like that. To be sure it was produced by the Society for Promoting Christian Knowledge, but the inmates generally ignored the fact. When Samuel opened his first volume, he was gratified to see an engraving of a giant boa constrictor from South America on the front page, with its jaws wide open and about to swallow a large animal. Thereafter, he passed many an hour at the crank handle wondering how many crushed prison warders such a snake could fit inside.

It didn't last long, however. Within a few weeks Speed was told he was to be transferred to the new prison at Chatham, on the lower Thames, whence he would in due course be transported to Fremantle and the Swan River penal station.

Prisoner 50's heart rejoiced in the news. If this meant release from separate confinement, then he was glad. It was almost like freedom. And certainly better than his solitary fantasies at the crank. Alas, however, Samuel Speed's happiness was premature.

8

TREADWHEELS

The old chap in his bed tried to laugh it off again.

'They had the hulks at Chatham,' he remarked. 'Have you heard of them?'

'Yes, of course,' replied Cribben the journalist, for he had also read *Great Expectations*, and the descriptions of the convict Magwitch escaped from the old, dismasted prison ships moored in the river, the rank mist rising over the marshes as the soldiers searched for him. 'I know about the hulks.' And wished he could write as well as Dickens.

'Like going to sea . . . and not going anywhere except to hell, ha ha.'

The words and intonation in his voice belied the old man's attempt at humour.

'Chatham could be an awful place.'

And wittingly or not – and the reporter did not pursue it, for people liked a small thrill with their breakfast newspapers – Sam left Cribben with the impression that he'd also spent his twenty months at Chatham in the prison hulks. But it was not so. The filthy, overcrowded, brutal vessels from which convicts were sent to labour on the Chatham docks before being transported to Botany Bay, had gone some years before Samuel Speed arrived there. A new prison had been built on St Mary's Island along modern lines, with a classical gateway and a high, square clock tower, and opened in the late 1850s.

Yet it was true that the vile reputation of the hulks had also transferred to the new place. Not just the convicts, but many of the warders and their practices went there as well; and so harsh was the regime that it led to a riot in 1861. It began when a group of several hundred prisoners, out working near the naval dockyard, were eating their dinner in a mess hall. One of them threw a bowl of soup in a warder's face, telling him it tasted horrible – and it broke into a melee, the men pushing the screws aside and trying to smash down the building with stone hammers. They were eventually forced back inside the prison . . . and although the ringleaders were kept in chains, the violence continued for several days, some prisoners unlocking cells with a skeleton key, smashing windows and furniture, and attempting to set fire to the place. It was only suppressed after the arrival of 1000 troops from the garrison barracks, and the floggings of 140 men that followed left an indelible impression. They lasted all day, administered by soldiers and seamen, and the screams could be heard by people well beyond the prison walls.

Still the tensions simmered. A few months afterwards another attempt to seize the jail was foiled, and at the end of the year a prisoner was sentenced to penal servitude for life for the attempted murder of a screw. The administration was changed and new warders brought in, but this was just at the time that an even stricter policy for the government of convicts was being introduced under

Edmund DuCane's influence. And it was well in place by the time Sam Speed arrived at St Mary's Prison, Chatham, in July 1864.

The food was better than Aylesbury, though the cells were smaller – only eight feet by four – with a slate floor and iron walls and ceiling. An ice box in winter and an oven in summer. But the accommodation was not as suffocatingly confined as it might have been; for having finished his obligatory term of separate confinement, Sam now joined the general prison population. And since most of them were employed on and off at the naval dockyards, to which the jail was connected by an underground tunnel to limit the risk of escapes, he spent far less time in his cell during the day, apart from breakfast and supper.

The labour was just as gruelling, however, even if Prisoner 6818 – as Sam now became at Chatham – had little complaint at first. Convicts with skilled trades – carpenters, stonemasons, metal workers and so on – had workshops within the prison or on site. But for unskilled labourers like Sammy, the gangs were put to breaking stones with heavy hammers, digging drainage ditches and levelling ground in and around the dockyards. Hard, solid work under the constant supervision of armed warders and the ever-present threat of force from the nearby military barracks, for the lessons of 1861 had sunk deep. But at least it was productive work again, after the futility of the crank. And for Sam Speed, how good it was just to be under the open sky once more, unshackled and without being enclosed, like an animal, by a high wall. How sweet to breathe the wind, flecked with salt, blowing up river from the sea. Or to enjoy the company of fellow human beings outside of an exercise yard . . . even to exchange a few words in low voices when the guards weren't listening . . . and to eat midday dinner with others in the mess hall, always conscious that this was where the riots had started.

It was even possible, sometimes, to see people in the distance who were not prisoners or enforcers of the law: the ordinary citizens of Chatham going about their daily business, reminding him that another life of liberty did exist beyond the penitentiary. Free men – and especially women, for Samuel, like most of the inmates, had not seen a female since the day of his arrest, apart from a hurried glimpse at the public gallery during his trial.

He had written a few lines in his awkward, untrained hand from the Oxford remand section to his sister in Birmingham, telling her about the fire and what had happened, hoping she could visit him. But it was months before the authorities allowed him to see her reply: a mere note to say she was sorry for him and would try to come when it was possible. But it was a long way to travel, even in these days of steam trains, and Samuel had heard nothing from her since. Nothing from his brother at all.

Still, he lived in hope. They'd never been close as a family – couldn't afford to be, when they all had to go out to work at a young age. Yet the knowledge that he *had* some close relations helped sustain Samuel in his isolation during the long months of separation. The prospect, however remote, that he might see his sister again before he was transported to Western Australia and separated probably forever, kept his spirits alive during the year and eight months he remained at Chatham.

They were helped, also, by the books he was able to borrow once a week from the prison library, and read to himself during that blessed, paradoxical hour of liberty in his cell at night before the gas lamps were turned out.

For a long time he stuck with *The Saturday Magazine*, finding his attention more likely to be held by its short descriptive, useful or historical pieces, on everything from looking after caged birds, the ancient cities of Mexico and the value of education for the labouring class, to the kings and queens of England. To be sure, it was often written in a high moral, verbose style that went over the heads of the very working people for whom it was intended. An article on 'Lessons from Clouds', for instance, talked for a page and a half about their grandeur as witness to God's creation, supported by extracts from the Bible and the poet John Milton. But it said nothing about how clouds were formed, or why they held the water vapour that fell to Earth as life-giving rain, which was the sort of thing a countryman like Sam Speed wanted to know. Still, there were always the engraved pictures, and enough elsewhere to keep his interest. A series of articles on the kitchen garden during the twelve months of the year – preparing the soil, planting, tilling, manuring and cropping – kept him going for weeks. Here was something to which the farmhand could really respond.

And he needed that buoyancy. For while Sam enjoyed his days out with the work parties around the docklands, the rest of the regime again weighed heavy on body and soul. Within the prison walls, the philosophy of jail as deterrence was enforced with rigour by the new administration.

The routine was much the same as Sammy had known at Oxford and Aylesbury. Meals in the cells; an hour of exercise, morning and afternoon; chapel once a day and twice on Sundays, where the gospel of love the minister preached was contradicted by almost every action of authority. The same hours of work were insisted upon – and when the prisoners were not outside with the dockyard gangs, they were put to the same dreary, wearying labours inside as they were everywhere else. Scrubbing floors. Polishing boards. Sometimes the crank. Sometimes the oakum trays sitting silent at long worktables. Sometimes, outside in the sun, picking up and putting down cannon balls for hours at a time – a practice they called 'shot drill', appropriately enough for a prison so close to the naval dockyard and a barracks occupied by the Royal Engineers. Edmund DuCane's corps.

Worst of all was the treadwheel: a long, stepped cylinder in a shed, onto which groups of men were forced to climb, each hidden from the other by a wooden stall. And holding onto a hand grip, once the screw released the brake they perforce had to mount the next step as the wheel began to turn. It was an endless, rotating staircase, rising to the next tread as every second passed. The strain on the legs and arms was acute. There was no chance to pause or slow down even momentarily to ease the muscles, as there was with the solitary penance of the crank or oakum tray. For the next step was always before you as the feet of twenty other men turned the wheel with your own, and the brain wanted only to block everything out with the agonies of it. Which, in Sam's case, he tried to do by screaming silent profanities and remembering extracts from his previous night's reading . . .

One-f—-you-all . . . two-the-blossoming-of-fruit-trees . . . is-one . . . shit-you . . . of-the-pleasant-sights . . . of April . . . oh-Christ . . . but-the-gardener-bugger-the-lot of-you . . . does-not-place-full-reliance . . . three-help-me . . . on-the-early-promise-Jesus . . . of-the-year . . .

The treadwheel was such that men could only endure ten minutes of it at a time, before they were given five minutes of rest – which was no rest at all, because the next ten-minute session was racing ever closer. It was a constant climb up a never-ending Jacob's ladder of sometimes fourteen thousand steps and more a day. And it led nowhere. Certainly not to Jacob's biblical vision of heaven . . .

. . . twenty-seven-William-the-Conqueror . . . twenty-eight-William-Rufus . . . twenty-nine-to-hell-with-you . . . thirty-Matilda-is-it-I-heard-of-her-she-escaped-from-Oxford-Castle-they-said . . . thirty-one-so-why-couldn't-I . . .? . . . God . . .? Blast-you!

In the early days, the treadwheels in some prisons were actually used to grind corn, as in any other mill. They had a practical purpose, and to this extent provided some consolation. The men who trod them could at least eat the bread made from their labours. But here, there was no such useful intent. The pain inflicted by the wheel was the end in itself. And Sam Speed, who might walk them for several hours a day, always stepping up and down in the same place and not going anywhere at all, could only retire at night to his cell – his 'numbered tomb', as Oscar Wilde called it – and try to blot the horrors of the day by reading something from the lives of the painters – *Hol-be-in*, say, who drew King Henry the Eighth – until lights out and the darkness would overwhelm, so that he'd sometimes cry himself to sleep, murmuring 'one day, you bastards . . .' for his prayers, and the words of Mr Justice Crompton hollowing out his smoky dreams:

You might suppose you'll have a pleasant time as prisoners getting into public works, but you'll find a good deal you don't like before you get there . . .

Oh, sweet Jesus, that was true.

. . . and I hope that in a little while it will be much more disagreeable than people in your position have any idea of . . .

No idea at all, your worshipfulness. And your hopes have come to pass.

Still, for a young man of quick wit, even Chatham Prison was not without its resources. Given he could now borrow books, there was clearly no point in Samuel asking to be taught how to read.

But there was nothing to stop him wanting to learn how to write properly. His hand was at best childlike, the letters angular and ill formed. So he made his request to a warder, who passed it onto his chief – who spoke to the chaplain, who consulted the Governor. And as Speed had a good character, avoided trouble, and whose previous efforts to educate himself were known, it was agreed that Prisoner 6818 could spend an hour in the schoolroom several days each week, to improve his handwriting.

Thus, Sam was able to cheat the treadwheel and shot drill for a little while in the normal course of a day. It wasn't a lot, but enough to constitute a small gain over the system and maintain his sense of self-worth. Sitting at the long wooden desk with his slate and pencil, writing over and over the looped and rounded letters ... *ooooo* ... *lllll* ... until they became more adept and easier in the neat copperplate handwriting that schoolmaster Canning required. Letters, groups of syllables, and then whole words strung together until they became short sentences. Ungainly, constricted words at first, but in time becoming more legible and uniform as Sammy practised them at night in his cell with his index finger on the little table, for slates and copybooks were not allowed in there.

Indeed, these lessons had one other advantage. Thanks to *The Saturday Magazine*, he was absorbing a great deal of random information about places, events and people he had never heard of before. Sam's knowledge was undifferentiated and untutored, but now with his access to the schoolroom, he could look at the map on the wall and ask Mr Canning where Yucatan was, what was meant by *in-ju-dic-ious*, and discover that the name of the painter Holbe-in, for example, was pronounced *Hol-bine*. In such ways did his reading acquire a little more structure – and even more so when the master thought he might attempt a whole book on a single subject, suggesting Mungo Park's *Travels in Africa* as a good start.

Samuel at first sought to disagree.

'Don't you have any books of stories? Something by Mr Dickens, say? I seen him mentioned in the magazine.'

'You mean a novel?'

'Suppose so.'

'We don't keep novels in the prison library, I'm afraid.'

'Why not?'

'I've sometimes heard that people who write novels complain that it's like hard labour. But essentially, novels are meant to be read for pleasure – and there is no place in a prison for pleasure or entertainment. These are meant to be houses of correction and reform . . . and the only books we keep here are those intended to instruct, improve and edify you.'

'But . . .'

'I really do suggest, Prisoner six-eight-one-eight, that you try Mr Park instead.'

Samuel could only comply and, given the restriction, it was by and large a sensible choice. The account of this young man's journey up the Gambia River at the end of the previous century, his difficult trek across the unknown interior of West Africa until he reached the mighty River Niger, the hardships of his return and his joyous welcome home was not hard to read. Park's writing style was easy and direct, with not too many difficult words (which Mr Canning could explain). It was full of incident – Mungo's capture and escape from a Moorish chief – and descriptions of the country and people, and their clothes, houses, food, customs, even language and words for counting. It was all very exotic to Sam Speed. Yet in a curious way, reading his few pages each night, he found himself able to relate to much of it. The lack of pictures he supplemented from memory of the hippopotamus and crocodile, for instance, in his reading primers. The African jungle he replaced with recollections of the Amazon from *The Saturday Magazine* (well, they were both tropical). And the image of chained African slaves being marched in long lines down to the coast was all too familiar. Almost every day, recalcitrant prisoners could be seen working in iron gangs at the dockyard.

So, as the months went by, new words entered Sam's silent litany of anger and transference as he lifted the shot and trod the wheel.

One-enory . . . five-footuck . . . six-footuck-enory . . . twelve-Wassiboo . . . twenty-oh-bugger-it . . . thirty-Peebles . . . Forty-bloody-Horatio Nelson (as, with immense satisfaction, he at last finished Mungo Park and turned to Southey's *Life* of the great Admiral) *. . . forty-two-Napoleon-effing-Bonaparte . . . forty-four-Trafalgar-and-Lady-Hamilton-what-a-goer-she-must-a-been . . .*

Well, it seemed a useful thing to do, given that the best Sam could expect at the end of his incarceration at Chatham was a long voyage himself in an ocean-going ship to the other end of the world. Something else to occupy his mind and keep the worst of the night-mares at bay by learning strange new words . . .

. . . fifty-sprit-sail . . . fifty-one-mizzen-mast-whatever-that-is . . .

He asked Mr Canning and looked them up in a maritime book – for Sam showed himself only too willing to continue his lessons in dictation and the proper forms of writing letters.

Dear Sir, With reference to yours of the seventh instant . . .

My dear Sister, I hope this finds you well as it leaves me at present . . .

(What a jest. She never replied again, and he wasn't 'well' there 'at present' – nor at any other time.)

In such ways, then, did Prisoner 6818 use Chatham's rudimentary education program to better himself, as in fact the system rather intended – to find some solace on the printed page from the physical privations of existence, and to protect and reinforce his sanity from the crushing, soul-destroying effects of the treadwheel. It also, in ways he only sensed, helped to save Sam from the more malign influence of certain other prisoners.

He made very few acquaintances at Chatham, other than the few men he laboured with at the dockyards and shared a table with at lunchtime. In part this was another function of the system: to avoid too much association between prisoners outside wherever possible, and quiet when in company. In part, too, it was a product of Sam's own nature. He became known as something of a loner, as someone who read books, who liked going to classes in the schoolroom – who talked to the teacher – and thus might be considered a possible nark. Nothing known, mind yer . . . but certainly someone many other inmates could not entirely trust or draw into their own. And this was to Speed's advantage.

It may have been because the Chatham prisoners, working in the dockyards, were in regular contact with the outside world – reminded constantly of the 'other life' they'd known and yearned to rejoin – but the tensions that led to the earlier riots had never quite gone away. Samuel was always aware of mutterings and abuse murmured *sotto voce* by men out with the work gangs or inside the prison yard moving from one daily drill to another. Complaints about the food, or the wheel, or the manner of a particular guard or prisoner they didn't like – hatred of the whole system itself – were there, like dust motes, in every breath of air. And, as ever, it was only fear of punishment that kept the inmates from acting upon them. Usually. For sometimes these resentments broke out into small acts of insubordination that were immediately leaped upon by the guards, and the men flung into the isolation cells – which at St Mary's were off the underground tunnel – deprived of daylight, and fed only stale bread and water, the so-called 'special diet', for days at a time.

Samuel knew of these things, and was glad the discontented kept their distance from him. Indeed, he was constantly afraid he might unintentionally be caught up in some act of defiance and his life made worse than it already was. So he kept almost entirely to himself. Solitary. Curled up small. Doing what was required, but forming little by way of friendships, even with other youngsters like himself. He saved his attention for the people he met in his books. Lord Nelson. Mungo Park's faithful African guide, Isacco. Fantasising, in his iron bed, about that regular goer, Emma Hamilton. He even began to reconcile himself to the belief his sister was unlikely to visit him. It was a long way, and in any case she would probably be full of blame. Better, perhaps, to cut himself off completely.

Separation within separation. Yet still the seams of trouble flowed like magma beneath the surface, and in the middle of 1866 they broke through again, erupting into open rebellion from a group of prisoners. Hooting and jeering in chapel. Warders were abused, then rushed and assaulted. Blood flowed. The triangles were brought out again: three men given thirty-six lashes, while another twenty-four were confined in the punishment cells for six months and thereafter forced to work in chains.

Even that didn't stop the violence. In September a prisoner called James Fletcher, who'd spent some days in the underground cells after having been reported by a guard for a breach of discipline, was breaking stones with twenty other men in the dockyard. The same guard, James Boyle, was standing nearby, when Fletcher of a sudden attacked and killed him, bashing Boyle in the head with his stone hammer. Arrested and charged with murder, Fletcher told the police he wanted to be hanged, as he was tired of the convict life, and of all the labours and privations to which he, and every other prisoner was subjected.

Fletcher got his wish.

But by that time, Samuel Speed was no longer at St Mary's Prison, Chatham. He was half a world away at Fremantle.

For the treadwheels on the jail clock had eventually ground out the allotted time for Prisoner 6818. The days that seemed like years, and the years that passed as decades, at length trod their way with exhausted feet into the past. In late March of 1866, Samuel was told he would be conveyed to the island of Portland, just off the Dorset coast; and there, with 276 other convicts and a small detachment of guards and their families, Samuel boarded the transport ship *Belgravia*, bound for the Swan River Colony in Western Australia.

He had heard nothing from his sister. And Sammy knew he would never see her again.

THE *BELGRAVIA*

'I've never been in a chain gang.'

Old Samuel reiterated this plea from his heart to the journalist: *Don't let your readers think* too *badly of me.*

But even as he spoke the words, the old lag knew he was not telling the whole truth. Why, he could think of half-a-dozen times when he'd been chained by the wrists to a line of other convicts, and paraded with every ignominy in prison clothes (the government's broad arrow on their backs) under armed guard through the streets. Exposed to the taunts – and, even worse, to the frightened whispers – of the crowd as they marched from one railway station to another. Aylesbury to London, to Chatham, to Portland, and from the prison there, high on its cliff, down to the waiting belly of the transport ship *Belgravia* at her anchorage below.

No, it wasn't a work gang. Sam never had to labour in irons, thank God. But they were troupes of men in chains and manacles, nonetheless. And he still grieved at the humiliation of it, three-quarters of a century afterwards. Still felt the old resentment flare,

like a match struck in the dark, when he thought of Tommy Jones
and the cause of it all.

If I could have got hold of him . . .

Quenching, for the moment, any kindling spark of gratitude
for that hint about the oakum twig and his evidence at Sammy's
trial. But Tommy had long gone: transported from Portsmouth to
Fremantle on the *Vimiera* six months before Samuel, and sent to work
up-country at the convict stations around Toodyay – a place well
known to Mr Cribben and also to the Director of Convict Prisons,
Captain DuCane of the Royal Engineers. It was some years, indeed,
before Samuel Speed and Thomas Jones were to meet again, and by
then they both had their freedom. The emotion may still have burned
like sulphur, but why commit a crime of violence, even had Samuel
dared to 'get hold' of Tommy the soldier, and go back to prison again?
Better to let it smoulder harmlessly – or at least hurting only himself –
and make the best of whatever opportunities life offered them on
these colonial shores where they'd washed up. Even if that meant . . .

It was cowardice. Admit it.

Whatever you please. But it was still chains of men linked by
iron, one to another, that marched down Portland hill, that April
morning of 1866, to the jetty, herded into a steam tug, ferried out
to the *Belgravia* and climbed aboard. And from the alien, unsteady
deck the guards removed their shackles, called the roll, gave them
a berth card and ordered them to descend the steep, ladder-like
companionways to the lower deck and the convict quarters.

'Tell me about the voyage, Sam,' the journalist's question
sounded in his ears. 'What was it like?'

'Oh . . . it were quite pleasant in its way. Halfway round the
world at the Queen's expense, as I thought. Enjoyable, you know.
Once you got used to it . . .'

But it was a strange, ambivalent habitation Sammy always found the convict ship – like a prison in some ways, confined between floating walls on the ocean, yet in other ways, unlike any other jail he'd known.

To be sure, high railings of iron bars divided the decks from one side to the other, the gates between them locked and guarded to keep the prisoners for'ard from the Captain, officers and civilians aft, like animals in a zoo. A barred cage, entered by another gate, surrounded the companionways to prevent any attempt at escape or insurrection that way. And all were manned by guards drawn from retired military men – volunteers, who'd chosen to come out to the colony, many with their families – and known as Pensioner Guards.

Pensioners, yes. But not yet decrepit, like me. They still knew their weapons and packed a soldier's punch.

Thus far was *Belgravia* like a prison: but there were no separate cells below. The lower decks behind the iron bars were further divided with railings to keep the 277 prisoners in smaller groups. Yet each man was given a bunk or hammock space of his own, assigned to a mess of some ten men for meals, a 'mess captain' chosen from among them to portion out the food and roster the cleaning. To this extent the ship was a form of communal living. No separate system of the model prisons here. And no silent one, either. For while there were regulations in force regarding when to rise, eat, clean, go to school for prayers and instruction, take the air on the upper deck, and lights out, it was impossible to stop men so crowded together for weeks on a long voyage from talking to each other. Not loud talk, mind you. No yelling. No ribaldry (except murmured quietly among themselves, followed by dirty laughter, when they spied a Pensioner Guard's wife on deck). No fighting – no rebellious or indecent songs at night. There was a lock-up like a kennel at the bows, and even a cat-o'-nine-tails in its bag, for any serious infraction. A noose, too, for the extreme penalty if required. But within these bounds, after two years and four months of incarceration in a separate cell, once aboard Sam Speed found himself returned to a community of fellow beings who were free to express themselves and reconnect to their essential human instincts. Released, too, in this new environment, from his self-protective reservations with other convicts.

It was natural that Sam, like everybody else, should find his immediate companionship from the men of his mess and the few others around them. Only to be expected that, once the gags of silence were removed, these prisoners should identify and position themselves by the most direct and hurried of questions and answers.

'What's yer name?'

'Sam. Sammy Speed.'

(So long since anyone had been allowed to ask his name. For over two years he had been no more than numbers – and when landed at Fremantle Sam was given another number, 8996, which he was to retain in the official mind for another five years until his sentence expired. Yet to his companions on *Belgravia* he was permitted to be Samuel again.)

'How long yer got?'

'Seven years. You?'

'Dick Leach. Ten-year stretch. What's yours for?'

'Firing a barley stack.'

'Me too. Sort of. Burnin' down a barn.'

'There's a young feller over there got twenty for manslaughter,' chipped in somebody else nearby.

'I got eight for sacrilege,' said a neighbour from the next bunk, and Samuel sympathised with him. He'd often felt the same reading the Biblical allusions to God breaking his chains asunder.

'Seven, for pinching eight shillings and sixpence,' another added to the conversation. 'It's cost them a thousand times that amount to keep me locked up and sent overseas.'

'Jimmy Carr,' one more introduced himself. 'Seven years for stealin' a pair o' boots.'

Though they weren't all trivial and minor offences. As the days and weeks passed, and local knowledge spread through the broader society of convicts, Sam came to hear of men among them sentenced for far more serious crimes.

'We had a few bad 'uns,' old Sam said to the reporter. 'Some who were lucky to escape the gallows.'

'What did they do, Sam?'

'Oh . . . there were several doing life for murder – one of them a soldier from the Indian Army. And several who'd committed rape, too – one, of a little girl under ten years old, and another, of his own daughter! I ask yer . . .?'

The old man could feel himself becoming agitated again, as if he were back on the *Belgravia* and hearing these things for the first time.

'A bad lot, you know. Wicked, some of them. I tried to keep myself well clear . . .'

Remembering. Sticking close to those around him. Dick Leach, only a young fellow like himself and Jim Carr, who'd taken the boots. Bill Davis, who'd stolen the eight and six. Richard Johnson, a man of forty, whose wife had died and was supporting a child, sentenced at Oxford – and a labourer, like Sam – to seven years for stealing a blanket.

Well, they had enough blankets on the convict ship.

But what happened to the child? Samuel always worried.

Gone to his family, Richard said. And from there, who knows? She could end up in the workhouse, as Samuel knew so many of them did. He'd been there himself.

It was some time into the voyage, of course, before these deeper personal confidences were revealed and shared. Once the essential facts of who, what, where and how long had been established and the necessary placements made in the pecking order, most minds concentrated on the business of survival in this foreign, floating world in which they found themselves.

There were a few sailors among them: some who'd been to sea before. But for most of the convicts, the guards and their families, this was a first voyage; and the constant motion of *Belgravia* beneath them, rising up and down, rocking back and forth upon the waves, was horribly unsettling. They'd been used to the stability of dry land – to the inescapable certainties of stone and brick masonry – to the immovable laws of regulation and command. But here, within the wooden walls of a sailing ship, everything was fluid, unsure, and subject to the vagaries of wind and currents over which nobody – except perhaps the crew – could exert any authority. And so they bobbed about below, or during the hour and a half the prisoners were allowed on deck each day, like sticks cast into a stream. Feeling helpless. Adrift. And utterly seasick.

It wasn't so bad to begin with. The ship departed Portland on 7 April, and with fair winds behind them they had an easy run down the Channel. Some of the younger ones imagined they'd found their sea legs already, and were inclined to swagger about like seasoned salts. Sam, indeed, half-imagining he was now at sea with Lord Nelson, began to boast to Dick Leach of his seafaring knowledge remembered from the maritime book at Chatham.

'They're the top-gallant sails,' craning his neck upwards, 'on the upper yardarm. See?'

'T'gallants,' muttered a passing sailor, 'and they be the royals.'

'And there are the rat-lines,' pointing to the rope ladders ascending from the sides of the ship.

'Ratl'ns,' the sailor murmured. 'Lubber.'

Dick Leach laughed. Sam, discomforted, kept any further explanations to himself, though the two of them, confident in their sea legs, were happy enough to keep telling the older felons the nausea they felt was all in their minds.

'There's nothing to it,' Sam sought to encourage John Browning, the shoemaker from Exeter who was there for sacrilege. 'You just have to let your body roll with the movement of the ship.'

But Browning could not have cared less.

'I'm not rolling nowhere, sonny. It ain't natural.'

At forty-seven, John was one of the older convicts aboard. He had lived long enough to know that the proper state of things was feeling a solid Mother Earth beneath his feet. Thus, he lay on his bunk, stomach churning as each wave lifted them up and dropped them down the other side, grieving for the wife and three children he was leaving in penury. And calling on the God he'd insulted to help him, and his family, and every soul aboard this swirling tub.

Not until they passed the Scilly Islands and headed into the Atlantic, did Samuel and his fellow swaggerers realise that their new-found sea legs were themselves an illusion. The wind shifted, and spring gales blew strong from the north. The billows turned into water mountains. The crew scurried aloft, under Captain Jackson's orders, to shorten sail and let *Belgravia* run before the tempest. But the lubbers battened down below turned to jelly – bond and free alike – as the pitching vessel climbed the foaming peaks and plunged into the abyss below. Down any moment, it seemed, to the drowned embrace of Davy Jones in his Locker. And what if they *were* to founder? On the convict deck, the fear they'd be left to drown behind bars with no chance of escape added not a little to the terrors of the storm.

Men and women clung to whatever they could for support – to their bunks, to ropes, to the oak bulkheads – as everything not screwed down skidded from one side of the ship to the other. Tables, stools, crockery, little knick-knacks with which the women passengers sought to pretty their cabins, were hurled about and smashed; and the convicts, who had no possessions to speak of, even grabbed the iron bars of their cages for protection and safety in this sundering deep.

Samuel was among them pretending, with his young companions, they could weather any storm by holding the uprights. But when Jim Carr first began to turn green, and Dick Leach followed by being sick all over his feet, it became too much. Sammy paled and quivered, lost his grip and any sense of balance and, slipping to his knees, vomited onto the heaving deck.

'Oh Jesus!'

And he kept on retching, in this contagion of seasickness, even after there was nothing left to bring up. Calling, like John Browning, on the Almighty he'd so thoroughly rejected in prison, to save him. And wishing only that he might die now.

But people generally do not die of mal de mer, as the ladies above politely called it. For Samuel came to discover that, once they crawl to their bunks, they can only lie there and suffer for days on end: sipping small mouthfuls of water brought to them by those of their fellows who are still mobile; unable to keep down any food; clothed in their own filth, despite the daily swabbing of the deck; hovering in a semiconscious place, where night and day are one, and lacking any sense of gravity. Where even Oxford Castle may come to seem preferable.

So *Belgravia* tossed its way across the Bay of Biscay, which not for nothing is sometimes known as 'the bay of storms'. The Medical Superintendent, Dr William Smith, making his third voyage, was too busy attending to the civilian passengers to spare very much time for the convicts of whom he was nominally in charge. On the whole it was left to the crew, the guards and any prisoners who were capable to clean the mess, serve what food was able to be eaten, and maintain order until such time as the weather improved and normal routine resumed.

The ship's religious instructor, William Irwin, was also busy about the convict deck most days, not teaching and sermonising, as his employment required, but rather helping in practical ways those who still needed it. Feeding bowls of warm gruel to the sick. Sponging brows. Reassuring those who lay wrapped like corpses in their blankets, that they *would* get better; and advising others who felt well enough to go on deck – when permitted, as the storm began to blow itself out – to keep their eyes fixed on the horizon, as it didn't move.

Mr Irwin was even seen on his hands and knees wiping up small pools of bile – the most that anyone had left to throw up – and sprinkling vinegar to take away the stink until such time as the hatches could be opened all day again, and the lower decks properly aired. A schoolmaster at Millbank prison in his regular profession, and now in his middle years, Irwin was an evangelical by persuasion, who took seriously the example of his Christ who washed the feet even of the humblest. And he was a humanitarian by conviction: still shocked by a system that saw those in poverty transported for stealing bread, or blankets, or a few shillings to feed themselves.

Or firing barley ricks, he thought, as he approached Sam Speed one afternoon, for William Irwin had read the convict manifest in order to know his charges better. Indeed, he was expert at it. The schoolmaster had made it his mission at Millbank to attend especially to the needs of those whom the law had forced *to leave our country for our country's good* as a convict poem had it. A literate man as well as a compassionate one, he had now volunteered to sail on his fifth voyage to the penal colonies of Australia, doing what he could to prepare the prisoners, morally and usefully, for the life ahead of them.

He'd even stopped by the sacrilegious John Browning to assure him that the God who protected those who went down to the sea in ships and had business on great waters, cared for him too, and would calm the winds.

Yet it was Samuel Speed's youth that attracted his particular notice. His age was given as twenty on the manifest; yet he seemed rather younger than that – still a lad almost – and for that reason was more vulnerable and in need of attention.

'I'm glad to see you're feeling better, Sam,' Irwin remarked as he approached. 'Good to see you up . . . if not yet about.'

'I'm getting there, Mr Irwin,' Speed replied. And to be sure he felt well enough to sit on the edge of his bunk and even keep down a little food, though not sufficiently recovered to return the schoolmaster's smile.

'I have some water if you'd like a drink, and a damp flannel and towel. It's been a while since your face last saw a wash basin, I think.'

'Yes.'

Samuel sipped from the proffered mug, and wiped his dirty visage. He felt grubby – not surprising after days of seasickness – and also curiously diffident talking to Irwin. His relationship with previous schoolmasters had always been strictly that of obedient pupil and teacher: never had they sought to serve him or engage in conversation, certainly not in front of other prisoners. Sam therefore busied himself with the towel.

'The weather's getting better too,' Irwin went on into the silence. 'We've changed course. Heading more southerly now, off the coast of Africa. We'll be passing Tenerife soon, and the sailors say that our days and nights are set fair.'

'That's a comfort.'

'I'm sure it is,' with a laugh. 'And we'll be getting back into the ship's regular routine. I hope you'll come to our daily classes, Sam.'

'I'd like that, Mr Irwin. I went to the school at Chatham.'

'I'm happy to hear it. You strike me as a bright young man, willing to learn – and there is much I could teach you.'

'I hope so.'

Sam was still feeling very tongue-tied, though the instructor seemed unfazed by it.

'Then I look forward to seeing you there. God bless.'

And he moved away to offer his ministrations to Dick Leach in the next bunk.

Things turned out as Mr Irwin had forecast. The seas at last grew calm and the winds blew warm and steady behind them. The hatches were opened and the 'tween decks began to dry and freshen again, so that the smell of cooked food wafting down from the galley no longer made people ill, but on the contrary served to stimulate their appetites. Routines were re-established – rosters decided with the mess captains for meals, cleaning, washing, instruction and exercise on deck.

Indeed, as Samuel discovered his sea legs again, so the joys he'd first found in the voyage renewed themselves. Those fantasies he was sailing with Nelson . . . the surge of the ship beneath him . . . the sharp tang of salt spray and the crisp bite of wind in the sails . . . a softer, perfumed breeze now, in subtropical waters . . . with the scent of Africa lying away to the east. Somewhere over that horizon was the great river Mungo Park had explored – the sweating, fevered jungles – and beyond, as Sam had read, the vast savannah plains where lions roared and gazelles danced.

Here, too, beside Samuel the flying fish whirred and dolphins arched into the running sea. So unconstrained and free they were, with all the world under the ocean to roam. No iron bars or shackled limbs for them. Such notions of liberty they stirred in the young man's mind. Such yearnings. And even though Sam sensed these things through the gratings on the deck of a convict ship transporting him to another prison on the far side of the globe, the idea that he might one day break loose from those bonds into which he'd been born, took hold – and never quite left him.

The feeling that he was being carried into some kind of liberation was just as strong in the daily classes Samuel attended with Irwin for an hour or so on the middle deck. A paradox it might be, but as he sat listening to the schoolmaster speaking to them – not lecturing, but rather talking easily as one man to another – it seemed that Sam was standing at the threshold of a room filled with people of liberal knowledge and ideas to whom he was a virtual stranger – and that he was being invited to step inside.

To be sure, William Irwin would read the Collects for the day and lead them in prayer, trusting they would all be guided by

Divine Truth to walk in the steps of righteousness, even in the wilds of Western Australia. That was part of his job; and Sam had been listening to that sort of thing daily in prison chapel, without the slightest interest, for the past two-and-a-half years.

It was when Irwin began talking about the places they were passing that he found himself starting to listen. Of how, apparently, the little birds that were native to the Canary Islands were naturally a kind of grey-green colour, and that it was only a disease that turned their feathers yellow. Interesting, because Sam's sister in Birmingham once had a canary in a cage, and he'd read about them in *The Saturday Magazine*. And even more to the point, his interest peaked when Irwin began telling them about Fremantle, and the prison, and the history of the colony to which they were bound.

Portuguese and Dutch navigators, together with the English buccaneer William Dampier, had been the first Europeans to explore the West Australian coast two hundred years ago, Mr Irwin told them.

'Buccaneer?' Samuel wondered out loud. He didn't know the word.

'A privateer, Sam. A sort of good pirate. He was on *our* side,' with a wry smile.

Oh. Was that possible? Talk of a good criminal? On a convict ship? But Sam sensibly kept these speculations to himself.

Irwin pressed on. It wasn't until 1827 that the western third of the Australian continent was claimed for King George, and a small convict settlement was established at Albany in the south. Two years later Captain Stirling founded the Swan River Colony of free men and women, with the main township up river at a place they called Perth and the port at Fremantle on the river mouth. Yet they'd struggled to survive in a harsh country, lacking both labour and sufficient capital; and as Britain was ending transportation to

New South Wales and Van Diemen's Land in the late 1840s, so the people agitated to have a penal colony established in the West, with a fresh influx of British Government money and a cheap convict workforce.

'The first ship carrying our people – our erring sons of the mother country – arrived at Fremantle in 1850,' the schoolmaster continued. 'All sons. No daughters, for women have never been transported to Western Australia. And they were mostly for minor offences to begin with, because there was no really secure place to put them. Not until the new jail was completed some years later, were people convicted of more serious things included among us. We have some today. But you know, the colony offers boundless possibilities to those who can put the past behind them, turn their lives around, trust God, and are prepared to work hard.'

What sort of possibilities? Samuel wondered again.

'At first, while still serving their sentences our people labour on public works. Road building, generally, and it's certainly needed. On my last trip I had to travel twelve miles from Fremantle to Perth over the worst roads I've ever seen. I spent more time out of the carriage than in it, helping to drag the wheels out of the very deep ruts. And they're building a new bridge over the river at Fremantle, so I suppose some of us will be working on that.'

Samuel considered there might be opportunities there for him.

'But once they give you a ticket-of-leave after a year or two – sometimes sooner, depending on good behaviour – it means you can work for wages for private people in specified parts of the colony. Of course, you're still under sentence and can't go anywhere else. But for those skilled at the work, copper and lead mining is very well paid to the north around Geraldton, and timber-cutting down south in the Vasse . . . and so are the building trades in a young colony. Carpenters, stonemasons, bricklayers, and so on. I know of one young blacksmith who got his ticket-of-leave almost as soon as he arrived, and when I last saw him was earning two pounds a week.'

Such riches! And what about farm labourers?

'Gardeners, shepherds, general labourers, servants . . . not so well. Wages are fairly low at present. But there is always work to be had in a growing settlement. That's why they wanted us in the first place. It's really a question of economics, and the laws of supply and demand.'

Oh yes. Samuel remembered them well enough from his *Fourth Book of Lessons*. Wages. Letting and Hiring. And he'd been at the end of the supply and demand chain often enough. Such laws created the circumstances that had brought him here. 'Ultimately, it all depends on us,' Mr Irwin concluded his opening remarks, 'and the extent to which we . . . our class . . . are prepared under Providence to make the most of the opportunities that the colony has to offer us.'

This capacity to identify himself with the convicts – to speak of 'us' and 'we' and 'our class' – was one of the traits that made William Irwin such an influence in the lives of many of those he was there to serve and instruct: not least Samuel Speed. And not just the prisoners. Some of the crew, and even off-duty Pensioner Guards, would attend his lessons as well; and the shared experience helped create a certain fellow-feeling between them, that in many cases lasted long after they'd landed and the old hierarchies were restored.

Irwin's practice of placing himself among the prisoners was also very evident in a newsletter he produced when the storms had passed in the third week of the voyage. *The Belgravian Weekly Journal* was laboriously handwritten and illustrated for distribution to the prisoners every Saturday, where it was read aloud to the assembled messes by one of the more literate men in their group: in Sam's case by a former schoolmaster, Joseph Rossiter, who was making his second voyage. Originally sent out in 1858 as a pupil-teacher, aged only eighteen and serving fifteen years for burglary, Rossiter had absconded and gone back home when still on his ticket-of-leave. He'd since been re-arrested, charged with being at large from transportation, and now was being returned to the colony.

Joe Rossiter wasn't the only absconder on that ship, neither, as I was to find out. Later.

Rossiter nodded in agreement one time when he read Irwin's account in the *Journal* of a monster picnic organised 'by certain members of our class' on the riverbank, which even the elite of Perth attended. And he laughed out loud with the others as he came to the bit that said the queen of the picnic, crowned with a garland of flowers costing six pounds – so much! – was Miss Fanny S— of Fremantle. 'She is yet single, seventeen, and what is more important wants a sweetheart.' Cheers on the convict deck. And puzzlement in Samuel Speed's mind that he should ever be invited to a picnic attended by the elite of anywhere.

Even more remarkable was the account of a grand testimonial dinner given in Fremantle by ticket-of-leave men in 1863 to farewell the retiring Comptroller-General of Convicts, Lieutenant-Colonel Edmund Henderson, a man much admired for his humane administration. It was the first time such an event had been held . . . the hall brilliantly lit, servants plying back and forth with savoury dishes, and attended by all the respectable members of the bonded class.

'Ticket-of-leave men hold a dinner, eh?' Mr Irwin had written.

'They know how to arrange and enjoy such an affair better than a lot of "gum suckers", as bragging colonials are called.'

And a few days later the ticket men erected an arch at the pier, and assembled at either side, cheering and shaking hands as Colonel and Mrs Henderson passed beneath it on their way to the boats. The free gum-sucking citizens stood by speechless at such a display of cordiality to former *convicts!* 'The officials belonging to the Colonel's staff were raging with anger, and I do not doubt if they had it in their power they would have locked us up.'

Joseph Rossiter looked up from the paper.

'It's true, mates,' the schoolmaster said. 'I heard it with my own ears.'

It sounded very strange to Samuel Speed to hear words written by someone in authority that showed not just sympathy, but a degree of understanding for themselves. Mostly these men knew only strictures and intolerance from those set over them. Yet here was their religious instructor telling them that, in Fremantle, 'the free class doesn't like to admit that ticket men are capable of holding such a function' as the testimonial dinner; or of Mrs Henderson turning aside to weep when she saw the farewell arch 'as a last token of regard she or her husband would receive in Western Australia for their many kindnesses'.

If the colony could produce such people as these, then perhaps transportation might be worth it in the end. The possibilities of a better life did seem to exist there. And Sam began to look forward to his journey's end with a certain hopeful expectation. He listened intently as Rossiter read the *Journal*'s descriptions of Fremantle: the plentiful crayfish; swimming at the beach; hot days and afternoon breezes; pleasant walks along the cliffs; and moonlight shining over the ocean and offshore islands. It even inspired poetry, and Samuel found himself strangely stirred by the words as Joe declaimed them in his best schoolroom style . . .

> *The soft creeping shades of the evening stole o'er me*
> *And brightly shot downward the beautiful star . . .*

After which he told his audience he didn't think much of it as verse. Though Samuel, who had read extracts of many poems in *The Saturday Magazine* without ever once hearing them spoken out loud, thought it sounded splendid.

Some things were less pleasant, such as the sketches of the old round tower on the hill, used as a jail and place of execution until the new and larger prison had been built from the local white limestone. The 'Establishment', Mr Irwin called it in his *Journal*, complete with all ancillary buildings for the Pensioner Guards and admini-stration, designed along lines of the best 'model' prisons at home. Samuel had an intimate knowledge of such places, and didn't share the schoolmaster's enthusiasm for them. He wondered, in fact, if such model instruments as the crank and treadwheel had also been imported from home? Joe Rossiter didn't seem to think so, unless they'd arrived after his sudden, illegal departure, but working the water pumps and stone-breaking with heavy hammers was certainly on the agenda.

This cheered Samuel up again. He didn't mind hard work in the out-of-doors. It was all he'd ever known. Until Joe added, ''Course, they call turning the pump handles "the crank". But that's only for the recalcitrant. The naughty ones. Of whom there are many.'

And Samuel quietly reaffirmed his resolution not to be among them.

I O

MR PICKWICK

There were some things in *The Belgravian Weekly Journal* with which Samuel Speed was completely unfamiliar – and in particular the literary allusions with which William Irwin would sometimes season his journalism. Sam was quite used to small, uplifting paragraphs from various authors in the margins of *The Saturday Magazine*, and had even read some of them. But this was different. Mr Irwin assumed you knew what he was referring to.

As they passed the island of Palma, for instance, he noted that the recent vine disease had ruined the wine industry and that 'a cup of good old canary is not to be had at any price. Falstaff now always drinks pale brandy and bitter beer.'

'Who? And isn't canary a bird? My sister . . .'

'Canary is also a form of wine, Sam.' Joe Rossiter – the school-teacher turned burglar – paused in his reading and explained. 'Named after the Canary Islands. And Sir John Falstaff is a charac-ter in Shakespeare's plays . . .'

'Shakespeare?' Sam remembered seeing his name mentioned

several times in the *Magazine*, and some lines of verse that were unlike any English he had ever spoken.

'Our greatest poet. Falstaff is fat and funny – a friend of Prince Hal's. Always after wine and women . . . Doll Tearsheet and Mistress Quickly . . . and running away from battles. *What is honour? A word. What is that word honour . . .? Air.*'

Samuel still seemed unenlightened.

'Falstaff gets tipped out of a washing basket into the river by the *Merry Wives of Windsor . . .*'

As if that would help. It didn't.

Then again, when Irwin was writing about Perth a few weeks later, he said it was in a chrysalis state like a 'village emerging into a town, as Mr Dickens describes Lamb Street of the Borough in *Pickwick . . .*'

'Is that the Charles Dickens, who writes stories?'

He was also mentioned in *The Saturday Magazine* and Samuel had once heard someone tell the tale of *A Christmas Carol* around the fire in a public house. But where was Picnic?

'Pickwick.' Joe Rossiter sounded terse and might have reached for his cane had he still been in a schoolroom. '*The Pickwick Papers*. It's another one of his books.'

'Oh.'

Samuel let it pass. But his interest in these literary matters soon came to the ears of William Irwin, who mentioned them to Sam one day as they were leaving the morning class.

'I hear you've been asking questions about some of the books I mention in the *Journal*,' Irwin said. 'Do you like reading stories, Sam?'

'I've never read a proper storybook, sir,' the young man replied. 'They don't allow 'em in prison, see. No novels. It's agin the rules.

But I read parts of the Bible when I had to . . . and me school primers . . . all about Mr Mungo Park in Africa . . . and also Admiral Nelson and Lady Hamilton . . .' (after whom he still lusted in his bunk). 'But, no, not a real story.'

'Quite a literary feast, all the same.'

'It didn't put any more food in my belly.'

'No.' The schoolmaster smiled. 'But I dare say Mr Park and Lord Nelson fed your mind a little, eh?' He allowed Sam time to digest his small joke, before going on more seriously. 'How are your eyes? The indent papers say you have a cataract in one of them.'

'Oh, I can still see a bit to read out of it. Cloudy sometimes, but the other one's all right.'

'And Shakespeare too, I hear. Have you ever seen the Bard performed?'

'No, Mr Irwin, I never did.' Pleadingly, not knowing quite what his religious instructor meant. 'I never done that, I promise.'

Irwin laughed gently.

'No need to apologise, Sam. One day when a theatrical company brings one of his plays to the colony – *Macbeth*, say, or a comedy like *Twelfth Night* – you must try to go. You'll enjoy it. The actors, the stage, the lights, the poetry . . .'

'If you say so, sir.'

'I do. There was a ticket-of-leave man I knew in Fremantle some years ago, who loved to quote passages from Shakespeare. "Shakey Coleman" they called him. Recited the Bard everywhere. The finest poet who ever lived, he used to say. An old Aborigine heard him once and declared, "I know Shakespeare too." And so he got his spear and started shaking it in the air with a loud shout!'

William Irwin was duly rewarded when Sam responded with a genuine laugh.

'It's a play on words, Mr Irwin!'

'It certainly is, Sam, though not as good as one of the Bard's own plays.'

Samuel was about to leave with a small tug at his forelock, when the schoolmaster stopped him again.

'And Mr Pickwick . . . I hear you've also been asking about him.'

'Yes, sir. I didn't know . . .'

'If it is of any interest to you, I have a copy of *The Pickwick Papers* in my cabin. I always travel with some of Mr Dickens' books for company. His characters are my constant companions. I could lend it to you if you wish, to read during the rest of our voyage.'

'But . . .'

'Now I know the rule against novels in prison. But we're not in a prison at the moment. We're halfway between them – and anyway, I know they have a few novels at Fremantle. So, while we're at sea, perhaps I can make an exception for you. Mr Pickwick is a most humorous gentleman – very genial – and I'm sure you'd like him. I can't let you take the book below, I'm afraid. Some of the others might . . .'

Samuel knew what he was trying to say without having to put the matter into words. Jealousies grew very quickly among so many people confined in a small place, especially if one were shown any hint of favouritism.

'. . . but you could read it up here during our daily classes. I could help you with any difficult words . . . or Mr Rossiter, of course.'

'Thank you, Mr Irwin,' Samuel answered with an unexpected lightness in his voice. 'I'd appreciate that, I really would.' And he meant what he said. Irwin's unprompted kindness towards him was the first he had known since . . . well, since the man had given him and Tommy that halfpenny on the road outside Woodstock going on three years ago. And look what that had led to. Or Tommy agreeing to say that Sam hadn't lit the barley stack – though neither the judge nor jury believed him.

But this offer by the teacher to lend him a book – his first real adult novel – had nothing to do with Sam's physical survival . . . with the need to eat or avoid going to prison. Rather it was concerned with . . . with . . . he found it very difficult to express in words . . . but deep down Sam sensed it had everything to do with the life of the mind and its nourishment, just as Mr Irwin suggested Mungo Park's book had fed his intellect. And in his gratitude it seemed as if he were no longer merely standing at the door of this room full of educated people, but that Irwin had taken him by the hand and was leading Samuel inside to introduce him to some of them.

'Thank you very much, sir.'

'It's a pleasure, Sam. I'll bring Mr Pickwick with me tomorrow.'

And so he did.

The first half-hour of Mr Irwin's sessions was always taken up with the daily prayers, Bible readings and his own short talks to the class about the history and prospects of the colony to which they were heading, together with a few moral exhortations to walk with God in their hearts.

'Love God . . . and love one another: they are the greatest of the Commandments,' the religious instructor sought to remind them. And to be sure, while love was generally in pretty short supply on board a convict ship, Mr Irwin always strived by example to show what it meant to 'love thy neighbour as thyself.'

After this homily, the gathering broke up into smaller groups, during which Irwin and some of the more literate among them would help the others with their reading and writing . . . going over the small primers and storybooks in the collection, or scratching the letters with unskilled hands on slates.

Sam had often been asked to help these monitors; but lacking the confidence of his own abilities, had always declined, preferring to sit with the more advanced men reading longer passages from approved texts, taking dictation or instruction on how to write letters and address envelopes.

As the class began to break up into these separate sessions on the day after his conversation about Mr Pickwick, Irwin drew Samuel aside and placed the book in his hands.

'Spend the next hour with it,' he said, 'and see how you like it. The first chapter's a bit dry, setting the scene. It reads like the minutes of a meeting – which is what it is, a meeting of the Pickwick Club. You might want to skip some of it – but give it a go, anyway. Essentially, it's about how Mr Pickwick, with his friends Tupman, Snodgrass and Winkle – such names! – decide to leave London and go on expeditions into the countryside . . . the people they meet and the adventures they have. After that, I think the stories and Mr Dickens' comic writing will draw you in.'

Samuel took the book to a seat, where the light was better through the hatchway, and opened it. He handled the volume like a precious object, caressing the smooth brown leather of the binding, his eyes lingering on the gold lettering of the title. He'd rarely – if ever – held such a beautiful thing as this before. The books he'd known at Chatham had all been worn and dog-eared from so much use. But here the pages still felt crisp to turn, and the type sat nice and clean on the paper, like the illustrations by 'Phiz', inviting you to read and enjoy their company. As indeed William Irwin had often done: for the leaves, as Samuel turned them, were carefully cut and much loved.

He smiled at the first page. To begin with, there was a drawing of Mr Pickwick – a stout, bespectacled middle-aged man, wearing pantaloons, waistcoat and a top hat – about to be assailed in a crowded street while the urchins looked on. Sam had often seen such encounters as a boy. Been involved with them himself, indeed. Then came the pleasant discovery that Mr Pickwick enjoyed the same Christian name as himself. Samuel Pickwick Esq. The young man tried it out, by squinting his good eye, to see if Samuel Speed Esq. looked as handsome in print. And thought that it did. For the rest, however, he soon found that the opening chapter was as hard going as Mr Irwin had predicted. It was all about gents arguing over points of order and minutes and apologising to each other, with not much in it by way of an interesting story at all. Besides, there were a good many long words with which Sam had difficulty. 'Philosophical transactions', for instance. What were they? 'Corresponding Society' didn't seem to make any sense, as he understood the words. He would have to ask. And there were quite a lot of very long sentences, more complicated than Mungo Park's writing, that took all his concentration to hold the sense from beginning to end – more so, as he spanned the arc of meaning in the even longer paragraphs.

Still, Sam persisted almost to the end of Chapter One (skipping only several extremely lengthy passages). He was just looking at Chapter Two, with Mr Pickwick rising like the beaming sun and calling a cab to begin his first day of adventures, when the hour was up and he perforce had to return the book.

'What did you make of it, Sam?' Mr Irwin asked as he placed it on his desk. 'Enjoy it?'

'The first pages were hard like you said, sir. But I laughed at the pictures, and I think it will be good.'

'So you'd like to go on with it?'

'Yes, please.'

'Then it will be here for you tomorrow.'

It was a long twenty-three hours to wait: a dragging day during which Sam sought to conjure up the image again of Pickwick and his friends as he paced the deck in his afternoon exercise, questioned Joe Rossiter in the mess about 'Corresponding Society', and dreamed of climbing mountains made of words piled into sentences. Yet the next morning came and shone eventually like Mr Pickwick's countenance, and Samuel was sitting under the hatch with the book once more . . . opening the pages and looking at the pictures to remind himself of what was to come . . . before settling down to Chapter Two.

The *Belgravia* rocked gently beneath him, as it bore steadily southward into that zone Mr Irwin called 'the Doldrums' in his chat that day, where ships often got becalmed. Yet Sam Speed was feeling anything but lethargic as he read of Pickwick asking the cabman about his horse – how old it was, and what it ate, and how often it was stabled – and writing the answers down in his notebook for a report to his club. And of the cabman, when they reached the coaching inn, jumping down, accusing Pickwick of being 'an informer', and punching him on the nose. Yes, and in front of the gathering crowd, knocking down, too, the poetic Mr Snodgrass, the sporting Mr Winkle and the romantic Mr Tupman who had rushed to help their friend. What fun that was!

Here was a book that made Sam want to laugh out loud. A story in which people talked to each other, thought things and had feelings, as they do in real life – quite unlike anything he'd read in *The Saturday Magazine*. And although Mr Pickwick and his friends belonged to a social class way above Samuel Speed Esq., they moved in an active world of other people with whom Sam was all too familiar. Thus, after they'd been knocked down by the cabman, he smiled broadly to himself with the arrival of a tall, rapid-speaking, rather threadbare young man – very – named Alfred Jingle, who came to their rescue. And winked to himself as well. Sam had been on the road long enough to know a confidence trickster when he met one – and thought immediately of his own persuasive Tommy Jones.

The wink was followed soon afterwards by a swearword, for the coach to Rochester had just been announced when the session came to an end. Reminding himself to ask Joe Rossiter what was meant by the expression 'jaunty impudence', Sam returned the book and left with the others under guard, to spend a further day and night in a state of keenest anticipation for the next instalment.

So the weeks passed, through May and into June. The wind held, even sailing through the Doldrums, and once *Belgravia* picked up the Trades again, she was logging well over a thousand miles between each issue of the *Journal*. Excellent time, Mr Irwin observed, speaking from the experience of five such voyages. They crossed the Line in mid-May, though there was no visit by King Neptune to the prisoners, even if the civilian passengers were indulged with some sport; and by the end of the month the ship had passed the latitude of Cape Town.

Each day now was reckoned as taking them not so much further from home, but rather closer to their destination – this 'prison within a prison', as Mr Irwin wrote in his weekly newspaper, referring to the trackless desert wastes that lay to the north and east of the settled parts of Western Australia. Only one Englishman – Mr Eyre, now the Governor of Jamaica – had crossed it from Adelaide with an Aboriginal companion, the others having been killed. Something,

indeed, for the convicts to look forward to: though the example of
Joe Rossiter was living proof that all hope of escape was not entirely
lost. Certainly, he'd been recaptured and was on his way back to the
penal colony – but that didn't mean the next man would be . . .

Actually it did, but I'll tell you that story later . . .

Every day, too, Sam Speed was drawn deeper into the adventures of Pickwick & Co: a couple of pages at a time to begin with,
but gradually increasing as he grew into it. The ball at Rochester,
where the oily Alfred Jingle impersonated Mr Winkle in his blue
coat, courted a lady, outraged her escort, was challenged to a
duel, and Mr Winkle only saved from a bullet when Dr Slammer
of the regiment recognised him as *not* the man who'd insulted
him. Apologies, and invitations to a military review (where the
Pickwickians became unfortunately embroiled in the manoeuvres).
Then to visit a Mr Wardle at his house in Dingley Dell. They arrived
at last, after a bolted horse and an upset chaise, to meet Mr Wardle's
two pretty daughters, his rather plain unmarried sister, Miss Wardle,
and a fat servant boy called Jo who kept falling asleep.

These ladies and gents were not people of Sam's world, though
he had seen their sort often enough in the street and glimpsed them
through the lighted windows of their houses. He'd worked for
enough yeomen farmers in his time, and the Pensioner Guards on
the convict ship might well once have marched with Dr Slammer's
regiment. So that Sam's laughter was not just a matter of mocking
his betters but softened a little as he began to recognise their human
follies and frailties in everybody. Even himself, to be honest, in the
laziness of Jo sometimes to his employer.

Each morning a little bit more, and the afternoon to tell Dick
Leach or Jim Carr of what he'd read: though mostly they were not
much interested, preferring to watch the sailors fishing over the

side, or the albatrosses swooping around the mastheads. For Sam's part, his imaginings at sailing with Nelson on HMS *Victory* declined in proportion as his engagement with Mr Pickwick rose. Indeed, to improve his reading skills, Samuel had taken to studying back copies of the weekly *Journal* when he could find them. Not that Mr Irwin's stolid prose was half so entertaining as Charles Dickens; but some of the stories were interesting enough, and they all helped to increase the speed with which he scanned the copperplate words and his ability to comprehend what they meant.

So, one afternoon, as he sat by a gunwale in the shade of an awning, Sam read a gory anecdote about a sea captain's son who, in these very waters, dived off the ship to rescue a man who'd fallen overboard – and had his brains pecked out by one of those large birds flying overhead. Not the most comforting thing for a voyager to read; and Sam peered over the rail to assure himself that he wasn't about to follow suit.

Not that death was ever far away. Two of the prisoners, William Hamilton and Michael Egan, both died of disease during the voyage, with Mr Irwin intoning the prayers as their bodies were committed over the side of the ship to the deep, and drawing the appropriate moral lesson that it was but a short step from life to eternity in his talks and weekly episodes of his *Journal*.

Then again, there was a long story in two parts about a boy called Harum-Scarum, who stole his mother's wedding ring set with a diamond, was thrashed by his father and ran away to join a travelling conjurer. He then went to Newcastle, was falsely accused of stealing from a jewellery shop and sentenced to prison for seven years. Happily, however, the chaplain put an advertisement in the papers, found the boy's parents who had moved to London, and they not only forgave their son but put his case before the Secretary of State. It was all very salutary – and a whole lot of tosh. Things didn't happen like that in real life, as Sam knew, and as the author of this nonsense was also well aware. It was signed by Laurence Crawleigh . . . and Crawleigh was with them on the convict deck, sent out on a ten-year sentence for stealing clothes to the value of twenty-eight shillings! Secretary of State? Hogwash! It was just wishful thinking.

Crawleigh's literary style was severely criticised by readers such as Joe Rossiter, who wrote frequent letters of complaint about spelling and grammar to the *Journal* under such pen names as 'Snap' and 'Iota'. Should words like *honour* and *labour* have a *u* in them or not? And is it more correct to say that 'Tomorrow is Sunday', or 'Tomorrow will be Sunday'? These were literary questions to which Samuel Speed had not given a moment's thought in his life. But thanks to Charles Dickens he now found himself interested in them. At least Laurence Crawleigh was a printer's compositor and worked for a newspaper – as had Dickens, Mr Irwin told Sam: and they agreed quietly between them, that the master of Pickwick would undoubtedly have made a better job of Crawleigh's 'Diamond Ring'.

Dickens had already done so, in fact. A little way into his book, Sam found inserted a short story called 'The Convict's Return', about a young man called Edmunds who had a brutal father and a long-suffering mother. Transported for robbery, he returned to his village after seventeen years to find his mother dead, everyone a stranger, and his father so terrified when he saw young Edmunds, he tried to strike him, burst a blood vessel and dropped to the grass.

He was a dead man before his son could raise him.

There, Sam Speed said to himself. That's *how you write a good story!*

He was becoming a critic!

Mr Irwin also had his repertoire of convict stories which he published in the *Journal*, and they never failed to gain the undivided attention of his audience. Some were funny – like the Perth policeman who challenged a man in the street one night after the convict curfew with the demand, 'Bond and free?' There were heavy penalties for not replying, so Cockney Charley answered 'Neither.' He was at once collared and sent before the magistrate – who released him the next day, and castigated the policeman by saying nobody could have answered what wasn't even a question. Bond *and* free? The correct challenge, of course, should have been 'Bond *or* free?' And the bobby wore his mistake, like a placard around his neck, from then on. It got a good laugh on the prisoners' deck, and let them know the sorts of restrictions they could expect to face when they got their own tickets-of-leave and were free to re-enter civil society.

Other stories related by the schoolmaster were not so amusing. Towards the end of the voyage he wrote several articles about the penal settlement at Norfolk Island. By then, William Irwin had largely exhausted Western Australia as a topic. He'd written about the poisonous black snakes that curled up in people's beds, his opinions of the local Aborigines and whether the black swans of Australia were true swans. He didn't think so, but deferred to Captain Cook on the matter.

Who's Captain Cook? wondered 275 prisoners below. Was he a convict overseer, perhaps? Even Joe Rossiter, the schoolmaster, wasn't entirely sure. But Mr Irwin told Sam next day that Cook was a famous navigator who had charted the east coast of Australia a hundred years before, claimed it for Britain, and had written about the black swans he found at Botany Bay.

Now that was a name that had resonated with every convict since the first settlement in 1788, but even more to be feared were the places of secondary punishment established in Van Diemen's Land and on Norfolk Island, a mere dot Captain Cook had also discovered, way out in the Pacific Ocean and from which there was no escape. William Irwin had visited the place, and wrote in his *Journal* about the difficulties of landing ashore by boat; the tall, straight Norfolk Island pines that Cook thought might be good for masts and spars, but which proved too brittle; the pleasant landscape; the convict settlement; and the graveyard, in which were buried many of those who, driven by the system to rebel, had paid with their lives. And it provoked Irwin to give a rare insight into his personal convictions.

A sudden end has closed in this island many a rugged way of vice, he wrote. *Born in a country which professes to be too religious to give education to its masses and to be reared in infamy, the day comes which has been so long in coming, when sectarian pride gives way to Christian Charity . . . The men who sleep here in the graves . . . are to be visited with human sorrow . . .*

Joe Rossiter was reading this out to the assembled messes, when he stopped short.

'That's an odd thing for our religious instructor to say, mates,' he remarked. 'Think about it. Old Irwin's supposed to be reinforcing the system – yet here he is criticising it. "A country too religious to educate the mass of its people, but allows them to be reared in infamy . . ." I don't say he's wrong: I just wouldn't have expected him to state it so openly here.'

At least, for those who *did* think about it, the passage helped explain the evangelical spirit that inspired Irwin, the prison schoolmaster, to make so many voyages as a religious instructor on convict ships. And which led him to encourage the further education of one of those struggling masses – young Samuel Speed, among so many others – by lending him a book.

In his article, Irwin described several outbreaks of revolt by Norfolk Island convicts that had been suppressed by force. One, in 1834, had led to the execution of some thirty men. The latest, in 1846, against certain brutal overseers, had seen more men go to the scaffold, including the ringleader, a man called William Westwood, known as 'Jacky-Jacky' to the natives of New South Wales, where he had been leading a lawless life. In the last issue of the *Journal*, indeed, the schoolmaster gave an account not only of the insurrection and Westwood's exploits as a bushranger, including his care for a woman wounded during a house breaking, but also the full text of what was said to be Jacky-Jacky's last letter to his parents, written on the night before he was hanged. He told them not to mourn, that he would meet them again in the realms of everlasting bliss, and that he hoped his disgraceful end would be a barrier to his brothers doing evil. Which showed, Mr Irwin again drew the moral lesson for his readers, 'how grace can grow in the most demoralised of human hearts'.

It was all very interesting to *Belgravia*'s prisoners, and may have served as a warning to tread the straight and narrow as they neared the end of their voyage. But there were some things that William Irwin would not tell them – and they remained a source of even greater fascination.

In an earlier issue of the *Journal*, he described the chain of three islands lying off Fremantle, and the nearest landfall to their destination. Rottnest was now used as a penal settlement for Aborigines. Carnac was a romantic rocky islet, good for picnics and possum shooting. And the third was called Garden Island, site of an early settlement, now abandoned, and which seemed to have a dark tale behind it.

'Who among our number will ever forget the affair of '58 after hearing its story?' Irwin wrote. 'It will not be told here, being unsuited both to us and our pages.' Talk about a spoiler . . . A moan went up on the convict deck as Joe Rossiter read the words. 'What story? What happened? Tell us, Joe. You was there about then . . .'

But for a long time he would say nothing.

'They wouldn't like it up there,' jerking his head to the deck above.

He persisted in this for weeks. But in the final days, Joe began to relent.

'Go on, tell us,' Dick Leach urged him one evening. 'What affair could have taken place that was so unforgettable yet unsuitable for us to hear?'

And as the other messes added their voices, Rossiter gave way.

'All right, mates. Gather round, so as I don't have to talk too loud and they might hear,' with another jerk of the head towards the barred grating and the guards outside.

They clustered around him, faces lit by the swaying lantern, as Joe told the story.

'Garden Island lies, oh, about ten or twelve mile off the mainland,' he began. 'By that time – eight years ago – there was only one family, by the name of Read, living there at a place called Sulphur Town.'

'Did it stink?' asked someone who knew about sulphur.

'No. It were named after a ship, HMS *Sulphur*, that was with the early Swan River colonists. Anyway, the island had good farming land, and the Reads grew crops and fattened sheep for the Perth market. They were doing well until one day in '58 five convicts broke out of Fremantle prison, stole a boat and sailed out to Garden Island.'

Dreams of escape. They were always with us . . .

'Old Mr Read was there by himself at the time. His family must have been away somewhere – no, Jim Carr, I don't know where. Well, they jumped him – beat him up very badly and tied him to a tree. Then they helped themselves to all his provisions, including liberal quantities of the best Jamaica rum . . .'

'They would have had a fine party!'

Laughter, overlaid with hints of longing and remembrance, from the audience.

'No doubt. And after destroying all but one of Read's boats, so he couldn't go for help, the five desperadoes set off in his whaleboat for some islands way up north, where they reckoned no one would find them. Well, it was some weeks before the authorities came out to the island and found Mr Read in a terrible state; and after taking the old man back to Fremantle and patching him up, they set off in a fast ship in pursuit of the runaways.'

'Did they find them?'

'Yes, Sammy, they did. And brought them back. Sent 'em to Van Diemen's Land, where I dare say they ended up at Port Arthur, or Macquarie Harbour, or somewhere dreadful like that. Still there, so far as I know.'

Breaths were audibly drawn in as Joe's listeners reflected on all the tales they'd heard of the savagery carried out by the screws at such places. Every bit as bad as Norfolk Island.

'Funny thing is,' Rossiter concluded his own story, 'of the five convicts that set out, only four were ever found. They reckoned the fifth had died but nobody knows how . . .'

Oh yes, they do.

Ancient Sam Speed stretched his thin shanks under the blankets on his bed at the Old Men's Home, and sought to make himself more comfortable. His bones ached, for he'd travelled such a long way in these past few minutes. In memory he was still aboard the *Belgravia* hearing Joe Rossiter spin his yarn and remembering his own first glimpse of the islands after they landed at Fremantle in early July of 1866.

'I went out there once,' he remarked to the journalist sitting beside him with pencil and notebook.

'Where, Sam?' Joshua Cribben asked. He could see this interview was going nowhere. The old bloke kept lapsing into silence, as if he couldn't remember anything. 'You haven't said . . .'

'To Garden Island . . . Sulphur Town. Nobody goes there now except to shoot a few pigeons and rabbits . . .'

'No.'

For poor Mr Read was so shaken by his experience that he never went back to the island with his family. They stayed in Fremantle, so it was said, living in very reduced circumstances. And as for the convicts . . . two of them did come back to the West after they'd endured their punishments, where a story emerged they had actually become cannibals during their escape in the whaleboat. Running out of supplies, they'd drawn lots to kill and eat one of their number. The fifth convict was dead all right. And it was said that one of those who returned from Van Diemen's Land had done the deed with a boathook.

But nothing too grim for the newspaper, Mr Rust had said. So old Samuel looked at Mr Cribben through his one watery eye and smiled.

'Whatever stories you hear, the officers were pretty good to us on the *Belgravia*. They were . . . and we had plenty of food.'

It was the plum duff served on Sundays of which he was thinking. And the schoolmaster William Irwin, who had lent him Mr Pickwick, and helped to turn Sam Speed into a reader.

'How did you go with it?' he'd asked as Speed handed back the precious volume on that last day before they landed.

'I didn't get anywhere near finishing, sir. I read about Mr Tupman courting old Mr Wardle's sister until her affections were stolen by that slimy Alfred Jingle . . . and how he borrowed ten pounds from Mr Pickwick and ran off with the lady to London . . . and Pickwick chased him there looking for his money and the lady but Jingle give 'em the slip, and he found the boot boy Sam Veller instead. I could take to him, Mr Irwin. Very amusing, as the funny bone said to the tickler. Same name as mine and Mr Pickwick . . . who has just taken him on as a servant and general look-out . . . But that's as far as I got . . .'

'I can see how much you've enjoyed it, Sam – how deeply you've entered into the spirit of the book. I told you once that the characters in these stories are among my closest companions, and they could become yours as well.'

'I don't see how.'

'They'll always be waiting for you, when you next pick up a copy of *Pickwick*. And the others. *Oliver Twist, David Copperfield* . . . So many intimate friends, always to hand.'

'But . . .'

'I know they have a library in the – er – Establishment at Fremantle, and while there are a few novels, as I told you, I don't know whether *Pickwick* is among them. I'll ask the chaplain. But when you get your ticket and can work for yourself outside, join the Working Men's Association. They have libraries with books you can read and even borrow.'

'I didn't know that.'

'Yes. They also have Mechanics Institutes in some places, but unfortunately they're not open to ticket-of-leave men. Not considered acceptable.'

'What about when we have our freedom again?'

'Not even then, I'm afraid. It's all that sectarian pride once more.'

Much as Samuel would have expected him to say.

'But never mind, I'm sure that somewhere in the Association libraries you'll find your new friends again, whatever else happens to you in life here. Sam Veller. Mr Pickwick. Remember that. And remember, too, that God loves you, Sam, and will always be there for you as well.'

They said their farewells. It was the last time they really spoke together, though William Irwin's humanity – and eventually his faith – was to influence Sam Speed for the rest of his life.

The schoolmaster was certainly there on the convict deck the next day as *Belgravia* came to her anchorage off Fremantle. There was much noise and jostle outside, lowering the anchors fore and aft in Gage Roads, and making the ship fast. Many orders were shouted and soothing words uttered as the boats came alongside, and the civilian women and children were encouraged down the gangway to safety, and rowed ashore. The guards and warders resumed their official selves, for they'd become rather relaxed during the voyage, as passengers always do. Now, as they began marshalling the prisoners below, Irwin moved among the men, offering words of comfort and wisdom.

'It all depends on yourselves now, whether the future is for better or worse,' he said. 'Don't pursue the phantom of dishonest gain, I urge you, but eat the sweet bread of honest industry.' Much as he'd written in his *Journal*. 'If you'd seen, as I have, the contrast between the prosperous careers of those who are always up and doing, and the death beds of utter misery that await those who follow evil courses, you'd always choose the good part that cannot be taken away from you.'

But his appeals were largely lost in the confusion of bells and orders, anticipation, fear, hope, curiosity and uncertainty. The civilians all ashore, the warders prepared to land their prisoners. And it was done by the same method with which they'd embarked. Up the companionways in small groups at a time to the deck. Where it was their turn to climb unsteadily down the gangway with untrained limbs into the boats, and be rowed through the spangled play of light on water to the jetty. It was the same jetty along which Comptroller-General Henderson and his wife had walked beneath a triumphal arch to the applause of the ticket men three years ago. But these were now convict men in prison garb, manacled one to another for security, and forced to march through the streets of Fremantle to the white limestone fastness of the prison, surrounded by armed Pensioner Guards.

Another chain gang. Though Samuel Speed kept that to himself. Again.

11

THE ESTABLISHMENT

The Convict Establishment loured over Fremantle like a perpetual warning of divine wrath. In every large town that Sam Speed was aware of, the summit of the most prominent hill was occupied either by a church to express God's benediction, or a fortress for protection by the civil power. But here, as the convicts came ashore from the *Belgravia* and were linked into their human chain, the white walls of the prison radiated nothing but fear of punishment. Dominating everything. From wherever you looked in the town, there it was proclaiming *I am the price of sin and crime*. The reason for your being here. Implacable. Inescapable.

Except, old Sammy thought, leaning against the pillows of his bed with eyes half-closed, remembering, except that a great many lags did try to escape – and quite a few of them successfully, too. Moondyne. That feller Williams. The Fenian O'Reilly, who got to America and wrote that book. They never thought the place was impregnable or their fate inescapable. Indeed, as the *Belgravia* lot set off that July morning of 1866, jangling in their chains along the waterfront and up Essex Street towards the penitentiary, Samuel now realised the thoughts of more than one of them were already turning to a breakaway.

'I knew them, you know,' he murmured to Joshua Cribben, sitting in the chair beside him with his reporter's notebook open and pencil poised.

'Who?' Hoping the old bloke would say something a bit more lively and newsworthy than he'd offered so far. 'Who did you know, Sam?'

'Moondyne Joe.'

The great escape artist!

'The Fenians. They were all there in my time.'

This seemed a lot more promising. The journalist felt his juices stirring with the prospect of a few never-before-told inside stories. But Samuel fell silent again for a moment or two. It was the felon, John Williams, of whom he was thinking. The one who, unbeknown to them all that July morning, was watching convicts make their way from the jetty towards the long ramp that led to the prison gates for the second time in his life. Joe Rossiter, the schoolteacher, they knew had already absconded back to England when out on his ticket-of-leave and been recaptured, but nobody knew – then – that Williams was another and far more dangerous returning escapee.

But of course, that was because he'd come back under another name. 'Goodenough', was it? Something like that, Sammy thought, sifting through the dregs of memory. John Goodenough . . . Badenough, more like. And it was true. A smooth-talking, artful and violent dodger, that one. Williams had first come out for burglary nine years back, when he was only twenty-three, and escaped twice! Once from the jail down south at Busselton – and again from the pen at Fremantle in '62. He'd even become something of a bushranger: stealing the prison doctor's own horse on the way out, grabbing the black tracker's pistol as he was caught crossing a river, holding up two places, stealing a boat, and finally making his escape from the Busselton coast on board an American whaling ship. They were never too particular who they picked up as passengers making their getaway from a penal colony . . .

The old chap smiled and grunted softly to himself. The memory had conjured up images of faces from the past. Busselton was a place Sammy knew well from his ticket-of-leave days . . . and that decent man, Henry Yelverton, who owned the sawmill where Sam worked when he first left Fremantle, and who'd actually built the town jail from which John Williams escaped.

So why, as Speed's mind jumped back to his original thought, had the silly bugger come back to the colony for a second time? He'd never been able to resolve that mystery. Some said at the time that he'd come out voluntarily as a sailor aboard the *Belgravia*. But that seemed a terrible risk, unless he was just tempting fate – which was always possible for a daredevil like Williams. Others said that he'd been caught for another crime back home and transported under an alias. In any event, it wasn't for a week or more after he got to Fremantle that one of the screws recognised Williams under his rightful name.

Whatever the truth of it, Samuel had never dared ask the man himself: for John Williams was one of those characters that he knew by instinct to stay away from, even when they were on the same work party building the first bridge over the Swan River. Someone who, just to admit a nodding acquaintance, was to risk being drawn into a circle of conspiracy and crime. As the chain of *Belgravia* convicts was trudging up the last of the ramp towards the prison gates on that first morning, Williams must have been wondering if he'd get away with it, and planning his next escape if he didn't.

Up the stone causeway . . . armed Pensioner Guards in grey-and-red uniforms beside them, the white limestone walls of divine justice glowering in the sunlight, dazzling their eyes . . . to the gatehouse towers – like a smaller version of Oxford Castle, though the place itself was huge. The doors opening to receive them . . . tramping through the shadowed archway and into the first courtyard . . . and slamming shut behind them with a sense of finality.

For the rest of their time there, the ritual was much the same as Sam Speed and every other convict had known in the purgatory of their English prisons. Reception. Name. Number. Sentence. Haircut. Bath. Everything they possessed, including their identity, taken from them. Indeed, as Samuel undressed in the bathhouse, the sense of liberation he had felt on board the ship began to slip from him, like the clothes he was shedding. And when he put on the new set of prison slops – his thick grey woollen uniform for winter (lighter calico in summer) stamped with the broad arrow – so he reassumed the garb of submission and penitence that was his only defence against the even more dreadful rigours of the system.

That, and his own escape Sam had found through reading to other places of the imagination. The jungles of Africa. The willing arms of Lady Hamilton. And now into the jovial company of Mr Pickwick and friends, sadly cut short when the ship berthed. As he marched with the *Belgravia* cohort from the prison reception block, through the iron gates to the inner courtyard and across to the cell block, Prisoner 8996 (as Speed now became) resolved to ask the chaplain at the earliest opportunity if perchance he had a copy of Mr Dickens' book in the prison library.

But that would have to wait. It was a vast building that opened to them as they entered the portals. Designed in the form of a truncated T, and opened only eleven years before, the extended wings had room enough to accommodate something like a thousand convicts, though they were rarely full these days. Crammed in the prisoners were, all the same, in cells measuring only seven feet by four, rising in four galleried storeys along the lines of every other 'model prison' Sam had known. Such tiny cubicles! You could touch the walls with arms stretched out: a hammock to sling from hooks on one side; a small, collapsible table on the other upon which to eat or read in those blessed few hours at night before lamps out. A bucket for sewage and another for water beneath the small, barred window, through which a patch of West Australian light filtered into the cell. A solid wooden door – strengthened with corrugated iron, a bolt, lock and peephole – to retain the heat, cold and misery. And the window at best could only be opened a few inches to let in the flies, mosquitoes and (if you were lucky and the cell faced the sea) a few draughts of the late afternoon sea breeze known as the 'Fremantle Doctor'.

The only other relief, in all of this, was the fact that you had to spend just half your time in the cells. The other half – from dawn until late afternoon – was committed to strict discipline, a regimented timetable for every action of the day, and hard labour on government works as the proper antidote to crime: supplemented, where necessary, by the lash, leg-irons, solitary confinement and a diet of bread and water as further encouragements to conform. Fremantle was a model prison of its time in this as in every other respect.

For the first week or so, the *Belgravia* men were kept inside the prison compound to become acquainted with the regimen. It was not so very different to Chatham, Sam discovered. The early morning bell to rise in the darkness and dress, fold your hammock and blankets, and clean the cell. Bucket parade with the stinking sullage to the latrine pits. Line up in military ranks for the daily work detail, to clean, scrub, dig, work the water pumps (for the obstinate) or repair jobs around the jail. Breakfast in the cell – every meal was eaten alone in the cell when inside the prison. Morning prayers with the Reverend Mr Alderson in the chapel upstairs in the short stem of the T . . .

Old Sammy stirred in his bed and chuckled quietly to himself. Another joke had occurred to him.

'There was something funny about that chapel.' He turned to the reporter again.

'What's that, Sam?'

'Well, a bit after my time I was told one of lags painted the Ten Commandments very nicely on the wall near the altar. But instead of the sixth, *Thou Shalt Not Kill*, he had to put instead *Thou Shalt Do No Murder*.'

'Why?'

'Because the authorities sent enough of the bad 'uns up to Perth to be hanged . . . and they later set up a gallows in the prison itself. Couldn't have a Commandment against themselves, could they?'

Joshua Cribben didn't see much to laugh at. He actually thought the worst of the 'bad 'uns' deserved the noose, and supposed he might have to witness an execution himself one day in the line of journalistic duty. So he said instead, 'You were going to tell me about Moondyne Joe . . .'

'No, not Moondyne. They didn't hang him, though Governor Hampton would no doubt liked to have strung him up because of all his escapes. But no, he died quietly in his bed at the Fremantle Asylum. That were . . . oh, nearly forty year . . .'

Drifting back into the past. Moondyne. His cell in the prison reinforced with jarrah planks studded with spike nails to keep him in. And still he escaped. As they all wanted to get away from the grinding monotony of labour and prison food. The same every day . . .

Bread and gruel, with meat and potatoes for dinner, though we only had one tin plate, and everything else had to be carried back to the cell in our neckerchiefs. You can imagine how they stank by the end of a week . . .

Much the same as every other prison with which Samuel Speed was acquainted. The difference was that here, at Fremantle, the discipline was enforced with a severity that exceeded even Chatham. At the lighter end of the scale were the multitude of rules about how convicts should conduct themselves. No talking or communication was permitted inside the cell block. But outside, any conversations had to be kept low and discreet, rather like life on the *Belgravia*.

One afternoon, early on, Sammy was talking to his shipboard mate, Dick Leach, in the yard, when Dick laughed out loud at one of Samuel's little jokes. He was overheard by a passing screw, who cautioned that next time he made a noise like that he'd get a black mark against his name. Jim Carr actually got his first black mark when he was caught whistling. Eight such marks added an extra day to your time before being eligible for a ticket-of-leave.

At the other end of the scale lay the horrors of physical retribution. The *Belgravia* men had only been at Fremantle a week or so when the presence of the returned felon John Williams – also known as Goodenough – was discovered by one of the guards. He was immediately seized, condemned to wear heavy leg-irons for a year, and ordered to be flogged: one hundred lashes administered under the supervision of the prison doctor, George Attfield, who no doubt felt a certain satisfaction at the punishment. After all, Williams had stolen his horse during a previous escape: and certainly, his screams at the triangle could be heard all over the prison.

He wasn't nearly 'Mr Goodenough' now . . .

Things had not been so bad at the prison under the more enlight-
ened administration of Lieutenant-Colonel Henderson – the man
who'd been cheered on his way by the ticket-of-leave men and
shook hands as he passed under their triumphal arch when he left
Fremantle for Home in '63. But since then a new Governor had been
appointed: a former Royal Navy surgeon, John Hampton, who'd
previously been in charge of the convicts in Van Diemen's Land, and
had a reputation for cruelty and self-interest. He immediately set
about replacing Henderson's approach with a much harsher regime.
Sentences were increased for the most minor infractions, and the
number of floggings greatly multiplied. In the six years Hampton
was in the colony, close to one hundred prisoners received more
than 6500 lashes, an average of over sixty each. The situation was
made even worse when, having succeeded in ousting the current
Comptroller-General of Convicts, Governor Hampton appointed
his own son George to act in his place: a fine act of nepotism for
which the family was notorious. George already held several salaried
positions at the colony.

All of this was taking place at about the same time that Sam
Speed and the *Belgravia* convicts arrived at Fremantle. And so
odious was the Hampton regime, father and son, that in the first
nine months of Samuel's incarceration no fewer than ninety convicts
tried to escape – three times the rate of any other similar period in
former times.

It was impossible for Sam not to overhear the mutinous whisper-
ings and plotting once he began leaving the jail with the outside
work parties to the port and road gangs. Difficult for him, indeed,
not to want to join them, still with the sound of John Williams'
flogging in his ears. But those same cries also warned of what would

happen to him were he to be caught, as he almost certainly would. And so, convict 8996 reverted to his habit at Chatham of drawing ever tighter into himself. Knowing everyone and knowing nothing. And finding the main companionship he needed between the covers of books.

Samuel did not have the consolation of his namesake, Mr Pickwick, however, or that other new-found friend, Sam Weller. He did ask the chaplain, Richard Alderson, about them when he was visited in his cell a few weeks after arriving at Fremantle.

'Ah yes, eight-nine-nine-six,' the clergyman said. 'My friend, Mr Irwin, mentioned you to me when he called just before he left again for England. Said he'd been lending you his copy of *The Pickwick Papers* . . .'

'That's right, sir.'

'Well, I'm sorry to disappoint, but we don't have a copy in the prison library. It's still only small . . . but growing.'

'Oh.'

Samuel could feel his stomach tighten, and tears started to his eyes. It seemed as if he'd just been condemned to another form of banishment, shut away even from the company of his imagination. When he'd told the schoolteacher, Irwin, on the last day aboard *Belgravia*, that Sam Weller was someone he could really take to, Speed had meant it. The street-smart boot-boy seemed like an older brother – or rather, a version of himself that Sammy would very much like to be. To be deprived of his company, so soon after meeting him, was like one more punishment, and Sam felt it deeply.

But it would not do to show that to the Reverend Mr Alderson. So instead he sought to make light of it and disguise his upset under a little laugh.

'Oh well, sir, I dare say they'll be waiting for me somewhere, when I get out.' Just as Irwin had told him.

'That's very true,' Alderson replied, 'and every incentive for you to become a model prisoner in this model prison, and get your ticket-of-leave as soon as possible.'

Which was Sam Speed's thinking, exactly.

'And of course,' the chaplain went on, 'we do have other books that I can make available to you. Copies of *The Saturday Magazine* . . .'

'I know them, sir, from Chatham.'

'Also books on the useful arts and manufactures, helpful hints for labourers, a *Life* of the Duke of Wellington, Milton's *Paradise Lost* . . .'

'I think that may be a bit beyond me, yet.'

'. . . And one or two novels. Nothing by Charles Dickens, I'm afraid. But we do have a copy of *Robinson Crusoe*. Written 150 years ago by Daniel Defoe. It's very interesting . . . about a castaway on a desert island. Based on a real experience, so I've been told. Would you like to try that?'

A castaway on a desert island pretty much reflected Sam's own state of mind at that particular moment. Thus he replied in the affirmative.

'That's very kind of you, Reverend. I would like to meet Robinson Crusoe.'

'Then I'll have it brought to your cell directly. Now, shall we say a little prayer together?'

They fell to their knees on the timber floor.

If that was what it took . . .

12

MOONDYNE

Once more, time ground itself out through the length of a prison day, each one the same as the other in the monotonous routine of work, eat, sleep and even pray according to the bell. The same day lived 365 times through the course of a year, as the Fenian John O'Reilly observed. The times of ease remembered from the *Belgravia* had long gone, and Samuel slipped into the old prison drill as readily and unconsciously as he wore into his new prison boots and hat. Days became weeks and turned into months. Winter was suddenly spring, and before long had given way to summer, bringing with it the heat and the flies and the dust for which the colony was infamous.

Dust everywhere. Blowing up the unpaved streets as the convict line tramped from the prison to the day's work down by the river or a new stretch of road. Dust getting into your eyes, already stinging from the sun and the glare of white limestone. Dust that was hard to rub out, especially if the convicts were linked together by a chain marching to and from the prison – and even worse for those undergoing further punishment, forced to wear a woollen black-and-yellow motley uniform known as a 'magpie', terrible in the heat, and their legs shackled with iron chains that could weigh up to fifty pounds so that the raw skin rubbed and blistered and erupted into dreadful sores.

Things were not a whole lot better even if your hands and feet were free, when mostly you only managed to rub the dust further into your eyes. Eyes that became red and swollen and gritty. 'Sandy blight' they called it, and not much that the prison authorities could do about it except recommend rinsing the eyes with water (which quickly filled with dust again). Dust that blew into the prison cell through the window left open for the few allowable inches against the heat and covered everything with fine particles of sand. The blankets, hammock, clothing, water bucket . . . every aspect of life was tormented by the grit. Even *Robinson Crusoe* became sprinkled with the stuff as Samuel read his few pages each night, though in that case he felt the sand rather added to the imagined difficulties of trying to survive on a desert island.

Curious, indeed, how his experience of life so enriched Sam's reading. No, it wasn't the city streets full of young Sam Wellers where he had grown up, or the rural byways he had traipsed looking for work as a farm labourer. But as he began reading of Crusoe's voyages, Speed was back aboard the *Belgravia*, remembering the song and swell of the ship, the glittering ocean and the free, leaping dolphins. And when the storm came he was aboard *Belgravia* again too, heaving and spewing his heart out, terrified at any moment of shipwreck and drowning, just like Robinson Crusoe. And while in the story it actually came to pass and he was cast up on his island, it didn't make Sam's conceptions of it any less real. Besides, he had seen a number of small islands as they made their way down the coast of Africa. There was Palma, where they brewed something called canary wine; Tenerife, with its summit piercing the evening clouds; and even here, working outside the prison, he could glimpse the offshore island of Rottnest, and hear the surf pounding upon the coast.

It was this that made existence bearable for convict 8996. Yet his enjoyment of the novel was rather episodic, as he was sometimes away from the prison with work gangs for days at a time, labouring on roads and bridges some distance from Fremantle, sleeping at encampments with the Pensioner Guards. And *Robinson Crusoe* was not permitted to travel with him on such occasions. Of course, only the most trusted prisoners were assigned to this work to begin with, and it was a mark of Sam's good behaviour that he was selected. He even went with a gang up to Perth for a few weeks – lodging in the Convict Depot by the river below Mount Eliza – to work with the teams building the Town Hall or laying out the extensive gardens at Government House, recently completed for Governor Hampton.

Here was work that young Samuel enjoyed – digging and planting and imagining how he would have planned it, remembering those pages about the kitchen garden through the year from *The Saturday Magazine*. Of course, it all had to be turned upside down in the antipodes, where summer at home was winter here, and broad beans should be planted in May rather than October. But it gave something to occupy his mind. And for the rest, as Sam laboured on the building or around the grounds, he sometimes supposed himself to be the absent Robinson Crusoe making his hut, fashioning his weapons and improvising just about everything to acquire the necessities of life on the island. After all, Samuel was a countryman, quite used to working with his hands in all weathers and conditions on practical things – from basic thatching and mending a plough, to feeding a motherless lamb – and often wondered if he'd be able to survive should he be cast adrift in the vast, trackless wastes of this land.

Back at Fremantle, though, he could return to Defoe's story based, as the chaplain had said, on the real adventures of a sailor called Alexander Selkirk, which made it all the more vivid for Sam. And while he could never imagine himself to have a faithful black servant like Crusoe's Man Friday, he knew from Mungo Park's devoted guide Isacco that such things were possible. And so Samuel Speed consoled himself that perhaps one day he might be able to employ a clever valet and general looker-afterer like Sam Weller, when he finally had his freedom and made his first fortune in the colony.

Fremantle . . .

The old chap stirred again in his bed, remembering those days out with the gangs, and especially when they were working on the first bridge over the Swan.

'I see in the paper that they're building a new bridge now,' he said, quite out of the blue.

'What bridge is that?' asked the journalist, taken by surprise at the sudden burst of words from the long silence.

'Over the river at Fremantle, o' course. I worked on the first one, you know, when I came out. Mostly built of timber . . . pylons, supports, paving . . . and iron bolts salvaged from the convict ships, too . . . the iron bars . . . Used it in the prison as well. A funny, hump-backed bridge it was. Still there in parts, under its replacement. I hope they build the new one as solid as we did.'

The reporter was scribbling down the words as quickly as he could before his suddenly loquacious subject sank back into reticence. And was duly rewarded when old Sammy went on to observe:

'They reckon Moondyne made one of his escapes over that bridge even before it was finished.'

'Yes, you were going to tell me about Moondyne . . .'

'Oh, there were a lot of escapes in them days. Or attempts to break away. But mostly they were caught again. Even Moondyne in the end . . .'

Ninety attempts in Sam's first nine months – and they didn't diminish all that much in the remaining months before Samuel got his ticket-of-leave. He could see the captured reoffenders now, in their shackles and 'magpie' clothes, scattered among the work gangs after their whippings and spells in solitary . . . hear the constant mutterings of discontent and plotting the next attempt. Even Jim Carr, singled out by the screws after his first black mark for whistling, started talking about it. Samuel told him not to be a fool – to have nothing to do with it – and he isolated himself once more, like Robinson Crusoe, on his own little island of books and story.

'They were almost always caught and punished . . .' the old fellow went on, remembering. 'Though that John Williams . . . he called himself "Goodenough" . . . finally got away for good. Yes . . . It was one of the most daring escapes, up there with Moondyne . . .'

'Tell me about him.'

'I'm telling you about *Williams*.' Sharply. No longer having to think or talk about himself, Samuel was quite content to open up about other people. He'd told these stories many times before – and Cribben knew his trade well enough to shut up and let his man get on with it.

'It was in early August '67, only a couple of months before I got my ticket-of-leave,' Sammy continued, his voice becoming stronger and more coherent as the story unfolded. 'Here, Bob . . . help me sit up properly. I'm sinking down in the bed.' Happy in familiar territory, he called the Tuppenny Orderly to lift him up, plump the pillows and make him more comfortable.

'Thanks, Bob. Now, where was I . . .? Oh yes. We'd just been marched back into the prison from the day's work, said evening prayers and been locked in the cells for dinner. The place was starting to settle down for the night – a wet night, I remember – when one of the cell block doors opened, and eight men came out apparently under the charge of one of the warders in uniform. He locked the door behind them . . . paraded them across the court to the workshop yards – where they have the machine shop and so on. He unlocked the gate, marshalled them through, waved to one of the other warders who observed them, and locked the gate behind 'em. Nobody thought that this was anything other than a normal part of prison routine.

'But once behind the gate it became anything but normal. It was that crook, John Williams, in the warder's uniform. God knows how he got it . . . or made the keys. But passing through the gate they locked and barricaded it – grabbed a couple of ladders – propped them against the perimeter walls – climbed over and let themselves down the other side on ropes. Pretty audacious, eh, Mr Cribben?'

'Very.' The reporter looked up quickly from his notebook.

'Trouble was they were spotted by one of the off-duty screws who lived in the nearby cottages, and he raised the alarm. But the rain came on again, and the night, and in the darkness they all got clean away. He was our "Mr Goodenough" at that.'

'Did they catch them?'

'Eventually, yes. They split up, you know, and it took the police some time to round them up. A couple turned quite violent . . . and one of them, a bloke called Woottan, was later hanged for attempting to murder a policeman.'

'And Williams? I thought you said he got away for good?'

'So he did. He escaped this life altogether and drowned trying to cross a flooded river. He weren't a Goodenough swimmer!'

'And Moondyne?' while the going was good.

'Oh, he could swim, right enough. A real bushman, he was. Could turn his hand to anything. Learnt his craft up at the Avon Valley in the Darling Ranges . . . the local blacks called it the "Moondyne" . . . catching runaway stock . . . horses and so on.'

'I suppose that's why he adopted the nickname?'

'Exactly. His proper name was Joseph Johns – Joseph *Bolitho* Johns, to be precise – a Cornishman, I believe, and a copper miner by trade. Convicted of burglary and came out here in the first year or so of transportation . . . early fifties . . . got his ticket-of-leave straightaway, went up to the ranges, and eventually was given a conditional pardon. But being a lag, the police kept a close eye on him.'

'I imagine they had to . . .'

'Oh yes, Mr Cribben, they're always suspicious of yer. We're never really pardoned . . .'

A small, uncomfortable silence fell between them, filled with pain, until old Sammy pulled himself together and went on with his tale.

'Which is why, when Joe caught an unmarked stallion and branded it for himself, the coppers . . . police . . . arrested him and put him in the Toodyay lock-up. It amounted to horse-stealing – a major offence – but Joe wasn't having any of it. He broke out of the lock-up that night, and so began his career as our most famous escapee. Four times he broke out of jail.'

'He was caught pretty soon, wasn't he?'

'Yes. The next day. But not before he'd made off with the horse, and the magistrate's saddle and bridle, adding insult to injury.

And not before he killed the horse and cut out the brand. Destroyed the evidence, see, and they could only charge him with jail-breaking, for which he got three years. He were clever like that.'

'Still a criminal, though.'

'Oh yes. But they were hard times. And Joe never really hurt anyone. He'd steal supplies and that, but he never seriously harmed anybody. Not like that Williams character.'

'I dare say that's why people liked him – sympathised with him – and laughed as he outwitted the authorities.'

'You got it in one, Mr Cribben. I knew him slightly – saw him sometimes in Fremantle Prison. A tall, lanky feller . . . nice nature . . . and a model prisoner. Of course, he had to be, to fool the screws with his good behaviour. He got his ticket a couple of years after the horse incident and went back to the bush. But not long afterwards he was accused of killing a runaway steer and was given ten years. He always protested his innocence about that, but he wasn't believed. They rarely believe you . . .' as drifts of smoke and the lick of flames in a barley stack stole into the old man's consciousness. 'Not often . . .'

I never done it. Wasn't me.

'So, anyway, Joe determined to escape again at the first opportunity,' Sam went on.

Unlike myself. I never dared.

'And that came when he was out with a work party on the Canning Flats. He got away for a month, that time. Committed a few robberies . . . and that's when people first began to hear about the nickname "Moondyne Joe". 'Course, they caught him at last, and this time he was sentenced to an extra twelve months in irons. A whole year in shackles . . .'

'But that didn't stop him.'

'Too right it didn't. That's when I first saw Moondyne, you know. In the yard of Fremantle Prison. We arrived on the *Belgravia* in July of '66 . . . and the next month Joe escaped by climbing clean over the wall. In his leg-irons! I tell yer, he was a determined man. Made his way that night to the tool shed at the bridge camp where we'd been working, took a hammer and chisel to cut off his chains and fled towards Toodyay with three other runaways. There were a lot of 'em in those days. Wanted to save Governor Hampton the cost of looking after them, I expect!'

'I imagine Hampton wasn't very happy.'

'He was mad . . . and his son, the acting Comptroller-General of Convicts. Ho! People were laughing at them and criticising their administration in the newspapers and everywhere. Sent a huge number of police to find Joe and the others.'

'They were trying to cross the desert to South Australia, I seem to remember . . .'

'That's right. Moondyne hoped the late winter rains would provide water and help cover their tracks. He was pretty well equipped too, because he had a lot of friends and supporters – besides helping himself to other people's goods at gunpoint when required.'

'Bushranger as well as bushman.'

'Yes, though there was little actual violence. That's why he caught the public's imagination. But of course they were captured eventually, a few hundred miles away . . . brought back to Fremantle . . . and that's where we saw Joe again. Chained by the neck to a window bar in the prison yard, although the papers later said it was to a post.'

'I suppose the Governor was making an example of him . . .'

'That son of his . . . George! He chained Moondyne like a dog in a kennel. That really upset everyone. And then Mr Hampton had a special cell prepared for his prisoner, lined with thick jarrah timbers, studded with nails, the barred window was screwed down tight, the hammock hooks removed. Joe had to sleep on the floor. And when it was finished and Moondyne put inside, George Hampton said, "If you escape from that, I'll forgive you." Or at least he'd get his father to.'

'He'd pardon him?'

'Words to that effect. But the cell was so cramped and suffocating, that within days Dr Attfield reported that Joe's health was starting to suffer. Reluctantly, George Hampton agreed to remove one small pane of window glass to let in a little air. But it wasn't enough. Moondyne's health was still deteriorating, until the doctor insisted he be allowed outside for a few hours every day to exercise in the open. So Joe was put to breaking stones in the prison yard . . .'

'Oh yes, I remember the story! His most famous escape!'

The journalist found himself becoming quite excited talking to someone who'd actually been there at the time.

'Certainly was. It set the seal on Moondyne's reputation. They delivered these heavy stones to the prison. Joe was breaking them in a corner of the yard where the wall abutted the back garden of the big house occupied by the Prison Superintendent, Mr Lefroy. The super . . . the doctor . . . the chaplain, they all had houses just outside, fronting the Esplanade. Anyway, George Hampton had given strict orders that Moondyne was to be watched at all times by a couple of guards, and that the pile of broken stones had to be removed from the prison every day. For some reason the last part of those orders was ignored . . . and so, as we left the prison in the gangs to work outside, and came back at night, we'd see the pile of Joe's broken stones growing larger and larger . . .'

'Until it was big enough . . .'

'Quite so, Mr Cribben! Until the day came when the pile was tall enough to obscure Joe from the view of the guards. And that's when, instead of breaking the rocks, he took a swing with his stone hammer at the prison wall. Then another swing . . . and another, until he'd made a hole big enough to crawl through the soft lime-stone into the Superintendent's garden.'

'And made his fourth escape.'

'But not before he set his hammer against the rock pile, draped his jacket across it on a bit of fencing wire or stick he'd found, and put his cap on top. So that the guards, looking across, thought it was just Joe sitting down and having a bit of a breather from the stone-breaking. That's what made him such a con-sum-mate escape-artist. Little touches like that.'

'And by the time they realised . . . Moondyne was well away.'

'Absolutely. The prison rocked with laughter. So did the public at the Hamptons' mortification, father and son. The newspapers waxed lyrical, as they say in books. And the urchins in the street started singing a little ditty that soon found its way into the mouths of free and bond alike . . . and even into the prison compound where it had to be sung very softly.'

'Do you remember it?'

'Certainly, young feller. It wasn't very difficult . . . Bob, would you pass over my falsies?'

There was a pause as the Tuppenny Orderly retrieved the dentures from the bedside table and fitted them into the old fellow's mouth. Then, lying back on the pillow, Sammy began to warble in a quavering voice to the tune of a nursery rhyme from far-off days.

The Governor's son has got the Pip,
The Governor's got the measles,
But Moondyne Joe has give 'em the slip,
Pop goes the Weasel!

There was a round of applause and laughter as Samuel finished the song, and cackling, too, as he wiped his eyes with his sleeve and caught his breath.

'Here, Bob, you can take me falsies out again.' He fumbled in his mouth, trying to extract the dentures and resume his haggard appearance, but the reporter intervened.

'I say, would you mind keeping them in, Sam? It's a bit easier to understand you with your teeth in place.'

'Oh. Well. If you say so, Mr Cribben. I suppose . . .'

The old man muttered to himself for a little in irritation – before coming to a resolution and deciding to go on with the story.

'Oh, the hue and the cry! That was in March of '67, and it went on for months – all during my time there. But, you know, on this occasion Moondyne Joe seemed to have disappeared completely into the bush.'

'Several years, wasn't it?'

'Almost exactly two years, during which the authorities didn't find neither hide nor hair of Moondyne. His friends kept Joe well hidden, see. And then he was only found by accident. He'd snuck into Houghton's wine cellar to take a bottle or two while the owner was away helping with a police search. Unluckily for Joe, they came back too soon, and Mr Houghton went down to his cellar to get some refreshments. Joe, thinking he'd been nabbed, tried to make a run for it . . . and so he did, right into the arms of the coppers waiting outside.'

'And then back to Fremantle, with years added to his sentence.'

'Yes . . . A year for absconding, and another four in irons for breaking and entering the wine cellar. For all the good that was supposed to do.'

A note of sadness crept into the old man's voice, as he remembered the futility and cruelty of it all. But then he added with a little laugh, 'Not that it mattered all that much to Joe. He soon talked his way out of it. Of course, I'd long gone by then. Got my ticket-of-leave and sent down to work in the Vasse district, around Busselton. The Hamptons had both gone as well. New Governor. New Comptroller-General of Convicts. And Joe went on to live a pretty honest sort of life for the next thirty years after that, they say . . .'

The old chap began to drift off again – tired, though stimulated, like the actor he was, after such a performance. Haunted, too, by the ghosts of those days who came briefly to life again as Samuel remembered them. Moondyne, the Hamptons, the pale faces of convicts and warders long dead. Jimmy Carr. Dick Leach. And the smell of eucalyptus and wood smoke from the forests down south . . . the scent of fresh-sawn jarrah logs as they carted them from the timber mill to the jetty . . .

Samuel Speed turned his head towards the reporter. 'But I only know what I heard, Mr Cribben. Some of it from Moondyne himself, when I was down in the Vasse, waiting for the day I was given my own freedom again.'

13

TICKET-OF-LEAVE

Sam Speed had known for some time that he was due for his ticket-of-leave – that longed-for moment when he would be released from the confined strictures of prison life and returned to society: able to seek work for himself and enjoy once more the free association of his fellow men and, as he hoped, of women. Of course, he wouldn't yet be truly free. A ticket man was still a prisoner and bound to the rules. He couldn't leave the district to which he was assigned without permission. He had to report his movements, employment and whereabouts to the police. Observe the ten o'clock curfew and avoid the watchman's call, 'Bond or Free?' Obey every law. Abstain from drunkenness and immoral behaviour. Not seek work aboard any ship, especially whalers. And accept that any breach of the above could see him returned to prison and his sentence extended, with or without the option of a flogging and hard labour in irons. A ticket-of-leave was more a halfway house than the old liberty, but within those limits Samuel would be permitted to think and act for himself again, acquire his own property – and even marry, without the constant supervision of warders and the ever-present Pensioner Guards.

The first intimation that he was about to enter this new phase of existence came one afternoon in the late autumn of 1867, when Sam returned to the Fremantle Establishment with the work gangs, and was about to go into his cell for supper and another session with *Robinson Crusoe*. He was met on the catwalk by a warder, who instructed Speed to collect his things and come along with him.

'You won't be residing in that cell any longer eight-nine-nine-six,' the warder observed. 'Or at least I hope you won't.'

'Why? Where am I going?'

Like everyone kept in an institution for any length of time, Sam found himself beginning to panic at the thought of a change to established routine – torn between hope that he might be moved to somewhere better, and despair that he'd been caught for some minor infraction and was about to be sent to the punishment block.

'What have I done?'

'Nothing wrong. Not that I know of,' the warder replied, knowing that there was a whole hidden life among the prison inmates of which the authorities were mostly unaware. Again, like every other institution. 'The guv'nor is of opinion that you have generally behaved yourself, and you are being moved out of your cell and into an association ward.'

Alarm turned to relief.

'Does that mean I'll be getting me ticket soon?'

'That depends on you. You'll be sharing the big room at the end of this floor with forty or fifty other men. Getting used to communal life again, in a manner of speaking. We relax the rules a bit in there. You can talk – quietly – among yourselves. No raucous horseplay or obscenities, mind – and there's a warder on duty all night to see that there ain't – else you go straight back to your cells. But so long as you continue to obey the regulations, don't make a disturbance and conduct yourself properly, it's usually the first step towards probation and getting your ticket.'

So Samuel went into his cell for a last time and collected the few possessions that a convict was allowed to have: his spare shirt and trousers, soap and towel for the weekly bath, mug and food bowl, the requisite Bible and his borrowed copy of *Robinson Crusoe*. And with scarcely a glance behind in farewell, he followed the warder along the catwalk to the association ward at the far end. He was greeted with murmurs of recognition by those men that he knew – even several jests of 'what took yer so long, Sammy?' – and was gratified to see that he was ordered to sling his hammock alongside a youngish *Belgravia* shipmate known as 'Jemmy', on account of his skill with that tool as a housebreaking implement.

It was as well Jemmy was there, for he helped smooth the newcomer's way into acceptance by the hierarchy of the ward. Shielding Samuel from taunts by those who objected at first to the entry of a stranger among them – like urchins testing the mettle of a new boy on the street. Showing him the way they went about things at collective mealtimes and at night. Laughing at his little jokes. And yarning of a late afternoon, when Sam laid *Robinson Crusoe* aside, of old times on board the convict ship and their mutual pals, Jimmy Carr and Dick Leach.

'Poor Carr ain't done too well,' Jemmy would say, 'not since he got his first black mark for whistlin' only days after we got here. The screws have never took their eyes orf 'im.'

'Three months, and he was put on bread and water for two days for disobeying orders,' Samuel added. 'And the next week he was given another ten days' bread and water. Ten days! There'd be nothing left of me.'

'There wasn't much left of Jimmy neither. I seen him not long after he come orf it.'

'It didn't stop him, though. Just last March they added eleven days in all to his probation time – for disobedience and idleness, so he told me.'

'And it gets worse, Samuel.' Jemmy lowered his voice further. 'The other week I was out with a work party, and there was Jim Carr wearing the black-and-yellow "magpie" togs. Three months in irons – 50-pound weight around his ankles and the skin already festerin' . . .'

'What for?' Samuel couldn't keep the shock out of his voice.

'Usin' filthy and disgustin' language to a screw. Said he wished he'd given 'im a bit more. Ha!'

But it wasn't funny.

'I just don't understand it . . .'

They shook their heads together, though in truth Sam understood only too well what had happened to Jimmy Carr. To be sure, the severity of the penal code was such that it succeeded in frightening some – perhaps the majority – of prisoners into submission and obedience. He and Jemmy were two of them, determined to earn their tickets-of-leave as soon as possible, because marks for good conduct could also be used to reduce the time they were incarcerated and increase the small gratuities they were given in lieu of wages for their labour.

But there were other men to whom the barbarity of the system succeeded only in driving their contempt for authority further inside – and instead of reforming their criminal characteristics, managed to make them worse. Jim Carr was such a one: and indeed, in the five years after he was eventually given his ticket-of-leave he had no less than ten convictions recorded against him, for two of which he served prison time at Perth and Fremantle.

Everything from stealing a shawl to loitering around the public houses to being caught out of hours. The screws had it in for Jimmy from the start . . .

Old Samuel twisted in his sheet. Poor fellow. Even after his three months in irons, Jim committed two further offences before he was given his ticket. One, for using more insulting and disrespectful language to a warder – and another for leaving his work party claiming to be sick, but then refused to go to the hospital. Foolishly. It was a sure giveaway for shirking, in consequence of which Jimmy was given another three days' bread and water.

I mean, if you're gunna tell a lie, you've at least got to act as if you believe it. Eh?

But then, who could tell how a man might respond? Look at Dick Leach. Not long after they arrived at Fremantle, he'd been given two months' special remission for some particularly meritorious bit of behaviour. An emergency, was it? Saving somebody? Sammy couldn't quite remember. Dick was even sent down to Busselton with a government work party, as a kind of bonus to get him out of jail. And then he'd blown it! When the two met some months later on Samuel's own arrival at the Vasse, Dick confessed that the sweet scent of liberty – so near, yet distant – had gone to his head after four years of breathing stale prison air.

'I was assigned to a road gang,' he said. 'But I lost me temper, refused to work, and was dismissed. Same thing a few months later. Got sick of it. Told the boss where to stick his pick. And was sent back to the guv'mint camp for what they called "Most contemptuous Insolence". Well, he asked for it, di'n't 'e?'

Even then Dick wouldn't learn. Before he got his own ticket, he was sentenced to a month's hard labour for pinching a new government blanket. Sold it, probably . . .

As for Samuel, he waited his time out in the association ward as patiently and inconspicuously as he could. His companions came and went. Some of them – even Jemmy – were returned to their cells for bad behaviour, for the call to assert oneself against the system could not always be resisted. But most submitted until their time for probation was up, were given their tickets and departed to their assigned districts: Northam and Toodyay, the Vasse region around Bunbury and Busselton, Champion Bay and a mining town called Geraldton . . . In time Samuel became one of the old hands in the ward and was giving advice about the routine of how to fold and stow hammocks each morning and empty the common latrine tub to another lot of newcomers.

Generally, though, he kept himself fairly self-contained, seeking refuge in his reading when he needed to from the close – often too close – community of the association ward, as if retreating to the privacy of his old cell. Thus, he finished *Robinson Crusoe* at last, finding that the tale of the castaway's survival and eventual escape from his island (courtesy of some pirates) held him to the end. There were certain things Speed found hard to believe. Crusoe's rediscovery of God, for instance, and his attempts to convert the natives and even the Spanish to his evangelical beliefs. In Sam's experience, abandonment on a desert island, no less than in a stone jail, was no place to find God; and while he went through the outward forms of religious observance in chapel because he had to, his rejection of the tenets of divine love remained much as they'd been from the first days of his incarceration, despite the example of William Irwin's kindness and his homilies on board the *Belgravia*.

Then again, Crusoe's making and losing of several fortunes left Sam feeling more than sceptical. Of course, everybody wanted to amass piles of money in the colonies once they got out of prison, and to return home in splendour. They'd all heard of the rich nuggets to be found in the goldfields of Victoria, or wealthy squatters grown fat as their sheep on stations that spread as far as the horizon. The thought that it might one day be them is what kept so many of the prisoners going – even if, like Moondyne Joe, a little bushranging sometimes seemed a quicker way to the easy money. Sam Speed was no less drawn by such dreams of finding a more prosperous life here, once he had his freedom, than he could ever have known in England. But he knew from Mr Irwin it would take a great deal of hard effort on his part; and as he closed the last pages of his book, Sam couldn't help wondering if Crusoe's several fortunes were not more a matter of wishful thinking, like the prisoner from that story in *The Belgravian Weekly Journal*, whose parents persuaded the Secretary of State to review his case!

Still, Samuel finished it. And as he suspected he was fairly close to his own time for release on parole with a ticket-of-leave, from then on borrowed only shorter works from the prison library. They had a comprehensive collection of the *Saturday Magazines* bound into volumes, and Sam spent many an hour after they came in from the day's labour refreshing himself in 'The Kitchen Garden Through the Year' (reversing once more the months and seasons for this upside-down country) and reading what articles he could find on the pastoral and mineral wealth of Western Australia, though as yet no gold had been found in the colony. But he could always dream of it, suspended in his hammock among the snores of fifty other men.

*

'When did you go down to the Vasse, Sam?'

The questioning voice of Joshua Cribben intruded into the old man's reverie. He'd said nothing for the past few minutes, thinking that Speed had exhausted himself after the dramatic recital of Moondyne Joe, and needed the rest. But time was getting on, and the journalist had to get his story together before the photographer turned up with his promised lift into town. So he asked again in somewhat louder tones:

'When did you get your ticket-of-leave?'

The old bloke opened one eye.

'It's all right, Mr Cribben, you don't have to shout.' Keeping his inquisitor at bay. 'I'm not stone deaf yet, you know.'

'Sorry.'

Bob the Tuppenny Orderly laughed from the bed opposite.

'You don't have to worry about old Sammy. He's as lively as a two year old.'

Rubbish. You should see me tottering about on me stick!

'Oh, yes. You know, we just prepare his weekly bath and he jumps in and out as nimbly as if he were getting ready to go courting again.'

What lies you tell, Bob. But thanks, anyway.

'He's just having you on, Mr Cribben. Take no notice of Bob.'

The reporter instead was scribbling down these remarks as a valuable illumination of the old feller's character. He must ask some more about that. Courting? At ninety-eight or whatever? That was something to perk up the interest of the *Mirror*'s weekend readers.

'Yes. Well, where was I . . .? Oh, me ticket. That was in October 1867 . . . to the very day I was entitled to release on probation for good conduct. I was escorted down to the office and told that I was to be given my ticket-of-leave to the Vasse, where I had to remain until I got my full release in three years' time. That was a happy day, I can tell you. My heart was singing like a two year old then. And the next morning I was given a lecture to behave myself, a warrant for me passage, a set of clothes and necessaries, and the small amount of money from the gratuities I'd earned in jail . . .'

'I didn't know they paid you?' The journalist sounded surprised.

'Oh yairs. It were a fortune. Two-and-two-thirds farthings a day based on my marks for good conduct.'

'Farthings?'

'You know . . . four farthings to a penny. I was in Fremantle Prison for 463 days, working with the labour gangs. At the end of it I were given one pound five shillings and eightpence – less one and six for three sixpenny postage stamps. I'd written a few times to my sister but she never replied, and I gave up after that.'

'One pound four shillings and twopence,' the reporter calculated. 'Barely a week's wages today.'

'Scarcely a month, then. But it was a hundred per cent more than I had when I entered the place, and I passed through the gatehouse for the last time feeling like a millionaire. A new man. So I thought. Down the long ramp I knew so well to the town, and would have had a tipple or two at the public houses in celebration, I can tell you. But I wasn't a millionaire, really – and anyway, as a ticket man I weren't allowed to drink liquor and get drunk. Besides, I was bound for the wharf and the coastal schooner to take me south to Busselton . . .'

Samuel could sense it all again now. That sweetest feeling of release as he walked up the gangplank unchained and unsupervised for the first time in four years, with only the jingle of coins in his pocket. The affirmation of belief that he was taking these first steps into a better life as he found a seat by the rail. Sensing the stink and pallor of confinement beginning to fall away like another skin, as the ship slipped her moorings and headed into the open sea. It was as if he were on board *Belgravia* again – the breeze whipping his hair and the salt spray stinging Sam's face as he rode with the slap and heave of the waves. There was even a dolphin or two to be seen keeping them company – those creatures that had come to represent for him such hope and liberation, so that he laughed out loud into the wind. To be sure, he was not yet free. He was still bound by the rules and prescriptions of servitude for another three years.

But I am on my own, he thought, *and I am on my way.*

And Sam Speed laughed again.

There were several other ticket men on board as well – older men, for the most part, who kept to themselves playing cards and drinking noisily during the voyage. Sam was as happy to keep his distance and enjoy the sail.

'Three days it took us in the boat, Mr Cribben. It might seem a long time, but it was much quicker than trudging 140 miles through the scrub and eucalypt forests with the bullock wagons. We had to walk almost everywhere in those days, unless you had the fare for the mail coach, which cost a fortune. None of your motor cars or trains like today. And mostly we didn't mind hoofing it. I don't reckon the young people are so tough these days.'

You do talk a lot of old man's bulldust, Sam Speed. You didn't want to hoof it to the Vasse. And you loved every minute of the voyage on that schooner.

The first port of call was the small settlement of Rockingham – only 16 miles from Fremantle, but there was some cargo that needed to be taken aboard for Bunbury a good hundred miles or so further south, where some of the ticket men also disembarked.

Old Samuel chuckled to himself. *There* were two place names to remember if we're talking about convict escapes. And he'd tell that story, too, in a moment; but for the present he was still savouring the tang of that remembered voyage into liberation, and all the desires of youth it had reawakened.

They landed at Busselton on the third day: a pretty town of limestone and timber buildings, founded thirty-five years earlier by the first settlers looking for suitable grazing land in this area of high rainfall, though the mighty forests of jarrah, tuart and karri trees also supported a timber industry that supplemented the prosperity of the Vasse district. The hard-wearing wood had been used to build the jetty where they berthed. It was modest enough now, though eventually it would stretch nearly a mile into Geographe Bay, named by the French navigator Baudin after one of his ships – as the river Vasse honoured a sailor of his who was supposed to have drowned when he fell overboard.

Along the jetty and across the sandy shore Samuel walked, carrying his few things in a bundle, until they reached the beginning of Queen Street and the welcoming embrace, as always, of officialdom. On one side stood the stone customs house and bond store, its location marked by a lighthouse. Well, it was more of a lantern in a barrel on top of a 30-foot pole, known as 'the tub', though its beam could be seen well out to sea by shipping, and especially the American whalers that frequented these waters in summer. The new lighthouse didn't come till a few years later. On the other side was the courthouse, police station and lock-up, built of solid limestone by local businessmen David Earnshaw and Henry Yelverton.

Good enough men, but the limestone wasn't. It was from one of these cells that John 'Goodenough' Williams escaped by pulling out the window frame from its surrounds. Ha ha.

They later strengthened some of the cells with jarrah planks attached to the walls, just like Moondyne's at Fremantle.

It was towards the police station that Sam Speed turned his steps. The importance of reporting his arrival had been impressed upon him the day he left the Establishment.

'Where yer going, youngster?' called the two ticket men who'd left the ship with him.

'Reporting in . . .'

'Ah, don't worry. We've got a week to see the traps. Come with us and look around the town first, see where the best grog's sold . . .'

'I'd rather do it now.'

'Suit yerself.'

And they left him to it.

Alone outside the police station, the sensations of liberty Sam had known on board the schooner flickered – and failed. The reality that he was still a bonded man came back with all the certainty of his sentence, together with the knowledge he was still three years away from true freedom. There was a moment when he wondered if he should make a bolt for it – but only a moment. He knew it was better to comply, and to do so at once before he forgot. To do otherwise would see that time stretch out still further when he was inevitably caught. And so, having reported himself to the police, Sam had his presence, number and occupation noted in the daybook with a copy for the Resident Magistrate and his ticket signed. Next Sam was directed to the local Convict Depot.

This was another stern government building a block or so further up the street. Here, the convict work gangs had their base,

to which men like Dick Leach would be returned when they weren't
camped out in the bush working on the new roads. And here too,
ticket men such as Sam could find a bed and a meal, courtesy of
the system, when they were between jobs or in need of temporary
shelter as they took their first steps back into civil society. Most tried
to avoid it, however, since a spell in the Depot meant returning to
the labour gangs, and Sam usually stayed at Earnshaw's Commercial
Hotel when he came into town. Fortunately, they could also find
work through the Depot, for employers frequently left notice of any
vacancies at the hiring office. It was cheaper than advertising and
gave them first pick of the new arrivals.

In this respect, Sam Speed was lucky. Happy, too, in his boss.

'I was taken on almost at once as a general servant by Mr Henry
Yelverton,' the old chap continued. 'He ran a big timber mill in
the bush at a little place called Quindalup, about 13 mile along
the coast. A decent man. Good employer to his men. He put me on
at one pound ten shillings a month – which was ten bob more than
the going rate at that time.'

He leaned against the pillows and thought back for a moment.
Then laughed.

'Mind you, the rules said that we ticket men had to negotiate our
own wages, and you can see I drove a hard bargain! 'Course, mostly
the odds were stacked the other way – more men looking for work
than there were jobs to give 'em. Just like now in the depression
time. But then, the mill was thriving. Big demand for Swan River
mahogany, as they called the jarrah in those days, and Mr Yelverton
had the first steam mill in the colony. So he paid good wages . . .'

A pause, as Sammy remembered something else.

'But I didn't get to keep it all! There was I thinking I was on the
way to making me fortune, when I discovered that Queen Victoria

wanted her share of it. I told yer, didn't I, that I'd been sent halfway round the world courtesy of Her Majesty? Well, I was mistook. As soon as I got a job and me first wages, she made me pay 'er back my fare! Cunning beggars. Government!'

'How much did they take?'

'It was in proportion to your sentence. I had seven years, so I paid seven pound one shilling. Ten years, ten pound . . . and so on. I don't know what the lifers had to pay! But it was spread over the three years you were on your ticket and conditional release, so it wasn't too bad. Made sure we didn't get too rich, eh!'

'Did you like the work out there?'

'Oh, it was bonzer. After four years under a prison regime, you felt as if you'd been given your life back. The bush breathed freedom. The scent of it after rain. Sitting around the campfire of a night, just having a yarn, and the smell of meat roasting for your supper. Pleasant days . . .'

And in memory he was back there again. Eucalyptus smoke rising . . . echoes of laughter . . . until he turned away.

'Of course, it was hard work. The trees were felled and dragged to the mill by bullock teams, where they were sawn into planks. And the boards then were taken about a mile to the jetty at Toby's Inlet on a little tramline with wooden rails, on trucks pulled by horses. We'd stack them by the beach, and load 'em onto the lighters that carried the timber to the ships anchored offshore. He was a clever man, that Henry Yelverton. He studied to be a doctor, you know, then went to America and came out to Fremantle on a whaler. Built up his business as a timber merchant and builder . . . built the police cells at Busselton, he did, and eventually started his mill. Bought his first steam engine from a shipwreck.'

'Quindalup must have been quite a thriving place, in those days.'

'Yes it *was*! Not much of it left now, so I've been told. The stump of the jetty . . . a few tumbledown buildings. But *then* . . . Mr Yelverton had his first mill near the beach, until he moved it inland and built the tramline. Built his own fine timber residence, Quindalup House, too, and huts for the single workers and even houses for the married ones with a bit of land to run stock. Had a post office and school, until they were moved closer to the beach. Regular little township it was. Police station, cells, bond store, a slab cottage for the harbour-master, Mr John Harwood, on account of all the shipping coming and going. Hard to believe now . . .'

'You mentioned the American whalers. Didn't that Irish convict, John Boyle O'Reilly, escape on board one of them?'

'Oh ho, indeed he did!'

'That would have been about your time down there, wouldn't it?'

'You're on the ball, Mr Cribben. Yes, I was still in the Vasse when it happened. Remember it well. Coppers and warders and black trackers everywhere. Early 1869, I think . . .'

Samuel groped in the ragbag of memory for a date.

'It's all right, I can check it later. Did you know O'Reilly, at all?'

'Well, I can't say for certain. He didn't enter Fremantle Prison until the beginning of '68, but I'd already gone by then, on my ticket. O'Reilly came out with sixty-two Fenian political prisoners on the *Hougoumont*, the last of the convict ships to arrive in Western Australia. They'd been convicted of sedition and planning an Irish rebellion. They were mostly civilians, but among them were a number of military prisoners, O'Reilly included. He was a poet and writer – a journalist like you, before he went into the army. Anyway, he was convicted of high treason – inciting a mutiny – and sentenced to be shot, though it was later changed to transporta-tion. A handsome, clever devil they say, and not very long after he arrived at Fremantle, he was sent down to Bunbury to work with the road gangs . . .'

Samuel paused a little, gathering his strength together. He was enjoying himself again, back on familiar ground retelling other people's stories, his words running fluently as a timber trolley along a pair of greased wooden tramlines.

''Course, that's where I might have seen O'Reilly . . . around Bunbury where I sometimes went. The timber business was a bit up and down, and when I was laid off from Yelverton's in a slow time, I worked for some of the farms in the district . . . George Dawson . . . a few others. I travelled around . . .'

'And that's when you met O'Reilly?'

'Very possibly. A lot of others certainly had some contact with him, because O'Reilly didn't labour with the gangs for long. He was a clever feller, as I said: educated, with a winning, command-ing personality. And he was soon asked to help the overseers with the clerical work. Writing returns. Taking messages back and forth between the gangs out at Capel, halfway between Busselton and the Depot at Bunbury . . .'

'I see.'

'And that's where he met the local Catholic priest, Father McCabe. Pat McCabe. Very sympathetic to the Irish cause, as you'd expect.'

'Quite.'

'Well, O'Reilly had always dreamed of escaping from the place. He couldn't bear it, for some of the overseers were terrible cruel to him.'

'How cruel? What did they do?'

'I heard that one in partic'lar had it in for O'Reilly. You never know why. They just pick on some poor feller . . . Anyway, O'Reilly was a few minutes late back to his desk one day, and this bastard screw took his chance. "You're late. No more letters for six months!" That's the sort of thing they'd do.'

'Very nasty.' Joshua Cribben was frequently late at his desk – had been so this morning and had to come out by bus. But being denied his mail for six months? 'A bit over the top.'

'It gets worse. Not long afterwards, a letter arrived for O'Reilly with a thick black border. He knew his mother had been sick and feared the bad news. "This came for you," said the overseer, as O'Reilly held out his hand for it. "You'll get it in six months." And this dog, who'd already opened and read the letter, shoved it in his drawer. It were six months before O'Reilly was told his mother had died. And yet, you know, he always refused to name the blackguard what did that. Said he must have been sick in the head and more to be pitied . . .'

'I'd have named him in the paper.'

'And so would I. That's the difference between us and a man of O'Reilly's sensibility. But we can understand why he so hated the place and was determined to flee east into the bush and try to cross the desert plains. He eventually confided his plans to Father McCabe, who told him that was one certain way to commit suicide. "Leave it with me," said the priest, "and I'll work out a plan and get back in touch with you".'

'Which is where the whaler came in?'

'Exactly. Well, weeks went by and O'Reilly didn't hear anything from Father McCabe. He was starting to worry when one day, towards the end of '68, he was approached by one of the local farmers – a feller called Maguire – and a friend of Father Mac's. He told him the American whaling ships would be calling into Bunbury during February to pick up water and supplies, and they'd arrange with one of the captains to take O'Reilly aboard.

'It was a long wait, but eventually Maguire contacted O'Reilly again and told him to get ready. They smuggled a change of clothes and another pair of boots to his hut in the convict camp . . .'

'Why different boots?'

'Because convict boots had the government broad arrow on the sole, studded with hobnails. Easy to track, see. Anyway, that night O'Reilly slipped away from his hut wearing the new clobber, and cut about three mile across country by starlight to an old convict camp at Picton. He waited by arrangement until a party of horsemen rode by and one of them started whistling "Saint Patrick's Day" or "Wearing O' the Green". Something Irish like that. It was the signal. O'Reilly stepped out of the bush, and with Maguire and his few friends rode hell for leather to the river north of Bunbury. There, they had a boat waiting, and under cover of darkness rowed quite a few mile into the bay and up the Leschenault Peninsula to wait in the sandhills for the agreed whaler – the *Vigilant* – to pick them up offshore. But it seems she was a day or so late in leaving. The escape party had forgotten to bring any food or water with them, and as it was the height of summer O'Reilly began to suffer dreadfully from thirst and hunger. So, his friends went to a settler's house nearby to get something to eat and drink – it was a Mr Jackson – and the convict waited among the sand dunes for his rescue ship.

'Next day *Vigilant* was sighted heading north under full sail. Quickly O'Reilly and his friends got into their boat and rowed out to meet her. But to their amazement – and dreadful disappointment – she took no notice of them, not their shouts or even waving a white shirt tied to an oar, and sailed away into the distance. Leaving them with nothing to do but curse and land O'Reilly among the sandhills again, arrange supplies from the Jacksons – who they had to trust and let into the secret – and go back to town to make other arrangements.'

'It must have been a terrible time for him . . . a pretty dramatic time for everybody, I imagine.'

'You're not wrong there, Mr Cribben. I was working for George Dawson on his farm at the time, and it was the talk of the district. Police and troopers searching everywhere. The black-trackers. Notices offering rewards for any information posted up. Five pounds, which you might have thought would be a temptation. Nearly half a year's wages! But it wasn't enough. The coppers never found him, and at last concluded that O'Reilly must have escaped on the whaler, when all the time he was hiding in the sandhills north of Bunbury, right under their noses. For nearly two weeks he stayed there, with the heat and the flies and sand and snakes, never knowing if he'd get away or be caught and flogged and sentenced to more years in irons. An awful time – agonising – you might say. He even rowed a small boat out to sea himself to try to hail a ship . . . It was important to get at least twelve mile offshore into international waters, you understand. He saw one whaler . . . perhaps it was the *Vigilant* . . . but she sailed away again. Nothing came of it, and when O'Reilly got to the beach again, he was so exhausted he slept for days.'

'But he *did* escape?'

'Oh yes. At the end of the month Maguire returned to say that they'd arranged with the Captain of the *Gazelle* to pick up O'Reilly the following day. Father McCabe had even paid Captain Gifford ten pounds for his trouble. The problem was that another convict, a real bad 'un called Bowman, had got wind of the escape plan, and threatened to tell the coppers unless they took him too. So there was no help for it but to bring Bowman as well when they rowed out to sea next day and waited until the *Gazelle* sailed by in the late afternoon. They hailed her. The Captain called out O'Reilly's name. And when he replied came the answering shout, "Come aboard!" Which he did. With Bowman in tow. And as the rowers pushed off from the ship, the brave Maguire stood in the thwarts and shouted, "God bless you – and don't mention our names until it's all over".' And in fact, their names were kept secret for a long time afterwards.'

'Did you know it at the time?'

'Oh no! It was years before the full story came out. And those who knew kept their mouths shut. O'Reilly eventually got to America, became a famous newspaper editor and writer and Irish patriot. He wrote that book *Moondyne*, you know, very loosely based on the real Moondyne Joe, but full of fantasy. Well, he *was* a journalist, wasn't he?' Samuel pointed a skinny finger from under the sheet towards the reporter. 'Always making things up. Aboriginal treasure trove! They never dug for gold. And he even had women convicts being transported to Western Australia. They weren't . . . but then I suppose O'Reilly wanted to have some love interest in his story . . .'

Not that you'll find much of that in mine. More's the pity.

'And it *was* a powerful plea against the evils of the convict system. He wrote from the heart.'

'And what happened to Bowman?'

'He was caught again. Deserved to be. When the *Gazelle* reached the island of Rodrigues, near Mauritius, it was searched by the British police. The crew pretended that O'Reilly had fallen overboard and drowned . . . somebody dropped a grindstone and his hat into the water . . . even though he was hidden below in a locker. But Bowman had made himself so disliked, that one of the sailors pointed him out. Back he came to Fremantle and the triangle. O'Reilly even named the villain in his book after Bowman, so his name lives on.'

'And O'Reilly himself . . .?'

'He eventually reached Liverpool and found a passage to America. I read that he watched his beloved Ireland disappear over the horizon from the taffrail in the golden light of the setting sun. Very poetic, don't you think, Mr Cribben? And he reached Philadelphia in November 1869 . . . almost two years exactly since that last convict ship, *Hougoumont*, left Portland with O'Reilly and the other Fenians aboard.'

'It's a good tale.'

'Yairs. Poetic justice, I calls it.'

14

THE *CATALPA*

The escape of John Boyle O'Reilly was not the end of the story. There was more of it to come, as both Sam Speed and the journalist well knew. But the old chap spun a good yarn, as one should who was there at the time. He judged his audience well; knew the value of a dramatic pause and a touch of comic relief; and became so involved in the telling, that when Samuel reached the climax of the Fenian's escape, he fell back against the pillow as one spent. His eyes shut, and the breath came in such short gasps through his ill-fitting dentures that the reporter looked across the bed to Bob the orderly with a quizzical look, as if to enquire whether Sammy needed medical assistance.

'Oh, he's all right,' Bob remarked. 'Sammy's just having a little nap. It takes it out of him, you know, all this storytelling.'

You're talking nonsense again, Bob. I'm not sleeping. Just resting. This is interval. Time for an ice-cream, if you care to bring us one.

The hint of a smile hovered about his wrinkled lips. But Samuel was grateful for the pause nonetheless; and while the others were content to let him have his forty winks, the old man used the curtain of silence and darkness behind the retina to take himself back across the decades to that time when he was young and which seemed, in retrospect, to have been as recent as last week.

Early 1870, wasn't it, when news of O'Reilly's landing in America appeared in the West Australian newspapers? Philadelphia, Sam seemed to recall, was where the Irishman made his appearance. The name means 'brotherly love', but that was the very last emotion expressed by the authorities in Perth. Brotherly outrage, more like. Indignation and foaming demands that the fugitive be returned to face justice. Some hope! Among the Irish section of the population, of course, there was general rejoicing; laughter among the convicts and ticket men, wishing it were them – but quietly, lest they be overheard and reported to the screws for sedition.

Sam Speed was especially careful, for he'd moved another step closer to his freedom. In May of 1869 he was given his conditional release, having satisfied the Resident Magistrate, Mr Harris, that he was respectably earning his living 'in a creditable and honest manner' and was in fair bodily health. The certificate gave him much more liberty to move about the district. He no longer had to report his every movement to the police, though he was still very much of the 'bonded class' and any breach of the law could see him returned to Fremantle Prison to serve the rest of his sentence plus any further penalties imposed by the courts. Thus, he kept his nose clean, as they say, and stayed out of trouble.

For the time being he remained in the Vasse, working on farms around Busselton: it was what he knew, and Sam liked the place. The demand for labour was there and the wages were reasonable. Indeed, he even opened an account with the government bank to deposit his small savings, for the farmers supplied board and keep, and there wasn't a lot to spend your money on in rural parts. He didn't drink much by way of liquor and neither did he smoke. Never had.

Flaming great waste of money, in my book.

Sam did come into town once a week or so, where he generally stayed at a pub. A branch of the Working Men's Association had just been formed in Busselton, and Samuel joined it as soon as he could. For one thing, it provided companionship among his own kind. Almost all of them were – or had been – ticket men, for the colonial stigma of having once been a prisoner was very strong, and the paths to preferment and success were limited for them among the 'free'. As Mr Irwin had foretold, they were not allowed to join the Mechanics' Institutes, for example. To be sure, some enjoyed a degree of commercial prosperity. Joseph Horrocks, who developed a copper mine and built the model village of Gwalla, north of Geraldton, was one of them. So, in his own way, was William Chopin, who practised as an unqualified chemist until his conviction and imprisonment again at the age of sixty-seven for procuring abortions. But on the whole, the former convicts remained within the lower echelons of society – labourers, tradesmen, the lesser professions such as school-teaching – and the Working Men's Association gave them the chance to establish some kind of social as well as business contact among themselves.

A chance, too, for self-improvement. Most of these associations tried to offer some form of educational program: perhaps night classes in basic literacy, much as the prison schools did, or trade instruction to develop manual skills. At the very least they provided a library for their members – and it was this, of course, that drew Sam Speed to the one in Busselton. He'd been pretty much starved of reading matter since leaving Fremantle, apart from the occasional out-of-date newspaper and discarded magazine. There were few novels to be found on the upturned boxes that served as bedside tables in the workmen's huts at Yelverton's timber mill or George Dawson's homestead. But when the association began in the back room of a hall at Busselton, Samuel hurried to join with his subscription to discover what stories might be found on its bookshelves.

The library was only in a small way to begin with. It tried to keep up with the latest newspapers from Perth and Fremantle, and in such manner did Samuel learn of O'Reilly's triumphant arrival in Philadelphia. There was a smattering of trade journals and manuals; a compendium of useful and general knowledge; several dictionaries; biographies of famous men and women through the ages; a copy of John Bunyan's *Pilgrim's Progress* among a group of religious books; and a small section of rather tattered volumes labelled 'Fiction'. One of them was *Uncle Tom's Cabin* – Harriet Beecher Stowe's novel of plantation life and black slavery in the southern states of America. It was a famous book. Even Samuel had heard of it, and he borrowed it for several weeks, reading it at night after work in his hut, returning the book at last, not only emotionally shaken by the story, but with a degree of understanding about one of the root causes of the Civil War that had so lately torn apart the United States. And in later years he often wondered if John Boyle O'Reilly had been as disturbed by the story as Sam was.

O'Reilly was certainly moved by the plight of the black Australians he saw during his brief time in the colony and wrote about them in *Moondyne*. But like most people of the day Samuel did not discern any parallels between the Negro slaves of the American South and the condition of the sad, wretched Aborigines he saw wandering the streets of town, living in squalid camps amid the surrounding bush. Forty years ago, these people had walked this country for their own, as they had for millennia. Now, they were seen as outcasts in their own land: of no value to the European intruders except as skilled trackers to hunt escaped fugitives; a constant threat to their sheep and cattle, not to mention that most important resource, the soil; and a problem to be solved by sending increasing numbers of them to a special jail built on Rottnest Island, not far from where the Governor had his summer home. There was even a separate cell for them in the Busselton lock-up, with iron rings fixed into the wall.

In the society of the Australian colonies, Aborigines generally were considered inferior even to convicts, who might look down upon them with hostility and contempt at worst, giving vent to their own mistreatment – or with indifference at best, like another form of native wildlife to be endured. Sam Speed, on the whole, found himself among the latter; and he was a child of his time. It would be years before the Aboriginal people found their own Harriet Beecher Stowe to voice in story the common humanity of every Australian – and John Boyle O'Reilly, for all the magnanimity of *Moondyne*, when Sam came to read his book, was not it. He even gave his noble Aborigine a Maori name.

More immediately, among the books at the Working Men's Association, Samuel found a slender copy of Charles Dickens' celebrated tale *A Christmas Carol*, with illustrations. What a writer he was! How he brought those characters to life, unlike the person Sam heard narrate the story in a country inn years ago. Ebenezer Scrooge . . . Sam had known enough misers like him both in and out of jail. The ghost of the dead Marley, loaded down with chains, might almost have stepped from Fremantle Prison, where Moondyne Joe had been kept in irons for a year and a half. And as for Tiny Tim, Samuel could scarcely claim to see himself in the little boy, for he had never known much by way of Happy Christmases and 'God bless us, every one'. But certainly when, in later years, he came to read *Oliver Twist*, there Sam was again among the children in the workhouse wanting something more to eat.

There was no *Pickwick Papers*, however. Not yet. Sam put his name down with the library keeper until such time as a copy came in, for some of the neighbouring landowners were fairly generous with donations of second-hand books. And in the meantime, he occupied himself on these visits into town with whatever journals were available and any other association activity that took his fancy.

Not least of these were the dancing classes. The hall where they met was the scene of several splendid balls held through the year. In the weeks before each ball, young men and women busied themselves practising the complicated steps of the popular quadrilles and cotillions of the day. Leading with the right hand, leading with the left. Dancing to your corners, dancing back to back. How to hold your partner when doing the polka, and even more carefully and gallantly when dancing the waltz . . . one-two-three, one-two-three . . .

Samuel sought to revel in it.

On the grand night of the ball, the hall was decorated with boughs of greenery and lit with lanterns and candles glowing on the faces of the couples, all wearing their best and weaving the patterns of the dance to the music of a fiddler. A circular waltz. A jolly Gay Gordons or rousing Galop. Sometimes a country dance, Corn Rigs or Sir Roger de Coverley. No alcohol was permitted to be drunk inside, except for the fiddler who was always stimulated by the beer and his playing seemed to improve as the evening wore on. It had the opposite effect on the young men who drank their booze *outside* the hall, and got progressively more unsteady on their feet and unsociable in their behaviour. Since there were always at least twice as many men as there were women at these balls, their growing intoxication made it even less likely they'd find a partner. Which tended to make them drink more. On the other hand, it helped Sam Speed's chances. Small and a little disfigured he may have been, with his scarred eye and the stigma of 'bondman' attached to his name. Always rather awkward on the floor. But at least he remained sober, kept himself clean, and remembered most of the steps. And as the evening grew late, Sam found his proffered hand taken more often by some pretty young Irish housemaid or seamstress, when other, more attractive partners, perhaps, were outside getting drunk.

Samuel could remember it still . . . the dark eyes of this colleen, no more than twenty, flashing in the lamplight as they went around the floor together in a polka. A Scottish girl, with a green ribbon in her auburn hair, laughing and holding her skirt as they danced towards each other in an Eightsome Reel. The heat and the noise and the sweet notes soaring above them as the fiddler worked up another sweat on the stage.

He began humming the tune to himself . . . 'De'il Amang the Tailors', was it . . . and a thin hand came from under the sheet and began tapping out the rhythm of the dance.

'Are you all right, Sammy?'

''Course I'm all right, Bob. You worry too much. I'm just remembering the dances we used to have in the old days. The girls and the music . . . They don't have nothing like it now.'

'You were fond of dancing, Sam?'

'Well, I weren't the most elegant cove on me feet, Mr Cribben. You'd probably call me more of a clodhopper. But at least I could stay upright and jig about in time to the music. The girls liked that . . . and the tunes were grand.'

'And when was this?'

'The early seventies . . . good times, then. Moondyne liked to dance, you know. Tall feller. Good-looking. Knew how to keep the women, too, when the music stopped . . .'

'Was he in the Vasse then?'

'Oh, yes. He'd been in Fremantle Prison for eighteen months in heavy irons after they caught him in Houghton's wine cellar. He pleaded with them to take the chains off. The weight of it! You can't imagine. So in the end, they agreed. But then the silly beggar was caught trying to forge a key in the carpenter's workshop . . . so they put him to breaking stones again.'

'That's how he escaped before . . .'

'Yes. But this time they weren't stupid enough to put the rock pile beside the outer wall. They put it in the middle of the court-yard where he could be observed by the screws at all times and from every angle.'

'So how did he get away, then?'

'By being honest! Well, he remembered the promise that George Hampton made when they put him in that special cell: "If you escape from that I'll forgive you." Word got back to the new Comptroller-General, who confirmed the promise with Superintendent Lefroy. And the upshot was that Joe was given his ticket-of-leave by Governor Weld and sent down by boat to the Vasse in May of '71.'

'Which is where you met up with him again?'

'Certainly did, Mr Cribben. He was working at Yelverton's mill, where I'd been. He'd come into town every so often . . . drop into the Working Men's Association . . . even attend some of the balls. He was a nice feller, you know. Everyone who worked with him said he was a decent, straightforward chap . . . popular . . . never shirked . . . and never boasted about himself. Whenever the subject of his escapes came up, he always swore his innocence of that original offence of stealing the steer. Of course, when riled his swearing could shock even a bullocky. But apart from that, the only people Joe didn't like were coppers and jailers.'

'Didn't he go back to prison again?'

'Yes. Briefly. Moondyne moved up to Bunbury for a bit but then got himself involved in a fracas and assaulted a constable. Found himself back in Fremantle clink for a month. Stayed up there as a boatbuilder and so on after he came out, and eventually got his Certificate of Freedom. Began to lead a respectable life.'

'And did he come back to the Vasse?'

'Not for a while. He did around 1880, after he got married. Her name was Louisa. A good woman. Joe loved her very deeply, they say. Yes, they worked on some of the farms around Margaret River for a while – Joe in the paddocks and Louisa in the kitchen. Funny thing, in O'Reilly's book *Moondyne*, his escaped convict is led by local Aborigines to a cave in the Vasse where they hoarded all their gold. Silly, but there it is. I don't know if the real Joe ever read that story – but he did find a cave near Margaret River that's still called Moondyne's. And he did go down there again to do a little prospecting. But there was no gold to be found in the Vasse. It was all out east – at Southern Cross and Coolgardie. Joe and his missus even went to try their hand . . . but by then Joe's luck was starting to run out.'

'You mentioned O'Reilly again. Of course, he was behind the most breathtaking escape in the colony's history . . .'

'The six Fenians who got away in the American whaler, *Catalpa*? Yes, that's right.'

'You'd remember that, I imagine . . .'

'As if it were yesterday. That's the thing about being old, as I dare say you'll find out. It's today we have trouble remembering. The past is always vivid.'

'Can you tell me the story?' Right on cue.

'Let me think. When was it? 1876. Yes. I'd got me freedom by then and were working back in Fremantle. So of course I was there on the spot, wasn't I? Living though all the drama of it. The colony nearly finding itself at war with the United States of America. The authorities bursting with fury and demands for justice. The rest of us laughing ourselves sick. Well, us old lags were at any rate, and all the Irish folk. The girls had an extra spring in their step at the next dance, I can tell yer!'

'The whole *Catalpa* plot began not long after O'Reilly reached America, didn't it?' The journalist sought to get his wayward subject back on the tramlines.

'Yes. He settled in Boston, I believe, and got a job on one of the newspapers as a reporter – just like you, Mr Cribben. The *Globe*, I think. Eventually became the editor . . . and maybe you will too, one day, eh? But he never forgot his fellow Fenians still imprisoned at Fremantle, and a promise to help them escape as well.'

'I think of the sixty-two Fenians who came out in the *Hougoumont*, most of the civilian prisoners had been pardoned by then and moved to Perth and elsewhere, from memory . . .?'

'Eventually, yes. But there were still seven of the military prisoners convicted of treason and mutiny at Fremantle. The government was making an example of them. And one of them, a feller called Wilson, smuggled out a letter to America pleading for help. It came into the hands of a man called John Devoy, another military Fenian, convicted of mutiny but later allowed to settle in New York, where he also became a newspaperman. There must be something about your profession and insurrection, eh, Mr Cribben? Because Devoy soon joined the Clan na Gael, a secret organisation supporting the Irish Brotherhood and armed rebellion in Ireland.'

'You're being a bit hard on us, Sammy,' the reporter murmured.

'Oh, I don't know about that. Look at all those nasty things you write about governments and other people.'

'It's our job. Keeping them on their toes.'

'You're certainly keeping me on my toes. And Wilson's letter kept John Devoy on *his* toes. Secret meetings of the *Clan's* supporters were called, and the upshot was that they raised about $20 000 – a lot of money in those days – to buy a merchant ship, send her out to Western Australia, and use it to rescue the Fenians still in prison.'

'Much the same way as O'Reilly had escaped . . .'

'Yes. In fact, it was O'Reilly who suggested that the ship be disguised as a whaler, because it wouldn't draw attention to itself off the coast of Fremantle. It was a good idea, which the Clan adopted, and they bought a three-masted whaler called *Catalpa* for $5500. She was put under the command of Captain George Anthony, himself a whaler, and a man of remarkable ability from all accounts. He had charge of fitting her out and selecting the crew. And when *Catalpa* left New Bedford in 1875, supposedly on a whaling voyage, only Captain Anthony knew the real purpose of the expedition. He told nobody the secret – not even his First Mate, until much nearer the rescue attempt.'

'Didn't they do some whaling, to maintain the disguise?' The journalist dredged his own seabed of memory.

'I believe they landed a couple of hundred barrels of whale oil when they reached the Azores.' Old Sammy sniggered. 'People used it to light their lamps in them days. That, or candles. It wasn't like today – flick a switch and turn on the electricity. You youngsters have it too easy!'

Age, as always, admonishing youth. But Joshua Cribben was equal to it.

'My folks still use lamps on the farm. We children had to trim the wicks and fill them every day.'

'That were different. You have kerosene.'

It was the journalist's turn to laugh.

'Go on!'

'Where was I? Why are we talking about kerosene lamps?'

'Whale oil.'

'Oh yes . . . well, it wasn't until the *Catalpa* left Tenerife that Captain Anthony told his Mate the real purpose of the expedition. He was a bit worried, because the Mate could have turned nasty, having been lied to all that time. But as it was, Samuel Smith – that was his name – willingly agreed to help with the rescue. And so, easier in mind, they faced the slow voyage down the Atlantic and across the Indian Ocean to the coast of Western Australia. It was a hard sail. They were hit by storms. Some of the crew deserted and they had to find replacements. There was constant trouble with the chronometer, until they bought a spare one from a passing ship. And there was one strange thing . . .'

'What's that?'

'As they were nearing Australia, *Catalpa* spoke an English ship heading for New Zealand. Captain Anthony went aboard her and had a pleasant hour talking to the Captain. Quite by chance, Anthony asked if he had any detailed charts of the West Australian coast, and the Master said he did. In fact, according to Anthony he'd been the skipper of the *Hougoumont* . . . you know, the last convict ship . . . the one that brought the Fenians out to Fremantle in '68. He fetched a bundle of charts he'd used on that trip and said to Captain Anthony, "Help yourself". Which he did.'

'What a coincidence! Is it true?'

'Apparently that's what Anthony said. The *Catalpa* spirited the escapees away using the very sea charts that had brought them to the penal colony in the first place.'

There was another pause as the implications settled in their minds.

'It was a long sail,' Samuel went on at last. 'It wasn't for eleven months after leaving New Bedford that *Catalpa* sighted her destination and dropped anchor off Bunbury at the end of March '76. Now came the hard part. The actual rescue. And the first task was for Captain Anthony to make contact with the local end of the operation . . .'

'There was a Fenian agent already in Fremantle, wasn't there? A man called Breslin?'

'Two of them, actually. One was John Breslin, who posed as a wealthy financier named "James Collins" looking for investment opportunities in the colony. In truth, he was a strong Fenian supporter, who'd arranged the escape of one political prisoner from an Irish prison already, before fleeing to America. The other was Thomas Desmond, who called himself "Johnson" and took a job as a wheelwright – though his real mission was to recruit sympathisers who would cut the telegraph wires between Fremantle and Albany on the day of the escape. Which he did, very successfully.'

'I saw a photograph of Breslin when I was reading up for this interview. He certainly looked the part of a plutocrat.'

'To be sure, Mr Cribben. A strong, good-looking man, with a large Victorian beard like a shovel, and manners that could charm the birds off the trees. He certainly charmed a servant girl at the Emerald Isle Hotel at Fremantle, they say, who bore him a son, though I doubt he ever saw the child. Charmed the Governor,

Sir William Robinson, as well, who entertained him with dinners and outings. Of course, "Mr Collins" had all the right letters of introduction and sufficient reserves of cash, courtesy of Clan na Gael and sympathisers in the colonies, who are said to have contributed something like £2000 to the enterprise. "Mr Collins" was so respected, that he was given a private tour of the Fremantle Establishment . . .'

'Really?'

'Yes. And he made contact with the six Fenians imprisoned there, and dropped the word to their leader, Wilson, that an escape attempt would be made. Actually, there were seven of them, but it was decided only to take six. The seventh was regarded as something of a traitor to the cause, but I don't know that for sure.'

Old Samuel paused a moment to regroup his strength, and drew in a deep breath before going on:

'Anyway, Breslin and Desmond had arrived in the colony in November '75, I think, and had a few months to get plans and contacts in place before the *Catalpa* arrived off Bunbury at the end of March. As soon as he got word, Breslin went down to meet Captain Anthony, talked over the arrangements and worked out the codes for their telegrams. In fact, they went up to Fremantle together in the little steamer *Georgette*, which was very fortuitous in the light of later events. Captain Anthony soon became friends with the skipper, and spent much of the short voyage in the wheelhouse with him, yarning in the way seamen do and picking up a lot of knowledge about the coastal waterways, especially around Rockingham where the rescue was to take place.'

'They surveyed it by land, too, didn't they?'

'Yes, indeed, Mr Cribben. You've done your homework, I'll say that for yer. When they reached Fremantle, they at once saw a problem. Anchored offshore was a Royal Navy gunboat, with another expected on a routine visit. It was likely that the attempt would have to be delayed. But they put the wait to good use. Breslin and Captain Anthony hired a fast, two-horse covered trap or gig, and timed the trip down the main road to Rockingham. It's 16 or 17 mile, and the first ten were covered pretty quickly down a well-made macadamised road. I can vouch for that. I was on some of the convict gangs that built it. But after that the road to Rockingham became fairly hard going, and the last part from the town to Cape Peron was just a rough track through the scrub and sandhills. The whole trip took two-and-a-half hours near enough, but it served its purpose. They found a good stretch of hard, sandy beach just near the point. And Captain Anthony raised a wooden marker post and declared, "Here I'll meet you with my boat, if God spares my life".'

'Very theatrical. Very Irish.'

'Ain't it, though? But I suppose the Irish always did have a sense of occasion.'

'And what happened then?'

'Well, Breslin returned to Fremantle. Captain Anthony took the mail coach to Bunbury – a good day-and-a-half journey then – to await the coded telegram to say the coast was clear, the navy ships had gone, and the escape was set. Even when it came there were still more delays. He would have been off Rockingham on Good Friday, when the prisoners are all kept inside the jail. Next thing, he discovered a runaway convict on board his ship, and had to hand him back to the police to avoid suspicion. Then a storm came up, the *Catalpa* dragged her anchor and risked foundering on a sandbank, which put things back another day . . .'

'A series of misfortunes,' the journalist remarked.

'Yes, but it all worked out in the end. The Captain telegraphed Breslin, got the signal, and *Catalpa* left Bunbury on the Saturday morning. By midday on Sunday he was off Rockingham, and late that afternoon Captain Anthony put his ship in charge of the First Mate, Mr Smith, telling him to stand well out to sea and keep a sharp lookout, launched the whaleboat with a sail and a crew of six, and set off for the shore. He didn't land that night, but shipped oars and waited off the coast . . . even hit a bit of a gale . . . but landed safely at the chosen spot on the beach just after eight o'clock that Easter Monday morning to await the arrival of his – er – passengers.'

'The hour had come.'

'Quite so, young man. You've a nice way with words. It was soon after half-past-eight for all of the actors in this little drama. For Captain Anthony and his crew on the beach at Rockingham. And on the coast road at Fremantle, just around the corner from the prison, two covered traps were waiting with Breslin, Desmond and another agent called Kelly, armed with weapons in case they were needed, as the six Fenians began their escape. They were all working outside the jail that morning – a stroke of luck. Another lucky break was that a good many of the guards and their families had gone off to watch the Easter Monday Regatta on the river. I was there myself, as a matter of fact, though I kept well out of *their* way. So, in ones and twos, their leader Wilson passed word to the overseers that the men were required elsewhere, and off they went. Around the corner to where the traps were waiting, slipped inside, put on long coats to disguise their convict clothes and took up a revolver or pistol.'

'How did they know to do that?' the journalist asked. 'How did they know this was the escape attempt?'

'Wilson had given them the word. Breslin told him on the Saturday that Monday morning was *it* . . .'

'But I mean, how did Breslin do that? They were prisoners and he was a civilian.'

'Well, "Mr Collins" was a well-known figure about the town. The guards would have recognised him from the previous visit.'

'And Wilson?'

'Oh, I see what you mean. Wilson and a couple of the others had been very well behaved . . . and had become so highly trusted they were made what the system called "constables" . . . convicts who had charge of a work party, say, under the direction of a warder – or were used to carry messages and so on, like O'Reilly had been. They had a bit more liberty than the rest of us . . . could move around. It wouldn't have been regarded as too unusual for the respectable "Mr Collins" to see Wilson from time to time outside during his strolls around the town and exchange a quiet word with him.'

'I understand it now.'

'Yairs. These constables first class got a much higher gratuity than us ordinary convicts: eight farthings . . . twopence . . . a day. Just like our "Tuppenny Orderly" Bob, here. Riches!'

Samuel cackled and paused a moment to let his joke sink in, before continuing.

'Anyway, once the six escapees were in the traps, off they set quickly down the road to Rockingham. Oh, how both horses and men must have galloped and sweated on that long race. Two . . . three hours, not knowing if the alarm had been given, even with the wires cut . . . if they'd get away or have to shoot it out. Uncertain if the ship and the whaleboat would be where they promised . . . The agent, Kelly, stayed behind in Fremantle for a while, to see if the alarm would be raised. Nothing. So he rode like the wind on horseback to catch up and tell them that all was yet quiet.'

'But of course it wasn't . . .'

'No. Somebody seen them. Somebody told the coppers, and they were already in pursuit. Worse, Captain Anthony discovered a jetty stacked with timber only half a mile down the beach from where he was waiting, and was told that the steamer *Georgette* was on its way to pick up the load.'

'The ship he and Breslin had taken from Bunbury to Fremantle . . .?'

'The very one. You're a good listener, Mr Cribben. And there it was . . . the *Georgette* coming around the point just as the horses pulling the traps breasted the sandhills and swayed down to the beach. Quickly, quickly, Captain Anthony ordered his crew to pull the whaleboat into the sea and for the convicts to get aboard and lie down on the bottom. 'Course the crew, being mainly Malays and Kanacks, didn't understand the language properly and thought they were being attacked by men armed with rifles and six-shooters. It took a bit of persuading in seaman's lingo for them to let the others aboard. And it was a good thing they did, for just as the boat had pushed off and was in open water, over the sandhills came a troop of eight mounted police armed with carbines. But the beach was deserted of people. All they found were the empty carriages and fagged-out horses. The whaleboat had got away.'

'Did they fire on the escapees?'

'Fortunately not. As the convicts were lying down, the traps couldn't be certain they were there. All they could see from shore were the seamen rowing, "Mr Collins", Captain Anthony and a couple of other civilians sitting on the thwarts, and had they fired they might have shot and killed an innocent man. And fortunate, too, that *Georgette* didn't see them. Night was coming on when at last they saw *Catalpa* standing off the end of Garden Island . . .'

Remember that? Sulphur Town and another convict escape by boat? Sam thought to himself, before continuing:

'. . . But it was too dark to get to her, and the wind was rising. So, there was nothing for it but to spend another night at sea in the whaleboat – heavily overloaded with nine more men, this time.'

'How many would have been in it?'

Old Sammy stopped and slowly enumerated on his fingers.

'About sixteen altogether, I reckon . . . Captain Anthony, his six crew, six convicts, Breslin, Desmond and Kelly . . .'

'And these boats are built to hold, what – eight to ten people?'

'Quite so, Mr Cribben. You can count as well, I see. The gunwales were just a few inches above the waterline, and they were in constant danger of being swamped. It was only that they emptied some water barrels and used them to bail out the sea that broke over them that the whaleboat stayed afloat at all. Captain Anthony put up the sail to try to keep her into the wind. But the mast snapped in the gale, and it was the superhuman efforts of the crew that kept them from going broadside onto the waves and overturning.'

'It's a wonder they survived. They must have been terrified.'

'No doubt about that. Captain Anthony tried to keep their spirits up by saying he'd been out in much worse weather than this – but I read later that, at the time, he wouldn't have given a cent for the lot of them. Their luck held, however. The winds calmed down towards morning, and as day broke they could see *Catalpa* standing in again towards the shore. How they bent their oars towards her then, with a cheer. But an hour after daybreak they saw the *Georgette* steaming out of Fremantle towards them. They all lay down low in the whaleboat so that nothing could be seen above the gunwale and waited until *Georgette* passed further down the coast. Once she'd gone, oars were unshipped, and for two hours they rowed briskly towards *Catalpa*. She must have seen them, because the ship began to change course towards the boat.'

'But then they noticed something else . . .' The reporter found himself quite caught up in the telling.

'Too right. Standing off *Catalpa* was a guard boat, with two sails, carrying thirty or forty coppers and Pensioner Guards. And as soon as they saw the ship putting on canvas, they did the same and started following her. "Put your backs into it, boys!" Captain Anthony cried to his crew heaving on the oars. "Give it everything you've got." And it then became a race between the whaleboat trying to reach *Catalpa*, and the guard boat wanting to cut them off.'

'And the whaleboat won.'

'By a whisker. As soon as he was within hailing distance, Captain Anthony called on his First Mate to hoist the Stars and Stripes – the American flag.'

'I know that.'

'Just checking, Mr Cribben. A man can't be too careful, you know. As soon as they reached *Catalpa* the men scrambled up the ropes . . . the whaleboat was hoisted on the davits . . . and as Captain Anthony stepped onto his deck once more, the guard boat passed across her bows. How the men rushed to the rails then, and began shouting and jeering, waving their rifles and calling fond farewells to the screws, many of whom they knew by name from the prison. And the guard boat, knowing it was useless to try to board the ship, turned for shore. The officer in charge even gave a smart salute as they departed. And the rescued men all tucked into the best dinner that could be provided by the galley and slept the sleep of the dead.'

'And that still wasn't the end of it . . .'

'No. There was one more scene to be played out. Next morning *Georgette* steamed up close, a loaded gun mounted on her foredeck, a detachment of armed soldiers at the rails, and a longboat swung out ready for a boarding party. Of course, the crew and all the passengers rushed onto *Catalpa*'s deck with their weapons and anything else they could find to repel them – harpoons, cutting spades, lumps of metal, wood . . .'

'Didn't the *Georgette* fire a shot across her bows?'

'Dead right. The ball sent a spout of water high as the topmast as it skimmed across the waves. "Heave to!" demanded the guard commander. "What for?" Captain Anthony replied from his quarterdeck. "You have escaped prisoners on board." "There are no prisoners here," came the response. "They are all free men".'

Old Sammy, the storyteller, was mimicking the voices of the players.

'The commander wouldn't have any of this. "You lie," he said. "I can see them on your deck." But Captain Anthony, cool as you like, answered, "They are my crew. Show yourselves, men." And they did. "Are you going to heave to?" "No." The wind was freshening, and 18 miles out to sea – well beyond the colonial limits – *Catalpa* was picking up headway. "I'll give you fifteen minutes to come about or I'll blow your masts away. You can see I have the means to do it." The soldiers aboard *Georgette* were swabbing the gun, ready for another shot. And now that the crisis had been reached, Captain Anthony pointed to the Stars and Stripes flying at his masthead. "This ship is carrying the American flag and we are on the high seas. I warn you that if you fire on me you are firing on the flag of the United States." And this shot went straight home. It was enough to sink the *Georgette*, or at least the purpose of its mission. There was no way the colonial government was going to risk going to war with America. Not over a handful of convicts. The *Georgette* followed *Catalpa* for an hour or so, circling her from time to time. But at last she turned tail and headed back to Fremantle, and *Catalpa* began her long voyage home.'

'Funny, isn't it, that the two skippers knew each other . . . Captain Anthony and his colleague on *Georgette* from the Bunbury voyage. Captain O'Grady, was it? Had even picked his brains about the coastal waters.'

'That's right. In fact, they say the two waved to each other in greeting during the exchange with the military. Oh, what a humiliation the Establishment did suffer! Governments issued angry statements. The newspapers thundered editorials, demanding reparations. But it were all hot air. Nothing came of it. We laughed ourselves silly in Fremantle, and I dare say they did down at the Vasse as well. *Catalpa* arrived in New York to scenes of rejoicing. The freed prisoners were treated as heroes. Captain Anthony retired from the sea, because it would be very unsafe for him to enter any British port after that, and was made inspector of Customs at New Bedford. The Clan na Gael actually presented him and a few others with *Catalpa* in recognition of his courageous role in the rescue, and in return, he presented the Clan with the Stars and Stripes that flew from the ship's masthead on that decisive morning off the coast of Western Australia.'

'His ship came in, quite literally.'

'Yes, it did. In every sense of that expression.'

There was a pause, as they wondered a moment what should come next.

'And *your* ship, Sammy . . .?'

'Oh. Well. As to that, Mr Cribben, you would have say I am still waiting . . .'

15

FREEDOM

Waiting. Always waiting, Samuel. For his freedom – and knowing what to do with it when he got it. For the opportunities it must surely bring his way – and the wherewithal to seize them. Yes, Mr Cribben, waiting for his ship of fortune that never came. For one of those girls, so dazzling and gay on the dance floor, to take his outstretched hand for *himself*, and not as a substitute for the flash lads outside. Because they cared for him – as he would care for them. But that time came and went – until in the end there was only God left, and the characters who peopled his books. Love, such as Sam Speed knew it, had to be bought like everything else. Waiting, with so many other destitute lags whose time had also expired, in the Old Men's Home, as he had for half a century near enough. Waiting to die. And now he was the last one left of them still breathing. Which was something, surely. An achievement to be remembered – the gift of a long life – with a newspaper reporter sitting beside his bed and asking how he did it.

'If I knew the answer to that, sonny, I would bottle it and sell it. Make a packet!' With a laugh. Nothing too maudlin. Or too grim. Like the Boss had said.

'The answer to what, Sam?' Joshua Cribben hadn't yet asked his question.

'Oh . . . nothing. I was just thinking . . . Hey, Bob,' changing the subject quickly, 'give us a hand to straighten meself up, will yer? The truss straps are slipping and the hernia's hurting again.' He'd slid further down the bed himself, in the drama of the *Catalpa* performance. 'It's the old trouble,' with a nod to the reporter.

'You're getting yourself too excited, Sammy,' the Tuppenny Orderly remarked, as he rose from the neighbouring bed, put his hands under the old bloke's shoulders and, with much fussing and scrambling of legs and feet under the sheet, got Samuel back into a sitting position. 'All this talk of escapes . . .'

'Has it been too much for him? Do you think we should stop now?'

The reporter sounded worried, for the photographer still hadn't arrived.

'No, no, Mr Cribben,' Bob said. 'Sammy's fine. He just needs settling. He thinks he's going to escape himself – eh, old-timer?' He turned with a benign chuckle to his patient and began plumping the pillows. 'And you're not going nowhere, are you?'

'The only way I'll get out of this place is in me box.'

'I say, that's a bit morbid,' Cribben observed, rather hastily. His readers wouldn't find that amusing. Not over their weekend breakfast cereal.

'Oh, but it's true, young man,' Samuel lectured from the pulpit of his bed. 'In life we are in death, as the Good Book says. You must know *that*, as a journalist chappie, even if you'd rather ignore it.' He paused a moment, before adding with a snigger: 'But don't worry. I'm planning on making me century. *Three* centuries if I could, like Len Hutton in the cricket. Eh, Bob?' as the orderly tucked in the blanket.

'You'll certainly drive me to my grave long before *you*, Samuel Speed.'

He rearranged the knitted beanie, which had become askew, on the old feller's skull. And they all laughed to escape an uncomfortable subject.

'Tell me, when did you get your freedom?' the reporter asked, safely back on the firmer ground of facts, figures and dates. 'And where?'

'Let me think now . . . I were still in the Vasse working . . . 1871 – well over sixty year ago.' Samuel paused, cogitating like mad and counting with his fingers like an abacus. 'July 1871. That's it!' A small note of triumph in his voice. 'I remember my Certificate of Freedom was seven months late in coming. I should have had it the November previous, but then they added extra time to cover the voyage out and I don't know what else. P'raps they included the eight days I spent crook in hospital during the winter of '70. It's not bad, is it? Queen Victoria sends me out here without the option, makes me pay back the fare, and then takes a second helping by filching more of me time. Governments! They're all the same. Never change.'

Cribben thought it seemed reasonable enough, though he sensibly kept this opinion to himself and asked instead: 'What did you do when your Certificate came through, Sam?'

'I went into Bunbury and got plastered.'

Cribben laughed out loud.

'I thought you didn't drink . . .'

'Not the *hard* stuff?' Bob the Tuppenny exclaimed, with a note of wonder in his voice. This was an aspect of Sammy Speed he hadn't seen before.

'I don't! And I didn't.'

Querulously. The old chap usually didn't mind a joke against himself – often told one, indeed. But he was suddenly afraid of having his reputation sullied in front of the *Mirror* reporter, and find himself publicly lumped in with the habitual drunks that frequented the Old Men's Home. A not dissimilar thought had occurred to Joshua Cribben as well.

'But you just said you propped up the bar of a Bunbury hotel.'

'There you go, Mr Cribben. Making things up again! I didn't prop up no bar. I bought two bottles of beer. Took them down the beach. Drank them. And was sick as a pig. Weren't used to it, see. I spent all night sprawled in the sand dunes and woke up next morning with a head like a dunny. And vowed I'd never touch the stuff again. And I haven't . . . Not often, anyway,' as an afterthought. 'Not so as to get boozed.'

Bob the Tuppenny laughed at the thought of it. Sammy blotto! He was unsteady enough on his pins at the best of times.

'And what else did you do?'

There was a note of resignation in the journalist's voice as yet another storyline went out the window. There was not a lot in the life of Samuel Speed – except his longevity – to titillate the customers.

'When I sobered up, I went back to my lodgings, put my head under the pump, and slept for three hours.' As if he were giving evidence in the police court. 'I then went to the Association library and borrowed a book.'

Of course he did.

'And what book was that?'

'*Pickwick Papers* by Charles Dickens. I'd been waiting to read it for a long time, and a copy had just come in.'

'It's an entertaining story,' said Cribben (*if rather old-fashioned*, in a private aside). 'I hope you enjoyed it.'

'It was the best present I could have been given to celebrate my liberty. I still rejoice in it.'

The reporter mentally rolled his eyes: a gesture that was not unnoticed by the old man. But he didn't care. He still remembered the joy with which he opened the pages and started again from the beginning. To be sure, it was not the clean and carefully loved copy that Samuel had borrowed from Mr Irwin. On the contrary, the book was rather weather-beaten and worn from rough handling in the bush. But the delight with which Samuel met his friends, as they stepped once more from the pages and into his life, was the same. More so, indeed, from auld acquaintance. Pickwick. Alfred Jingle. Messrs Tupman, Snodgrass and Winkle. Sam Weller. Exactly as Irwin had said it would be. And so was the pleasure with which Speed was introduced to a new circle of companions – men and women of such rich and varied character – as he read deeper into the book during those nights in his quarters at the surrounding homesteads.

He smiled once more in remembrance of the ridiculous news-paper war between rival editors at the Eatenswill election. No wonder governments were so bad if *that's* how they were chosen! The elder Mr Weller – Sam's father – a coachman by profession, who always pronounced his Ws with a V in the cockney way, and his Vs with a W, as in 'Veller vanting wegetables.' The poetic Mrs Leo Hunter declaiming her 'Ode to an Expiring Frog' . . . on a log . . . by a dog, which Samuel actually found rather touching. His taste in verse was still rudimentary, though he knew that rhyme was important: in any case, he had seen many such pocket tragedies in the course of his rural employment, even if he recognised that Mrs Leo Hunter's ecstatic performance might have been funny. Above all, there was the running narrative throughout of Mr Pickwick being sued for breach of promise by his landlady, Mrs Bardell; of his losing the case but refusing to pay either the damages or the costs of her lawyers, the unscrupulous Dodson and Fogg, progenitors of many a legal firm offering a no-win-no-fee service that didn't turn out to be quite what it sounded; and of Pickwick thereby being committed to the debtors' prison in the Fleet.

Here, in the later stages of what was supposed to be a comic novel, was a catastrophe with which Samuel Speed, ex-convict number 8996, could fully identify. And he burned with the injustice of it. He knew all about wrongful convictions, and was at one with Mr Pickwick in refusing to yield to it. Of course, he was a gent and had the means to do so, whereas Mr Speed did not. Sam knew all about the insides of prisons too, and their hatefulness; and he wasn't at all upset that the slimy Alfred Jingle (or, subsequently, Mrs Bardell herself) had ended up in the Fleet as well. But what astonished him was that Mr Pickwick had been offered his own reasonably spacious room in the prison (at a fee); was able to furnish it comfortably; have Sam Weller come every day with his meals and run errands; and receive as many visitors as he wished (until the night bell rang), as if he were in his own drawing room. This was not the sort of prison with which Sammy was familiar. Nobody had offered him the choice of a nicely appointed room, specially cooked dinners and a stream of guests. Quite the reverse. The cropped hair, phenol bath, small stone cell, iron bed and the daily grind of 'hard labour, hard fare and hard board' was applied without exception to every inmate. Yet here was Mr Pickwick . . .

'He was a rich man, and that made all the difference in them days,' old Samuel muttered to himself. 'Still does.' And understood that this was another reason why the experience of reading *Pickwick* at the time of his freedom had remained so influential for the rest of his life.

'What was that about a rich man?' The questioning voice of the newspaper reporter intruded once more into the old man's reverie. 'Did you make your pile and then lose it, Sammy?' Anything for a story.

'No, Mr Cribben. It was somebody else . . .'

It had taken Samuel months of reading and several painful interviews with the Association secretary, pleading for an extension to the library loan, before he finished the book. But the thing was that, when Sam did at last return *Pickwick*, it led him to other stories by Mr Dickens. *David Copperfield* for a start. Then *Oliver Twist*. And a little later to *Great Expectations* and the convict Magwitch who still stalked his dreams. Not always in an unpleasant way necessarily, for Samuel had known real ones who were much worse: John Williams, for instance. No. It was mainly because Magwitch was one of those lags who'd made his fortune in the colonies and gave it all to young Mr Pip, whom he'd so terrified into bringing him food as a child.

Samuel knew perfectly well, of course, that such expectations were hardly ever realised, and that most expirees remained shackled to the working class with the shameful placard 'bond' forever hung around their necks, until at length they fell into penury and dependence on a public institution again. Just like himself. But that didn't stop them aspiring to fantasies of wealth. And even when Sam Speed, in his honesty, eventually was forced to admit that his treasure ship would never come home, it didn't prevent him from continuing to project those hopes onto others.

'Who, Sam?' The insistent, prying, irritating voice of the journalist stung like a mosquito in his ear.

'Tommy Jones.' It blurted out. Just like that.

'Who's Tommy Jones? You haven't mentioned him before . . .'

'Haven't I? No . . . Perhaps not . . . He was the mate convicted with me of burning the barley stack.'

'And did he become rich?'

'I don't know, Mr Cribben. I like to think he did. I seen him once, just before he went off to New South Wales. Newcastle. Heading for the goldfields. But whether he struck it rich or not, I can't say. I never heard from him again . . .'

'Where did you see him?'

'In Fremantle. Early part of '75, I think it was. About that. Did I tell you that I'd moved back to Fremantle by then?'

'Yes.'

'Thought so. Funny, isn't it? I couldn't wait to escape from the place when I was a prisoner . . . and here I was with me freedom living back there in the shadow of the jail once more. Like a villain returning to the scene of the crime. Well, I was getting far more interested in the gardening side of things, you know.' He added this last bit hastily, lest the conversation did in fact return to the crime. 'The kitchen garden . . . rolling the lawns . . . tending the flowerbeds. I was thirtyish, see, and the back not able to lift too many heavy sacks and logs no more on the farms, and the old eye was starting to give trouble. So, when the family I was working for in the Vasse bought a house in Fremantle and asked me to help with the garden, I jumped at the chance. We travelled up from Bunbury in the *Georgette* . . .

Them up top, and me in steerage.

'That's the little packet steamer that was involved with the *Catalpa* a bit more than a year later. Strange, isn't it, to think I might have been there at the famous encounter. Could have been part of history . . . What am I telling you this for?'

The old man paused, fumbling around in the here and now for a reason.

'Your pal, Tommy Jones . . .'

'Oh yes. We hadn't been back in Freo for more than a few weeks. I was returning to my lodgings one day after work, when I saw him strolling down the street towards me, large as life and twice as cocky. Recognised him at once.'

'Course you did. Could never forget what he done to me.

As soon as he saw him his heart began pumping, Sam remembered. Fists curled into a ball and venom starting in his throat.

I'll tell him! Knock him flat!

Then he took a second look. And realised that Tommy was altogether older, bigger and tougher. Always had been. Ex-army. And Sam's own fighting spirit drained out the soles of his boots.

What was the point of me being pummelled? We'd both end up in the clink again. And he had been decent to me at the trial and showing the oakum stick. Trying to make amends . . .

'Howzit, Tommy?' As the late afternoon sun chased the shadows down High Street.

'Little Sammy Speed! Well, I never . . .'

All togged out he was in travelling clothes. Clean moleskins. New boots. Small beaver hat on his head and a large wad of notes in his pocket.

'Come and have a drink, Sam-u-el . . .'

'So what did you do?' The reporter persisted.

'We went into the nearest pub, of which there are many in Fremantle, and had a beer. For old times' sake.'

'I thought you'd sworn off it after the last time you got shickered.'

'I did *not* get shickered or anything like it. You must stop putting words into my mouth. Do all you people do that?' Sammy was rather enjoying snapping at the journalist whenever opportunity arose, like a small terrier keeping a larger hound on the defensive.

'I was partic'lar careful what I drank as I had very little money in my pocket.'

Though Tommy had a bundle. Offered to keep on buying.

It was very different to the last occasion they met as free men. Both were starving, then. Begging for a halfpenny on the road out of Woodstock.

But this time I were afraid of what I might say if my tongue got loose on liquor and started running at the mouth, and so I only sipped the glass.

'I suppose you had a lot to catch up on. What you'd been doing out here . . .'

'Oh, yes. All of that. He'd been up Toodyay way even before I arrived on the *Belgravia*, so naturally we hadn't seen each other. Done well for himself. Saved his money. And told me he was going to the New South Wales diggings. It was only a year or two since that Mr Holtermann found his vast nugget at Hill End. Over 300 pounds of pure gold, worth £12 000. Imagine! Tommy had the gold fever good and proper. Asked me to come along with him . . .'

'Why don't yer? We could both strike it lucky . . .'

'I ain't got enough saved, Tommy.'

'That's orright. I can stake yer till you find yer feet. Got more than enough for two. Make up for what happened, eh? Back then . . .'

'I dunno.'

Even at the time, Samuel was fully aware that here was an opportunity . . . an opening on the path to a fortune. He'd been reading *Great Expectations* – nearly finished it – and the wealth accumulated by Magwitch loomed large in his imagination. But faced with the need to make a decision, he hesitated, unsure which choice to take. What if he didn't strike paydirt but only mullock? He'd be in debt to his nemesis Tommy Jones for the rest of his life. And he wasn't as strong as he used to be . . . And the eye . . . And he liked his work here . . .

Go on with it! You were frightened.

And besides, he knew what transpired last time he had any personal association with Mr Thomas Jones Esq., baker and pastry cook, late of the Royal Engineers.

The smell of burning barley thatch and white blossoming smoke rose from the subconscious once more to accuse . . .

'Let me think about it, Tommy.'

'Well, don't think too long, Sam-u-el. The ship leaves the day after tomorrer. I'm staying at the Emerald Isle. (Another tenuous connection to the *Catalpa* story.) Let me know if you're coming wiv us . . .'

'And did you?'

'No, Mr Cribben. I never did. I thought about it. Often wished I had. Wondered if Tommy had his big strike. Hoped so. It would have been nice . . . But no. In the end I stayed here, and his ship sailed without me. Well, you know . . . Everything. I had me gardens. I worked for some of the big families around here. Oh yes . . .'

Trying to keep any regrets and tears for what might-have-been out of his voice.

'Merchant families, mostly . . . The Mannings of Fremantle. Their old man built that big stone house they called "Manning's Folly" in Pakenham Street, down near the waterfront. Turned it into a warehouse later, until they pulled it down ten year ago. Lovely walled garden . . . and other houses they had. The Batemans, too. Big interests in whaling. They built the tunnel there, under the old prison they call the Roundhouse on the cliff, to carry their goods up from the beach into High Street. Business is still going strong,

I hear . . . And the Samsons are another firm still thriving. Father and sons. Some lived in Freo and some in Perth. That's when I moved up here to the city, you know. Mrs Willie Samson . . . she would remember me. Beautiful roses. And I grew cucumbers and melons and tomaters for the summer salads . . .'

Samuel's voice trailed off into the shallows of reminiscence and irrelevant detail as the emotions stirred by talk of Tommy Jones kept infiltrating, like bandits, to subvert. Had he struck it rich at Gulgong? Gone home to England as a swank at last?

Did I make another blunder not going with him?

Sam really hadn't heard a word of him since the day Tommy left for Newcastle. And that very silence opened the way to all kinds of imagined possibilities: from the fortunes of Robinson Crusoe and the convict Magwitch, to the prospect that some good might have come from that fateful Saturday evening when he and Tommy bought a box of matches instead of a bun in that Woodstock shop . . .

'Mr George Leake, here in Perth, I worked for him too. His father was the Police Magistrate . . . his uncle, Sir Luke, was a big sup-porter of the Working Men's Institute as it became known . . . and *he* was the Crown Solicitor with a new wife. She liked gardenias. Very Important People, Mr Cribben. Young Mr Leake, he played a big part here at the time of the Federation debates, and even became State Premier in 1901. But he died the next year. Politics can do that to yer. Eh?'

The old man tittered softly. But then, with this thought of death, Samuel was forced to acknowledge another truth to himself. For along with his cordial good wishes for Tommy on the goldfields, there was also sometimes the far more malicious hope – privately expressed, as he trudged the streets from these grand mansions to his room in some straightened boarding house in the cheaper quarters – that things had not turned out any better for Tom Jones than they had for him.

I wasn't being nasty, God. Truly. Just realistic.

After all, tens – hundreds – of thousands of people were drawn to the Australian colonies by the gold rushes. Look what happened when they struck it in the West at Southern Cross in '87, and even more so at Coolgardie and Kalgoorlie in the early nineties. But almost all of them quit with less than they came. Few saw much more than a flash in the pan if they were lucky . . . and the number of Holtermanns and others, like the chap who unearthed the Welcome Stranger nugget worth a king's ransom, could be counted in mere double digits. So it was more than probable that Mr Thomas Jones had also ended up, like the vast majority of diggers, down on his luck. Poor, and sick, and with nothing much to show for his life. As had they all . . .

That's what I meant, God. Honest.

Liar.

Again.

16

GOD

A silence had fallen in the room as Sam pursued these meditations. The reporter was scribbling the eminent names of the old lag's employers in his notebook, thinking they would add some distinction and interest to the article. Bob the Tuppenny lounged on the other bed looking at them both, sensing that the interview was beginning to wind down and that the photographer must soon arrive. Time to spruce Sammy up again.

Dust could be seen drifting in a beam of watery light through the window, and somewhere a fly was beating against the glass in search of escape. When suddenly through the quiet came the cracker of another question.

'Did you ever get married, Sam?'

Tuppenny Bob sat up straight. Ooh. Here was something he hadn't thought of in relation to the old bugger. Samuel Speed? Married?

'Me, Mr Cribben? Me marry? Not on your life. I didn't have to.' With a touch of whimsy in his aged voice. 'Not with all the girls chasing me like they used to, ha ha!'

Yet another lie.

Samuel tried to pass it off as a joke, though the reporter had taken the remark seriously enough and was scribbling it in his book. It would go down well with the readers. *All the girls chasing me!*

No, they weren't. Not in the seventies and eighties they weren't, when there were three to four times more men than women in the colony. It was a consequence of the fact that the nearly ten thousand convicts transported to Swan River after 1850 had all been males. And with so much choice available, any single girls were unlikely to select a small, squinting jobbing gardener and expiree of few means as an outstanding prospect for a spouse. Not until the rushes after Southern Cross did the balance between the sexes start to reach anything like some equilibrium in the West. Which didn't mean that this most basic of instincts was any less potent, or that competition among the men to fulfil it was less intense. If anything, the shortage of women – and denial while the convicts were in prison – made it the stronger; and a flourishing trade among the brothel madams and streetwalkers had grown up to cater for it, especially around Fremantle portside and the alleys just north of central Perth and along the riverfront.

Samuel Speed, being human, was no less driven by his desires. And his fantasies. Even in old age they had not entirely gone away: *All the girls chasing me*, indeed!

To be sure, he kept subscribing to the occasional dances and balls (such as were open to people like him) in pursuit of a conquest among the tail-enders. He continued to practise his steps at the Working Men's Institute classes when held, was abstemious and clean in his habits; and in any case the music always drew him. But he was not alone in his stratagems: and in a large town like Perth, while there were certainly a plentiful number of drunks at the end of a social evening, there were generally also enough men who'd remained sufficiently sober to provide more seductive partners. So that rarely, these days, did Samuel find his hand accepted for a last waltz. ('No, thank you. I'm sitting this one out,' only to find her in another man's arms the next moment.) Even less often was he able to walk her home afterwards . . . along Adelaide Terrace, say, to the larger townhouses of East Perth where his pretty young kitchen maid may have worked . . . or attempt to steal a kiss at the back gate. ('What do you think you're doing, Mr Speed? The mistress would go mad if she found out. I could lose my place!')

Another rebuff.

Then again, Sammy was not above setting his cap at some of the young servants who worked in the various houses where he tended the gardens. The Irish girls, for instance, generally had no particular objections to going out with ticket-of-leave men and expirees – of marrying them and bearing their children, even if Speed had not yet found one who had no particular objection to *him* as a potential husband. But he had to be careful about making his advances – to be certain that the head gardener was out of sight, and that a meeting appeared entirely natural. Anything else, and they could *both* lose their places.

Still, he had to try. So, of a morning, if Sam were picking apricots or apples in the kitchen garden and Bridie, the new laundry maid, came out with a basket of washing to hang on the line, he'd find a way to work around to her, making a great show of moving the ladder. And, once screened behind a sheet, he'd offer her a piece of fruit with a smirk on his lips, and try to tempt her like some lesser devil in Eden with his Eve.

'Oh, Mr Speed, I don't think you should take a plum just for me. Sure, the cook would have words to say if she knew . . .'

'It's a windfall, Bridie. Just picked it off the ground. Honest. Cook wouldn't want it in the house, and it will only go to waste otherwise. Better off in your pocket, eh?'

'Oh. In that case . . .'

'Give us a smile.' And upon her obliging, 'There's a dance at the Institute on Saturd'y week. Would you like to come?'

'Well, now, I'm not at all sure I can get the time off. I'll have to ask the mistress.'

Which she may or may not do. Even if she did, Bridie may or may not go to the dance with him, chaperoned along the street among a party of other young maids and their beaux (as young men a'courting were called in those days). And even if she did go to the dance with Samuel, it was ten to one that she'd walk home with somebody else.

'Sure, I missed you in the crowd, Mr Speed,' she would say when they came across each other in the garden a few days later. But he didn't believe her.

The cooks in these establishments were usually well aware of Samuel's flirtations (as they knew everything that went on in the house), and would frequently tease him about them. There is nothing like the contest of the sexes to raise a few laughs among the onlookers.

'Sam Speed, you sly dog . . .' cook might say when he brought in a box of potatoes or lettuces for the table, a basket of cut flowers for the house. 'I seen you at the clothes line with young Bridie.' (Or Kitty, or Ethel, or whomever the girl was at the time.) 'Thought nobody was lookin', eh? You'll turn her head, you will!' With a loud, embarrassing guffaw.

'No, but seriously, Sammy,' as she gave him a sandwich to take outside for his lunch, 'you want to watch your step with her.

She hasn't been out here long and is only young . . . And I know what you men can be like, ha!'

If only that were true.

Far from discouraging these amorous excursions, his boarding house landladies generally sought to urge Samuel on. The weekly rent included early breakfast and a cooked dinner at night: it cost more than just a bare room, and ate deeply into his wages, but was worth it. He'd never learnt to cook for himself, and it was far cheaper than buying his meals at the local hostelries.

'If you don't mind my saying so, Mr Speed,' Mrs Gurney might say of an evening when he came in late from work (her half-dozen other guests having already eaten) and putting a mutton chop in front of him on a plate kept warm in the oven, 'but what you want is a wife.'

'That's true.' Cutting through the layers of fat to the meat at the bone.

'I mean, here you are, a nice man in your thirties, is it? Steady worker. Not a drinker. You've been with me for – what, three years? Time you found yourself a good woman to look after you, instead of spending all that time up in your room reading books and whatnot.'

'It's not for want of trying, Mrs Gurney. Trouble is, there are so many others looking for a wife as well.'

'Well, I should try harder, Mr Speed, if I was you. There'll be someone for you, I'm sure of it. Looks aren't everything, are they?'

Oh, but they are. In the marketplace of sexual attraction, a handsome appearance is the first unit of currency. Followed by a healthy bank book.

Old Samuel smiled wistfully at the remembrance, and turned his face to the reporter.

'No, I never married, Mr Cribben.' And suddenly changing tack as another joke came to him, he added brightly: 'I was a regular "Nineteener".'

'A regular what? I don't know the expression . . .'

'Don't yer? Bit before your time, p'raps. It comes from a Mark Twain story, 'The Man That Corrupted Hadleyburg'. The nineteen most upright, virtuous families in that town were known as the Nineteeners . . . until a trickster comes along and exposes them as hypocrites and frauds.'

'Oh, I see.'

'Well, I lived as pure and sober a life as the Nineteeners.'

'With all the girls chasing you?'

'Figure of speech, Mr Cribben.' Quick as a wink. This feller really kept you on your toes.

'And were you a hypocrite too, like the Nineteeners?'

Oh.

Then smartly, to blunt the inference: 'If you'd read the story, young man, you'd know that one of the families *kept* their reputation for goodness.'

'And that was you?'

'I tried, God knows.'

I did, God. And you know I'm as much of a hypocrite as they all were. Even the last family that was never found out. They knew in their hearts at the end . . . We are all human.

Yes, indeed. For all that Samuel tried to live decently and honestly to avoid spending even another hour of his life in custody – dividing his time between work, his books borrowed from the library and the occasional evening lecture or dance at the Working Men's Institute – the primordial tides that drove every species to reproduce itself surged relentlessly on. And they didn't ebb simply because Sam Speed had not found a wife. Thus, of a night-time in the darkness under his blanket, he might seek the solitary pleasure of self-gratification, hoping that God wouldn't notice, and knowing it was wrong from everything he'd been told as a boy. But he needed the urgent release, or who could tell what he might not do in frustration? Besides, he still had a good head of hair in those years – and as for going blind, the other great evil said to be brought about by masturbation, he'd been losing his sight in one eye before he ever started doing that!

Even so, when 'that' was no longer enough to satisfy, Sam would sometimes find himself driven onto the evening streets in search of other company, a saved shilling or two in his pocket for the necessary.

'I'm just going to the Institute, Mrs Gurney, to change a book.'

Another Dickens – or perhaps, as his reading broadened, the novel *Vanity Fair* by his great rival, William Makepeace Thackeray. That Becky Sharp sounded a real little corker, like Nelson's Lady Hamilton . . .

'Goodnight, Mr Speed. You've got your key?' as he shut the front door of the North Perth terrace behind him.

And he *would* go to the library in the Institute's new hall not far away in Beaufort Street, telling himself this was the reason for his going out. He'd dawdle over the books and the illustrated newspapers in the reading room, chat to one or two others about the story he'd just returned, confirm the dates for the next social dance and classes . . . when all the time he knew he was fooling himself – being the hypocrite – and that the moment he went back outside he'd be drawn down to the open ground near the boat terminals or some dark alley off a back street in search of a young woman selling herself.

'You looking for a friend, dearie?'

'How much?'

His few coins would change hands, and they'd go off to find some convenient shrub, some midnight crib in a hovel, hidden from the view of everyone except conscience, for several desperate, perfumed minutes of intercourse . . . this irresistible sexual act that was not love . . . until Sam had finished, and they would as quickly part ways.

'Thanks, dearie. See you another time, perhaps.'

Probably would. If she were still about, when desire once more could no longer be suppressed.

Samuel was never able to afford the more expensive bawdy houses of North Perth . . . and not always the 'rubber goods' some shops sold to protect himself. Hence his need for younger women, in the belief they were less likely to be diseased. But it was ever a risk – and the feeling of sexual relief that came from these furtive encounters was always followed, as he walked home, by a sense of dread that he might perhaps this time have caught the pox. Syphilis? Gonorrhoea? He'd look them up in the Institute's dictionaries when he returned *Vanity Fair*. And if he had the symptoms they described, how could he possibly afford the mercury cures he'd read about? Samuel couldn't, of course, which meant that he'd likely go mad and die. Which led inevitably to successive sensations of remorse – guilt – and self-loathing. And with that fear came determined promises to himself never to go with street women again. Until the next time. When the cycle would begin again.

Is there never any end to the struggle, God?

But God didn't respond to that question, or to anything else that Samuel may have asked. The only answer the man knew – denial and celibacy – was no answer at all. He wasn't a monk; and in any case he suspected that most of them were as compelled and self-deluded as he was, hiding their human weakness under the blanket of night and secrecy.

At such times when he was low, Sam would frequently find himself questioning the meaning of everything he had ever done, asking whether his life amounted to anything at all. Scared and scarred by the years of imprisonment. Unloved. Approaching forty and no longer a young man, unlikely now ever to marry. He had his work, which he liked, and he knew his employers respected him as a trustworthy gardener, referring him one to another. But rent and travelling and clothes and his few social pleasures at the Working Men's Institute (not to mention the street girls) meant Sam had very little in his savings bank. Certainly not enough to think about going east to Southern Cross when exciting news of the first gold finds came through, even supposing he'd retained all his youthful strength. Still less with Coolgardie and Kalgoorlie, because by then . . .

The old man suppressed the unwelcome thought. Time enough for that. But still, these new rushes were, for him, more opportunities passed by. And while Samuel would never lose the companionship of those splendid people he knew from his books, the mere act of reading was becoming more difficult. The sight in his bad eye was failing – and even the good eye was feeling the strain of reading lengthy paragraphs of small type by lamplight in his room at night . . .

Sometimes, when he couldn't even think of a joke to mask his depression, Samuel Speed wondered just how long he would be able to go on like this.

I was a 'regular Nineteener', all right. In Mark Twain's true meaning of the expression. But I won't tell the reporter that.

And it was not all without hope.

Late one winter's afternoon in the mid-eighties, Samuel was walking up St George's Terrace – thinking such dispiriting thoughts as these, still feeling unclean and worried by another assignation two nights ago – when he found himself outside Trinity Congregational Church. It was an attractive red-brick chapel with a high-pitched roof and two slender turrets at the front, standing somewhat back from the street. Sam had often admired it, though as he'd never set foot inside a place of worship since his last compulsory attendance at the chapel in Fremantle Prison and still had no time for its teachings, he'd never entered Trinity. This evening, however, the front door stood ajar, lamp-light streaming down the steps. And into the dusk he heard the sounds of an organ playing and a choir singing. One of the old hymns that came back from his Wesleyan childhood . . .

> *My trespass was grown up to heaven;*
> *but far above the skies,*
> *in Christ abundantly forgiven*
> *I see your mercies rise.*

He knew the tune – had sung it sometimes in those prison services he'd been forced to attend – and stood on the footpath awhile listening and even humming along. Sam was about to walk on, back to Mrs Gurney's boarding house and supper when, to his surprise, he instead opened the gate and walked across the church-yard to the front steps, drawn by the music. Extraordinary, for there was no compulsion about it. He went further and opened the door a little wider, then crept inside. Choir practice was being conducted down at the front, singers and organist concentrating on their books and the leader, so nobody took any particular notice when Samuel sat in a corner at the far end of the back row and listened. Nobody bothered when he coughed in the midst of another hymn he knew, for their voices were raised, and it was as if he were hearing the words properly for the first time.

> *Long my imprisoned spirit lay*
> *fast bound in sin and nature's night*

Samuel knew all about that in a quite literal sense.

> *Thine eye diffused a quickening ray –*
> *I woke; the dungeon filled with light!*

Not in his experience, it didn't. Yet the choir rejoiced:

> *My chains fell off, my heart was free,*
> *I rose, went forth, and followed thee.*

Charles Wesley's words were the same as ever. But this time they sounded different to Samuel Speed. He'd long ago rejected that nonsense from the psalms: *He shall break thy chains asunder.* Sam had lain in his prisons for more than four years waiting for his chains to break, and nothing had happened. And yet, listening to the hymn again this evening, alone in the chapel of his own free will and with no one to tell him otherwise, he began to think it need not be taken quite so literally after all. He'd served his time . . . and yet who could deny that his heart was still bound? He had his freedom . . . and yet how his spirit continued to wallow in the dungeon of 'nature's night'! Perhaps the choir was singing that, should he find again some faith in the light of God, he might also find a release from the disgust he so often felt for himself.

Maybe.

Certainly nobody noticed, as the practice came to an end, that Samuel got up from his corner and tiptoed out the door. Or if they did, nobody minded especially, for the chapel was open to all. But it is true that the man walked home that night considerably easier in spirit than when he'd entered the church an hour before.

I can't say you'd found me, God. But I reckon you'd started looking!

To be sure, it was no miraculous conversion. No blinding moment or 'quickening ray' on the road to Damascus: but the start of a journey that took Sam in halting steps from the depth of self-hatred and the feeling there was no love for him here among mankind, except in payment for a shilling, to a belief that he was more than the sum of his parts and that he had the love of the divinity to sustain him, even in his wretchedness.

God is Love.

The words of the framed text that had hung on the grubby walls of the workhouse above his bed as a child came back to him on that first evening. He sat in his room after he'd eaten (Mrs Gurney scolding him for having been *very* late), *Vanity Fair* unopened on his table, thinking over the experience of the last few hours. The chapel. The choir and the joyous organ as they repeated the last lines of the verse.

My chains fell off, my heart was free . . .

Everything quiet and still, save for the music of the hymn hanging in the air, and the feeling of serenity that came over him when he heard the words as he'd never understood them before.

God is Love.

He'd not thought about it much, except as one of those platitudes that stood like signposts through life, carrying a general nub of wisdom but with no particular relevance for himself. *Suffer the children. Look before you leap.* That sort of thing. But now, as memory of the stained little text came back to him, Samuel began to ponder the meaning of it as an adult and not as a child. And when at last he undressed and went to bed, lying awake thinking in the darkness until he fell asleep, the words kept recurring. Even in his dreams. So that when he woke next morning, it was with a sense in the dawn that the Love it spoke of was the light that had filled the prisoner's dungeon. And that even if nobody else cared for him in the world, he at least had that.

This feeling of calm – of relief (was it?) that he was not entirely alone, however worthless he sometimes felt – stayed with Samuel for the rest of the day. And the days after that, until it began to settle into some kind of conviction. So much so that, come Sunday morning, he put on his best set of clothes – the ones he wore to the dances – and went back to the church. He made sure that he arrived late, after the respectable citizens were all seated in the pews, and stood quietly at the back listening to the service. He noticed one or two fellows that he knew – expirees all – and nodded to them in recognition. But mostly he concentrated on the service: on the ritual that had become so familiar, if neglected, since prison days; on the words of the pastor in his pulpit exhorting them to love God with all their hearts and souls and minds. Yet, above all, it was the singing he heard, especially when he lifted his own voice in the hymn that so touched him the other night.

I woke; the dungeon filled with light!

It was far too early in this pilgrim's journey to say that the chains on his spirit had fallen away, but indubitably, as time went by, Samuel felt them beginning to loosen. He asked Mrs Gurney if she had a Bible he could borrow.

'It's only a New Testament, I'm afraid. Mr Gurney used it in his last illness. Dyspepsia. Nice big print though, for your eyes.'

'That will be fine, thanks.'

'I didn't know you was religious, Mr Samuel.'

'No . . . er . . . I need to look something up for my book . . .'

And also much too early to acknowledge anything like that publicly.

Still, he kept the late Mr Gurney's Testament on the table by his bed, reading a page of it every night before blowing out the lamp: not as he had done with those schoolmasters in prison, as an exercise in duplicity to gain access to the library, but rather for its own sake – to see if it could further illuminate those thoughts that had so stirred him in the chapel. He'd lie in the bed, hands behind his head, pondering what the minister had said last Sunday, and finding the same text spelled out as he read through Matthew. *Thou shalt love thy God* . . . And it made perfect sense. Naturally, if he believed that God loved *him*, it was only right that he should try to love God back with all his heart and soul and mind. Unlike anyone Samuel had ever loved before – except, perhaps, the Irish girl with the flashing eyes he'd danced the polka with at Busselton, though it had never been returned. That, and the faint presence of his mother, now almost forgotten, he sometimes sensed in his dreams.

No, this was not as he'd read the Testament in jail. There, it was all mouthed by rote in an underhanded way, pretending to stumble over the words in order to persuade the chaplain to let the school-master keep visiting him in separate confinement. Now, Samuel was trying to understand what the words *meant* to him – and besides, he still had his library books!

He'd started reading novels by some of the women writers of the day. *Jane Eyre*, for instance, which Sam enjoyed not just for

the romantic story – for she got her Mr Rochester in the end – but
also because her trials at Lowood school, and of finding herself lost
and forsaken on the moors, reflected something of his own experience in life. Jane Austen, he didn't care for as much. Her characters
belonged almost entirely to a world he knew nothing about, and
their problems seemed trivial. Why should Elizabeth Bennet take
such profound offence simply because Mr Darcy wouldn't dance
with her? Samuel had to put up with that sort of thing at every social
event he attended. She just had to persist, like he did . . . though, on
reflection, he acknowledged it might be different for young women
than it was for young men. And then again, there was this other
book . . .

Old Samuel heaved a sigh and dragged himself back to the
present.

'Have you ever read the story of *Silas Marner*, Mr Cribben?'

'Eh? No, Sam, I don't think I have.'

'It's a good book. By a feller called George Eliot. Except that *he's*
a woman! Pen name. She was really Mary Ann Evans.'

'I must have a look at it.'

'You do that. She's a fine writer. You want to watch out, or the
ladies will be taking your job away from you . . .'

The memory of how he found *Silas* was quite clear. It was the
first book Samuel ever bought for himself. He'd kept up his church-
going – not every Sunday, perhaps, for there were inevitably still
those times when he felt himself defiled. But they were sufficient to
get himself recognised as a regular member of the congregation –
earning a smile from some of the women as they left, a nod from one
or two of the men, and a handshake from the pastor as he went out
the door. There was always a reserve about this, a slight distance,
for everybody knew without being told that Mr Speed, like several

of their other members, had once been 'bond'. He, like they, always sat in the back pews. But as part of Christ's – the Good Shepherd's – flock, they understood it was their Christian duty to welcome Samuel into their communion if not quite their hearts.

He began to attend one or two of the social activities: the annual Sunday School picnic – indeed, in March of '88 he donated a sum of two shillings and sixpence to the Sunday School appeal to help flood victims at Greenough to the north, near Geraldton. It was a small sum in the scheme of things (though large enough for him), and sufficient to get Sam a little more purchase among the worshippers. He attended a church musical evening that was very pleasant, but nothing like the exhilarating dances at the Institute. And then one Saturday he went to a church bazaar, run by the ladies as a fundraising effort in the Sunday School hall: for some thought was being given to building a new church in front of the old one, with the increase in population following the first gold strikes.

Samuel spent a happy enough hour browsing among the fancy needlework stalls, the cakes, potted plants and morning tea tables. There was nothing he particularly wanted to buy, until he came to the 'white elephant' stall selling second-hand books and other knick-knacks. Rummaging through the goods, he picked up a copy of *Silas Marner, The Weaver of Raveloe*, in pretty fair order apart from a few dog-eared pages and some slight stains on the cover and binding. Still, quite readable: and leafing through it, Sam found himself becoming engrossed in the tale of this gaunt, pale figure in black carrying his bundle of woven cloth through the landscape – peculiar of appearance and with poor eyesight, just like himself. A man who, also like Sam, was accused of a crime he didn't commit and was cast out from his community, until he ended up at a distant village, living in a cottage near the stone-pits: withdrawn into his loom; miserly; in despair and anger with himself and the world.

Here was somebody that Samuel not only recognised but understood might have been himself.

'How much do you want for the book?' he asked the lady behind the table.

'I was looking for sixpence,' Mrs Collins replied. 'But it's somewhat worn and I recognise you from our congregation — would threepence be all right?'

'Yes.'

Samuel searched his pocket for the coins, passed them over, and stood beside the table still reading. He was holding the book very close to his face because the bad eye was watering; the light in the hall was rather dim and the print was quite small, even for the good eye.

'It's Mr Speed, isn't it?' Mrs Collins ventured once more. She was a kindly woman of about his own age, dressed in grey with a frilled apron to show that she was among the 'helpers'.

'Yes. Samuel Speed.'

'Forgive my being personal, Mr Speed, but I notice you're having a little trouble reading . . .'

'It's the light . . . and me eyes. Not what they were.'

'It's just that we have several pairs of used spectacles here on the stall, all in good order with no damage to the glass. And I thought that if there were any that suited your eyes, they may be of some assistance . . .'

'That's kindly of you, madam,' Samuel replied rather formally, touched by her thoughtfulness. 'I never considered glasses. New ones are a bit out of my reach . . .'

'Well, try these on and see what you think.'

He did so, and after several trials found a pair with fine steel rims that suited him perfectly. The tiny black words on the page were altogether larger and easier to read with one eye.

'Bless my soul!' he exclaimed. 'Why didn't I think o' this before? All those nights peering by the oil lamp . . . I'd better have 'em. How much are the specs?'

'How about threepence?' Mrs Collins replied. 'That will make up the even sixpence. I'm so glad you found something to suit.'

'I'd 'a bought *two* pair at twice the money if you had another set this good,' Samuel laughed. 'Thank you, madam.'

'My pleasure, Mr Speed.' And she left him with a smile.

So Samuel took the book back to his room and sat reading it in the sunlight all that Saturday afternoon and every night for the next three weeks, alongside his page from the Testament, until he finished it. How the spectacles did magnify everything – and not least Sam's own sense of identification with the wronged weaver, isolated as a hermit and having barely any contact with the village. And, likewise, how greatly the second-hand glasses improved that perception of hope and joy that came to Marner when the orphan child Eppie unexpectedly entered his home, and through her innocence and devotion to her new 'father' led Silas back to love and to life.

It was almost too late for Samuel to suppose that he'd find a wife now, let alone have a child to comfort him in his old age. He was getting on, set in his ways, and any infant found lost on the streets of Perth would be taken straight to the orphanage.

Besides, I wouldn't know what to do for it, and Mrs Gurney would undoubtedly charge extra rent for having another mouth to feed.

Better to leave things as they were, with his weekly round between work, the Institute library, the boarding house and church where some in the congregation, in fact, were offering him small gardening jobs for themselves or their friends. He'd be satisfied with that. Except, in his heart, Sammy wasn't really satisfied.

As time went on, he began to realise that something was still missing, and it wasn't just the lack of a family or anyone by way of a close friend. There remained a void in his inner life that hadn't entirely been filled by the hope that God loved him and that he, for all his failings, was trying to love God in return. Part of him was still empty – and it wasn't for some while after he got his new specs that Samuel thought he'd found what it was.

Reading Saint Mark's gospel one evening before bed, he came to the passage where Jesus was reiterating the great Commandment to love God with all one's heart and mind and soul. Sam nodded to himself in agreement. *That's right*. But it was the next part of the sentence that this time struck him with clarity and force: Christ's second Commandment to *Love thy neighbour as thyself*. He'd read it many times. *Love one another*, as John put it – and as Sam remembered, with all the power of rediscovery, Mr Irwin used to tell them on board *Belgravia*. But Samuel had never really comprehended the import until now. It seemed enough that he had this two-way relationship between himself and the Almighty. For years he'd kept a distance from almost all of his neighbours: necessary perhaps in prison, to prevent him being drawn into any conspiracies at Chatham or Fremantle; scarcely less self-protective outside, where any chance encounter with another Tommy Jones could see him arrested again.

Now Samuel began to realise that it wasn't sufficient: he had to show and to share this love he felt with other people, just as Silas Marner had been guided by Eppie's little hand from the stone-pits to rejoin the life of Raveloe, and to know once more the beauty of nature.

I already had that from my gardening, but the other . . .

Again, like the first evening in the chapel, this was no sudden rev-
elation. It took Samuel time for the teaching and its implications to
fully influence him. But certainly, from around this period, the man
began to open himself to other people – and allow the personality
traits that had always been there to reveal themselves more completely. His general cheeriness, his little jokes and asides, tempered
now by a sympathetic understanding that everyone had their burden
of faults – sin, as the minister put it – to carry within.

Thus, for all the mental energy Samuel put into his books and
his beliefs, the needs of the flesh remained and had to be satisfied as
well. There were still those evenings of solitary pleasure under the
blanket, and occasionally a dark rendezvous with the harlots in a
back alley. Followed, inevitably, by shame and a determination not
to do it again – though knowing that he undoubtedly would. Speed
was no Saint Augustine possessed of the self-irony to pray *Lord
make me chaste, but not yet.* Sammy was a countryman. He knew
the same essential instinct drove every living creature; and the plain
man in him gradually came to the view that the God who implanted
the sexual drive could surely not be too upset at the physical expression of it. Yes, it would be nice if he, Samuel Speed, might do so in
the respectable context of married life. Yet as that probably wasn't
going to happen, the best he could hope was to hurt as few people as
possible. To be sure, he was contributing to the harm of the prosti-
tutes he met: but that was happening anyway, and he was not alone
in that. Which was something Sam found of comfort, even when he
was feeling his most sordid.

Occasionally, leaving church, he would catch the eye of a well-
to-do gentleman with his family, and wonder what contempt for
him they'd have if they knew about the other night. No doubt

they would be chief among those who drew lots and cast out poor Silas Marner from among them. But then Samuel would pause and consider that every single one of these people were also carrying their shameful secrets – of sex, of business, of family – hiding in the deep recess of conscience. And he'd smile to himself – not with any sense of superiority, but with a day labourer's common tolerance and knowledge that we are all one. God loves us, despite our imperfections, and thus we should love one another.

We are all Nineteeners, Mr Cribben.

Sam didn't know if this was what the pastor meant when he'd preach to them of 'being saved' and the 'state of grace' to be found in the love of God. If it was, then he'd reached it. But if not, then he had at least established a way to live with himself.

As for the other teachings of the church – those miracles of virgin birth and resurrection from the dead – Samuel didn't really have a belief one way or the other. Christmas and Easter had been the two festivals of the year from time immemorial, and he accepted them as such. The two great Commandments were the only things that ultimately mattered to him, and everything else was by the bye.

In such manner Samuel Speed entered his middle age with some contentment at his lot, and a good deal more peaceful in mind. Until an event occurred that was to change the course of his life irrevocably.

17

GEORGE LEAKE

In the autumn of 1889, Sam Speed had an accident that put him out of work for several months and left him destitute.

He'd been working in the garden of a house owned by George Leake and his wife in St George's Terrace, helping to cut, remove and stack the overhanging limb of an ancient jarrah tree that had broken away in the night and crashed into the flowerbed. It was heavy labour, especially working at one end of a crosscut saw, for the timber was thick and dense. They'd stopped for an early lunch; and when the head gardener left to enjoy a smoko and return the empty plates to the kitchen, Sam went off to finish loading the wheelbarrow. Stupidly, with his bung eye, he tripped over a log, fell heavily onto the sharp edge of another and sprained his knee. It didn't hurt too badly, however, and even more foolishly he decided to carry on – straining to lift three or four heavy sawn chunks into the barrow, and putting more pressure on the injured joint.

'Are you all right, Sammy?' the head gardener asked when he returned, for the man was limping noticeably.

'Fit as a fiddle, Mr Jarvis. Just a little tumble. The exercise will do it good.'

But it didn't. The afternoon labour of loading, barrowing and stacking the sawn timber behind the woodshed to season in fact made the knee considerably worse; and Sam was in a good deal of pain as he hobbled the mile home to North Perth and Mrs Gurney's boarding house.

'What's the matter with *you*, Mr Speed?' she enquired, when he appeared for his dinner. 'You look wrung out. Too much dancing ag'in, is it?' with a bracing laugh to her other guests seated around the table. 'All your gallivanting!' Wagging a naughty finger, to much amusement.

'No. I hurt me knee at work. It's a bit sore. I think I'll rest it up a bit.'

'I should say.'

'It will be all right by morning. Hope so. I need the work.'

Yet as Sam had spoken with false hope to Jarvis, so also to his landlady. The act of climbing up and down stairs did his knee no good at all: and when Mrs Gurney knocked at his door the following morning to ask why he hadn't come for breakfast, she found him in bed moaning with agony, unable to get up much less stand on two legs.

'Ooh, Mr Speed,' she exclaimed, after delicately examining the knee poking beneath his nightshirt. 'Ooh, that don't look no good at all. It's all swollen. I should get the doctor to you.'

'No! No doctors! I got no money for doctors. Can't *you* do something for it?'

'Well now, I'm not sure. I remember when Mr Gurney had something sim'lar after he fell down in his cups, I treated him with hot flannels. That helped a bit. And a bread poultice. I'll see what I can do direc'ly I've seen Mary about the tidying up, and bring you a cup of tea. It will be a bit stewed, I'm afraid.'

She went to the bedroom door, paused holding the handle, and then asked the question that bothered her the moment Sam mentioned doctors.

'You still got enough for the rent, Mr Speed? Only paid to the end of the week, see . . .'

'Oh yes, I'm all right there, Mrs Gurney. Wouldn't let *you* down, would I?'

'Good-oh,' she replied, much relieved in mind. Landladies cannot afford to let their rooms for nothing, and there had been plenty of enquiries lately with the number of diggers coming into town, headed for the new goldfields. 'I'll be back with you in a jiffy.'

It was more than a 'jiffy' – almost an hour before Mrs Gurney returned with her ministrations and her chatter, none of which did Samuel much good, except perhaps one suggestion later that afternoon.

'You know, Mr Speed, that knee o' yours is still swolled up like a balloon.' She had examined it again in her matronly way, pulling down the bedclothes and removing the wet flannels. 'And sore too, I dare say.' Prodding the joint with capable fingers, until Samuel winced with the pain. 'As I thought. Mr Gurney was just the same. He couldn't move for days, and I reckon you'll be laid up there for quite a bit yerself. I doubt you'll be going back to work any time soon . . .'

'No. That's what I'm worried about,' Sam confessed from his pillow.

'Well, if I was you, I'd send a note to your employer and let 'em know. There'll be money owing to you in wages.'

'Yairs.'

'I can pop it in the evening post, if you like. Sooner the better, I say.'

'Not sure I'm up to writing just now, Mrs Gurney . . .'

'That's all right, Mr Speed, I can do it for you. Just want to do what's best for my lodgers, don't I? Look, there's a pencil and paper on the table here with your books. You just tell me what to say and I'll write it down. Keep it simple, mind. I were never a great speller. Ha!'

With much deliberation, then, the good woman transcribed to Sam's dictation: *Mr Speed is sick with a bad knee and can't work for now. Please send wages owing care of Mrs Gurney at the above address. With thanks. Signed Sam'l Speed.*

He demurred at the latter proposal, suggesting the money should perhaps be sent care of himself. But Sam conceded the force of his landlady's reply that he was a sick man, and his wages might otherwise go astray if left sitting on the hall table waiting for *him* to collect them, 'specially with everyone else in the house.

'This way we know they will be safe,' she said firmly. 'You can't be too careful with money these days, Mr Speed.'

When could you ever not *be too careful?*

But he was in no state to argue, and let it go. Mrs Gurney directed the letter to Mr Leake at the address Sam gave, and hurried downstairs to send the maid off to the post with it, calling as she went, 'We'll put the penny stamp on your next bill, Mr Speed . . .'

His money arrived a few days later, together with a note from Jarvis, which cheered up both of them: the landlady, because there was sufficient cash to cover two weeks' rent; and her tenant, as Mr Leake told Sam he would still have a job when he was better. Alas, their pleasure lasted only a matter of days, for it soon became clear that Sam's knee was not healing at all quickly, and that he'd be off work for quite a long time.

'I really do think we should call in a doctor, Mr Speed.'

'No. Please. I can't afford it.'

'Well, p'raps go to the hospital then, when you're able to walk a bit.'

'That's an idea, Mrs Gurney. I'll do that.'

It was a good week or more after his accident, however, before Sam felt strong enough to make his way downstairs and, with the help of a stout walking stick, formerly the property of the late Mr Gurney, limp the mile or so to Murray Street and the old Perth Hospital. It was a distance he normally covered quite briskly. Today, it took him an hour and a half, shuffling along through the city crowd, with frequent rests leaning against the shopfronts. It was far more than his knee could manage so soon after the injury. The joint had swollen badly again and was hurting like hell by the time Samuel found a seat in the waiting room, eventually to be examined by a young physician dressed in striped trousers, starched shirt with wing collars, cravat and a frock coat.

'I sprained it real bad, doctor.'

'It's rather more than a sprain, I'm afraid, Mr Speed,' he said, not unkindly. 'It's arthritis.'

'What's that when it's at home?'

'A kind of rheumatism, you might call it. It comes from years of putting heavy strain on the knee joint and wearing the cartilage down to the bone. I imagine you've done *your* share of hard labour over time . . .?'

The young man raised his head and looked Samuel clear in the eye.

He knew.

'Yes. You could say that.' No need for disguise with him.

'We've now got bone grinding on bone in your knee. That's what gives the pain, and the fluid causes the swelling.'

'And what's the cure?'

'I'm sorry to say there isn't one. It will ease up for a while . . . and then come back again if you put too much stress on it.'

'I thought it was just a sprain from falling over that log.'

'That might have triggered it, Mr Speed, but the condition has been developing for years.'

'Will I be able to work again? Still be a gardener?'

'Not heavy labour, I'd suggest. A little light weeding or pruning around the herbaceous borders . . .'

'Some chance.' Everyone wanted a job like that. 'Can't you do *anything* for me?' Sam was beginning to sound rather desperate.

'I can prescribe some pain-relieving medicine extracted from willow bark.'

'How much will that cost me?'

'Five shillings . . .'

'Oh God.'

'. . . unless you're being supported from the public purse. Have you been declared a pauper, Mr Speed?'

'No!' Indignantly.

'Then I'm afraid it's another five shillings to me.'

'How can I pay that? I've only got a few savings, and you tell me I can't never work properly no more.'

Tears started in Sam's eyes, and his voice began to break with nerves, as it had all those years ago when he stood in the dock before Mr Justice Crompton.

'Well . . . have you got a shilling? That will satisfy *me*. But I'm afraid the price of the medicine is fixed.'

Collecting himself in the surgery, Samuel fumbled in his pocket and found one shilling.

'I'll have to give your medicine a miss, but.' And he picked up the walking stick, ready for the tough walk home.

The young doctor stood and held Sam carefully by the arm to steady him.

'You know, Mr Speed, if things are in a bad way at present, you could always get yourself into the poorhouse at Mount Eliza for a while. The Invalid Depot . . .'

'Never! I know that place.'

Didn't I, though? The Perth Convict Depot, it used to be. Kept there when we were labouring at the Town Hall and the Government House gardens for the bloody Hamptons.

'Yes. I expect you do.' Gently enough.

I spent the last twenty years of my life trying to keep out of that Depot. Any depot.

'It need only be for a few months. Until the knee settles down again and you can get some light work. Dr Lovegrove is the principal medical officer. He goes out from here regularly . . . fairly regularly, anyway . . . to see the old men. He can prescribe medicines and treatment without charge where necessary. I can speak to him if you like . . .'

'I'll die first.'

The young man smiled, trying to lighten the mood.

'There's always that option, I suppose. But Mount Eliza seems preferable. And it need only be for a short time.'

'Thanks, Doctor. But I've still got a few means.'

And me pride, too.

Muttering to himself angrily as he limped out the door and into the street.

'Bloody cheek . . . wanting to send me to the poorhouse . . . the Invalid Depot . . . Convict Depot . . . I worked like a dog . . . kept myself decent . . . stayed out of trouble . . . now this . . . not fair . . . I'll get better . . . show him . . . blasted doctors . . . five shillings for a bottle o' flaming medicine . . .'

And so on, thumping with his stick on the pavement, venting his fury on the doctor, though in truth it was himself with whom he was most upset. All those years trying to make something of himself, now gone to waste.

Shoulda gone to the diggings when Tommy Jones give me the chance.

Coulda tried harder to go out to Southern Cross couple of years back.

So his thoughts blamed him.

'I'd have been sitting pretty by now. Made me packet. Tommy's ship has come in, I bet. Gone home a regular toff, no doubt. And me? Three pounds eleven shillings and sixpence in the bank is all that stands between me and the brink . . .'

All for bloody nothing.

Samuel was in the midst of these soliloquies when he found himself passing a branch of his government bank. He had his deposit book with him, and on a sudden impulse he went inside and withdrew the three pounds, leaving only the shillings and pence as his remaining savings. At least he was not yet utterly destitute. He still had money in his pocket – most of which he gave to Mrs Gurney when he got home as an advance against future rent, together with a substantial outlay of opinion on doctors in general and this one in particular.

'He wants to put me in the Invalid Depot, Mrs Gurney. What do you think of that?'

'Well, he might be right, you know,' as his landlady carefully counted the notes and entered the sum in her book. 'Got to face facts, Mr Speed, when you get crook. As I told Mr Gurney when he had his relapse near the end . . .'

Facing facts was the last thing Samuel had in mind.

'I'll be all right,' he replied, climbing the stairs to his room, where he lay on his bed with the knee throbbing, trying to recover from the long walk into town and back.

So anxious was he for his life to resume its normal, rudimentary course, that Sam went back to work far sooner than he should: hobbling down to the lower end of St George's Terrace with the aid of the Gurneys' walking stick, reporting to Mr Jarvis and, after insisting he was 'fit as a fiddle', was given the job of pruning the last of the autumn roses. It wasn't strenuous work, but it did require a lot of bending and moving around; and Samuel was feeling the knee starting to bite, when he saw the mistress of the house, Mrs Louisa Leake, coming into her garden.

'Mr Speed . . . how nice to see you again,' she said in her pleasant, ladylike voice. Louisa was one of the Burt daughters – from a distinguished colonial family – as indeed was Mr Leake, at present the Crown Solicitor with political ambitions of his own. 'I heard you'd been away sick. I hope you're quite recovered.'

'Pretty well, m'um, thank you.' Removing his hat and touching his forehead in the time-honoured way. Pretty well, when his knee was screaming *Liar!*

'I'm very glad to hear it. The garden hasn't been quite the same without you, and cook tells me the kitchen garden has been far less productive.'

'It's good to be back, m'um.'

She moved on a little. And as she did, Samuel turned too quickly back to the rosebush, and twisted the injured knee so suddenly that he cried out in pain.

'Why, Mr Speed, whatever is the matter?' Louisa came hurrying back.

'Nothing, m'um. Quite all right. Just the knee . . .'

The thing jabbed at him again. Savagely.

'Ahh . . .'

Samuel groped the air, trying to find something other than a rosebush to support him.

'Wait!' Louisa came hurrying forward. 'Lean on me.' And as he put his arm on her shoulder she called out, 'Mr Jarvis! Please, come quickly! We need your assistance.'

The head gardener came running, and together they helped Samuel to a garden bench. He sat there awhile, trying to suppress a groan and waiting for the grip to subside.

'Mr Speed, I can see you're not at all as well as you say you are . . .'

'Just me knee . . .'

'Sammy hurt it here a few weeks back, m'um,' said Jarvis, 'when we was cutting up that fallen branch of the jarrah tree.'

'I can't bear to think of you working here in pain because of an injury sustained on our property,' she said. 'It is far better for you to rest up until it is fully healed.'

'But . . .'

'No. I insist. Did you walk here today?'

'Yes, m'um, just from North Perth.'

'Well, you clearly can't walk home. I'll get John to bring around the dogcart and drive you back. It's not far, and he can help you up the steps.'

'That's good of you, Mrs Leake.'

'It's the least we can do. And Samuel . . . if you need our help again, just let me or Mr Leake know.'

'Thank you, m'um.'

So events ran their course. Samuel returned home, causing quite a stir when he returned in a trap and was helped upstairs by a coachman. The phrase '*That* Mr Leake' did the rounds of the neighbourhood, and for a week or two Sam enjoyed a shade more respect from his landlady than he ever had before. He was laid up in his room waiting for the knee to improve: reading *Silas Marner* again and his daily pages of the Testament, missing his Sunday outings to the church, and the regular visits to the Institute library, with the occasional detour to the street girls. Trying to pray to God to make the knee better – but knowing that it wasn't going to happen quickly, and that even when it did he would have long run out of funds. Feeling sorrier for himself. More bitter and regretful. Sensing that Mrs Gurney's brief moment of respect was returning to business-as-usual, as she calculated that Samuel's payments in advance would soon reach their due date. Preparing himself – even as he sought to resist it – for the inevitable.

Thus, the morning came when, feeling rather better and coming downstairs for breakfast, Samuel was met by his landlady at the dining room door.

'Oh, Mr Speed, just a quick word, if I may. I was wondering what arrangements you've made . . . Your rent only goes until Saturday, and after that . . .'

'I don't know, Mrs Gurney. I've only got eleven shillings left in the bank . . .'

'That will cover you for a few more days, Mr Speed, but after then – what? I can't afford to extend terms, you know. Mr Gurney always told me, "Never give credit, Lena," and he was right about

that if not much else. Every day I get an enquiry from some pros-
pector or other. So . . .?'

She was met with silence.

'Um . . .'

'So I was thinking, Mr Speed,' as she supplied the answer to her
own question, 'that it's getting near time you listened to the good
advice of that doctor you saw at the hospital.'

'Yes.' At length, and with a deep sigh. 'I'll have to think about it,
Mrs Gurney.'

He ate his porridge stoically, knowing that the eyes and thoughts
of every boarder at the table were upon him, for they'd heard their
landlady's voice clearly at the door. Looking at him not in embarrassment, necessarily, though that might have been her intent, as
warning, but rather with a kind of sympathy – a fellow-feeling that
this might one day be them. As Samuel had often felt sadness and
relief in his turn, when he saw another, whose feet were clinging to
the lower rungs of society, find the supports break and fall to the
bottom of the ladder.

No help for it now. Nowhere else to go.

And therefore, later that morning, Sam Speed shuffled slowly
back into town and along St George's Terrace, until he came to the
building that had the brass plate 'Leake and Harper Solicitors' at
the entrance.

He climbed a wide stone staircase, holding the cast-iron balus-
trade for balance, to the first floor, and entered the office.

'Can I help you?' enquired a young man, one of the articled
clerks.

'My name is Samuel Speed. I was hoping to see Mr Leake. He
knows me.' Sam added the last phrase hurriedly, to establish his
bona fides.

The clerk eyed him up and down. A poor working man, obviously: not the sort of client the firm usually had through the doors. But clean and fairly neat. And Mr Leake *was* the Crown Solicitor, an important legal officer, and who knew what cases he might be involved with?

'Mr Leake is in court at present. But he will be back directly, if you'd care to wait.'

Sam took a seat near the outer door, where his late employer would be sure to see him when he entered the office. Which he did within the half-hour, bustling through carrying his wig in one hand and black robe slung over his arm. A clerk followed with his briefcase — and trailing behind came all the ghosts suddenly awakened in Sam's mind from his Lordship's courtroom at Oxford. He'd seen men in wigs and black gowns before. He knew what they could do – and was at that moment seized with Mr Leake's official importance.

Surely he'll *be able to help me.*

'And who's this?' asked the Crown Solicitor, pausing before the man whom he vaguely recognised.

'Mr Speed, sir. He says you know him.'

'Do I . . .?'

'Yes, sir. I work in your garden sometimes. Hurt myself recently . . .'

'Oh . . . of course. My wife mentioned it to me. Samuel, isn't it? And what can I do for you?'

'Begging your pardon, sir, I was wondering if you could write a letter for me . . .'

'What kind of letter? Please, come into my room and tell me . . .'

Samuel followed him into the inner sanctum, sat delicately on a carved chair in front of the desk, and related the circumstances of his injury, the long time his knee was taking to heal, and the fact that he was now almost destitute.

'I've only got a few shillings left, sir, and they will run out by early next week, and after that, nothing. I'm very sorry to bother you, but Mrs Leake said to ask if I needed help . . .'

'Well, of course I'd employ you immediately, Samuel. My wife speaks highly of you. But with your knee as it is . . .'

'It's not that, sir. I was wondering if you could write a letter for me to the authorities asking if they could find me a place at Mount Eliza. At the Depot . . . Just for two or three months. I don't know who else to ask . . .'

'Course I did. Just turn up at the door. But a letter from Mr Leake would carry more weight like, and get me in.

'Well, that would be Mr . . . Mr Dale, that's right. Superintendent of Poor Houses at the Colonial Secretary's office. I could certainly write to him if you wish. I'll do it now, if you like.'

'I would be grateful, sir.'

Knew he'd have the right contacts.

George Leake took a sheet of office letterhead, and taking up his pen wrote the following:

The bearer Samuel Speed is anxious to get into the Invalid Depot for two or three months. He has lately been in my employ, and unfortunately met with an accident and sprained his knee. He is now quite unfit for work, and having been laid up for several weeks is quite without means. I have no hesitation in saying that he is a man worthy of assistance. I should employ him if he were fit for work.

He signed and dated it 20 June 1889, and handed it over for Sam to read.

'Will that do?'

Just the ticket. Clever me.

'Certainly, Mr Leake. Thank you, sir.'

'Can you take it around now to Mr Dale at the Colonial Secretary's office . . . do you know where that is? Just along the street. We can set things in motion . . .'

'Yes, sir.'

'I expect to hear back fairly promptly. When I do, I'll send a message to your lodgings if you'll leave the address. I believe my wife sent you home in the dogcart the other day, Sam?'

'It was very decent of her, sir.'

'Well, it's clearly too far for you to walk the two miles or so to Mount Eliza with your belongings. Once we have approval, we'll send John around again to take you out there.'

'That's very kind of you, Mr Leake. I can't thank you enough.'

'I am glad to have been of service. And Sam, when the knee is mended, let us know. I'm sure we'll find work for you in the garden. In the meantime . . .' fishing in his pocket and bringing up two silver crown pieces, '. . . here's an extra ten shillings, just to help things along a little.'

A small matter it may have been in George Leake's daily round, but the difference this one act made to Samuel Speed was enormous. Within a day the application had been officially recommended and approved (would it not?) with his age given as forty-six; Mr Leake informed; and a note sent by hand to the boarding house to advise Sam that the dogcart would be there at ten o'clock next morning to drive him and his possessions to the Invalid Depot at Mount Eliza.

And so it was.

18

THE DEPOT

'They were very good to me, Mr and Mrs Leake . . .'

It seemed ages since Sammy had mentioned them to the journalist as among his clients from the old days, but in truth it was less than a minute. Rather like the Boss, when one of those films he showed in the hall broke down and he had to rewind it on the spool. Scenes you'd already watched flashed by in the half-light – and yet you knew exactly what was in them and what the people were saying. So with the cinema of old age, when the memory is constantly rewinding to the past. Fast forward . . . and fast backwards.

'In what way were they good to you, Sam?' Joshua Cribben sought to focus the old fellow on his subject.

'Oh . . . I fell on hard times, you know. Jiggered my knee, and they looked after me. Got me a place in the old Mount Eliza Depot with all the other broken-down old lags.'

'I was going to ask you about that. They've still got one of the original buildings here at the Home, haven't they?'

'Yairs. The old bungalow, we call it. Moved it out here when they pulled down the Depot years ago. Remember when they were still building it . . . and a lot of the blokes who lived there. Me among 'em.'

'Just near the Swan Brewery on the river, wasn't it? Handy for the drunks . . .'

'That's right. But I were never one of *them*. I had my stories, see. And they had nothing . . .'

He could see it again, in the flickering frames of his mind. Coming downstairs with his bag and his books that June morning of 1889: handing the Testament and the walking stick back to Mrs Gurney. 'I would of let you keep 'em, Mr Speed, but they were my late husband's and a treasure to me.' No matter. There'd be plenty of sticks at the Depot, and Bibles too, no doubt. John helping him into the cart and driving through the city to Mounts Bay Road . . . and Samuel sitting in the back, teary and disconsolate, just as he'd been that morning he set out with Tommy Jones down the Bladon road out of Woodstock. And look where that had led. Nowhere. Still broke. Still with nothing. And still with no prospects. In all, it seemed Samuel Speed's journey through life had led him back to exactly the same place from where he'd started.

And yet . . . that was not entirely true. Sam's native optimism sought to reassert itself. He still had his bank book . . . slightly enlarged since yesterday, when he'd deposited one of the two silver crown pieces George Leake had given him. He still had his few books and the companionship of all the others he'd read. Even his own little library had expanded somewhat, with the purchase of three second-hand books with the other crown on the way home from the bank: *Moby Dick*, *Tom Sawyer* and a copy of John Boyle O'Reilly's *Moondyne*, which Sam had already read from the Institute library, but wanted for himself as a keepsake of a man and a time he had known.

So he had that, a good breakfast in his belly, change of three shillings and sixpence in his pocket from the books, fellow lodgers – even Mrs Gurney – waving farewell. More than that, he was riding in a dogcart down the road this time – not tramping in broken shoes – with somewhere to go, courtesy of the recommendation from a gentleman having influence in the colony. Which he hoped would duly impress itself on the Master of the Invalid Depot. In this, Sam Speed was not mistaken. His instinct to seek George Leake's protection had been spot on. And twenty-five years ago, he'd known nobody of any influence to assist him whatsoever. Not even the workhouse night porter.

The Depot had started in the early fifties, at the same time they were building Fremantle Prison, as a Perth base for those convicts sent up river to work on government projects in the town. Sam Speed had been one of them in his time. It had been added to over the years, and now was a collection of around twenty weatherboard or rubble-filled masonry cottages – really not much more than sleeping huts – shingled or covered with tin roofs, squatting at the foot of Mount Eliza, the high point of a large paddock reserved as public land at the western edge of town, that would one day be named King's Park.

When transportation ceased in 1868, the Depot was converted to an invalid home for destitute men, almost all of whom in the early years had been ex-convicts. Still were, when Samuel arrived. And as he made his way to his allocated hut (the magical influence of his letter of recommendation having secured him an actual bed, which was not always the case for those unfortunates who had to sleep upon mattresses on the floor), he was greeted by noises of recognition from those he'd known.

'Samuel Speed, well, well . . . upon my word . . . welcome home among us ag'in, Sammy . . . Howzit, Jemmy? . . . bound to come to this one day and watch where yer puttin' that clobber . . .' Much as it had been when he first entered the association ward at Fremantle clink all those years ago, and the walls began to close in on him once more.

Yet again, this was not quite the case. The letter had more far-reaching consequences than the mere fact of Sam's sleeping accommodation. For the first twenty years of its existence as an invalid depot, the place had suffered from a succession of incompetent or unsuitable Masters, some of whom had even been accused of selling food for their own benefit, and the place had developed a pretty unsavoury reputation.

All this had apparently changed a couple of years ago, with the appointment of Mr John Price Wade as the Master: a man who took his position seriously, to the point where he adopted a high cocked hat, boots, tight trousers and a swallowtail coat as part of his official costume, quite like the Beadle in *Oliver Twist*. And, with Mr Bumble, he asserted his authority with zeal, though for the most part leaving the actual day-to-day running of the place in the bullying hands of the orderlies, matron and a couple of nurses. Discipline and display was his *forte*.

Now, a man of much self-importance is naturally very deferential to those of even greater consequence in the official hierarchy above him. And when Mr Wade received an instruction to admit Samuel Speed to the Depot on the basis of a recommendation signed by the Superintendent of Poor Houses, the Crown Solicitor and the Colonial Secretary no less, he jumped. Samuel had his undivided attention from the moment he presented himself at the door, having been driven in Mr Leake's dogcart. Any complaints, and the roof could fall on the Master's head.

Of course, Mr Wade would be happy to accommodate him for the short period of two or three months (was it?) until he got on his feet again. (They all said that, on arrival.) Naturally, he could see that Samuel was clean ('I had a bath last night'), so they might dispense with the customary scrub in disinfectant. And the haircut too.

Clothes? It was usual to issue new inmates with a fresh set (white duck trousers and shirt, dark jacket not unlike a prison uniform); but as Sam was only staying briefly, he could keep his own and ask for new ones if his visit became extended. There were pegs in the dormitories, but perhaps he'd like to leave his valise in the office where it would be safe. ('You can never tell, with some of our residents.') And yes, there was a locker with a key where he could keep his books secure. (*That was good, for I still had my savings bank book hidden behind the dust jacket of* Moondyne – *what better place? – and didn't want anybody finding that.*) And the Depot had a small library if he'd like further reading matter.

Anything else? Certainly, Samuel would be free to go into town from time to time with one of the carters. Yes, he'd be entitled to his tobacco ration, and the small amount the men were paid for the work they did about the Depot. A gardener, wasn't he? Well, there was a vegetable patch here in dire need of expert attention. Oh, it was usual for new arrivals to hand over whatever money they had, to defray expenses at the rate of ninepence a day until the money ran out. Samuel was prepared for that, and handed over his three shillings and sixpence. It seemed only fair and added to his cachet with Mr Wade – though the savings book he still kept to himself.

After which, with many felicitations and hopes that Sam would enjoy his stay, the Master called one of the orderlies to show Samuel to his berth . . . and to find a walking stick he could use in the locker room, where they kept any items of ongoing value from the deceased.

That evening, Mr Wade composed a note to the Superintendent, requesting that he inform both the Colonial Secretary and the Crown Solicitor that their wishes concerning Samuel Speed had been attended to with satisfaction. In his line of business, you store up merit points when you can.

So Sam settled into the daily round of institutional life once more . . . which, with only a few intervals of respite, had remained his lot to the present day. Indeed, it sometimes seemed he'd never really escaped it, from the hour he and Tommy Jones handed themselves in at the Woodstock police station. From workhouse and prison to ticketman, farmhouse and boarding house to Invalid Depot, almost every essential function of life – eating, sleeping and working – had been governed by a timetable; and everything else ruled by punctilious observance of the regulations – which, by the 1920s in the Old Men's Home, came to cover fifteen close-typed pages. Though, like every other article of bureaucratic faith, there were generally ways around them to be found by a person of experience and quick wit.

'How did you find it there?' the reporter asked. 'The Depot came to have a pretty grim name, as I recollect . . .'

'Oh, it did, Mr Cribben. You're right there. And deservedly so. There was no proper dining room . . . had to eat meals in our rooms, off of tin plates. No proper washroom or lavatories. No dispensary for the infirmary. Everything had to come from Perth Hospital . . . including the doctor, who managed a visit once a week if we was lucky. I know of one feller who lay five days with a broken leg before they took him to the hospital . . .'

'What?'

'Yes. And the Master . . . he was a peculiar man, that Mr Wade.'

'In what way?'

'Well, in some ways he could be very strict – bossing people around, punishing blokes for the smallest infraction of the rules. Putting 'em in the cooler. Docking them of their money. Forcing them to give up what little cash they had. Though I have to say, in fairness, he were generally pretty good with me. Let me go into town every so often . . . hitching a ride with the carrier . . . to do a spot of work here and there with Mr Jarvis if he wanted me at the Leake residence . . .'

That always worked a treat.

Even more so when Leake went into Parliament and became Attorney-General . . . on his way to be Premier soon after Federation, when the six Australian colonies turned into states, and the old Queen died. One cross word from Sam Speed in the right quarters, and the whole apparatus of government might descend upon the Master.

'Sometimes I'd go up to the Institute if I wanted to read the paper. Or into the church if there were a service on. I loved the singing. Buy another second-hand book with my savings. I found *Alice* there, and *Treasure Island*. Even stayed overnight, occasionally, if I could find a bunk . . .'

And down to the riverbank.

'Coming and going . . . though to be sure as time went by, the "going" became a lot less regular with me. The old knee, you know . . . The doctor was right. It never come good.'

Thus, the 'two or three months' of George Leake's letter turned into six. Which quickly became a year. And, in the nature of things when someone who's lived a hard life settles into a routine that provides some minimal convenience, the years accumulated into a decade. And then another . . .

'Oh yes, I stayed around the place a lot more. Fishing sometimes with the other old 'uns in the river. You could get a good catch in those days. Helping in the garden. And I must say the vegetables served with our dinners showed a considerable improvement,' he said with a twinkle. 'I grew a nice cabbage. Potaters. Got my small allowance each week, and the 'baccy ration.'

'I thought you didn't smoke.'

'No. Never touched the stuff. Didn't like it. But I took it at the Depot, and sold it on to the others. Just good business . . .'

The shillings mounting up in the savings bank when I went into town.

'Did it here, too,' remarked Bob the Tuppenny Orderly from the other bed, and a kind of surreptitious giggle went around the three of them.

'So there was *that*,' Samuel went on. 'The better side of Mr Wade. But then there was the "dark side", as they say. Not so much in what he *did* as in what he didn't do.'

'Which was . . .?'

'Not keeping a proper eye on them orderlies. The paid ones and the Tuppennies as well. And they could be cruel. No one half so decent as young Bobbie here. No. They could be monsters if they thought they could get away with it.'

'Were they monsters with you?'

'No, not really. They knew Mr Wade kept an eye out for me. But some of the others . . .'

'There was an enquiry into that place, I remember reading about . . .'

'Yes, Mr Cribben. You do your homework, as I said before. It got so bad things started appearing in the newspapers.'

'What sort of things?'

'Well . . . there was one old-timer in the Depot, nearing his end. He was sick in bed, and not long to go. And he got a visit from a lady who was a friend of his. She sat by his bedside, trying to soothe him, you know. Talking to him soft. Fanning him in the heat. But there was no damp sponge to wipe his forehead. No towel. Not even a glass of water for him to sip and ease his thirst. Nothing! And so she sent someone to ask the orderly for a glass of water – and he refused to give it her. Said it was against the regulations. I ask yer, How cruel was that? And that poor old feller went to his Maker without even a drop of water to moisten his lips, because they said the rules didn't permit it. They put that in the paper!'

'Struth!' Bob the Tuppenny exclaimed. 'I never heard o' that before.'

'Yes, old mate,' Sam continued. 'People can be very unkind to aged folk. It's just that some show it more than others. Except perhaps for rich old 'uns.'

'And not always then,' observed the journalist, thinking of the recent homicide of a wealthy widow at the hands of her relatives.

'Too right, Mr Cribben. Mount Eliza could be worse'n what happened to the old chap who died without his glass of water.'

'How *much* worse?'

'An old bloke . . . name of Bob Douglas . . . came into the Depot in the late nineties, I think. Yes. From Northam way. It was just before that enquiry you mentioned. In fact, his treatment triggered the whole thing, and eventually led them more or less to build this new place out here on the river at Dalkeith. Remember it well . . .'

He drifted off into a quiet lagoon of recollection, until both the journalist and the orderly could bear the suspense no longer and asked at the same time, 'What happened to Bob Douglas?'

'Oh, yes . . . I was telling you, wasn't I? Well, he came into the Depot late one autumn suffering, so he said, from yellow jaundice. Could've been, too, which can be rather contagious. But instead of putting him in the infirmary with the nurses, they stuck Bob Douglas on a hard mattress on the floor of a sleeping hut that had seventy other men in it. All sleeping on the floor . . . some on raised stages either side, and some, like Bob Douglas, in the well, as it were, down the middle of the room. It was terrible. He had trouble walking. Blokes had to lift him and carry him outside to the toilets such as they were. Wash him. It was a week before that Dr Lovegrove came out to see him: said he had cirrhosis of the liver and didn't prescribe anything much by way of medicine to ease him. Bob couldn't keep his food down. Well, the tucker wasn't suited for a man in that condition. He needed soups and soft porridge. And still he lay on that mattress, getting weaker and filthier. For nearly three weeks. Can you imagine? It wasn't until a few days before he died that they carried Bob into the infirmary . . . and not until the actual day that Dr Lovegrove bothered to come out and see him again. By which time, o' course, it were too late.'

'That's terrible!'

'Yes. And just to rub salt into the wound, Bob Douglas came into the Depot with something like three pounds ten shillings in his pocket. A lot of money, even in these days. So they took eighteen shillings of it to pay for his board, if you could call it that, and handed the rest over to the government.'

'Didn't he have any family to leave it to?'

'Don't know, Mr Cribben.'

'Then in that case, I suppose . . .'

'You may say that, sticking up for 'em! But I tell you, it riled some people enough to write to the paper, and they put it in an article. Yes, said that Mr Wade was like some character out of Charles Dickens, which were true enough, and blamed him for what happened to Bob Douglas – which weren't true, because he was away at the time and his assistant so-called was in charge. Called him incompetent and should be sacked. O' course they didn't do that but had this inquiry you spoke of instead. Bit of a whitewash by Mr Roe, the Police Magistrate, I reckon. Only lasted five or six days. Called quite a lot of witnesses from among the inmates . . .'

'You?'

'No, not me. There were no way I was ever going to give evidence to the beak again. But in the end, they exonerated Mr Wade of cruelty and put the blame on the orderlies instead.'

''Course they did,' remarked Bob the Tuppenny with feeling.

'Oh, it was right enough, Bob. But the inquiry was very critical of Wade for not supervising the place properly . . . and also of the doctor, who they said should come out at least once a day to hear any complaints about the food and everything. Not once a week, and then just a quick walk through the infirmary. Spoke very sharp about the lack of hygiene . . . toilets, vermin, no dining hall and overcrowding because of all those failed diggers coming back in from the goldfields. Said there should be a new place built for destitute old blokes like me . . .'

'And in due course they built it out here.'

'Took 'em eight years. But yes . . . we came out here in 1906 and they pulled the old place down. Altogether different now. Much better, if a lot further from town. Though Mr Wade, who came with us, remained much the same, I have to say. We used to call him "the Quaker" sometimes from the way he was togged out and his severity. Insisted on having a fence built around the acreage, with a pair of gates that he kept locked, and you needed his permission to get out. It was like being back in prison again for three years until the new Boss, Mr Rust, took over . . .'

'Did Wade let *you* out?'

'From time to time. I'd go to Gallop House occasionally in the early days, to help a bit in the garden. Big place. Do you know it? Got fairly run down in the end. Overlooks the river, not far from here. Little outings. But I was starting to get on in years by then. And when Mr Rust came he opened the gates and never shut them again, so there was no need for permission to leave. Besides, we started getting visitors. The concert parties – did I tell you about them? – coming from town in a ferry. And then the ladies from the Braille society with books . . .'

'You learned Braille?'

'Eventually, Mr Cribben. It was a lifesaver for me. Especially when the good eye started to get a bit dim and the specs were not so useful no more . . .'

And that is no lie.

It wasn't until the early nineties that Braille books generally became available to the visually impaired of Perth, with dedicated people able to teach the skill of reading the raised dots with their fingers. But it quickly caught on – opening the world of literature, music and mathematics for those to whom it had previously been denied. By 1897 the Victoria Institute for the Blind was founded to celebrate the old Queen's Diamond Jubilee, with premises a couple of miles out of Perth, and soon to have one of the largest Braille libraries in the Australian colonies.

The Institute was a little too far out of town for most readers to trek to the library. So, it was arranged that the Braille books could be left and picked up from Gee's stationery shop in Central Arcade, just around the corner from Trinity Church: the new one, built of red brick in front of the original chapel in the high Romanesque style, and opened in 1894. Sam Speed still went to the occasional service if he happened to be in town; and certainly, in these days around the turn of the century, he made every effort to attend the fundraising bazaars. Who knew what interesting books or more powerful spectacles might be picked up at the 'bring and buy' stall?

The Trinity congregation took a good deal of practical interest in the Braille movement – naturally, given the hope it brought to those in need. A few years later in 1913, just before the outbreak of the Great War, the first meeting of what became known as the Braille Society to help produce the books was held in Trinity's assembly room. Even before that, the ladies behind the stalls had a keen awareness of the project; and from time to time drew nice Mr Speed's attention to the merits of learning Braille, as he stood peering at a decent copy of Stevenson's *Kidnapped*, say, or a cheap edition of Thomas Hardy's *Tess of the d'Urbervilles* held up close to the spectacle lens of his good eye.

'I'm sure you'd take to it very quickly, Mr Speed. They hold Braille lessons in town here, weekdays as well as nights. A reader of your ability would pick it up very quickly. So much easier on your remaining sight.'

'Thanks very much, Mrs Collins,' (or Mrs Graham, Miss Sharpe or whomever else it might be), he'd reply. 'But you know, I'm over my half-century now, and I think this dog is too old to learn new tricks.'

'You underestimate yourself, Samuel. I know how much you like to keep up with the latest authors. That was a very nice copy of Mr Kipling's first book of *Jungle Stories* you bought from me last time. Did you enjoy it?'

'It was a corker. Took me right back to the time I first started reading about tigers and the jungle and India . . .'

It was when I was doing my primers with that Mr Martin in Oxford Castle. But I won't tell her that.

'I don't know if they're available in Braille yet, but they will be one day, and then . . .'

'The peeper is all right for the moment I think, Mrs Collins, so I'll leave the Braille at present. But I will take this copy of *Tess of the Dubber . . . Doober . . .* is it . . .?'

'*D'Urbervilles*. A tragic story, I think you'll find. Controversial, so I haven't read it. But a powerful one, they say.'

'Sounds right up my alley.'

And it was too, he remembered. This relentless tale of love and desire, class and power, poverty and the double standards of communal morality, took place in a rural England where the new machines were just coming in. An England that Sam Speed knew all too well. He, too, had been caught in the constant struggle of life to satisfy those basic needs of sex, hunger or shelter, and the weight of a social system that so often prevented the poor from doing so in the end, and drove them to crime. Rick-burning in his case. Rape and murder for Tess. The book reminded him, in a way, of Silas Marner, seen through a mirror in reverse. He'd been accused and cast out, until he found the love of a child. Poor Tess had discovered too much love too soon: violated by one, abandoned by the other, and then cast out. Forever. At the end of a rope.

At least in this country, once he'd served his sentence, Sam had been given openings he'd never have been offered in England. The chance of going to the goldfields to find his fortune, for instance. And though he'd not taken it up – and doubted he'd have struck it rich even had he done so – the societal barriers were not so rigid and ancient, as they were in England, that he'd be denied the opportunity. Or acceptance should he find a fortune. There was an easiness, even a certain generosity, between the classes here in Australia, that Sam had never known at home. Where in England would an

under-gardener find a Crown Solicitor to give him a recommendation to the poorhouse? Where in Birmingham would old Mr Speed
have a lady of means and position recommending a book to him,
putting aside a good pair of spectacles for him, or suggesting that
he learn to read Braille because she thought highly of his abilities
and quick mind? Never. And thus, the more he thought about it, the
more Samuel came to feel a degree of gratitude for his lot. No, he'd
never amounted to much in terms of material wealth. But with his
books, his small degree of freedom at the Invalid Depot, proximity
to town, and the faith that God still loved him, he knew he was a
damned sight happier than he would have been had he remained at
home. To that extent, Queen Victoria and her penal code had done
him a favour.

The more, too, that Sam thought about the Braille idea, the
more it appealed to him. His bad eye was now almost useless, and
he didn't know for how much longer the good eye would hold out.
The typeface on the books he'd been reading lately seemed to be
getting ever smaller. The notion of reading with his fingers had some
merit to it. Besides, everybody at the Depot knew they were building
a new home for the old men at Dalkeith, some miles down river,
and the chances of getting into town once that happened to take
Braille lessons (or for anything else) seemed slim. So, he made some
enquiries at Trinity, was put in contact with the people who taught
the method, and with Mr Wade's permission enrolled for a course
of lessons.

'Did you have trouble learning it?' The reporter's voice dragged
him back to the present.

'Well, yes and no, Mr Cribben. There's a different combination
of these six dots for each letter, see, not to mention the contractions.
You have to learn those by touch, before you can start to read it.

Trouble is, I had rough workingman's hands in those days. Wouldn't know to look at 'em now.'

He poked his thin hands from beneath the blanket, the skin wrinkled paper-thin and blotched over crests of bone, and examined them for a moment.

'No. It was all the outdoor work in the gardens, see. A few callouses. Scratches. Hard skin. That sort of thing. Good hands, but they didn't have the sensitivity to feel the little dots easily. I mean, it's like trying to read when the letters are all in a foreign script. Chinese, say. So it took me some time – a month or two – to remember them all, and then put the letters into words. And then to remember what the words *were* as you scanned a sentence. It was very slow. Like learning to read for the first time. I was starting to get there after a year of it, but then . . .'

He wandered off again down a side track of reminiscence.

'But then . . . what?' These incessant questions.

'Well, then we moved out here to the new Home and I lost contact with the teachers. Had to close me little bank account. And I started doing small jobs away from here. Gallop House, did I tell you? Yes. And then, when it opened around 1910, I went to the Children's Hospital at Subiaco to help out in the garden. Mr Rust assisted me there . . . he does a lot of work with the kiddies, you know. Next thing, the War came along, and the Braille people were needed to help all those poor soldiers coming back from the Front . . . gassed . . . blinded . . . Their need was much greater than mine, Mr Cribben. Besides, I didn't really need the Braille in those days. I still had the good eye with some sight in it. The specs helped . . . and then I got me magnifying glass as backup.'

Sam paused a moment, remembering the impact that terrible

War had on everyone. Catching his breath, and groping for the thread that would lead him back to the here and now.

'It weren't until well after the War that I really had to learn Braille. Began to lose the sight in *both* eyes, and I was faced without being able to read much at all. It was *need* that drove me on, then. Necessity, you understand. And Mr Rust's encouragement. He was building up the library here. I gave him my small collection of books because they weren't no good to me any more. And he got a few Braille ones. "You should give it another try, Sammy," he said. "There are other old-timers out here who could benefit as well. I'll help you." And the Boss was as good as his word. He even asked those nice people from the Braille Society to visit from time to time, to give us lessons and bring some books with them. They built a Rest Home, you know, out at Victoria Park, for the blind. Pleasant place. Much smaller than this . . . the Reverend Gunning comes to visit . . . I stayed there for a few years in the later twenties, helping in the garden, you know, as best I could. Getting better at the finger reading until I could scan a whole page in under five minutes. Enjoying the spell away . . . Went back a couple of years ago, and returned here only last month from the hospital. The old hernia again . . .'

Mention of his ailments produced a twinge of pain down there, and he winced somewhat before deciding to ignore it. Another thought had come into his mind.

'Did you know they've started bringing out gramophone records of people reading stories? "Talking books" we call them. Lots of us can listen to 'em at once. They have some at Victoria Park and here, too. None at the hospital, I'm sorry to say. Saves all the trouble of finger reading. And some of the readers are as good as Clarrie Short used to be . . .'

'What sort of books did you like to read, Sam?'

'Oh, whatever was going. Adventure stories, but there generally weren't much in them to remember. Kipling, o' course. Some of those crime stories when they started to come out. Sherlock Holmes . . . Mrs Christie . . . Wilkie Collins, *The Woman in White*, do you know it? Mark Twain. But Dickens is the one that still stays with me. Mr Pickwick. Copperfield. Oliver Twist. They've been old friends for years. Everything turned out all right for them at last. Pip, especially, from his convict inheritance in *Great Expectations*. Wonderful stories. Happy endings . . .'

Samuel stopped a moment. Wondering. And drew a lungful of cold air.

'I wish life was really like that, Mr Cribben. Don't you?'

'Yes, Sam. If only it were.'

PERCHANCE TO DREAM . . .

The interview had been going for well over an hour, and Samuel could feel the tiredness starting to drape him like a pall. He'd given it his best with the Moondyne and Fenian recitations; and the effort of his last speech on learning Braille had almost drained the remaining strength from him. He lay against his pillow, eyes closed, hoping the whole thing would soon be over.

And so was the journalist. For his part, Joshua Cribben was dissatisfied that the session had yielded very little by way of entertaining copy for his readers. No secret exposures. No juicy titbits on life behind bars . . . or even in the Old Men's Home, for that matter. Sam's tales of the bushranger Moondyne Joe and the *Catalpa* escape had been interesting from a contemporary's point of view, but they were well-known incidents and he hadn't shed much by way of new light on them. It was his long life, and the fact that Speed was the last of the expirees still alive in Western Australia, that constituted the guts of the story; and the old bloke's forgetfulness about himself could be explained simply as the result of his extreme age. Part of the colour Joshua would weave into the piece when he sat down at the typewriter, and the historical bits he'd try to look up later to knock the thing into shape.

Cribben looked at his watch. Surely the photographer would be here soon? He leafed back through the pages of his notebook to see if there was anything he'd missed and was getting ready to put the pad away when he casually remarked, 'I suppose you came across all sorts who'd come here in the convict transports, eh Sam?'

The old chap opened his one good eye.

'Oh yes, Mr Cribben. I mean, it *takes* all sorts, don't it? Good 'uns and bad 'uns. The odd professional person. Coves like school-masters and shopkeepers. The occasional shirt-soiled gent. But mostly, you know, they were just people like me. Poor men, who got caught up in crime because too often there was nowhere else to go.'

'Social outcasts . . .'

'I suppose *you* might put it that way.'

There was another silence, pierced with meaning, as Sam let the barb sink in. These young people had no sense of how their words could hurt. Or, if they did, thought that old folk wouldn't under-stand the intent. *But we know, too well.* And then, to soften the dart a little and to show he meant no harm, he added, 'Moondyne Joe came into the old Mount Eliza Depot with us, not long before he died.'

'I didn't realise that.'

'Yes, it were very sad. He'd lost his wife, you know, and Joe missed her terrible. Began to lose his marbles as well, and they found him on the streets of Perth all confused and derelict. So they charged him with being a vagrant and sent him to Mount Eliza. Well, most of us had been there at some time when it was still the Convict Depot, and Joe must have thought it still *was*. You know him and prisons. So, he ran away after eleven days. He was caught quickly enough, and taken back before the beak. Removed to Mount Eliza. Escaped. Caught again. Returned. Ran away once more. And the fourth time they didn't send poor old Moondyne back to us.'

'Where did they send him?'

'Where would you think? Where else but Fremantle Prison! I mean . . . thirty days back in *that* place. For all that Moondyne had suffered there – and broke out from under their noses. I dare say the authorities saw a kind of justice in it and they excused him from doing hard labour. Well, he was in his seventies . . . and you could say at least they ensured he was safe and reasonably fed.'

'There is that.'

'And there were also places other than Fremantle clink where they could have looked after him.' Sam spoke sternly in reproof. 'But no. They broke *him* in the end. He spent most of his time in the prison hospital that last time, they say. And when Joe came out, he was transferred to the Fremantle Lunatic Asylum . . . another convict building, you know it? A fine-looking place. Peaceful, too, I hope. Because four months after he went in, Moondyne went home to his Maker and his wife . . .'

'When was that?'

'Turn of the century . . . 1900, I remember, the year before Federation and we all became citizens of the Commonwealth of Australia . . .'

They paused again, wondering what else they had in common. Until at length:

'You've had a long life, Samuel Speed. Any regrets, looking back?'

'What's the use of regrets, Mr Cribben? Wishing won't change anything . . . and even if it could, who can say life wouldn't turn out for the worse, though we might hope for the better? I'm here – and you're there, writing up an article for the paper about me. And you wouldn't be doing that if I'd stayed in England and dropped dead in the workhouse at half me age.'

Regrets? Sam pondered the answer he might have given. 'Of course there are regrets,' he thought. 'Tommy Jones. The fire. Prison. Sure, I wish it hadn't happened. But it did, and it brought me here, like I told him. And I might not have had my books and the friends I've made through them, had I stayed at home. Not much chance. No way I'd ever have met that Mr Irwin and all those new paths he opened for me. No Pickwick. No Silas. No Tess. No understanding the great Commandments and finding my faith again. Still, it would have been nice if one of those bright-eyed girls at the dance fancied me enough to waltz off with me, and marry me, and have our children. I regret that. But then, what would've happened when me knee went? I'd have had a wife and a family with no means to support them, and we'd all have ended in the poorhouses, split up and abandoned. No. Better as it was. Unless I'd gone east to the goldfields with Tommy and found another Holtermann Nugget. But the knee still would have been jiggered – and it would still be all daydreams . . .'

There was one thing . . . No, Samuel wouldn't mention it to the journalist, who'd think he was foolish and pretentious. But there was one thing Samuel regretted. And it was this: he'd not really been able to appreciate Shakespeare – 'the Bard' – in the way that Mr Irwin did. 'Our greatest poet,' he'd said. But Sam had never learned to understand the plays in the way that others did . . . or at least not until recent years, when they'd had an inmate at the Home here, one Clarrie Short, who knew how to recite the verse, but then only in bits when he was sober.

Before that, however, Samuel had struggled on his own, but for the most part found the heroic blank verse beyond him. He'd see lines from Shakespeare in the newspapers advertising everything from patent medicines to paint, meat, soap, beer and shirt collars: *Perfect and so peerless.* Sometimes in a journal or anthology he'd find passages printed as separate poems containing some of these famous words.

Tomorrow, and tomorrow, and tomorrow, creeps in this petty pace from day to day . . .

And if he read them very slowly and patiently, more as prose than verse, and they were in the kind of English he knew, Sam could disentangle the sense and glimpse something of their merit.

Life's but a walking shadow, a poor player, that struts and frets his hour upon the stage, and then is heard no more . . .

He could see that. Yet when he took a volume down from the library shelf at the Working Men's Institute, the tight rows of poetry and even prose written in this heightened, sometimes archaic language, quite overawed him.

Out, damned spot! Out, I say! One, two. Why, then, 'tis time to do 't. Hell is murky! Fie, my lord, fie! A soldier, and afeard?

Sam had no idea how such words should be spoken, let alone grasp what they meant. Lady Macbeth might as well have been sending her damned dog Spot outside. And even when he once borrowed a copy of Charles and Mary Lamb's *Tales from Shakespeare*, the stories themselves appeared so convoluted, reduced to the bare essentials of 'then, and then, and then,' that the man lost interest in them. Besides, even the great speeches rarely appeared. There was no *Out damned spot!* or *Tomorrow, and tomorrow, and tomorrow* in the Lambs' version of *Macbeth*.

It wasn't until the late seventies, when he'd moved to Perth, that Samuel saw in the newspaper that there was to be a reading of the Scottish play at the Mechanic's Institute by the Church of England

Young Men's Society. He paid his shilling for a seat at the back, foregoing other pleasures, and while it was an amateur reading, the words were spoken in the main fluently and coherently and Sam understood the gist of it.

The trouble was that, without scenery and costumes and acting, the theatrical drama of the play was lost – and it was the music sung by a choir that he remembered most. Some years later, in the middle eighties, a professional touring company staged a production of *Macbeth* at St George's Hall, Perth's first dedicated theatre, in Hay Street. It cost two shillings this time for the cheapest seats up in the 'gods'. Samuel went, and was utterly absorbed by the spectacle. At last it made sense to him. The witches. Lady Macbeth's urging of Duncan's murder, and her remorse. *Out, damned spot!* It was Duncan's blood she was trying to wash from her hands. Banquo's ghost. And Macbeth's defiance . . . *Tomorrow, and tomorrow, and tomorrow* . . . before the final battle.

He went home to Mrs Gurney's full of it, and next day borrowed a copy of the play from the Institute, determined to learn it by heart. But again, the dense slabs of verse, lined up like battalions on the page, defeated him. The struggle of trying to rescue sense from the closed ranks of words proved a victory too far, however valiant the effort – and before long, Sam had returned the book to the library and gone back to *Silas Marner.* He saw no more productions after that: for then came the Depot, and the move out to the new place, so that by neglect, distance and disuse his interest in the Bard almost rusted away.

It wasn't until around 1930 that Clarrie Short turned up at the Old Men's Home with his booze and a barrel chest full of Shakespearean quotations.

The quality of mercy is not strained . . .

To be or not to be, that is the question . . .

He reminded Samuel of that ticket man, 'Shakey Coleman', Mr Irwin had mentioned on *Belgravia*, all those years ago. The one who recited the Bard all over Fremantle – and the Aborigine who could also *Shake* his *spear!*

And now, here was Clarrie. A big, solid man of some education, he'd arrived in the West from the Old Country during the gold rushes of the nineties, intent on making his fortune. And he had started out well: staking a claim in the early days at Coolgardie and filling a bag with very promising 'shows'. But then Clarrie lost the lot – claim and all – in one mad weekend of champagne, fornication and gambling; and while he'd trailed around the outback these past thirty years 'prospectin'', he'd never found anything to equal those early strikes. Now, with the onset of the depression, he turned up at the Old Men's Home with nothing but the rags he stood up in, his strength turned to fat and alcohol – though his voice still retained its English elasticity, and the mind its memory of the Bard's endless flow of iambic pentameters. At least it did, before Clarrie started the day's drinking.

'Ah, Samuel, my dear fellow, what shall we have today?' he'd bellow of a morning into the recreation room, where Sam was studying, with his magnifying glass, headlines from the newspapers.

He discerned in old Sammy a fellow *litterateur*, one with a taste for the classics. And in turn, Sam recognised something of himself in Clarrie: not merely his delight in the kind of verse recommended by Mr Irwin, but also as a sad paradigm for what Sam might have – probably would have – become, had he followed his heart and Tommy Jones, and gone to the diggings.

So he'd put down the paper with a smile, and say, 'Howzit, Clarrie? What's for today? Anything you like, my friend.'

'Ah, Samuel. It's not what *I* like but *As* You *Like It*. Jacques from Act Two, in the Forest of Arden . . .'

And striking a pose while the others gaped at him, Clarrie would start to declaim:

'*All the world's a stage, and all the men and women merely players; they have their exits and their entrances; and one man in his time plays many parts, his acts being seven ages . . .*'

'Put a plug in it!' somebody might complain from the billiard table.

But Clarrie would take no notice and spout on to the end, to *second childishness and mere oblivion . . .* before coming to a stop and asking, 'Which age shall we be today, eh Samuel?'

The seventh age, of course. Sans teeth, sans eyes, sans everything. *I were thinking of it only this morning when I woke up.*

'Hey Clarrie,' would come another voice from the door, 'get a move on. The pubs are openin'.'

'Quite right, Buster. We'll play Falstaff instead, go down to the tavern and *drink ourselves out of our five senses*.'

Until at length poor Clarrie drank himself into the grave. But his memory and the words remained, with all their potency, for Sam Speed.

'He could have gone on the stage himself . . .' the old chap murmured from his bed. 'Or the films. Could've been a fine actor.'

'Who are you talking about, Sam?' asked the reporter.

'A feller we used to have here. Do you remember him, Bob . . . Clarrie Short?'

'Yeah. Just. Hopeless case. They put him out in that old bungalow from the original Depot you mentioned, Mr Cribben, with all the other poor sots.'

'But he knew his Shakespeare. That's something, too. Oh yes, we get all sorts through here, as you asked me. Gold diggers and post diggers. Wowsers and tipplers, though rather more of the latter as you keep reminding us, Mr Cribben, but all God's children. Fancy men and poor men. Thieves and working men. Con men and honest men. Horse-breakers, house-breakers and safe-breakers . . .'

Ah. Should I mention him? Sam checked himself. *Old Charlie?* Mr Rust wanted some amusing anecdotes and here's one. The Boss locked himself out of his office one day and couldn't find the keys. Charlie was passing at the time; and knowing he was an experienced safe-breaker, who had served many a long stretch for his skills, the Boss asked if he could unlock the door. He did it in no time. 'There y'are, Boss.'

Being a cautious man, Mr Rust had the lock changed next day, just in case Charlie succumbed to temptation. But he merely laughed. 'Boss, the new lock is easier than the old one!' And it was, too. He had it open in seconds. And the Boss, being a good-humoured man as well, laughed with him. In fact, he even asked Charlie if he could open the office safe? Which he did, without too much trouble. Then added, 'I wouldn't bother changing the locks again, Boss. I won't rob the place. If I did, I'd be the first person you'd come looking for!' Ha ha. Charlie became quite a useful sort of cove around the Home after that.

It's a nice little story, Samuel thought. *But if I tell that chap and he puts it in the paper, people might ask what sort of place is Mr Rust running, letting safe-breakers into his office, and get into trouble. No. It ain't worth it. I'll tell him something else instead.*

'We had old soldiers and seamen among us as well. One feller . . . he was a Norwegian called Olaf, I think . . . been a merchant sailor but retired from the service in all but the grog. He got back here one night dead drunk. In fact, the orderlies thought he *was* dead, and put him on the slab in the morgue.'

'You've got a morgue here?'

'Certainly have, Mr Cribben,' Bob the Tuppenny replied. 'We have a great need of it here. Out the back. Masonry building, to keep it cool.'

'And it works!' Sam grinned. 'Olaf woke up next morning . . . and came to breakfast complaining it was the coldest night's sleep he'd ever had.'

He was gratified with a round of laughter.

'Mind you, he's the only customer I know of who's ever got up and walked out of the place,' Samuel went on. 'The rest of us sleep there soundly, until the man comes to take us away in our box. Will do so myself, eventually.'

'I wouldn't want to dwell on it . . .'

''Course not, Mr Cribben. You're a young man, and it ain't natural to think about death. Though if what I see in the papers is right, there's another war coming soon, and as a journalist you'll find yourself in the thick of it, I dare say.'

'That's my own feeling,' said Joshua Cribben, thinking suddenly of his wife and two baby girls.

'But until then, death is a long way off for you. Out here, though, we're all old 'uns and the end is getting ever closer. Dying is part of living, you know, and you learn to accept your lot.'

'Do you, Sam?'

'I think so, young feller. By and large I reckon I've made a reasonable fist of what I were given. The minister comes out here every Sunday to try and keep us on the straight and narrer, but the hymn singing ain't all that wonderful. We should be learning to play the harp . . . all us old codgers getting ready to join the angels, eh?'

He paused a moment, lying back on the pillow as if he were asleep. But he suddenly opened one blind eye and added a postscript:

'We had six of us pass away here one night. Half-a-dozen old stiffs put out in the morgue "at rest". It got so crowded that somebody put a sign on the door "Standing Room Only". Standing room . . . and not one of 'em who could remain upright no more! Just as well it wasn't the night Olaf slept in there. The shock when he woke would of killed him outright.'

With his little chuckle Samuel fell silent — and indeed seemed to doze off for a minute or two, for he woke with a start to the sound of voices and footsteps coming towards him down the ward. Through his misty sight he made out Albert Rust with a young man in an overcoat and carrying a large camera.

'Hello, Sam. This is the photographer come to take your picture for the newspaper. Mr Parker . . .'

'Tom Parker. How d'you do?'

'Howzit, Mr Parker?'

Nosey parker, more like.

'What does it feel like to be the last of the old convicts, eh?'

'Still alive. But I try not to think about it too much.'

'Sorry I'm late,' Tom remarked to Josh Cribben, taking off his coat and getting his camera ready. 'Held up with the other job too long.'

'That's all right. We've just finished. It was a long interview.'

During which the old bloke said everything and nothing, Cribben muttered beneath his breath.

Samuel silently reciprocated the sentiment, hoping that was indeed the case.

'You feeling all right, Sam?'

'Oh, fine, fine, Mr Rust, thank you.'

'You happy?' the Boss enquired of his fellow journalist. 'Anything you need from me?'

'I don't think so, thanks. I seem to have it all.'

'And what about *me*?' came a shrill, piping voice. 'Where do you want me for the photo? I can't get out of bed, you know.'

'Then I'll have you propped up against the pillow, if that's all right.'

'Perfectly all right, Mr Parker. Here, Bob, give us a hand . . . My beanie okay?' as the Tuppenny heaved and grappled the thin body to sit him up straight.

'Beanie's fine, Sammy.'

'And Bob, I think I've still got me falsies in.'

'Yeah, that's right.'

'Well, take them out, Bob. I don't want 'em.'

'No, no!' cried three other voices in unison. 'Leave your teeth *in*. Much better for the photo.'

'No, I don't want to,' the old lag insisted. 'Me gums are hurting.'

'They weren't hurting a moment ago.'

'Well, they are *now*,' he said cantankerously. 'Too much chitchat.'

'But your face looks all shrunk and hollow without them.'

'I can't help that. I'm an old man of ninety-something. Shrunk and hollow is exactly what happens when you get to my age. Here, take 'em away, Bob.'

And he put the dentures into the orderly's hand.

'He'll look more dead than alive,' the photographer murmured. 'But if that's what he wants . . .'

Old men can be very stubborn. And that was precisely what Sam wanted. Sympathy and vulnerability were all that mattered now. *Sans teeth, sans eyes, sans everything.*

'Is this all right?' called Samuel, straining from the pillow and smiling a toothless grimace. He looked even more like a cadaver.

'I suggest you keep your mouth closed,' the photographer replied. 'And turn around slightly, looking up to the light from the window . . .'

Samuel complied, the bad eyed closed, and the other blinking spontaneously from the light off the flash bulb. A startled corpse in his beanie and flannels, Mr Parker thought. Rather creepy, in fact . . .

'And another . . .'

He took three or four photos, in every one of which the old man looked as if his face had caved in. God knows what the picture editor would make of them, but it wasn't Tom Parker's fault. The old bloke had refused to follow any other request, and he was . . . well, an old bloke.

'Thank you, Sam,' as he closed the camera. 'I think that's about it.'

'Yes, thanks for everything.' Joshua Cribben put away his pencil and notebook, picked up his hat and coat, and prepared to depart. 'Goodbye, Sam.'

He shook the old man's extended index finger.

'Goodbye, Mr Cribben. I enjoyed our little conversation. You make sure you write something nice about me in your paper.'

'I'll do my best, Sam.'

'You do that. It's the most any of us can hope for.'

Samuel lay there awhile, listening to the fading echoes of their voices as his visitors walked down the ward. The Boss asking if they wanted a cup of tea . . . the photographer saying he had to get back . . . Cribben apologising with thanks, but he had to return with his colleague.

Silence. And rest, after all that talking.

Samuel put his arms beside him, thinking over what he had said. Nothing that he shouldn't have revealed, so far as he could remember. Nothing personal, very much. Moondyne and the Fenians, but everyone knew about them . . . A few funny little stories . . . harmless, like the Boss wanted.

And all I want to do now is sleep.

'The dinner bell will be going soon,' said Bob the Tuppenny close by. 'Do you want to get up for your lunch, Sam, or will I bring something on a tray?'

'I'm all right here, Bob. And don't bother about a tray. I'm not hungry at present. You go off. I'll stay here and get a bit of shut-eye.'

'It's been a big day for you, old-timer.'

Bob removed the pillow props from behind Samuel's head, and gently eased him down beneath the sheets again. Nursing his legs into a comfortable position, and smoothing the blanket over him.

'I thought you handled that reporter feller very nicely, Sammy. All his poking questions into your life. Played him on a bit of a break, I'd reckon . . .'

'Thanks, Bob. Tried to, at any rate . . .'

Keeping the truth at bay.

'You have your nap, little mate. I'll come back later.'

And he tiptoed to the door.

Samuel slipped further beneath the bedclothes, pulling the night-shirt around his legs to keep them warm. A chilly wind had come through the door as the others left and he could hear rain falling on the tin roof, but his body heat would soon warm him under the blanket. Warm as toast, as he sank deeper into Lethe's arms.

He thought everything had gone well. Hoped so, as he told Bob the Tuppenny. But even as he drifted into slumber, Samuel knew it was one thing to avoid telling the truth to other people – and quite another to keep it from himself. The whole dramatic of his hour with the journalist had been precisely that dichotomy. And Bob said he'd played him on a break . . .

Comfortable in the knowledge, Samuel Speed settled into his sleep. Until, as it so often did, from the depth of his unconscious came the smell of smoke. And fire. Those inflammatory dreams of fear and indictment he'd known these seventy years or more . . .

Black smoke and grey, rising with the sparks and cinders from long ago and Joseph Heynes' field, up past the workhouse along Hensington Lane. Woodstock, 1863. The same as always . . .

And yet, this morning, into the dream came something Sam hadn't seen before. He was waiting for the cry *It wasn't me!* But it didn't happen. Not today. Instead he saw the shadows of two figures – silhouettes against the glow. Tommy Jones, yes. And then himself. Little Sammy Speed.

Knew us at once.

Oh, the sound of the rain, and the gnawing ache of a stomach with nothing in it. The smell of damp barley, as they pushed the stooks away to get to the dry inside.

One match struck.

'Sammy . . .'

Thomas Jones passing him the box.

And then the flare of a second.

A moment of hesitation before the flames took, hissing along the stalks like serpents of fire. And then they stood back watching, as the stack ignited and dazzled their faces, red and dancing against the night sky.

'Christ! What have we done . . .?'

'What? What was that you said?' Mr Justice Crompton calling down the decades.

And from the darkness, they were standing once more in the dock before the scarlet King of Hearts on judgement day.

'How do you plead?'

Guilty, your Lordship. Guilty as charged.

Tommy Jones lied to your court.

And so did I.

The flames paled and died away. But the ashen smoke still billowed until it surrounded him, as it ever did. And yet again, this morning, it was different. It had always tried to choke him before . . . to suffocate. But today it seemed to caress him, as though Samuel was being wrapped in a shawl . . . a white woollen blanket . . . and he was being rocked as a cradle ever deeper into his dreams and all his yesterdays . . .

Smoke from the kitchen oven, where Mrs Gurney was roasting a leg of mutton . . .

The billy boiling on the campfire at Yelverton's mill . . .

Smell of cooked salt beef wafting down from the galley to the convict decks on the transport *Belgravia* . . .

Whiff of stale cabbage in every corner of a workhouse . . .

Dust disturbing . . .

And before that, even further into the past, came the faint perfume of Samuel's mother, and the scent of milk dew on her breast.

Dreams.

Sweet dreams.

*

Samuel Speed died at the Old Men's Home, Perth, on 8 November 1938, a little more than two months after his photograph and interview were published in the *Mirror* newspaper on 27 August. His funeral was arranged by the Braille Society for the Blind of WA, and he was buried in the Karrakatta Cemetery on 10 November. The Reverend F. W. Gunning of the Anglican Church, Victoria Park, officiated.

AUTHOR'S NOTE

Talk about the serendipity of a writer's life!

For fourteen years I'd been wanting to write the story of Samuel Speed, believed to have been the last of the transported convicts to survive in Australia. He died in 1938, not all that long before I was born – and consequently is almost modern. Yet during those fourteen years of digging we could find very little about him beyond the bare facts of his career recorded on his convict indent, a few official documents in Britain and Western Australia, and the reports of his trial and conviction for arson at Oxford in 1863. Even now we don't know precisely who, of the many Samuel Speeds born in England during the 1840s, was the convict. So I kept putting off the work in favour of other projects . . . coming back to it . . . and laying it aside once more . . .

It wasn't until January 2018, having just sent off the final pages for a new edition of *Captain Cook's Apprentice*, that I decided this time I really *was* going to write Speed. I pulled out the old files, began reading them again, and contacted people in Perth who'd been so helpful with the research before. The very next morning my wife called out, 'Have you seen the ABC?' And there, on the website, was an article about Speed, written by two British academics from Liverpool University. More than that, they'd discovered a photograph of Samuel and an interview he'd given from his bed in the Old Men's Home to the Perth weekend *Mirror* newspaper, published in August 1938, just over two months before he died. A day or two earlier, and we might have missed it. As I say, talk about luck!

All at once I had not only a face, but also some flesh with which to clothe the mere skeleton of a figure that we'd disinterred to this point. Clearly, the article had been digitised on the National Library of Australia's brilliant Trove site after I'd done my earlier sweep. And while we may well have found it during the new round of research, nevertheless the novelist now had something substantial for my imagination to work upon. Within a couple of weeks I began putting the first words down, and over the coming months the characters of old Samuel, Bob the 'Tuppenny Orderly', and the reporter (unnamed by the newspaper, but who now contains many fragments of my younger journalistic self) began to emerge fluently and indeed urgently, as ideas that had been germinating inside the head for fourteen years at last began to find their expression.

There was something of a hiatus in the writing mid-year – halfway through the work and Sam just landed at Fremantle – when we made our own research journey to the West, visiting Perth, Fremantle, Busselton and the scenes Sam would have known. They included, in another rare bit of serendipity, finding Harwood's Cottage with a few remaining buildings from the convict years at Quindalup, a mere dot on the map south of Busselton – and, through that, an introduction to a descendent of Henry Yelverton who owned the timber mill where Sam had toiled during part of his ticket-of-leave.

The visit also made plain that I needed to rework some of the earlier material. I'd been to Oxford, the castle, courthouse and Woodstock during a previous trip to the UK; but I realised that I needed to show in more detail how the English prison system, for all its nineteenth-century horrors, did try to give the inmates some basic education. It was Sam's passing reference in his interview to a story by Mark Twain that suggested to me he'd become a reader: if Twain, why not Dickens and the others, whose characters might become his lifelong friends? Sam's funeral, in fact, was arranged by the Braille Society, and the records show an association between them over many years. Thus the necessity to show how the system could bring a semiliterate labourer to this stage; and while Sam's involvement on the convict ship with the religious instructor William Irwin is imagined, Irwin's compassionate, educated character, as revealed in his on-board *Journal*, suggests how he might well have guided the young Samuel along the paths of literature.

The rewriting done, I was able to return to the narrative, and it was completed exactly one year and four days from the day I began. Remarkably quickly for me: and the shade of Samuel Speed who, like every character, took up residence in our house like an extended visitor from the day I resumed work on his story, at last began talking of packing his bags and moving in with somebody else, namely his readers.

In all these aspects of his life I have taken my lead from the few hints given by Sam in his *Mirror* interview – even where they seemed to be fantasies, as in 'all the girls chasing me like they used to'. His return to the church was suggested by the donation he gave through the Trinity Congregational Sunday School to a flood relief appeal as reported by the *West Australian*. Two shillings and sixpence (twenty-five cents) may not seem much these days: it could be half a week's wages in 1888. These are the sorts of assumptions that have to be made by every historical novelist, and I emphasise that this essentially is a work of historical fiction.

Even so, I have sought to remain true to the historical facts – so far as we know them – concerning the actual Sam Speed, and referenced in the Chapter Notes and the Appendices. The George Leake letter, for example, still exists in the archives. Sam's actual age I have left fluid. He said in the 1938 interview that he was ninety-eight; the contemporary records indicate he was ninety-two or -three; his death certificate said ninety-five. No matter. Old men in novels (as in life) are allowed to be liberal with their age and antecedents.

I should add that it has been said there was another transported convict who died in 1939–40 – after Speed – but no name has to date been mentioned. Whether that turns out to be correct or not, the fact remains Speed believed he was the last convict, the newspaper interview reported him as such, it has been repeated many times since, and it is Sam's story of survival into the modern era that I have been telling.

Anthony Hill
Canberra, 2020

ACKNOWLEDGEMENTS

As with every work of historical fiction, the internals of thought, speech and emotion in *The Last Convict* can only be the author's. Yet the externals of life in the English and Western Australian prison systems, the convict experience, the specifics of time and place, are as accurate as I can make them. Where I had to make assumptions I tried to base them on reasonable hypotheses as shown in the Chapter Notes. While I thank everybody who has helped me along the way, I particularly wish to pay tribute to the indefatigable research assistance of Loreley Morling of Perth, Western Australia, and Audrey Holland who have been on this journey with me from the beginning and rescued me from many a threatened mishap; also Lorraine Clarke who did much research in the later stages. Olimpia Cullity and Eleanor Lambert gave continuing help from the Fremantle Prison Museum during the writing; Dr Alan Cowan has been the medical advisor for most of my books – as I have talked them through with Suzanne Wilson, whose editorial opinion I value above all others. My friends Richard Morris, Jeremy Salt and Jane Tanner read the manuscript and made valuable suggestions; and my very understanding publisher Ali Watts has been a constant support. Above all, let me as always acknowledge Gillian, the best and most supportive of wives, whose morning call, 'Have you seen the ABC . . .?' brought this whole book into being.

While any errors of fact or interpretation are of course my own, I acknowledge the kind assistance, whether great and small, of the following people, many of whom are also mentioned in the Chapter Notes: Norma Andrews; Richard Beck; Rob Bennett; Ruth Boreham; Busselton Library staff; Bevan Carter; Lorraine Clarke; Dr Alan Cowan; Olimpia Cullity; Sir Daryl Dawson; the late Rica Erickson; Professor Barry Godfrey, University of Liverpool; Virginia Grant; Pamela Harris, Fremantle Library; Andrew Henry; Gillian Hill; Audrey Holland; Eleanor Lambert; Loreley Morling; Richard Morris; Gillian O'Mara; Diane Oldman; Oxford Castle Museum guides; Oxford City Council; Carl Pekin; Rev Ian Powell; Sarah Proctor; Andrew Sergeant, National Library of Australia; Jeremy Salt; Tim Stimpson; Jane Tanner; Vicki Thomas; Paul Vallerius; Ali Watts; Suzanne Wilson; Chip Yelverton.

APPENDIX I

Mirror, *Perth, Saturday 27 August 1938*

LAST OF THE EXPIREES
Came Out On Convict Ship
Now Nearly 100 He's An Inmate
At The Old Men's Home

Now in the Old Men's Home, Samuel Speed is the last survivor of the men who were transported to the Swan River Colony as convicts. Almost 100 he landed at Fremantle in 1864 aboard the troopship Belgravia under sentence of seven years for arson.

He was then 25. Three years later he was released as a bondsman; and in 1871, having served his sentence, he became an expiree.

That was 12 months after the last convict ship, the Charles Fox, arrived in Western Australia.

Lost in the mists of years that have passed since Samuel Speed first heard a warder's harsh command, listened to the heavy beat of the hob-nailed boots of the chain gang men, is a story that would startle the world. But, intelligent as he is today, old Sam's memory is clouded with time, and there is none to stir it for him.

He was never a member of a chain gang; carries no lash marks on his back as other unfortunates did; remembers Garden Island when it was known as Sulphur Town; helped build the old Fremantle bridge; has never smoked in his life.

"Never cared for it," said Sam to a "Mirror" representative. "Besides, I could always sell my tobacco rations to the other prisoners."

Not Another Black Mark Against Him

He was born in Birmingham in 1840. Still a young fellow when he received his sentence of transportation, Samuel Speed left behind a brother and sister, neither of whom he has heard of since.

From the day he landed at Fremantle he has never had a black mark against his name; and so exemplary was his conduct that, after three years, he was released as a bondsman. In those grim old days, a convict whom the governor regarded as trustworthy was released to work for a private person. It was cheap labor for employers, and one way of easing the congestion in the prisons.

A bondsman received no wages, but was clothed and fed. If his employer reported any misbehavior on his part he was liable for 100 lashes at the triangle and work in the chain gang.

Escaped The Rigors Of The Chain Gang

A wise man was Samuel Speed. He kept free of the trouble of many of the hot-heads he ran into; and the authorities were quick to recognise his sense of responsibility. So Sam escaped the monotony and rigors of the chain gang.

Among those unfortunates transported, he recalls, were men in every walk of life; doctors, lawyers, shirt-soiled gentlemen and social outcasts tipped together in the hot-house of humanity that was the Swan River Colony.

Vividly Sam Speed recalls the trip out on the *Belgravia*. The waiting on the hulks at Chatham was an awful time. "Whatever stories you hear," he said, "the officers were pretty good to us. We had plenty of food, and my back bears no lash marks today."

On his release as a bondsman, Sam Speed went to work for Manning of "Manning's Folly" fame. Later he was with the Batemans, the Gallops of Dalkeith, and the Samsons.

"Mrs Willie Samson will remember me well," he said.

Many a bolt he drove building the old Fremantle bridge; and he grinned as he added: "And now they're telling me it's being pulled down for a new one. Let's hope they make as good a job of it as we did in those days."

Moondyne Joe, a romantic figure to us of the present generation, was a very real person to old Sam. He knew the ex-convict; knew of his dramatic escape to the bush around Bunbury; knew of the fruitless hue and cry that was raised by the prison authorities. But "Moondyne Joe" got clear away – was smuggled away on a ship to Boston where he became editor of a newspaper.

"As Lively As A Two-Year-Old"

"Did you ever marry, Sam?" we asked the old-timer. "Marry? Me, marry? Not on your life, not with all the girls chasing me like they used to. I was a regular 'nineteener'."

Sam recalls well the dramatic escape of the Fenians, and the occasion on which a number of convicts broke prison, escaped to Sulphur Town and burned down the shops. "Those were the days when you had to walk wherever you wanted to go – unless you had the fare for a coach ride. None of your motor cars or trains. We didn't mind hoofing it – I think the young people aren't so tough these days."

Tucked up in his bed during the week with the mercury dropping quickly, old Sam was as cheerful as ever.

"He's as lively as a two-year-old" said one of the attendants. "We just prepare his bath and he jumps in and out as nimbly as though he were getting ready to go courting again."

[Printed as written. There are a number of historical errors I've sought to correct in the narrative: The *Belgravia* arrived in July 1866; the *Hougoumont* was the last convict ship to arrive in Fremantle in January 1868; ticket-of-leave men were paid wages and Sam's monthly rates with Yelverton and Dawson are noted on his convict indent; it was John Boyle O'Reilly – not Moondyne Joe – who escaped from Bunbury by ship and became editor of a Boston newspaper; escaped convicts fled to Garden Island and Sulphur Town in 1858, eight years before Speed arrived in the colony (see Chapter 10). Sam's age was given as ninety-five on his death certificate; his true age remains uncertain.]

APPENDIX II

JACKSON'S OXFORD JOURNAL

Saturday 5 December 1863

OXFORDSHIRE WINTER ASSIZES
[Extracts]

Mr Justice Crompton arrived in Oxford on Saturday morning by the 11.10 train, travelling from Reading in the same train with the Crown Prince and Princess of Prussia. His Lordship was met at the station by the High Sheriff (Thos. Taylor Esq.) and the Under-Sheriff (J.M. Devonport Esq.) with the usual retinue, and was escorted to the County Hall, where the Commission was opened. The Learned Judge was then conducted to his lodgings in St Giles's, and shortly afterwards was waited upon by the University and City authorities, who made the usual presentation of white kid gloves, fringed with gold.

On Sunday morning his Lordship attended Divine Service in the Cathedral. There was an Assize sermon, the Rev. Dr Stanley delivering an eloquent valedictory discourse to the University.

The Court opened at ten o'clock on Monday morning, and the following gentlemen were sworn on the Grand Jury: The Right Hon. J.W. Henley, M.P. foreman [and twenty other names].

His Lordship, in charging the Grand Jury, said he found that in this county, as well as in Berks, a vast proportion of the crime consisted of rick-burning, which had now become so prevalent all over the country. In the county of Berks there were six, and in this county there were eleven persons charged with this offence, and they appeared almost universally to be strangers to the county who, in a state of destitution, resorted to this crime apparently for the purpose of being put into prison and sentenced to penal servitude.

A long period of penal servitude seemed to be just what they wanted, while a short term of imprisonment would not mark the enormity of their crime. He hoped they would not find penal servitude so pleasant as they seemed to expect, and it had occurred to him in Berkshire that, if corporal punishment was to be resorted to at all, it might be in these cases, and might have some effect in deterring men from committing this crime.

The law, however, did not allow the administration of corporal punishment except to persons under 16. At Reading he ordered a boy to be flogged, and in the first case in the calendar, where a child nine years of age was charged with arson, it would evidently be no use keeping such a child in prison. It was a subject for consideration whether corporal punishment might not be extended to other persons. He thought they would find all of them quite clear cases, except one or two which he would bring under their notice.

[He then mentioned a case of forging receipts by a workhouse officer; evidence to be given in a case of rick-burning; a painful case of manslaughter where a man was defending his mother from an assault; and another case of rick-burning against two labourers where the evidence was doubtful as so many tramps were going about the county committing such cases. The other charges of arson, he thought, were very clear, the parties mostly having admitted the fact before the police and magistrates.]

All this to the Grand Jury before the trials even began. Then followed brief reports of the separate cases brought before the court.

RICK-BURNING AT BLADON

Thomas Jones, 24, baker, and Samuel Speed, 18, labourer, were charged with setting fire to a stack of barley at Bladon on the 8th of August, the property of Joseph Heynes. Jones pleaded guilty; Speed stood his trial. Mr. Sawyer prosecuted.

Charles Ferrabee, porter at the Woodstock Union, deposed to seeing the two prisoners standing outside the workhouse, and then going up to the gate of Mr Heynes's field. A few minutes afterward he looked out of a window and saw a rick on fire.

Lewis Coates, inspector of police at Woodstock, on hearing the alarm of fire on the night named, saw the prisoners standing together near the police-station. Witness asked them if they had set the rick on fire, and both replied that they had, and that it was because they were starving.

They both stated that they put matches to the rick, and Jones said he had a halfpenny given him while coming along the road, and that they went to a shop and bought matches with it. Witness took them into custody, and went to the spot where Jones said he had thrown the box of matches, and found it there on the road, about 50 yards from the rick.

Speed's defence was that he stopped at the gate while Jones went up the field for, as he thought, a different purpose.

Jones alleged that he committed the act alone, and that he threatened Speed to make him say he did it as well.

The Jury, having found the prisoners guilty, they were sentenced to seven years' penal servitude.

[Among the other arson cases]

ARSON AT ISLIP

John Watson 23, labourer, Thomas Johnson, 22, cigar maker, and Henry Turner, 18, collier, pleaded guilty to setting fire to a stack of straw at Islip, the property of Geo. Alley, on the 6th of November. They stated that they had nothing to say.

His Lordship observed that they had committed a very grave crime, apparently under the idea that they had better get imprisonment for a long term of years than continue going about the country. They had said they did it to get victuals, but it was a shocking thing to destroy property in this way, doing no good to themselves and infinite mischief to the people to whom it belonged.

The crime was very common, and it was necessary to treat it with great severity. They might suppose they would have a pleasant time, going into public works, but they would find a good deal they did not like before they got there, and he hoped that in a little time it would be made much more disagreeable than people in their position had any idea of. They would be sentenced to six years' penal servitude.

APPENDIX III

SAMUEL SPEED'S TIMELINE

[From public records]

1840?	Born, Birmingham? [Perth *Mirror*].
1863	8 August, set fire to barley rick at Woodstock with Thomas Jones [*Jackson's Oxford Journal*]
	28 November, Speed and Jones sentenced to seven years' penal servitude [as above, which gives Speed's age as eighteen].
1864	3 May, Speed to Aylesbury Prison from Oxford Castle where his age is also given as eighteen [Ho23/1 Aylesbury].
	15 July, Speed to Chatham Prison from Aylesbury [PCOM2/2 Chatham].
1866	22 March, Speed to Portland from Chatham. Transport *Belgravia* sailed 7 April [PCOM2/7 Chatham].
	4 July, *Belgravia* arrived at Fremantle. Speed to Fremantle Convict Establishment [Convict 8996 indent which gives his age as twenty].
1867	13 October, Speed ticket-of-leave to Vasse district. Employed by Henry Yelverton [convict indent].

1868   Speed employed at Quindalup by George Dawson, farmer [convict indent].

1869   20 May, Speed given Conditional Release [convict indent].

1870   May/June Speed spent eight days in hospital [convict indent].

1871   18 July, Speed received Certificate of Freedom [convict indent].

1871–88   Speed stated in *Mirror* interview he worked for the Manning, Bateman, Samson and Gallop families.

1888   16 March, Speed donated 2/6 to Greenough flood relief through Trinity Church Sunday School, Perth [*West Australian*].

1889   20 June, George Leake letter requesting Speed's admission to Mount Eliza Invalid Depot as he has a sprained knee and is destitute [SROWA, see Leake in References].

1910   Gardener at Children's Hospital, Subiaco [electoral roll].

1916   Labourer at Old Men's Home, Claremont [electoral roll].

1919–25   Pensioner at Old Men's Home [electoral rolls].

1925–28   Gardener at Braille Society Rest Home for the Blind, Victoria Park [electoral rolls].

1936   14 July, to Perth Hospital with enteritis from Victoria Park, discharged 21 July to Victoria Park [Hospital and Braille Society records].

1938   9 June, Speed in bed at Victoria Park with double hernia [Braille Society records].

              8 July, Speed admitted to Perth Hospital from Victoria Park with debility [Braille Society and Hospital records],

1938 cont.   discharged 16 July [Hospital records]. He appears to have returned thence to the Old Men's Home.

22–26 August, Speed had interview at Old Men's Home with the Perth *Mirror.*

27 August, Perth *Mirror* article and photograph of Speed published.

8 November, Speed died at Old Men's Home [Death Certificate].

10 November, buried by the Braille Society at the Karrakatta Cemetery [Death Certificate].

APPENDIX IV

PHOTOGRAPH OF SAMUEL SPEED

[From Mirror front page]

LAST OF THE EXPIREES

AGED 105, according to some records, but officially accepted as 98, Samuel Speed, now at the Old Men's Home, is the last surviving expiree. He came to Australia in the convict ship Belgravia, and was released three years later. He has no other black mark against him, and has since been an excellent citizen. (Story, page 16).

CHAPTER NOTES

CHAPTER 1

Author visit to the Old Men's (later the Sunset) Home, Dalkeith, June 2018. Many thanks to Carl Pekin and Paul Vallerius of the WA Department of Local Government, Sport and Cultural Industries for arranging a splendid day. The Home closed in 1995 and is now a cultural and heritage precinct. Speed interview published Perth *Mirror*, Saturday 27 August 1938, see Appendix I. I assume the interview took place on the previous Wednesday. Thanks to Dr Alan Cowan for advice on the double hernia and Speed's health generally. Details: 1920 *Regulations for Homes for Aged and Infirm WA*; Whyntie for Tuppenny Orderlies, background to Home and system. Sincere thanks to Loreley Morling, Audrey Holland and Lorraine Clarke for their research assistance with this project, and Ruth Boreham who helped with material in the UK National Archives.

CHAPTER 2

Author visit June 2018. The dining hall and stage are virtually unchanged since the 1920s. Details and anecdotes from Whyntie, Jack Rust memoir. Born in 1918, Jack lived at the Home where his father was Superintendent (Master) until 1938. *West Australian* and *Daily News* 23 August 1938 for cricket. I knew the late Jack Fingleton as a young reporter in Canberra's Parliamentary Press Gallery during the early 1970s, and remember his kindness to me with much pleasure.

CHAPTER 3

The *Mirror* article 27 August 1938 gives no by-line. Joshua Cribben is imagined, though he contains many fragments of my own days as a journalist. The article makes clear Speed was in bed during the interview. *West Australian* and *Daily News* 24 August 1938; *Mirror* 11 April 1936 for 'Exciting Boil-Over', also 5 March 1938 for 'Night at the Hot Pool'. Speed's age: despite every effort, we have been unable to establish from the UK BDM registers exactly which Samuel Speed we are dealing with. Of the five Sam Speeds we examined born in the general Birmingham region during the 1840s, as he claimed in the interview, one died in 1862 and four were still living with their families in England in 1871. It is quite possible that the convict Speed's birth was not recorded in the official registers, or that he lied about his background to the journalist (although Speed's convict indent names a married sister at Birmingham as his next-of-kin). As a novelist I have left it fluid, but his actions at the trial suggest he was a quite young man and eighteen, as the trial report and his Aylesbury Prison 1864 record state, seems close to the mark.

CHAPTER 4

Author visit to Woodstock 2012. *Jackson's Oxford Journal* gives
a full account of the trial and the evidence on which I have reconstructed in fictional form the crime. Bladon is a small village a couple
of miles from Woodstock. It was also (as the English manage to so
confound researchers) the name given to that part of Woodstock
where the workhouse was located in Hensington Lane.

CHAPTER 5

Author visit Oxford 2012. Thanks to Oxford County Council and
Tim Stimpson for showing me the old County Hall courtrooms and
cells. *Jackson's Oxford Journal* for the trial. Thanks to my friend Sir
Daryl Dawson for reading the chapter and his valuable advice. The
truly shocking words of Mr Justice Crompton in his charge to the
Grand Jury before the trials began, are as reported: see Appendix II.
They provided the angry, emotional impetus for me to press on
with Sam's story. *Alice in Wonderland* by Lewis Carroll (Charles
Dodgson), a lecturer in mathematics at Christ Church, was published in 1865. I sometimes mused whether the white kid gloves
worn by the White Rabbit had any literary connection with those
presented to the Assizes judge on circuit. The case of nine-year-old
John Smith is from *Jackson's* report of the Assizes.

CHAPTER 6

Author visit 2012. Thanks to the guides of Oxford Castle and
Tracey who played 'Queen Matilda'. Speed's number 139 is
invented, as no personal details are in the records from Oxford.
Aylesbury and Chatham, see records below Ch 7. Details of prison
life for convicts, including the libraries, schoolroom, separate and
silent systems from Mayhew & Binny, and illustrations including

the veiled caps worn at Pentonville. Published in 1862, it is exactly contemporaneous with Speed's imprisonment and can be seen online at Google Books. Also search Victorian prisons, Oxford Castle, oakum picking, silent system, etc. School primers from collection in the National Library of Australia. Rev Hartnett and Amos Martin are imagined. The model prison at Oxford Castle is now a prestige hotel called, appropriately enough, 'Malmaison'.

CHAPTER 7

Jack Rust for padded cell memoir, Gammon is imagined. Prison: see above Mayhew, Smith T and online searches. Also search Aylesbury Prison. Speed's movements in UK National Archives: from Oxford to Aylesbury Ho23/1 (where his age is given as eighteen) and PCOM 2/2 to Chatham, see under Speed in References. Picture of the crank and a good description of how it was used in the prison exhibition at Oxford Castle. Other photographs online. See also 'Victorian Crime and Punishment' from the National Archives (UK) Education Service online. The Prisons Act of 1865 imposed a uniform regime in which punishment, not reformation, was to be the primary object. Lord Chief Justice Cockburn told a Parliamentary committee in 1863 that the aim of treating prisoners should be 'deterrence, through suffering, inflicted punishment for crime, and the fear of the repetition of it'. *The Ballad of Reading Gaol* by Oscar Wilde, imprisoned at Reading 1895–97. Edmund Frederick DuCane (1830–1903) was in Western Australia 1851–56 with the Royal Engineers. He was appointed director of convict prisons in July 1863. He retired in 1895 with a knighthood and the honorary rank of major-general. Oliver Tweedie is imagined. Thomas Jones' movements from his convict indent (WA convict records No 8593). Toodyay WA was formerly known as Newcastle, but I have retained the modern name as there are already two Newcastles in the tale (UK and NSW) and one more could be confusing. Toodyay is also a most evocative name for a novelist.

CHAPTER 8

Chatham riots: 'Life in Kent Jails before 1877' in Kent History Forum, available online; *The Times* 19, 21, 29 January 1861, also *The Illustrated London News*. Article 'New Prison for Convicts' from *Kentish Mercury*, 16 December 1854, on Kent History Forum website. Copies of *The Saturday Magazine* can be seen online through Google Books, also Park and Southey. Schoolmaster Canning is imagined. For 1866 riots see *The Times* 11, 13 September 1866. PCOM2/7 Speed to Portland 22 March 1866, *Belgravia* sailed 7 April. O'Reilly Bk 4 Ch VI has details of boarding a convict ship at Portland in 1867.

CHAPTER 9

Irwin's *Belgravian Weekly Journal* is the main source for the progress of the voyage, and the material read on the convict decks. The journal had nine issues, beginning three weeks into the voyage after the storms passed. Irwin was clearly a man of remarkable sympathy and compassion for the convicts. A Testimonial thanking him for his services on *Belgravia* was signed by a number of officers and passengers at the end of the voyage. Irwin sailed again the following year on board the transport *Norwood*, making six voyages as religious instructor on the convict ships. Born in Dublin in 1821, he was schoolmaster and religious instructor at Millbank, and later Parkhurst Prisons. He died in 1901. See Pease *Catalpa* pp 62–3 for a journal being read between decks on a convict ship. Edmund Henderson (1821–96) was promoted to Lieutenant-Colonel in

1862: Irwin refers to him in the layman's short form 'Colonel' in the *Journal*. Back in England he was appointed Surveyor-General of Prisons and later head of the Metropolitan Police. The convict George Barrington reputedly spoke the lines: *True patriots all; for be it understood/we left our country for our country's good* at the opening of the first Australian theatre at Botany Bay in 1796. He is sometimes wrongly credited with having written them, see ADB entry. For the convicts on board *Belgravia* search convictrecords.com.au/ships/belgravia.

CHAPTER 10

Irwin's *Belgravian Weekly Journal* for the voyage; Bateson for life aboard the convict ships. Speed's association with Irwin is imagined; however, Sam clearly became a reader as his reference to Mark Twain's 'Nineteeners' shows, and his funeral was arranged by the Braille Society. See also note Chapter 18. Summers makes clear that novels were generally prohibited in prison libraries in the mid-19th century. Vogel Ch 1 tells of a failed attempt to introduce novels at Sing-Sing, USA in the 1840s. There was at least one novel at Fremantle Prison library, see below Ch 12. *Daily News*, Perth, 17 November 1926 for the story of Read and the convict escapees.

CHAPTER 11

Author visit to Fremantle Prison, June 2018. Sincere thanks to the curator, Olimpia Cullity, and assistant curator Eleanor Lambert for generous research assistance, including Convict Department of WA *Rules and Regulations* and continuing advice on daily prison routine. Thanks also to prison guide Andrew Henry, Pamela Harris of Fremantle Library, and others who assisted during my visit. Ayris and Smith for Fremantle Prison; Bosworth, Erikson, Hasluck and

Stannage for general overview of convicts in Western Australia. For John Williams' escapes see *Perth* Gazette 1, 7, 21 November, 1 December 1862; *Perth Gazette and Western Australian Times* 27 July 1866, 16 August, 27 September 1867. The 27 July 1866 edition states that Williams had returned as one of the crew on *Belgravia* and gives details of his punishment. There were four John Williams on the *Belgravia* convict manifest, but none were the escapee. Nor does the surname Goodenough appear among them. Goodenough appears as an alias on Williams' 1857 convict indent 4302. I have been unable to locate Williams' convict indent for the period after he returned to Fremantle on the *Belgravia*, but see newspapers above. Ayris p 55 for floggings under Hampton regime; Elliot p 87 for ninety escape attempts. Richard Alderson was the Establishment chaplain during Speed's time there.

CHAPTER 12

Speed's individual life in prison is imagined. His convict indent (number 8996) gives his age on arrival in WA in 1866 as twenty. There is no record of his movements until he got his ticket-of-leave in October 1867. He has a clean sheet so far as any further infringements or punishments are concerned. The 1850 Fremantle Prison chaplain's register (CONS 1156R/21A) notes the books delivered to each prisoner during the year. I counted about fifty titles, mostly instructional or non-fiction books. *Robinson Crusoe* was the only novel I found, but there may have been more later. Thanks to Bevan Carter for his advice. This list of books does not appear on prisoners' records in following years. Elliot for both Williams and Moondyne; p 78 for *The Governor's son has got the Pip*. There are some variants. Elliot p 67 says Joe was chained by the neck to a window bar, the *Perth Gazette* 12 October 1866 says he was chained to a post. The *Gazette* 15 March 1867 states that George Hampton made the promise to forgive Joe if he escaped the cell (but only his father, the Governor, could of course confirm it, see Elliot p 93.) John Williams convict indent 4302 can be seen online, as can Moondyne (for whom there are eighty-four records, search Joseph Bolitho Johns) under WA Convict Registers on Ancestry.

CHAPTER 13

One of the association wards at Fremantle later became the prison library eventually with more than 10000 books, another was converted to the Roman Catholic chapel. Convict indents for James Carr (8816) and Richard Leach (8913) can be seen online through Ancestry's Australian Convict WA Records (search their numbers). Their association with Samuel Speed is imagined. Daily gratuities calculated from the 1862 Convict Department *Rules and Regulations*. Speed's indent character is marked Good (as opposed to Very Good), which entitled him to two good conduct marks a day. Each mark equated to a gratuity of one and one-third farthings, thus two and two-thirds farthings each day. I calculated Sam's 463 days at 307.89 pence or 25.66 shillings. Interestingly, escaped convicts were required to pay from their gratuities the cost of their recapture and any floggings. Speed's ticket-of-leave movements and employers through his convict indent (8996). Author visit to Bunbury, Busselton and Quindalup, June 2018. Sincere thanks to Busselton Library staff, Rob Bennett and Norma Andrews of Harwood's Cottage Quindalup, and Chip Yelverton who kindly sent a photo of a family-owned painting from the 1860s showing convicts loading timber from the Quindalup jetty. Harwood's has been beautifully restored and has several buildings from Speed's time. Liam Barry has an excellent account of O'Reilly's career and his escape from

Bunbury on the whaler, pp 68–9 for the letter; see also Elliott B Introduction to the 1975 edition of O'Reilly's *Moondyne*. O'Reilly called his Aboriginal king by the Maori name Te-mana-roa, which he said meant 'the long-lived'.

CHAPTER 14

Horrocks and Chopin, see Erickson. Rotary Club's *Busselton Heritage Trail* for the Working Men's Institute and dance practice in the hall. The Busselton Working Men's Institute was formed in January 1867, see *Inquirer and Commercial News* 24 January 1872. Moondyne, see Elliot Ch 11 ff. For the *Catalpa* rescue I have relied on Pease (1897) who got his material directly from Captain Anthony; but Fennell and King p 23 point out a discrepancy in the story of the *Hougoumont* charts (Pease p 62–3). The ship was skippered in 1868 by William Cozens; the vessel spoken by *Catalpa* was *Ocean Beauty*, which Lloyd's Register apparently shows a Captain Pearce as Master. I have left it open in Sam's narrative. I've been unable to establish a connection between the twopence paid to the convict constables and the 'Tuppenny Orderlies' at the Invalid Depot and Old Men's Home, but it seems more than a coincidence.

CHAPTER 15

Speed's Certificate of Freedom, 18 July 1871, see his convict indent (8996). Speed's subsequent career and meeting with Tommy Jones is necessarily imagined until 1888–9 when he reappears in the records. Jones received his Certificate of Freedom on 7 December 1871, and departed for Newcastle, New South Wales on 2 March 1875, see his convict indent (8593). Jones' age was twenty-four in the report of his trial with Speed in 1863. I have been unable to trace him since he left for Newcastle. The families Speed worked for are from his interview with the *Mirror*; some of them were based in Fremantle and some, like the Leakes, in Perth.

CHAPTER 16

Speed says he didn't marry in the *Mirror* interview, and we have found no record of any such marriage; also 'all the girls were chasing me' and 'regular Nineteener'. The term 'Nineteener' occurs in *The Man That Corrupted Hadleyburg*, a short story published by Mark Twain in 1899. It was this reference that formed my belief Speed became a reader. If he'd read Twain, I supposed he'd also have read Dickens, etc., as described in this novel. His long association with the Braille Society supports this view (see Ch 18 below). The Perth Working Men's Association was formed in 1864; the new hall was opened in Beaufort Street 1 June 1881, when it generally became known as the Working Men's Institute. There were over 200 couples at the opening dance. In 1880 some thirty-five members visited the Association's reading room each evening, and 900 books and over 2500 periodicals were issued by the librarian. By 1891, during the gold rushes, these numbers had fallen by about a third. See the *Inquirer and Commercial News* 1 December 1880, 20 April 1881, 8 June 1881, 28 October 1891; *West Australian* 31 August 1880. The first Trinity Congregational chapel was built in 1865 with a hall added behind in 1872. The current church, built in front of the first one, was opened in 1894. Speed's donation of 2/6 to the Greenough flood relief through Trinity Sunday School, *West Australian* 16 March 1888. This is the basis for my assumption that he attended the church. See also Thompson and Cox for church background.

CHAPTER 17

George Leake letter dated 20 June 1889 states that Speed had 'lately been in my employ', recommends his admission to the Invalid Depot as he had a sprained knee and was unable to work. It was recommended by the Superintendent of Poor Houses and approved by the Colonial Secretary on 21 June. Thanks again to Dr Alan Cowan for advice on the possible nature of Speed's injury, osteoarthritis of the knee. Speed's age is given as forty-six on the Minute Paper, which means he would have been born in 1843, two years older than his age of eighteen given in *Jackson's Oxford Journal* at the time of his trial and on the Aylesbury Prison records. A dogcart is a light, horse-drawn cart, originally used for sporting shooting, with a box behind the driver's seat to carry a dog or two.

CHAPTER 18

Report by Augustus Roe into the *General Management of the Depot at Mount Eliza* dated 27 August 1898. The *West Australian* 4 July 1898 for the death of Douglas; 18 July for the inmate lying five days with a broken leg and refusal of water to a dying man, also attack on Wade as a Dickensian character unfit for his position and Dr Lovegrove's infrequent visits. Hetherington has an excellent detailed section on Mount Eliza pp 79–148, and Whyntie gives more background. She states p 65 that Wade was also known as 'The Quaker' from his costume and harsh attitudes to old men; p 66 decision in 1904 to build the new Old Men's Home at Dalkeith and opened 1906. Laffey is very good on the early years of the Braille Society, founded in 1913. Victoria Park Rest Home built 1924. Speed is recorded as a resident and gardener 1925–8, February 1935 and various dates in 1936–7 to 8 July 1938 when he was taken to Perth Hospital and thence back to the

Old Men's Home. Talking books were introduced from the early to mid-thirties.

CHAPTER 19

Whyntie, general background to the Old Men's Home. Elliot pp 115–6 for Moondyne. Shakespeare WA *Times* 4 February 1879 (reading), *West Australian* 29 April 1886 (*Macbeth*); Clarrie Short is imagined but see *Belgravian Journal* No. 9 for 'Shakey Coleman' and the Aborigine 'shaking spear'. Jack Rust *Memoir* for Charlie the safe-breaker, the Norwegian seaman and six in the morgue. Parker is imagined. Speed's funeral *West Australian* 10 November 1938; also *Sunday Times* Perth 4 December for an account of Speed's funeral. It states, '. . . there were only a few of his companions at the Old Men's Home present at the grave-side'. He is buried in the Anglican section of the Karrakatta General Cemetery, grave No. 638. The death certificate gives his age as ninety-five.

AUTHOR'S NOTE

See Godfrey and Williams for the ABC website article on Speed, and thanks to Professor Godfrey for his correspondence. Again, sincere thanks to Loreley Morling and Audrey Holland of Perth and Ruth Boreham UK, for their research assistance from the start of this project in 2004, also Lorraine Clarke during the writing. Erickson and O'Mara (1994) note under Speed p 520 that a possible expiree may have died in 1939–40, information which is repeated on the Fremantle Prison roll of convicts, but in twenty-five years no name has to date been given.

REFERENCES

SROWA = State Records Office of Western Australia

Australian Dictionary of Biography, online version.

Australian Hymn Book, The (Collins, Sydney, 2001 ed). Hymns 50, 138, both by Charles Wesley (1707–88).

Ayris, Cyril. *Fremantle Prison – A brief history* (self-published, West Perth, 1995/2016).

Barry, Liam. *The Dramatic Escape of Fenian John Boyle O'Reilly* (The National Gaelic Publications, Australind WA, 1992/2008).

Bateson, Charles. *The Convict Ships 1787–1868* (Library of Australian History, Sydney, 1983).

Bennett, Rob and Norma Andrews. *Harwood's Cottage* (BB Media, Quindalup WA, 2003).

Bosworth, Michal. *Convict Fremantle, a place of promise and punishment* (UWA Press, Perth, 2004).

Braille Society for the Blind of WA, later Association for the Blind of WA, now VisAbility. *Minutes of Victoria Park Rest Home for the Blind*, mentions Speed 1936, 7 July, 8 December; 1938, 9 June with hernia, 8 July sent to Perth Hospital.

Clarke, Marcus. *For the Term of His Natural Life* (Australian Journal 1870–72; Book Agencies of Tasmania, undated c. 2000). The classic Australian novel of the convict system on the east coast.

Cox, Rev. Sydney Herbert. *The Seventy Years History of the Trinity Congregational Church 1845–1916* (E.S. Wigg and son, Perth, 1916).

Electoral Rolls. Western Australia. Samuel Speed appears:
Subdivisions of Subiaco 1910; Claremont (Old Men's Home) 1916, 1919–25; Canning (Braille Rest Home, Victoria Park) 1925–28;

Eliot, George. *Silas Marner, The Weaver of Raveloe* (1861; Penguin edition 1973).

Elliot, Ian. *Moondyne Joe, The Man and the Myth* (UWA Press 1978; Hesperian Press 2014).

Elliott, Brian. Introduction in O'Reilly *Moondyne* (1975) *q.v.*

Erickson, Rica. *The Brand On His Coat, Biographies of Some Western Australian Convicts* (UWA Press, 1983; Hesperian Press, 2009).

Erickson, Rica and Gillian O'Mara. *Convicts in Western Australia 1850–1887* (UWA Press, Perth, 1994). Reference to Speed p 520 states another expiree possibly died 1939–40, but no name has been put forward to my knowledge.

Fennell, Philip and Marie King, eds. *John Devoy's* Catalpa *Expedition* (New York University Press, New York, c. 2006).

Godfrey, Barry and Lucy Williams. 'Australia's last living convict bucked the trend of reoffending' (*The Conversation* and posted on the ABC website 10 January 2018).

Hardy, Thomas. *Tess of the d'Urbervilles* (first published by James R. Osgood, McIlvaine & Co., London, 1891).

Hasluck, Alexandra. *Unwilling Immigrants, letters of a convict's wife* (Oxford University Press, 1959; Fremantle Arts Centre Press, 2002).

Hetherington, Penelope. *Paupers, poor relief and poor houses in Western Australia 1829 to 1910* (UWA Publishing, Perth, 2009).

Irwin, William. *The Belgravian Weekly Journal* (handwritten and illustrated copies produced aboard the transport *Belgravia* in nine parts between 28 April – three weeks into the voyage – and 23 June 1866. Copies at the State Library of NSW and Battye Library, Western Australia; some pages also online.)

Kennedy, Julie. *The Changing Faces of Woodstock, Book Two* (Robert Boyd Publications, Witney, 1997).

Laffey, Paul. *In Braille Light: a history of the early years of the Association for the Blind of Western Australia* (UWA Press, Perth, 2004).

Leake, George Jnr. Letter recommending Speed be admitted to Mount Eliza Invalid Depot, 20 June 1889. SROWA Colonial Secretary's

Correspondence Files (Accession 527 Item 1889/1731). Later became Attorney-General, delegate to the Constitutional Conventions, Premier 1901. Died 1902. Also see below under Speed.

Mayhew, Henry and John Binny. *Criminal Prisons of London and Scenes of Prison Life* (Charles Griffin and Co., London, 1862).

O'Reilly, John Boyle. *Moondyne* (Geo Robertson, Sydney, 1880; Rigby, Adelaide, facsimile 1975 with introduction by Brian Elliott).

Oxford Castle Unlocked (Official Guide, Oxford Preservation Trust).

Park, Mungo. *Travels in the Interior of Africa* (first published 1799).

Pease, Z. W. *The* Catalpa *Expedition* (George Anthony, Massachusetts, 1897; Hesperian Press, 2002).

Perth Hospital. *Admissions and Discharges* record book (1936, 14–21 July, Speed admitted with enteritis from Victoria Park and discharged; 1938, 8–17 July, Speed admitted suffering debility and discharged).

Richmond, Carol. *Banished! Sentences of Transportation from Oxfordshire Courts 1787–1867* (Oxfordshire Black Sheep Publications, Witney, 2007).

Roe, Augustus S., Police Magistrate. *Report of an Inquiry into the General Management of the Depot at Mount Eliza* (WA Government Printer, 27 August 1898).

Rotary Club of Busselton. *Busselton Heritage Trail* (Busselton, Geographe Bay, 2017).

Rules and Regulations for the Convict Department, Western Australia 1862 (printed at the Convict Establishment, Fremantle W.A. 1862). Copy generously supplied by Olimpia Cullity and Eleanor Lambert.

Rust, Jack. *Remembrances: Old Men's Home; Sunset Isle; Amongst the Elite* (SROWA AU WA S2115 cons5649 16. Typescript, memoirs of growing up at the Old Men's Home 1918–37, where his father was the Master. Albert Rust retired in December 1938, not long after Samuel Speed died.

Smith, E. Langley. *Convict Prison Fremantle, an Overview* (self-published, Perth 1999/2014).

Smith, Thornton. 'The English Convict System' (in *Cornhill Magazine*, July 1865).

Southey, Robert. *The Life of Horatio, Lord Nelson* (1813).

Speed, Samuel. Official records. **Australia:** Convict indent 8996, SROWA, available online through Ancestry, see Chapter Notes; details of Fremantle Prison 1866–67, ToL to the Vasse 13 October 1867; Conditional release 20 May 1869; Certificate of Freedom 18 July 1871.

England: H023/1, Aylesbury, No. 50, received 3 May 1864 from Oxford Castle, age eighteen; PCOM2/2 Chatham, No 6818, received from Aylesbury 15 July 1864; PCOM2/7 Chatham to transport *Belgravia* 22 March 1866, sailed 7 April from Portland, arrived Fremantle 4 July 1866, age given as twenty. SROWA Box 196 ALB4, Minute 75/89, George Leake letter and recommendation approved to admit Samuel to the Mount Eliza Invalid Depot. See also *Jackson's Oxford Journal* under Newspapers and Appendix II for report of his trial.

Stannage, C.T., ed. *Studies in Western Australian History IV, Convictism in Western Australia* (University of Western Australia, 1981).

State Records Office of Western Australia [SROWA]
Colonial Secretary Correspondence 1889, see under Leake, George above.
Colonial Secretary's Correspondence, Mount Eliza Enquiry. AU WA S675 – cons527 1898/2280.
1850 Fremantle Prison chaplain's register (cons1156R/21A).
Public Health Department, Old Men's & Old Women's Homes Rules and Regulations, 1920, PH 1629-17. Law 847-20.
Jack Rust's Remembrances. AU WA S2115 cons5649 16.
Sunset Hospital, Old Men's Home, inmates' cards Accession 3395 Item 2, Speed S number 564-38.

Summers, F. William. In *Encyclopedia of Prison Libraries*, ed. Wiegand et al (Garland Publishing, New York, 1994).

Thompson, Peter. A Brief History of the *Trinity Uniting Church Buildings 1865–2013*, (available online under Trinity Uniting Church website).

Twain, Mark. *The Man That Corrupted Hadleyburg* (*Harper's Monthly*, 1899).

UK National Archives: PCOM – Prison Commission records. See above under Speed: H023/1 Aylesbury; PCOM2/2 Chatham Kent; PCOM2/7 Chatham to transport *Belgravia*.

Vogel, Brenda. The Prison Library Primer (Scarecrow Press, Maryland, 2009).

Whyntie, Ann T. 'Sunset Hospital: Its History and Function' (in *Early Days*, Royal Western Australian Historical Society, 8:5, 1981).

NEWSPAPERS AND MEDIA

ABC website, 10 January 2018, for Godfrey and Williams *op. cit.*
Illustrated London News, January 1861, for Chatham Prison riots.

Jackson's Oxford Journal 5 Dec 1863, full account of Speed and Jones' trial.

The Mirror, Perth, 27 August 1938, 'The Last of the Expirees', article and photo of Samuel Speed; hot pool 5 March, 11 April 1938.

Perth *Daily News*, various dates, see Notes Ch 3.

Perth Gazette and independent Journal, various dates, see Notes Ch 12.

Perth Gazette and West Australian Times, various dates, see Notes Ch 12.

The *Inquirer and Commercial* News, Perth, various dates, see Notes Ch 14, 16.

The Saturday Magazine, London, four-page weekly magazine published for working people by the Society for Promoting Christian Knowledge 1832–44, available on Google Books.

The Times, London, various dates, see Notes Ch 8.

The *Sunday Times*, Perth, 4 December 1938, Speed's funeral.

The *West Australian*, various dates, see Notes Ch 3, 16, 18, 19.

ONLINE RESOURCES

Ancestry, online Western Australian Convict Records; UK and Australian Births, Deaths and Marriages.

Australian Dictionary of Biography, online entries for Barrington, DuCane, Hampton, Henderson, Joseph Johns ('Moondyne Joe'), O'Reilly.

Convict ships. For *Belgravia* manifest search convictrecords.com.au/ships/belgravia. Other convict ships can be searched on this site, or enter the ship as a search term.

Kent History Forum, www.kenthistoryforum.co.uk.

Perth Directories, 1891–1938. I could find no mention of Samuel Speed in the individual entries. The inmates of the Invalid Depot and the Old Men's Home are not listed by name, although the Superintendent's name is given; the same is true for the Braille Society Rest Home for the Aged Blind in Sunbury Road, Victoria Park.

Also by Anthony Hill

The enthralling story of Captain Cook's voyage to Australia, as seen through the eager eyes of a cabin boy. When young Isaac Manley sailed on the *Endeavour* from England in 1768, no one on board knew if a mysterious southern continent existed in the vast Pacific Ocean. It would be a voyage full of uncertainties and terrors. During the course of the three-year journey, Isaac's eyes are opened to all the brutal realities of life at sea – floggings, storms, press-gangs, the deaths of fellow crewmen, and violent clashes on distant shores.

Yet Isaac also experiences the tropical beauty of Tahiti, where he becomes enchanted with a beautiful Tahitian girl. He sees the wonders of New Zealand, and he is there when the men of *Endeavour* first glimpse the east coast of Australia, anchor in Botany Bay, and run aground on the Great Barrier Reef.

Acclaimed and award-winning historical novelist Anthony Hill brings to life this landmark voyage with warmth, insight and vivid detail in this exciting and enlightening tale of adventure and discovery.